SOHO CRIM
By
Peter Thur¦

• • •

In the grey post-war world, Soho was the most exciting and dangerous place in Britain. Crime, sex, foreign food, and jazz, all lived side by side in this melting pot of approximately one square mile in the centre of London that is Soho.

There were no flowers near to where Jack Comer was born; as a Jew from the east end of London, his earliest memory of a vibrant colour was the scarlet red blood that gushed from the gaping wound left by a cut-throat razor, during a street fight between two rival illegal bookmakers.

With such childhood memories it was no wonder that Comer wandered into a life of crime. A life that took him from his humble east-end beginnings, to the top of his chosen profession, as the boss of the London Underworld.

Wage snatches and gold bullion heists featured heavily in Comer's line of work, as did protection rackets, gambling, and taking over west-end nightclubs. None of this however, could be achieved without a high level of violence, some of which ended in death, gang warfare, bent coppers, and double dealings from all sides.

There were however, two sides to Jack Comer; the side that everyone saw was Jack Comer the vicious gangster, but the other side of the coin was Jack Comer, the family man, who would have laid his life on the line for his wife and daughter.

Jack Comer made many enemies along the way, from Darby Sabini and the early racecourse gangs during the 1930s, to the 1940s wartime racketeers, and through to the Messina Brothers, who ran the first organised sex trade gangs and who were threatening the well-being of his clubs and spielers in the west end.

As the 1950s was coming to an end, the old guard were also in decline and new faces were starting to make their presence felt around Soho. Reggie and Ronnie Kray were about to become the new face of British crime and Comer was starting to feel the heat, but being the man he was, he was not about to take this new threat lightly.

Chapter 1

It was dark; it was always dark lately for Jack Comer. This time however, it was more than darkness, it was an impenetrable pitch black. What was happening to him, where was he, was he dying, was he dead?

Suddenly a pinpoint of light seemed to pierce the blackness, like some far away star in the night sky. It started hurtling towards him, getting closer and more intense. Noises started to accompany it, whooshing and then banging, followed by unintelligible growling sounds.

"He doesn't seem to be breathing properly," said a voice from somewhere on that distant star. "Who was that?" thought Comer, "were they talking about me?" As if to confirm it was him the voice was speaking about, a tremendous weight was suddenly dropped from a great height onto his chest. Comer tried to scream, but like in a nightmare, no sound came out; the weight was dropped on him again, and again he tried to scream, but it was no use, who were these bastards that were trying to kill him? If only he could see, if only they would let him out of the darkness.

Jack Comer was lying on an operating table in St Thomas' Hospital, London, surrounded by a surgeon, his assistant and two nurses. The surgeon placed the two pads of the cardiac defibrillator onto Comer's chest; "Clear" he called, warning the staff to stand clear of the patient.

Bang, the pads seemed to jump up in the surgeon's hands; he turned to look at the AED screen, where faint blips could now be seen; he continued to watch the screen for another few minutes, the heartbeat now growing stronger with every second that passed. He smiled to himself and replaced the pads onto the table next to the rather cumbersome looking AED screen. "The patient has a normal heartbeat once again, but I want him closely monitored around the clock for the next twenty four hours" The surgeon never even looked up as he issued his orders, picked up his notes and walked out of the room.

• • •

Rita Comer was a few years younger than her husband, beautiful, with long dark hair and dressed in the height of fashion, in a navy blue suit and matching high-heeled shoes. She had first met Comer in her native Dublin, when she was just twenty years old. He was there on what he described as a 'business trip' and introduced himself to her in the meeting room of a pub where her brother was attending an important function at the time. Comer was besotted with her from the moment he met her, and within a few months she had moved to London, where she shared a flat with him.

Comer and Rita were married a year after she moved to London, and a short while after that, Rita gave birth to a daughter, whom they named Miriam, after Comer's mother.

There was little sign of the stress she was suffering, on the face of Rita, as she sat there beside her husband's bed in the private room at the hospital. She gently stroked his hand and gazed at his heavily bandaged head and face. "Oh Jack, Jack," she whispered.

Was that a movement of his eyelids, did he hear her? She stared intensely at him, willing him to hear her, and to come out of his coma, "Jack," she again whispered, "please hear me Jack – please?"

• • •

Although his world was still dark, Comer was starting to get more glimpses of light, as he had earlier on, like tiny shooting stars that suddenly exploded like fireworks, leaving dim shadows on his retina.

"Please hear me Jack – please?" Was that his mother's voice? "Please hear me Jack – please?" It was, but he couldn't answer her, no words would come out, no sounds; like an awful dream where you are falling and scream for help but no one can hear you.

The grey mist in front of him was starting to clear, he could see a figure standing before him, it was his mother, dressed in black as she always was, her long apron tied around her waist. She held her hands out towards him, "Please hear me Jack," she said, "please listen to me – you can change things Jack, it doesn't have to be like this"

"What do you mean," he replied, "how can I change anything? I'm not a kid any more mum" The words came out this time, but did she hear him? For even as he uttered those words, so her image started to fade, gradually merging into the grey mist that surrounded her.

• • •

Rita stood back nervously from the bed as a nurse took her husband's pulse, while just behind them, a police officer watched from the half open door. The nurse explained to Rita that his pulse was normal, and he seemed to be doing quite well, but Rita wasn't convinced, "His eyes were moving" she said, "they wasn't open but I could see his eyelids moving and his face contorting as if he was in terrible pain"

The nurse coaxed Rita into a chair and explained to her that Mr Comer was not suffering any pain at that moment, as he was on a course of painkillers. What he was experiencing was something known as REM or rapid eye movement, which is common in many people, especially when on painkillers. The amount of time one spends in REM sleep has a lot to do with certain psychological factors, people with depression tend to experience this for short but intense periods of time, exactly like Mr Comer had just undergone. "Does your husband suffer from depression at all Mrs Comer?" she asked.

Chapter 2

Rita didn't answer the nurse, her mind was miles away as she sat and stared at her husband and remembered the night this had happened, the night that had ended with her husband being attacked and left for dead; the night he was brought into the hospital, where he now laid, like a zombie, unable to speak or move.

Rita had accompanied her husband that night, to a pub in north London, where he had a business meeting with an Irishman. Rita wasn't sure what the meeting was about, but Comer did seem to be pleased with the outcome, so pleased in fact that he said they should celebrate by having a meal at the Ritz.

They toasted each other with Champagne, had caviar for a starter, followed by roast pheasant for their main course. Rita recalled to herself how happy her husband seemed that evening; certainly not acting like a man consumed with depression. After a second bottle of wine, Comer said he felt on top of the world, and as it was such a nice evening, that they should walk back to their flat in Cumberland Mansions, "I want to walk and get some fresh air," he said. Rita was a little concerned, after all the problems they had endured over the past few months. "Are you sure we'll be alright?" she said, "Shouldn't you give Moisha a ring and get him to pick us up?" Moisha was one of Comer's oldest friends and confidants, who also acted as his driver and minder. "I've given Moisha the night off" Comer replied "This is the start of a new life for us now" he said, "and if all goes according to plan, I might be able to give Moisha a lot more time off from driving me about and looking after me"

Rita smiled and hung onto her husband's arm as they left the Ritz and started walking to Park Lane, onto Hyde Park Corner and then to Edgware Road. It was about 10.45 pm as they turned off Edgware Road, and into George Street, and Seymour Place, where Cumberland Mansions were situated.

Rita was laughing and holding onto Comer like a lovesick teenager as they approached the entrance to their flat. Comer took the keys out of his pocket and started up the steps leading to the street door, with Rita following close behind. "Bloody light has gone," he murmured as he looked up at the darkened doorway. As he took another step, a figure stepped out of the darkness, it was a man with a mask covering his face and holding an automatic pistol, which he was pointing directly towards him.

Comer's first thoughts were to protect his wife; he turned and grabbed Rita, throwing his whole body around her like a protective cloak, as he tried to rush her back down the steps, away from the masked gunman.

But even as he did so, a large American car screeched to a halt in the kerb directly in front of them. Rita screamed as the doors of the car flew open and another man, also wearing a mask over his face, leapt out and rushed towards them. The man leading the onslaught was brandishing yet another pistol in one hand and a large knife, possibly a machete, in his other hand. Comer's mind was in turmoil, he knew he had to save Rita at all costs; he had two options, stand and fight, or make a run for it with Rita?

From behind him he heard the voice of the man who had been hiding in the doorway, shout to him, "You're a dead man Jack" Comer took a brief glance over his shoulder and saw the man now advancing towards him with his pistol pointing directly at him and Rita. He now had no other options left. He leapt down the steps, pushing Rita to one side as he did so. The second man from the car now raised his gun and fired it directly at them. Rita screamed and fell to the floor as both assailants started to close in on them. For one moment Comer thought his wife had been shot, but then he noticed the blood dripping off his own fingertips; he had been shot in the shoulder.

There was nothing Rita could do to help apart from scream, which she continued to do. She was on the ground and looking up as the man wielding the the pistol and the large knife leapt over her and struck out at Comer; the blade slashing into his flesh and ripping open a deep wound down the left side of his face. Comer looked around for a weapon, anything that he could use against the man. An empty milk bottle was all he could lay his hands on; he grabbed it and hurled it at the man with the knife, catching him full in the face, causing a rush of blood to start seeping through his balaclava, which he immediately ripped off, allowing his face to be seen by both Comer and Rita. A face they both knew well. It was one of his old arch enemies, Teddy Baxter.

Now it was the turn of the other man with the pistol. He raised it and aimed carefully at Comer, firing off two shots in rapid succession. The first shot missed, but the second shot grazed Comer's head, sending him reeling back and collapsing in a pool of blood on the stone steps.

"Finish the bastard off," shouted Baxter. The other man now jumped down the last step towards Comer's prostrate body, at the same time as Baxter, both moving in for the kill, like a pack of hyenas, but at this precise moment the sound of police cars' bells (they didn't have sirens at this time) grew suddenly close, "It's the old bill," shouted the second man. Baxter now had his pistol pointed downwards at Comer's eye, his finger tightening on the trigger as the police cars raced into the far end of the street. He quickly took his finger off the trigger and rushed back towards their car, "Go, go" he shouted as both he and the second man tumbled into the car and it raced away into the night.

Rita's screaming, coupled with the sound of the gunshots had alerted several neighbours, some of whom had phoned for the police. A passing motorist, who saw the attackers running to their vehicles and making their getaway, later identified the thug with blood running down his face as Teddy Baxter. Rita also later identified the second thug, through his voice, as a man named Mickey Reilly.

Not only had the police arrived within minutes of the attack, but an ambulance had also arrived and Jack Comer was taken to St Thomas' Hospital, London. He was unconscious all the way, and remained in a coma and on a life support machine for the following forty-eight hours. Rita remained at his bedside the whole time.

Comer had also undergone emergency treatment for gunshot wounds to his temple and his right shoulder, as well as twenty-three stitches down the left side of his face.

He was completely unaware of anything that was going on around him, such as Rita being interviewed by the police, and how she picked out both Mickey Reilly and Teddy Baxter in an identification parade, as the two men who had attacked them.

It didn't take long for this story to leak out, and within hours of Comer being admitted to the hospital, the press had infiltrated the hospital corridors and waiting rooms, all eager to speak to Rita. Under normal circumstances, Rita would not have spoken to anyone until her husband had given her his permission, but when she looked at him, still lying unconscious in that hospital bed, covered in bandages and with a saline drip attached to him, she felt it was her duty to do all she could to help catch his cowardly attackers.

Rita went out into the corridor and held an impromptu press conference, where she told the reporters that she knew who was behind this attack and that she had given names to the police. She also said that the men who carried out this attack were both armed and intent on murdering her husband. "My husband would not be lying in this hospital now, but on a mortuary slab if he wasn't so brave and able to defend both me and himself," she told the onlooking circle of reporters. "Is this the start of another gang war Mrs Comer?" called one of the reporters. Rita looked at the man for some moments while she considered her answer, "I am hoping it will be the end of all gang wars – especially those waged against my husband"

Chapter 3

Roy Marshal stood in his office, looking down, through the enormous plate glass window, at the big red buses, black cabs, and other traffic that was choking up Fleet Street. "It's getting worse down there," he said, "d'you know, it's quicker to walk in London now than to go by cab – and as for buses, bloody great things belting out all that shit – bring back more trolley buses that's what I say"

Marshal was the editor in chief of the Sunday Express newspaper, and he looked every inch of what one would expect of such a position, with his greased back grey hair, wire framed spectacles, grey chalk stripe suit, and a red bow tie.

Without taking his eyes off the traffic in the street below him, he threw a question at David Palmer, his head crime reporter, "So what's the latest on this Jack Comer thing?" he asked, "is he out of hospital yet?" Palmer said that the last he had heard, Comer was still in a pretty bad way, and was being kept in there, "Under observation, as they say"

"Under observation? These people need to be under permanent observation if you ask me" replied Marshal sneeringly," but unfortunately Palmer, they sell newspapers, and newspapers are my business, do you see what I'm getting at?"

Palmer nodded his head, "So what do you want me to do?" Marshal spun around to face Palmer, "I'll tell you what I want you to do." He said, "I want you to get over to whatever hospital it is that they are holding him in, and get him to sign an exclusive deal with us for his life story" "But he's still unconscious" replied Palmer. "I know he's fucking unconscious," Marshal bellowed, "but when he comes to – then I want you to sign him up – and if he won't sign, then get his wife to sign – in fact, that might be a better idea than waiting for him, get her to sign a deal first, offer her anything – we can always do some swings and roundabouts later"

Marshall looked pleased with himself, yes, he thought, jolly good idea of mine that was, me thinking that up like that. He took his silver cigarette case out of his inside jacket pocket and opened it, "Blast, I'm completely out of fags," he said, "wouldn't have one to spare would you Palmer?" Palmer dug deep into the side pocket of his jacket and pulled out a somewhat crumpled, blue and gold ten pack of Wills Woodbines, which he opened up to discover just two cigarettes left inside. "I've only got two left," he said, almost apologetically, hoping that his boss would say, oh that's alright then, instead of which Marshall just snatched the packet from his hand, "That'll do me nicely," he said, "Remind me to replace them for you"

"Yes" Palmer replied as he opened the door and left the office, "I will"

● ● ●

Jack Comer opened his eyes for the first time in three days. The first thing he saw was the uniformed police officer, who was standing guard on his door. His mouth was so dry, his eyesight blurry. He tried to lever himself up against his bed, but could hardly move: was he too weak? Had he lost all his muscle power? The police officer must have alerted one of the nurses, as she came bustling in, her starched white pinny rustling as she drew closer to him and started to straighten his bedclothes. "How do you feel Mr Comer, can I get you anything?" she politely asked in her Irish lilt. "Water" he hoarsely replied, "I need water"

Comer looked around the room as the nurse went over to the small sink and started pouring him a glass of water. "Has my wife been here?" he asked. The nurse came back and placed the water down on the table beside him. "Just a moment," she said, "I just need to loosen these restraining straps," she said as she started undoing the straps, which were holding him down. "Your wife's been here for three days Mr Comer – in fact she's only just gone home this morning, I'm sure she'll be back soon, so don't you go worrying yourself about her"

No sooner had he drank the water when the door opened again and two plain-clothes police officers entered the room, "Just a few questions we need to ask you Mr Comer"

How many times had he heard that over the last ten years? Just a few questions, they always need to ask just a few questions. I've been shot, I've been slashed and I've been beaten, I could be dying for all these bastards know or care. Comer closed his eyes; maybe they'll go away?

"Mr Comer – can you hear me Mr Comer," Of course I can fucking hear you, he thought, why don't you just fuck off? "Mr Comer," said the police officer, a little louder this time, "do you know who attacked you Mr Comer? Would you know these men if you saw them again?"

Comer kept his eyes closed and started to groan – he raised his hands up to his throat and groaned even louder as if gasping for breath. The two police officers looked at each other, not sure what to do. The nurse had obviously heard the noises coming from the room and came running back in as quickly as she could, ordering the two police officers out at the same time. "Are you alright Mr Comer?" she asked, "what do you want, can you breath?

Comer nodded his head and pointed to the water glass again, "Water" he gasped, "water"

Time seems to pass so slowly in hospital. It had only been just over an hour since the two detectives had been there; trying to interview him, but it seemed more like twelve hours. He kept thinking of what had happened that night, and more importantly, why? Although he knew in his mind, the identity of his attackers, he was still not one hundred percent sure of the exact motive behind it. He was on the verge of making a big come back, but as far as most people knew, he didn't have any interests, so to speak of in west end clubs or spielers, and he wasn't exactly loaded, as far as money was concerned, so why had they tried to murder him?

The more he thought about it, the angrier he became; it hadn't exactly been an easy ride to the top of his chosen profession, and he had taken his fair share of knocks along the way, so why should he let someone else step in and take what little was left away from him?

Pictures of that night started to flash up before him in his mind, he saw Rita lying on the ground and that simpleton thug, Baxter, leaping over her, missing her head by a fraction of an inch as he did so. Comer's fists tightened into two balls of steel; how he wished he had that maniac in front of him now.

At this point the door to his room opened and his lovely, friendly Irish nurse looked in, "Two visitors to see you Mr Comer – do you feel up to it at this moment?"

"Not more reporters?" replied Comer, "I don't want to see any more reporters" The nurse looked somewhat perplexed as she looked at the business card she was holding, and read the names from it, "says here, Ronald and Reginald Kray, business advisors"

Comer nodded to the nurse and told her to show them in. What was this about, he wondered? The last time he had encountered the Krays they had told him in no uncertain manner that at his age he should be sitting back in comfort and relaxing, instead of waging wars and being threatened on a daily basis. So why were they now visiting him like this, could it be they had reconsidered and were looking to renew interest in his team once again? They had worked well with him to start with, if only he could talk them into forming a new alliance, he would be a force to be reckoned with once again. He quickly pulled himself up in his bed, ran his fingers through his hair, and straightens his pyjamas as Reggie and Ronnie Kray entered his room. "Nice to see you boys" he said, "pull the curtain round the bed would you, I don't want those nosey bastards listening to everything," referring to the police officers just outside the room.

Reggie and Ronnie looked immaculate, as they always did; Reggie in a pale grey, single breasted suit, white shirt and a dark blue silk tie. Ronnie, in a navy blue double-breasted suit and matching tie. Comer smiled to himself as he watched Reggie pull the curtain around the bed; he was obeying his orders.

He had always found Reggie to be the more amiable of the two brothers; it would be Ronnie, who would need convincing. Ronnie did not mince his words; if he didn't like something, or someone, he would say so, and God help anyone who dared to oppose his views. But they had come to see him, not the other way round, and as such, surely he, as the older and more wiser man, would command respect from the two upstarts whom he himself had helped in their early days?

Reggie smiled as he sat down on the side of the bed, next to Comer, while Ronnie, as morose as ever, stood at the end of the bed and stared directly at him. "How are you feeling now Jack," Reggie asked, "Who did this to you – have you any idea?" Before Comer could even think of an answer, Ronnie lent forward and whispered, "I hope you don't think we had anything to do with it Jack – you don't think that do you?" Ronnie spoke very slow and deliberate; his voice always carried, what a judge might possibly describe as an air of menace. Comer looked at Ronnie; there wasn't a hint of any real feeling in either his face or the way he had delivered those words. What could he answer to such a question? Of course he didn't think they were anything to do with the attack on him, but there again, why was Ronnie now even posing such a question?

Comer shook his head, "Of course I don't Ron," he replied, "we go back years – we come from the same part of London, why should I think something like that?" There was silence in the room for a few seconds, with all three men looking from one to the other. "You know what it's like Jack," said Reggie, "word gets about" Comer looked quizzically at Reggie and asked him what he meant, but before Reggie could answer, Ronnie interrupted; almost growling, he told Comer that they had heard that he was bandying their name about in context with the attack, "We don't need this Jack" he said, "we told you our plans some time ago didn't we?"

Comer pulled himself up straight, trying to make himself appear bigger, which is not an easy job from the confines of a hospital bed. "I swear on my mother's grave I have not mentioned your names to anyone regarding this attack on me," he said, "why should I, we all know who carried this out don't we?"

Ronnie walked slowly around the bed, opposite his brother and placed his hand gently on Comer's face and ran his fingers down the scar and stitches, "I don't know who did it Jack – it's things like this that get us a bad name - tell me who it was and I'll cut their fucking balls off for them"

After the initial veiled threats from Ronnie, the mood of the conversation was hopefully starting to come round in Comer's favour. He placed his hands on both Reggie's and Ronnie's arms, "All I want is for you boys to declare you're with me – let those pricks who did this know I am back, bigger and stronger than ever"

Ronnie looked at Reggie, and Reggie looked at Ronnie. "When we last spoke," said Reggie, "you told us you were on the verge of retiring; now you're talking about making a come-back – bigger and stronger than ever?"

Comer sensed he was being pushed into a proverbial corner. One minute they were talking as if they were his best friends and offering to cut his enemies up for him, and now they are virtually writing him off. Reggie was staring at Comer, a look of bewilderment on his face, "What's it to be Jack – I'd hate to think you were making fools of us?" Comer was starting to sweat as both brothers lent even closer to him. He had never felt so vulnerable in his life. Reggie, he could possibly argue his point with, but Ronnie was a different story – there was madness in his eyes, like two pieces of black coal, burning into you.

"I'm not trying to make fools of anyone," he stammered, "for fuck's sake, what am I supposed to do? I was nearly killed by those bastards – I thought you had come here today to offer your support?"

"You've got to look at this from our point of view Jack," said Ronnie as he took a packet of cigarettes out of his pocket, "You don't mind if I smoke do you Jack?" He said as he lit his cigarette. "You've got to face up to it Jack, you're not getting any younger - the west end and the club scene are a young man's game – we did warn you some time ago about this didn't we?"

Comer could feel his heart beat starting to race. He had known the twins since they were just a pair of juvenile delinquents in the east end, and here they were talking down to him, as if he were some benign old uncle – didn't they know who he was? He was Jack Comer, king of the underworld, and with them or without them, he would hold that title once again.

Ronnie then took a metal tube out of his pocket, unscrewed the cap, and took out a large Havana cigar, "Nearly forgot Jack," he said, "a little retirement present for you - I know how much you appreciate a good cigar". He pressed the cigar into Comer's mouth as Reggie struck a match and lent forward, offering the flame to the cigar. Comer snatched the cigar out of his mouth and placed it on the bedside cabinet next to him, "I'm not supposed to smoke," he said dismissively.

Ronnie Kray shook his head, "Such a shame to see you like this Jack, letting these people tell you what you can and can't do" "That's right," added Reggie, "not like the old Jack Comer we used to know – take our advice Jack, get out now, while you still can" The twins stood up in unison, "Brighton's a nice place to retire to Jack" said Ronnie as he patted Comer on the arm and turned to leave. "Or Ireland" added Reggie as they both walked out.

Comer was incandescent with rage. He grabbed the glass of water from his side cabinet and practically threw it down his throat. His eyes then settled on the cigar Ronnie Kray had given him, "Bollocks to them" he growled as he picked up the expensive cigar and crumbled it between his fingers, "Fuck 'em – fuck 'em – fuck the fucking lot of them – I'll show them all who's the boss of the underworld"

Chapter 4

A short while after the Krays had left, Comer's condition started to deteriorate again, his heart started beating erratically and he was put back on a saline drip. He issued strict orders to the hospital not to release any details of his condition to anyone, not even his wife, as she had enough problems over the past few months, and now needed to relax and look after their daughter.

Fortunately for Comer, his condition improved dramatically by the following morning, and by the time Rita arrived to visit him, they had taken the saline drip away, and to all intents and purposes he looked almost his old self again. They kissed and he asked about their daughter and if Moisha was taking care of things for her.

Rita told him to stop worrying, "I am perfectly alright Jack" she said, "It's you we have to worry about I want you well again and home with me and Miriam, where you belong," "But what about money?" he replied, "Have you got enough – there's still some left in the other safe, you know that don't you?"

Rita smiled at Comer and nodded her head. He was still the same, always worrying about her. They call him names, say he's a gangster, and that he hurts people, but to her, he is, and always will be, Jack Comer, her loving husband and family man. "Fortunately Jack, I haven't had to touch any of that money" she said, "I've done a deal with one of the Sunday papers" The smile dropped from Comer's face like a ton of bricks as he heard this, "What have you told them Rita?" he asked, "You haven't give them any names have you?" Rita's lip started to tremble and tears welled up in her eyes, as she explained to her husband that she thought he was going to die when they first took him into hospital after the attack. "Oh Rita" Comer exclaimed, Rita, Rita, Rita – we'll have half the London underworld after us now, calling us grasses – why did you do it Rita?"

As Rita wiped the tears away from her eyes, she explained to her husband for a second time that she thought he was about to die, and all she could think of was revenge on the people who did it.

Comer leaned forward and took Rita in his arms, "Alright" he said, "It's done now, so tell me about this deal you've done with the paper – what have you said to them?" Rita tried hard to regain her composure but her voice still quivered with emotion as she spoke, "I haven't told them anything Jack" she said, "They want to do a brief interview with you from here in your hospital bed"

"Yeah, I bet they do," replied Comer, "I hope they don't think they're going to get an interview out of me for nothing?" Rita grasped her husband's hand reassuringly, "They're paying us £3,000 Jack," they've already given me a thousand"

● ● ●

Three thousand pounds wasn't a bad deal at all, it is the equivalent of £50,000 today. Comer was more than pleased with his wife; this could be the fresh start he was looking for, although which way he was going, was still undecided at this point.

At 4.30 that afternoon, Moisha looked in, "Two blokes from the Sunday Express to see you Jack – shall I send them in?" Comer nodded and pulled himself up in the bed, while Rita took a small mirror out of her handbag and started re-applying some fresh make-up.

Moisha showed the Sunday Express journalist, Ronnie Marshall, in, along with his photographer, Mick Humphreys. Jack Comer may have been poorly, but his mind was still functioning as efficiently as ever where money was concerned. The first thing he asked the two men when they walked in the room, was did they have a contract, "It's alright Mr Comer," said Palmer, "Your wife's already signed one" Comer shook his head as he looked at Palmer, "Come off it boys" he said, "you should know better than that – you may well have entered into a contract with my wife, but now it's me you want to talk to – is that right?"

Palmer and Humphreys looked at each other, both realising they had made a mistake here.

"I haven't got all day boys," rapped Comer, "You're not the only paper that wants my story you know" Rita looked worried, was Jack about to mess this deal up she wondered.

Palmer apologised to Comer and said he would need to get onto his boss before he could authorise any fresh deals. Comer waved his hand dismissively at Palmer, "You've got ten minutes – there's a phone box outside" (no mobile phones at this period in time)

Palmer rushed out of the room, leaving his photographer, who immediately started setting up a wooden tripod for his rather bulky camera. "I wouldn't bother with that just yet if I were you," snapped Comer. Mick Humphreys looked somewhat worried as he dismantled the tripod again.

There was an uneasy silence in the room as Comer sat up in his bed, his eyes fixed firmly on Humphreys, who stood awkwardly facing the door, waiting for Palmer to return. "Three minutes to go," snapped Comer, looking at his watch.

The door suddenly burst open again and a breathless Palmer rushed back into the room, "My boss isn't there today," he stammered. "That's it then" Comer shouted, "no contract no interview" Palmer was sweating now, he knew he had to get that interview with Comer; his job could be on the line if he didn't. "Listen," he said, "I have a friend who's a solicitor in Fleet Street – I could get him to run one off quick for me"

Comer was a first class poker player; he could sit in at a card school, holding just a pair of deuces and con the other players into believing he had a full house or better. Rita often said he should have been an actor. He now decided to play his trump card. "Tell you what I'll do," he said, "I'm a businessman, I know how to draw up a contract – keep it short – keep it simple, give me a piece of paper and a pen and I'll draw one up now– take two minutes"

Palmer had no other option; he had to take the chance. He opened up his briefcase, took out a note pad and pen and passed them to Comer.

True to his word, the contract was ready within the allocated time. It was short and straight to the point, with him, Jack Comer, agreeing to an interview, to be published in the Sunday Express, for the sum of £3,000.

The interview took nearly three hours. Comer gave David Palmer exactly what he wanted; a tough, no nonsense story, parts of which he made up on the spot, "Yes, I am king of the underworld," he boasted, "and no one is going to force me out – got that? No one"

Palmer was relieved when the interview was finally over. He opened his briefcase and took out a bottle of Scotch and four glasses, which he poured for everyone. "Lovely Jack" he said, "now a couple of photos if you don't mind?"

This was exactly what Comer had been waiting for; his coup de grace as it were. "What are you doing?" he asked as Humphreys started to focus his camera on him, "I didn't give you permission to take any photos of me"

Humphreys looked at Palmer, a look of helplessness on his face. Palmer was shocked as he realised that Comer had conned him. "But we signed a contract Jack," he stammered. "And I adhered to my part of that contract," answered Comer, "and nowhere in that contract did it mention photos – surely you read it?"

Another £1,000 for the photographs, it was daylight robbery, but when you are dealing with a man like Comer this is his game. The newspaper could use old shots of Comer that were in the public domain, but this is not what the public wanted to see; they wanted to see Comer in all his glory, scars and all.

The article, along with the headline 'Jack Comer – Still King of the Underworld' appeared in the Sunday Express the following Sunday, alongside photos of a very battle scarred Jack Comer and his exquisitely dressed, and made up wife Rita. Comer looked proudly at the paper and the article; this'll show 'em, he thought to himself, he had always believed that money bought power, now he would show the world; no one gets the better of Jack Comer.

• • •

On the very day the article was published, Comer was allowed out of hospital. Moisha picked him up and drove him home, making sure to use the back entrance, as the usual gaggle of reporters were huddled around the front door. No sooner had he put his key in the door and started to push it open than he heard the excited squeals of his daughter, Miriam, "Daddy, daddy" she almost screamed as she rushed towards him and hugged and cuddled him. Comer obliged his daughter, kissing and hugging her, even though it caused him some pain in doing so.

Rita followed close behind Miriam, kissing him and gently hugging him, "It's so nice to have you back home again Jack," she said as she led him into the living room. Comer eased himself into his favourite red leather armchair and smiled at Rita as she picked up a little package from the side table and handed it to him. "I've bought you a little present," she said, "I know you aren't particularly religious, but I would like you to wear this as a sort of good luck charm, to protect you in the future"

Comer looked puzzled as he unwrapped the package, his big hands fumbling with the dainty wrapping and bow, which Rita had tied it so lovingly with. It was a gold Star of David, on a gold chain. He just stared at it without saying a word. "If you don't like it Jack, I can change it for something else?" Comer looked up at his wife; in all the years she had known him, she had never seen him this emotional, there were tears in his eyes as he silently nodded, and then murmured, "I do like it Rita – put it on for me" Rita unbuttoned his shirt collar and slipped the thin chain around his neck, letting the Star fall down onto his chest.

Chapter 5

The Star of David had always featured prominently in Comer's house when he was growing up, because his mother always wore one around her neck, it was unusual, in the fact that it was a silver Star outlined in black, probably jet, and was on a very fine silver chain. She would always touch it as she said the blessing before sitting down to eat their evening meal.

Jack Comer was like most boys of his age growing up in an east London tenement during the 1920s, not at all interested in religion. Money was his religion; his father worked as a tailor's cutter, bringing in a very modest income, and his mother stayed at home most of the time, looking after the family, which consisted of himself and three younger sisters. She did a part time cleaning job once a week for a local doctor, but even with that extra money, the family always struggled.

Young Comer did all he could to help the family finances. Pretending to go to school, he would hang about the local street market instead; where he would steal fruit and whatever else he could lay his hands on, from the stallholders, to take home to his mother, telling her that he earned it for helping the stallholders to set up their stalls.

By the time he was fourteen, he was almost six feet tall, and had a very good physique. He had also graduated from stealing fruit and vegetables, to being a lookout for a local burglar, named Solly Feinstein, which brought him in a pretty regular wage. This partnership lasted over a year, until Comer found out that Feinstein had been conning him out of his percentage by telling him he had only received a certain amount of money for the goods he had stolen, when in fact he had sometimes doubled that amount.

When Solly Feinstein swaggered through Wentworth Street market one Sunday morning, in his brand new dogtooth check suit, silk muffler and tweed flat cap, he saw himself as some sort of Raffles character; a gentleman thief, who people looked up to. A nod here, a wave there; yes, people knew who he was, and he was proud of it. He even paused for a few moments to look at a stall selling walking sticks and canes; the silver headed one looked very nice, but was it really him? Maybe not, bit too 'toffish' for Stepney, he thought as he moved on.

As Solly Feinstein crossed the road at the corner of Old Castle Street and Wentworth Street, a hand suddenly grabbed him from behind and pulled him back into the narrow confines of Old Castle Street, and from there, into a dark doorway. Jack Comer slammed Feinstein up against the wall, his hand gripping the silk muffler around Feinstein's neck and twisting it tight. "You owe me money Feinstein," growled Comer. Feinstein could hardly speak or move, "I don't know what you're talking about," he wheezed. Comer brought his knee up into Feinstein's groin, causing him to groan in pain. "I heard how much you got from that last job, and it was a lot more than you told me" Feinstein struggled to pull himself free, but Comer just twisted the muffler tighter. "I figured you owe me at least fifty quid," he snarled. He then stuffed his hand into Feinstein's inside pocket and took out his wallet, whilst still keeping a tight grip on the muffler. He quickly riffled through the wallet, took out the few banknotes, which were in there and threw the wallet onto the floor. "Ten fucking quid? Is that all Mr Big has, ten fucking quid?"

Feinstein continued to struggle, but Comer quickly put an end to this by smashing his head back against the huge oak door behind him; once, twice, three times, and then letting go of him, leaving him to slump, half unconscious to the floor. "You've got until Tuesday to get me the rest of my money Feinstein – you understand? Forty quid – you can meet me here at two o'clock – and if you're late you'd better make it fifty" Comer gave Feinstein a final kick in his stomach as he walked away.

● ● ●

It was Monday, just after 6 pm., raining, and already dark. The small block where Comer lived looked exactly the same as all the other blocks in that grimy street. A gaslight was flickering from behind the grimy and broken window, where yellowing lace curtains, shielded Comer's flat from the eyes of passers by.

Across the street, the shadowy figure of a man was sheltering in another doorway. It was Solly Feinstein, his face still heavily bruised from his earlier run-in with Comer. He squinted his eyes and peered through the dim light and now quite heavy rain towards Comer's flat opposite, where he could see the silhouettes of figures as they passed by the window inside. One of the figures was unmistakably that of Jack Comer, his size and build would be recognised anywhere, especially when coupled with his voice, which could just about be heard through the broken window pane, as he called out, "Bye mum"

Feinstein braced himself, swallowed hard and took a large iron bar from out of the waistband of his trousers, then pulling his coat collar up close around his face, he hurried, half limping, across the road towards Comer's flat. As he got almost there, the street door opened; it was too dark to see inside but an umbrella was thrust out from inside the dark passageway; it must have been slightly broken as whoever was holding it seemed to be having trouble opening it. It probably only took three or four seconds to get the umbrella to open, but it seemed like an age to Feinstein, who could hear his own heart beating.

At last the figure stepped out of the passageway, pushing the umbrella above their head to shelter them from the heavy rain, "This is what I owe you Jack" shouted Feinstein as he raised the iron bar and brought it smashing down, tearing through the umbrella and onto his victim's head; not once but again and again.

The tattered, torn and blood stained umbrella was blown into the gutter, leaving the figure of Jack Comer's mother, Miriam, lying prostrate on the ground, with blood forming on a pool on the pavement from the back of her head and tricking with the rain, into the gutter. Solly Feinstein stood for a moment, looking aghast as he realised that he had attacked the wrong person; he dropped the iron bar and then stooped down to rip the silver Star of David from Mrs Comer's neck before running off into the night.

• • •

Comer never collected the debt owed to him by Solly Feinstein; he was too busy visiting his mother in the London Hospital, where she passed away three days after the cowardly attack on her. By the time he did decide to look for Feinstein again, he was told by various people that Feinstein had moved up north, to Liverpool. Comer put this sudden move by Feinstein, down to the fact that he owed him money; he never once thought that Feinstein had anything to do with his mother's death.

Comer never completely got over his mother's death, especially the way in which she died, but time, as his father would often say, is a great healer, and by the time he was 20 years old, in 1932, he had moved on, and was living in a flat of his own in Cobb Street, close to Petticoat Lane.

He had also moved on with his business interests, for now he had his own gang, consisting of two very close friends, Sonny, and Moisha, both of whom he had known since he was a boy, plus a number of friends and acquaintances whom he could call upon when he required their help.

Comer was now running what he called the Jewish Protection League, which he had set up to protect Jewish shops, pubs, and stallholders in the area from gangs of mainly Russian thugs who were terrorising them, demanding protection money and smashing their shops and businesses up when the refused or couldn't pay them.

"Why are you paying these foreign bastards money?" he would say, "I'm one of your own – we need to stick together" Comer now looked the part, he was 6 feet 4 inches tall and very well built. When he walked into a shop or a pub, people took notice of him; he had affected the look of the American gangsters in the movies, with his double-breasted Crombie overcoat, and snap-brim Fedora hat.

The sight of Comer, Sonny and Moisha, all very big men, turning up on a Sunday to collect the League's fees was enough to frighten most opposition away, and to ensure regular payments were always kept up. There were occasions however, when the inevitable did happen, and Comer, Sonny and Moisha had to enlist the help of a few extra men, all armed to the teeth with iron bars, hammers, knives, and cut-throat razors; guns were very rarely used by London villains at this time. Needless to say Comer and his men won the day every time, and eventually took over the protection business relating to almost every Jewish business in east London.

● ● ●

Most young men in the early twenties spend a great deal of their time running after the opposite sex, and Comer admired women as much as the next man, but beneath his extrovert persona, he found it very difficult to relate to women.

Like most people, he found that drink would often loosen his tongue, and that is exactly what happened on the night of March 1 when he attended a friend's birthday party, and spotted a girl across the room that he immediately fell in love with. Ruth was a raven-haired beauty with the most amazing smile. She was talking to a group of people, but Comer couldn't help noticing how her eyes seemed to stray away from her group and focus on him much of the time.

He poured himself another large Scotch and decided to take the bull by the horns by marching up to the group and pushing in, somewhat awkwardly next to Ruth. His friends around the room couldn't believe it as they watched him laughing and chatting to Ruth within minutes of joining her.

It was 1934; Ruth was twenty years old; two years younger than Comer. She didn't have a boyfriend, and lived at home with her parents in Mile End. After just a couple of hours, Comer, who by this time was more than a little inebriated, felt that he had met the love of his life in Ruth.

"Are you Italian?" he asked her, to which she laughed and explained that she was always being taken for an Italian, probably due to her dark hair and bone structure, but in actual fact, she was a good old fashioned Jewish girl, "See," she said as she lifted out the Star of David from her blouse to show him.

Comer smiled, but as he focused his eyes on the Star, the smile dropped from his face and he sobered up within seconds. This was the Star of David that had belonged to his mother; he would recognise it anywhere. He asked her how long she had owned it and where had she got it from. Ruth said her uncle had bought it from a local dealer, and had given it to her for her birthday.

Comer couldn't tell Ruth the truth about the Star, as it might frighten her off, so he fabricated the story somewhat, by saying it brought back so many memories to him, as his mother used to have one exactly the same, and how much he would like to buy one. His amorous overtures to Ruth now forgotten for the time being, he asked for her phone number, and if she would mind him phoning her.

Ruth seemed happy to give him her phone number, which she scribbled down on a scrap of paper. "You will phone me won't you?" she said. Comer smiled at her and promised to phone her first thing the following day.

Chapter 6

Saturday morning, March 17 1934. One could have been forgiven for thinking it was late evening, when in actual fact it was only 9.15 am, windy, raining, dull and overcast; a typical March day. A man in a homburg hat and long black overcoat with an Astrakhan collar hurried along the narrow side street in Whitechapel. He ran up the six steps of his local synagogue, paused for a few seconds to shake some of the rain off his coat and entered the building. From the other side of the street, a bearded man, who was similarly dressed to the first man hurried across the road and also entered the building. It would soon be time for first prayer.

Inside the entrance to the synagogue a few homburg hats were hanging on a hat stand, while inside the main hall of the building a few men sat here and there, some huddled together, talking quietly to each other, while others sat alone, as if deep in their thoughts. Most men were wearing yarmulkes (small skull-cap type hats), although here and there, others, including the first man who had entered earlier, were still wearing their homburgs.

In the centre of the room, sat the Ark, its curtains still closed, hiding the Torah Scrolls, which are kept inside. The Rabbi, resplendent in his robes and shawl, peered through a chink in the curtain in front of him, to count the number of worshippers in the synagogue. Just nine souls in the whole building. He shook his head in disappointment; there has to be at least ten worshippers present before he can begin the service.

As if in answer to his prayer the entrance door opened again and another worshipper entered, and quickly took a seat towards the rear of the auditorium. A deathly silence engulfed the vast hall; the group of men who were chatting to each in hushed tones, also lapsed into silence as the curtains covering the front of the Ark opened to reveal the Torah Scrolls, as the Rabbi made his entrance. The worshippers got to their feet, facing the Ark as the Rabbi took out the Torah scroll and carried it solemnly to the reading desk, where he solemnly laid it out, ready to read.

The sound of the main doors creak as they swing back and forth as somebody, unseen to the Rabbi passes through them. Pushing his spectacles up over the bridge of his nose, the Rabbi squints his eyes and pauses for a moment, staring towards the back of the hall in the hope of seeing maybe another worshipper who has just entered the room, but instead of seeing an extra worshipper, there now seems to be two missing.

Everyone in the vast hall, including the Rabbi who continued his reading were completely unaware of what had happened to the two missing men at the back of the auditorium. It wasn't until the end of the service, as the worshippers started to file out that one of them screams out in Yiddish and a crowd quickly gathered to look down at the body of the man lying on the floor between the rows of seats. The man, still wearing his overcoat, his homburg hat now on the floor next to him, was lying on his side in a massive pool of blood; his throat had been cut from ear to ear. Some of the men knew him, as a local jewellery dealer, his name was Solly Feinstein.

• • •

A few streets away, the bearded man, who had entered the synagogue just after the murder victim, was hurrying through the rain soaked streets as quickly as he could. He passed several street market stalls, busy with customers buying fruit, vegetables and Kosher chickens, hanging from hooks, looking more like skinny featherless pigeons than poultry.

It was by now almost lunchtime and the Duke of Sussex pub on the corner of a small side alley was doing a roaring trade, with stallholders and shoppers alike bustling in and out through the well worn swing doors. The bearded man in his overcoat and homburg hat didn't look out of place as he entered the pub, as many in there were dressed in a similar fashion. Once inside he made his way directly to the men's toilets, where he entered a cubicle, making sure to lock the door behind him. He then took a coloured silk handkerchief out of his pocket, from which he unwrapped a bloodstained switch-blade knife. He quickly wiped the knife clean, flushed the handkerchief down the toilet, and stuffed the now clean knife into his trouser pocket.

Peering closely at himself in the small wall mirror, he removed his metal-framed spectacles and his homburg hat. His fingers now carefully removed the two metal hair-grips, which were holding his wig in place. Attached to the wig were two long, almost pigtail like sideburns, which all came off together, revealing his own hair to be short, dark and slightly curly. Next to come off was the false beard and black overcoat, revealing the light coloured raincoat he was wearing underneath.

The transformation of Jack Comer was unbelievable, from a portly middle-aged Orthodox Jewish man; he had now become the well-built, good-looking young man about town, maybe even a businessman. He stuffed the hat, spectacles and wig into the centre of the overcoat, rolled it all into a ball and placed it on top of the toilet cistern before walking back into the crowded pub and out onto the street once again, without anyone taking a second glance at him. This wasn't an area he normally used very much, so his face was not familiar here; he was just another face in the crowd, and justice, he felt, had at last been done.

● ● ●

By Monday, the story of the man found murdered in an east London Synagogue was headlines in all the papers. Pictures of Solly Feinstein stared out from the front pages, along with the gory details of how his throat was slashed from ear to ear. He was described as a small time dealer in stolen goods.

Comer smirked to himself; he was pleased with what he had done to this miserable creature who had murdered his mother, but it also had its downside, which was the fact that he would not be able to see Ruth again, for when she saw the newspaper headline, as she inevitably would, she just might put two and two together and link him to the murder, even though it had been over two weeks ago since they had met at the party.

Chapter 7

There was only one way that Comer knew of drowning his sorrows, and that was to immerse himself in his work, which he did with great relish, as his work was something he absolutely loved.

He loved being able to walk through the streets of east London and to be greeted every few yards by people who knew him, others who wanted to know him, and those who made out to know him. Comer hardly ever went anywhere on his own, he was nearly always accompanied by at least two of his cronies, more if the occasion called for it. Sonny the Yank and Moisha Blueball were his most constant companions, mainly because he had known them since his teens, and now they also worked for him.

It had now been over a year since his brief yet memorable meeting with Ruth. He still carried the scrap of paper she had given him with her phone number on it, in his wallet, but in his heart he knew he would never contact her again; he couldn't, it would be far too dangerous. As much as he knew all this, he still couldn't help turning round to look, every time he saw someone who looked like her. What would he have done if he had seen her? Would he stop and talk to her - who knows? He wasn't here in Brick Lane this Sunday morning looking for love; he was here on business.

Comer, Sonny, and Moisha had been to Blooms Restaurant in Whitechapel for breakfast, and were now making their way down Brick Lane to collect the weekly contributions from the shops and stallholders. They passed the Great Synagogue on the corner of Fournier Street, and then the Truman's Brewery.

Their work would start when they actually entered the part of Brick Lane where all the stalls were situated, which was just after the huge iron railway bridge, which straddled the street. An elderly man was turning the handle of a large old barrel organ and smiling at passers by, in the hope of receiving a penny or two. "Who's he looking at?" snarled Sonny the Yank. Comer looked round at Sonny, "He's only trying to earn a few pennies for Christ sake" Sonny wasn't talking about the organ grinder, he was talking about one of two men who were standing on the corner of Pedley Street, opposite them.

Both men were well built, and were wearing dark suits and black roll-neck jumpers. The man with his back to them was looking up and down the street all the time, as if he was expecting someone, but the other man was staring straight at them.

There was something about these men that Comer didn't like. Why were they, or one of them to be precise, paying so much attention to him and his group? Even the police wouldn't be that blatant; would they? But if they weren't plain-clothes police officers, then they had to be a rival gang.

Comer wasn't worried about the men; he had handled bigger men than them in the past, but it did play on his mind as he carried on along the street, with Sonny and Moisha.

As they got to the railway bridge, a sudden deafening din assaulted their senses, and their path was almost entirely blocked by a huge crowd, which had gathered at the junction of Sclater Street and Brick Lane. The Lane was always crowded on a Sunday morning, but never this dense, and what the hell was all this noise?

One of the advantages of being tall is that you can always see over the heads of those in front of you. This came in handy for Comer at sporting events, such as boxing, and he put it to good use now, as he raised his head up more and managed to see a man standing on the back of an open lorry. The man was Oswald Mosley, the Blackshirt leader of Britain's Fascist party. He was shouting through a megaphone, ranting, raving, and taunting the Jews.

Comer, Sonny, and Moisha pushed their way through the crowd; they weren't about to let this insane Fascist denigrate their own race without giving him as good as he was giving other people, who for some reason, seemed too frightened to answer him or shout him down. It wasn't until they reached the front of the crowd that Comer saw why the crowd were too frightened to oppose this loud mouth, for there were at least twenty of Mosley's men, circling the lorry, all facing the crowd, and nearly all with one hand in their pocket or inside their jacket, as if hiding a weapon of some sort.

Although he had heard about them, this was the first time Comer had ever come face to face with Mosley or his Blackshirts. Not all big men, he thought, that was for sure, but an awful lot of ugly ones, and nearly every one wearing a black roll neck jumper, which answered the other problem, which had been nagging away at the back of his mind; the two men they had seen earlier, they were obviously Mosley's lookouts.

Comer, Sonny, and Moisha, were undoubtedly big men who could hold their own in a fight, but when Comer looked at Mosley's men, he realised they were hopelessly outnumbered. He felt like he was boiling inside, standing there and listening to the anti-Semitic taunts of Mosley, whilst being pushed from behind, closer and closer to one of Mosley's thugs, who sneered at him and uttered, "Move away Yid, before you get hurt"

Comer didn't mind being called a Yid, as that is exactly what he saw himself as; his parents both spoke Yiddish, so as far as he was concerned this was no big deal, but what made his hackles rise, was being told to move away; no one told Jack Comer to move away.

He grabbed the Fascist oaf by the collar of his jumper, pulled him forward and head butted him, immediately opening up a large gash on the man's eyebrow. As other Mosley men rushed forward to help their stricken comrade, so Sonny, and Moisha waded in as well, and not just with their fists, but with a brass knuckleduster, and a policeman's truncheon, which Sonny had acquired somewhat surreptitiously at a earlier fracas he had been involved in.

Within minutes the street looked like a battlefield, with many of the Jewish shopkeepers and stallholders now also joining in. This is what they had been waiting for, someone to lead them.

Stalls were overturned and shop windows were being smashed, but at least the Jews were fighting back, and Mosley was starting to look decidedly scared. The look on his face suddenly changed however, when another gang decided to join in, but this gang was the police.

• • •

Comer, Sonny, and Moisha appeared at Thames Magistrates Court the following morning, alongside eight other men, all Jewish; not one of Mosley's men were charged with anything.

Having been kept in police cells overnight, all the accused, including Comer, looked very tired and bedraggled indeed. They were paraded before the Magistrate, one at a time, all the shopkeepers and stallholders were charged with the same offence, that of causing an affray. All pleaded guilty and were fined five pounds and bound over to keep the peace for twelve months.

Comer, Sonny, and Moisha were last to be charged, but not with causing an affray like the other men, Comer, Sonny, and Moisha were charged with causing a disturbance in a public place; Comer was also charged separately with causing grievous bodily harm to a police officer.

Sonny and Moisha were dealt with first, being fined twenty pounds each and given six months imprisonment, suspended for one year.

Comer now stood alone in the dock and listened to Police Sergeant Harris of Bethnal Green Police Station giving evidence about him; telling how he had seized his truncheon from him and battered him over the head with it. Sergeant Harris also told the court that Comer was known in the area as a villain and a thief.

That was the final straw as far as Comer was concerned, he hadn't had any form of weapon on him that day, and the only person he knew who had a policeman's truncheon, was Sonny the Yank, but he could hardly use that as evidence in court. "You're a liar," he shouted, "I never had a truncheon and if I had hit you on the head with anything, then where's the bruises?" The Magistrate banged his gavel on the bench and told Comer to be quiet. "No I won't be quiet," shouted Comer, "He's lying, and he's got no right to call me a villain and a thief, I've never been nicked for anything in my life – he's a dirty rotten liar"

"Mr Comer," interrupted the Magistrate, "one more outburst like that and I shall hold you in contempt of court – you will be invited to state your side of the story after the police officer has finished giving his evidence, do I make myself clear?"

"Yes" answered Comer nodding his head, but even as he spoke, he could see from the contemptuous look on the Magistrate face, exactly whose side he was on. Sergeant Harris continued with his evidence, telling the court that local people were too frightened to give evidence in court about Comer and his gang, and that was why he had never been arrested before, and as for the injuries he had suffered at the hands of 'this thuggish man,' he assured the court that he did have bruises, which were fortunately hidden under his hair-line.

When it finally came to Comer's chance to give his side of the story, he was interrupted after less than one minute into his speech, "What do you do for a living Mr Comer?" asked the Prosecuting counsel. Comer felt his lips moving but no sounds coming out as he searched for what to say. He looked beseechingly at the Magistrate, "Do I have to answer that?" he asked, "I don't see that my profession has anything to do with what I'm being charged with here"

"It is a perfectly reasonable question Mr Comer," rapped the Magistrate, "and one which all defendants are asked – now if you don't mind, I would like an answer from you on this?"

When Comer reluctantly replied that he was a business consultant, the prosecuting counsel smiled and nodded his head in a mocking gesture, which caused a few sniggers from around the court, "Do you find business consultancy to be a well paid job Mr Comer?"

If only he had agreed to the services of a solicitor, but Comer had thought this was a simple case of causing a disturbance or similar, something that he could handle quite adequately himself. He explained to the prosecuting counsel that he had only recently taken up this profession, so he couldn't really say at this point whether it was well paid or not.

At this point, the prosecuting counsel called Sergeant Harris of Bethnal Green Police once again. Sergeant Harris was asked exactly how much money did Mr Comer have on him when he was arrested, to which Sergeant Harris produced his notebook and read out, that Mr Comer had fifty six pounds, eight shillings and four pence on him. This, he said was equivalent to a whole year's wages of one of his constables.

The prosecuting counsel thanked Sergeant Harris and addressed the Magistrate, saying, "Hardly the sort of money one would expect to find on a person who didn't even know if his new chosen profession was going to be well paid or not"

The prosecution then went on to ask Sergeant Harris if he had heard of Jack Comer before this incident had occurred, to which Harris replied that he had indeed. As a local police officer, Comer's name had come up on many occasions when he had been investigating crimes of beatings and intimidation, but, said Harris, in every case the witnesses would not testify or add their name to a witness statement against Mr Comer, in other words they were afraid of him.

Sergeant Harris was then asked if he had been examined and treated for the wounds he sustained that day. Sergeant Harris produced a medical certificate, which he had obtained from the police doctor who had examined him. The certificate pointed out that Sergeant Harris had severe bruising of the cranium area of his skull, which the attending doctor attributed to being struck with a heavy object, such as a truncheon.

As far as Comer was concerned, the police, the prosecuting counsel and the magistrate were all out to get him, no matter what he said he was going to be found guilty. The magistrate turned over the pages of his notes and adjusted his glasses on the end of his nose as he looked down at Comer and asked if there was anything further he wished to say in his defence.

This was the face of oppression, the face that Comer had been battling against all his life, the face of Oswald Mosley and his anti-Jewish thugs. Comer could feel the rage boiling up inside him; who did this person think he was, who could sit up there and look down his nose upon him? "Yes," he blurted out, "I do have something I want to say – I want to say that you can do what you want to me, but you won't ever break me or my resistance to people like you, because you are nothing but a fat slob"

A multitude of voices erupted in the courtroom; nothing like this had ever been heard before. The magistrate had to bang his gavel to restore order before he could continue. "Mr Comer," he declared, "Far from trying to break you, as you so inarticulately put it, I have studied my notes on the allegations against you, and have decided that there was not enough conclusive evidence against you to convict you of the alleged crime"

Comer could hardly believe his ears, this pompous, blown up fool of a magistrate had actually just found him not guilty. A broad smile broke out on his face as he turned and looked up to the public gallery where Moisha and Sonny were sitting.

"Before you become too overjoyed with my findings Mr Comer, I would like to add that although I am finding you not guilty of the charge against you, I am however, finding you guilty of contempt of court, which I warned you about earlier, and I sentence you to six months in prison - take him away"

The smile immediately dropped from Comer's face as a uniformed police officer took hold of his arm and led him out of the court.

Chapter 8

Later that same evening, Comer was transferred to a prison bus along with eight other prisoners, and transported to Brixton Prison is south London.

The smell was the first thing that Comer noticed as he was ushered into a large, dimly lit room with green tiled walls, a sort of mixture between a hospital and washing being boiled; it made him feel sick. Along one side of the room was a long table with piles of clothing laid out upon it, whilst on the other side, was another long table with four men sitting behind it.

Comer and the rest of the new inmates were ordered to the first table, where they were asked various questions, name, age, medical history, religion, etc. At the end of that table sat a doctor, at least that is what Comer assumed him to be, as he had a white coat on and a stethoscope around his neck He told Comer to strip down to his underpants, and then proceeded to give him a thorough examination, which included getting him to drop his underpants and bend over, while the doctor did a quick examination of his anus. What did he hope to find up there, thought Comer, a hacksaw and a rope ladder?

After the questions and medical examination were over, he was then directed to the second table, where he was issued with a grey uniform, which looked like it was made from old blankets. To add to this ghastly, ill-fitting monstrosity, he was also issued with woollen underwear and an enormous pair of black boots.

Still dressed in his underpants and carrying his new uniform in a pile, he was directed to the bath-house, where he was ordered to leave his clothing on a chair and get into one of the half dozen yellow stained and cracked baths that filled the small room. Needless to say the water was just about lukewarm, so he was out of there as quickly as he could, and drying himself down on a towel, about the size of a face-flannel and rough enough to sandpaper a piece of wood with.

There were no mirrors anywhere, so he couldn't see what he looked like in his new uniform and boots, but he got a good idea by looking at the others, who had come in with him; they looked like something from a Charlie Chaplin comedy, so God knows what he looked like.

"Supper" called a disembodied voice. What little delicacy had they rustled up for us, he thought, as they were marched into the next room, where yet another long wooden table was set up in the centre of the room, with benches each side of it. "Line up at the hatch" screamed a warden with a bright red face and bulbous eyes.

In almost any group of men, there is always at least one fat one, and sure enough there was in Comer's little team, and it was he, who managed to get to that hatch first; Comer was fourth. The men were all given a wooden tReggie with a small dish containing the supper on it, plus a tin mug full of something slightly resembling tea.

What the hell was on that dish? Comer wasn't sure what it was, but at least he now knew where the terrible smell was coming from. As hungry as he was, there was no way he could eat this. He pushed the dish away from him and took a sip of the tea, which didn't taste a lot better than the mess on the dish looked. "Aren't you going to eat that?" It was the fat man, who was sitting opposite him, "Eat it?" replied Comer, "I don't even know what the hell it is?" "It's bread pudding," said the fat man, "I'll have it if you don't want it?" Comer pushed the dish of stodge over to the fat man, "Help yourself"

Ten minutes later another warder came into the room, ringing a hand bell, "Right, come on then, let's be having you," he shouted, "It's beddy-byes times boys" He walked up and down the line of men, ringing the bell as loud as he could, and as close to the men's ears as he could, "You got to be a bit quicker than that in here boys – when I tell you to do something, you do it, and you do it quick – do you hear me?"

He shouted this last order into the ear of an elderly looking man, who jumped to his feet immediately, apologising to the warder as he did so. Comer gripped the edge of the table in order to hold himself back; he felt like knocking this ignorant pig out.

A great introduction to prison life this was, a cold stinking place, rotten food, and jumped up little warders who thought they could make your life a misery. No one was going to make Jack Comer's life a misery!

• • •

A single cell; this was a luxury most prisoners craved for. Most had to share a cell with another prisoner, some even had three men to a cell. It didn't bear thinking about; the smells, the closeness of their bodies, the constant inane chattering, the petty bickering, which quite often erupted into violence, and if you were very unlucky, you might even be locked up with a sexual offender, who sees you, not as his cell-mate, but as a piece of meat, to be used. This, of course wouldn't have happened to Comer, who could easily fight off such things, but just to be on the safe side, he had hidden some money in a bar of soap, which he was allowed to keep, and handed two pounds to the warder who was allocating the new prisoners their cells.

Comer quickly adapted to prison life; he never accepted it, but he used the system to his own advantage. He soon found out who were the friendly 'screws' (prison wardens) who were susceptible to a bribe, and who were the Prison Governor's 'blue eyed boys' Extra bedclothes? See Mr Barrett, the head screw on his landing. Writing paper and pen – see Mr Barrett. His own shoes returned to him in place of the prison boots – see Mr Barrett.

Brixton was mainly a remand prison, which meant that prisoners who were awaiting trial were allowed to have meals sent in to them by relatives or friends. Comer saw an opportunity here to indulge in some of the finer things in life other than prison stodge, and so with the help of his 'friend' Mr Barrett, he arranged for either Sonny or Moisha to have his favourite foods delivered to the prison for him every day. They also passed packages and envelopes to Mr Barrett, who in turn passed them onto Comer. The packages contained everything from cigarettes and cigars, to whiskey, money, books, even his favourite white linen shirts, and proper underwear.

The exercise yard was where prisoners met and discussed the orders of the day. It was also where Comer conducted his latest business venture, which was that of prison bookmaker. He took bets on almost anything, from the weather, to horse and dog racing, the results of which he obtained from his friendly screw, Mr Barrett. Prisoners could use either hard cash or cigarettes to bet with, Comer accepted almost anything.

It was on one of his daily walks around the exercise yard that he met Billy Munro, a Scot, in his fifties, with vivid red scars down each side of his face. Comer took a liking to Munro straight away; he reminded him of himself, a big man with a swagger and an air of bravado about him.

Munro had only been in Brixton Prison a couple of days, but had already been told that Comer was the 'guvner' there; if you want anything, ask Comer. "So what are you in here for?" Comer asked.

Munro explained that he had been 'fitted up,' which is underworld slang for having a false charge brought against a person.

Have you heard of Darby Sabini? Munro asked. Comer smiled; of course he had heard of Darby Sabini, everyone had heard of him. He was of Italian stock, and controlled most of the illegal gambling in southern Britain. It was said that he could call upon an estimated 300 gang members at any one time, including local criminals and imported Sicilian gunmen.

Munro was impressed with Comer's knowledge, and carried on to tell him how he had once worked for Darby Sabini, but had fallen out with him because Sabini had overheard him laughing and running down the Italians as a race of ice cream sellers. It was just a joke, explained Munro, but something that he had to grin and bear.

Munro explained how he then went to work for another gang, the Collins family from south London, who also worked the racetracks. A few weeks ago, whilst waiting for a train at Liverpool Street Station, he was suddenly approached by two very big men, one with a strong Irish accent and the other a Cockney. "I didn't know them," he said, "but they certainly knew me, hello Billy said the Irishman, do you know who we are?" Munro continued to tell Comer that he didn't have a clue who they were and told them so, but as he did so, the Irishman pushed his face into Munro's and told him they were Darby Sabini's men. "I didn't believe them," said Munro, "I had worked for Sabini for a long time and I hadn't seen these two before, so I went to walk away from them, I'd only got about two paces away when I felt what I thought was a blow to my head, it sort of spun me round, and then I saw the pair of them coming at me, both with open cut-throat razors – they slashed at me again and again, catching my face down both sides – I could feel the warmth of my own blood pouring down my face – the strength just went out of me and I collapsed to the floor, but as I did so the Irishman leaned over me and warned me not to go near any of the racetracks Darby Sabini controlled ever again – if I did, he said it would be a bullet in my head next time, not just a couple of tram lines"

Comer was puzzled, "So how did you end up in here then?" he asked. Munro explained that he passed out and after the attack, and the next thing he knew was waking up in hospital with a detective sitting by his bed. The detective cautioned him and then charged him with being in possession of an offensive weapon, which was one of the cut-throat razors that had been dumped down upon his body as his assailants had ran away.

Comer could hardly believe his ears, "The copper must have been a complete idiot," he said. Munro shook his head, "No, he wasn't an idiot, I was – the copper works for Sabini"

Over the course of the next few weeks Comer and Munro became close friends. Comer even cut Munro in on his gambling business in the prison. Munro was earning money from Comer, while Comer was learning all the time from Munro.

When Munro spoke about Sabini for instance, he spoke of him with reverence, not with hatred, as one would think he would, especially as it was due to him that Munro was slashed, and had also ended up in prison on a trumped up charge.

"You know why Darby Sabini has so much power? Two reasons – one, because he looks after his own – especially the Italians, or at least that is what he leads people to believe, and two, because he is a self publicist, and the more people that believe in him, the more powerful he becomes"

Comer was fixed in his ways and beliefs in a great deal things, but he was always ready to listen to the perceived wisdom of his elders, which was probably due to his Jewish upbringing. Munro's words made sense, and were something he would remember and make the most of when he got out of prison.

Four months into his sentence, he was suddenly told he was being released the following day. He gave Billy Munro five pounds and told him to contact him when he got out. He also arranged with his friendly screw, Mr Barrett, for Munro to take over his cell after he was gone, as Munro was still awaiting a trial date.

● ● ●

The ever faithful Sonny and Moisha were waiting for Comer when the gates of Brixton Prison opened and he walked out into the early morning sunlight of mid July. Moisha was sitting behind the wheel of a magnificent black Packard, Straight Eight saloon, while Sonny stood with one of the back doors open, ready for Comer to step in.

Comer leaned back in the lush interior of the huge limousine; the smell of the leather and the wood trim around the doors; the plush carpets on the floor; this was luxury as was surely befitting for a man of his demeanour. The car headed out into the traffic on the main road; it didn't drive as a normal car, it purred, like a Rolls Royce. Moisha looked at Comer in his rear view mirror, "Where to Jack, fancy some breakfast – Blooms maybe?" Comer looked down at his crumpled trousers, and told Moisha to take him straight to his flat in Cobb Street, "I need a bath and a change of clothes before I do anything," he said, "after that I want you to take me round to my dad's place, Oh, and I need some money," he said, turning to Sonny, who immediately obliged with a wad of banknotes. Moisha meanwhile had manoeuvred the car into the direction of the east end of London.

● ● ●

The hallway of the flats where his father lived was as dank and gloomy as ever. Comer, now resplendent in a freshly pressed suit, clean shirt and tie and highly polished shoes, hammered on the door with his huge fist; the door knocker had been missing for at least five years. He had to knock again, remembering to call out and identify himself this time, as it was rent collection day, when so many tenants were reluctant to open their street doors.

The door was finally opened a crack and his sister Rebecca peered out. When she saw it was him her face lit up and she threw her arms around him, "Oh Jack, Jack" She had tears in her eyes as she let him into the flat.

The big change in the flat was of course that his mother was no longer there, but the old, and well worn furniture was all still the same, as to was the smell of cooking, which he remembered from his childhood, and which his sister Rebecca was now contributing to.

There was one other change, and that was Jacob, his father. He was sitting in his usual chair, not looking at Comer at all, but staring through the thick lace curtains, to the street outside.

Comer called to his dad three times without receiving an answer, "Dad?" he called again, "It's me, Jack" His father pointed to the Packard, which he could see parked outside, "Is that your car?" Comer looked round at his sister, "What's wrong?" he asked. Rebecca quietly explained that he had been like this since their mother was killed; he had packed his job in and now just sat at home all day looking out the window.

Comer walked over to his father and placed his hand on his shoulder; "I'm going to take care of you now dad" His father pushed his hand off his shoulder and for the first time looked up at his son, "Bit late for that isn't it? I don't need your help Jack; your mother needed help, and look what happened to her"

For one of the first times in his life, Comer was lost for words; he just stared down at the little old man, who was once so big in his eyes. His father never returned eye contact and instead turned back to staring out the window once again.

Comer turned back to Rebecca and took his wallet out of his pocket. He took out the bundle of money, which Moisha had handed him earlier, and started to count some off. He suddenly stopped counting, folded the whole bundle in half and gave it to Rebecca. "Here," he said, "get whatever he needs, whatever you both need, and there'll be more where that came from, every week, I promise you" Rebecca took the money from her brother, kissed it and tucked it into her apron pocket. She couldn't say thank you to him as her eyes welled up with tears as she opened the door to let him out and silently mouthed the words, good-bye Jack.

• • •

Back in the lush interior of the Packard once again, Comer was now doing exactly the same thing as his father had been doing; looking out the window with his back towards Sonny, who was sitting next to him.

"I'll need some more money Sonny," he said, "and a drink" Sonny mumbled his reply, "no problem Jack – no problem"

After a couple of calls on local east end pubs, Comer was at last starting to relax. "Do you feel hungry Jack?" asked Moisha as they left the pub in Salmon Lane. Up to this point he hadn't given food a thought, but now it was mentioned, he started to feel a few rumbles from deep within his stomach. Moisha told him to leave it to him as he swung the car around again and started heading towards the west end of London.

The Packard drew to a halt outside the Nightingale Rooms in London's prestigious Mayfair district; no need to search for parking places in 1930s London; traffic was very sparse, even in Mayfair, where many people would use their chauffeurs to drop them off and pick them up again later. Moisha left the car where it was and joined Comer and Sonny; all three walking into the club together.

Comer had been in a number of clubs over the past few years, but nothing prepared him for this place; it was sumptuous to say the least, with its marble pillars, and a sweeping staircase leading down to a parquet lined dance floor, which was surrounded by tables and chairs for the diners. A pianist was leading a trio who were performing a jazz number on the stage, with a young and beautiful female dancer performing in front of them.

They were shown to a table near the dance floor by the maitre d' who then beckoned to a waiter to serve them. "Nice place boys," Comer said, as they sipped their first bottle of Champagne, "how'd you hear about it?" Moisha explained that a young guy named Albert Redman, whom he had met in a spieler a couple of weeks ago had told him about it, he said a well-known face about town part owned the place.

This intrigued Comer; who was this well-known face that part owned such a place? Neither Sonny nor Moisha knew or seemed to care. Moisha seemed to be more interested in the exotic dancer, who was now performing very close to them, accompanied by the pianist who played and sung his rendition of Begin the Beguine.

As the waiter took their orders for dinner, Comer scanned the faces of the diners. A couple of big men over the other side of the dance floor; could one of them be this mysterious Mr Big, who part owned this establishment? Or what about the diner with the very glamorous woman who was absolutely dripping in diamonds, who was sitting quite close to them? "What?" he exclaimed as the waiter interrupted his train of thought and asked him for the second time, what he would like for dinner. "Oh, er, steak, yeah, I'll have steak and chips" "And how would you like it cooked sir?" enquired the waiter, to which Comer answered, "I want it cooked properly, I don't want it bleeding raw do I?"

An hour or so later and all three men had finished their meals, and were on their third bottle of Champagne. Moisha beckoned to the scantily clad cigarette girl, who slinked her way to their table with her tray slung around her neck, which allowed her breasts to hang over the top like a pair of turtle doves about to burst into song. "What brand?" she simpered, "we'll have the biggest," he paused, "cigars you've got" said Moisha, roaring with laughter.

Comer, Sonny and Moisha were certainly enjoying themselves as they sat back, with their cigars, listening to the music and watching the dancers on the floor. They were now on their fourth bottle of Champagne when Sonny suddenly jumped to his feet, "There he is, that's Albert, the young guy who told me about this place" he said, pointing to a well dressed young man who had just entered and was making his way through the crowd.

Albert Redman saw Moisha waving to him and came over to their table. "Nice to see you Moisha – well, what do you think of it here?" Moisha said they all liked it and invited Redman to sit down and have a drink with them, "That is alright isn't it Jack?" he intervened for Comer's approval. Comer waved for him to pull up another chair and sit down next to him, "of course it is," he said as he leaned across and took another glass from the table next to them.

Comer's initial reaction to Redman was that he was a jumped up little spiv, probably a couple of years younger than himself, eager to prove himself by loud mouthing about his connections in the underworld. As far as Comer was concerned, his local publican had connections, but that didn't put him in the number one league. He was determined nevertheless, to use Redman to find out what he wanted. This was a class place and whoever owned even a part of it was worth knowing. "Champagne?" he said with a smile as fake as the diamond ring on Redman's finger, as he poured a glass for him.

Half an hour later, he had found out all he needed to know about Redman, he was what we would today call a 'gofer' someone who does almost anything for a pittance, just to be near the rich and famous, or infamous in this particular case. As for the man who owns a part of the fabulous establishment they were now in; "Billy White" exclaimed Redman, "Talk of the devil, here he comes now"

Comer looked to where Redman was indicating, and saw Billy White for himself, as he entered with a beautiful blond on his arm, and a minder trailing behind them, who was as large as a bear, and with a face to match.

The staff were all over Billy White, taking his hat, his young lady's fur stole and showing him to the best table in the house. Comer noticed how so many people waved or said hello to him and how he acknowledged them with a casual nod or wave of his hand. He was acting like Royalty, but this, thought Comer, was a man who had most definitely arrived.

"Well?" said Comer to Redman, "are you going to ask him over or what?" Redman somewhat nervously smiled over towards Billy White and gave a little wave. What an absolute fake this guy is, thought Comer, I wouldn't be surprised if he didn't even know him at all. At that very moment he saw White get to his feet and start to walk towards his table, and he wasn't with his minder, which indicated to Comer that he felt safe. Maybe he had misjudged Redman?

The smile dropped from White' face the moment he reached their table. He looked directly at Redman and asked him what the fuck did he think he was doing sitting there boozing. "You was supposed to be checking out the punters before I got here" Redman started to splutter out some feeble excuse, but White wasn't interested, he told Redman to get over to his table and make sure his fiancé was alright and to help her with the menu and wine list.

Redman obeyed without further questions and scuttled off to do what he was told. Billy White immediately switched the charm back on, and apologised to Comer for Redman' behaviour. Comer brushed the incident to one side and asked White if he would like to join him for a drink. White had a better idea, "Why don't you all come and join me at my table, there's plenty of room?"

As the evening wore on, the two men got on very well. When asked, Comer described himself a sort of insurance agent, "I look after people who are being bullied and threatened," he explained, "and in my area of east London that is one hell of a lot of people" Billy White smiled knowingly, "You sound like a man after my own heart," he said.

Some time later, White looked at his solid gold Patek Philippe watch and declared it was time to go. He reached into his inside pocket and took out a slim gold case, from which he produced a business card, "here," he said, as he gave one to Comer, "any time you're in the area, pop in and see me, you never know, we might be able to do some business together?"

Comer looked at the business card as White and his party left the club, it read 'William White, Entertainment and Business financier, 83 Park Lane, London, W1. He then turned to Moisha and Sonny, "I want you to find out everything you can about Mr White," he said, "Where he's from, who he mixes with, and where all his money come from?"

Chapter 9

Over the following few weeks, while Moisha and Sonny were busy putting themselves about London in their quest for any information they could find about Billy White, Comer was equally busy; not in London, but on the horse race tracks, such as Kempton Park, Epsom Downs and Sandown Park. Like so many Jews from the east end of London, Comer loved to gamble, but his predilection was for cards rather than horse racing, which he knew hardly anything about, apart from his very brief spell as a bookmaker in Brixton Prison.

What he did know however was that there was big money in gambling; he remembered what Billy Munro had told him during his time in Brixton Prison, of how Darby Sabini controlled the race tracks and how he could call up a vast army of men at any given time. He had been brought up hearing about Darby Sabini, the man was a legend, but he didn't really know anything about how he operated. Now, he thought, was the time to find out.

• • •

Comer normally liked the luxury of being chauffeured around in a limousine, more so since he had become the proud owner of a beautiful Packard, but today he had decided to travel by train, from Waterloo to Epsom Downs. This was for two reasons, the first being that he had ordered Moisha and Sonny to scout around London, finding out what they could about Billy White, and they would need the car for that. The second, and probably the most important reason, was that he didn't want to be seen at this important race meeting with Moisha and Sonny; two large men, who alongside himself, could possibly stand out in the crowd. In order to mingle and go unnoticed he needed to be alone.

It was a beautiful late August afternoon when he got there. He had even gone to the trouble of swatting up on what the average racecourse punter wears, and had dressed accordingly, in a tweed jacket, silk cravat, and a brown trilby, accompanied of course by the obligatory pair of binoculars around his neck.

The course was particularly busy as Comer strolled through the crowds, looking every inch like the seasoned race-goer he was trying to portray. He paused at every bookmaker's stand, studying the prices as they chalked them up on their blackboards, but it wasn't just the prices that he was studying, he was also studying the men who were standing around the bookmaker's stands; these men were heavies, who more than likely worked for Darby Sabini. They didn't bother to look at the prices, but were looking instead at the punters, people like himself.

He couldn't afford to keep in one place for too long in case the heavies who were minding the pitches became aware of him. He placed a couple of small bets here and there, always on the favourites; only mugs bet on outsiders with their big odds, and about as much chance of winning a race as he would have of being a jockey.

An argument was taking place at the next stand he came to. A punter was shouting at the bookmaker, saying he had been fiddled out of his winnings. He was insisting he had laid out five pounds to win on True Blue, a horse that had just won the last race. The bookmaker however, insisted he had placed his money on Blue Boy, another horse in the same race, which had come third. Comer watched intently as the man became more angry and threatening. The bookmaker looked around towards three large men, who were obviously more of Darby Sabini's boys. The heavies wasted no time in barging their way forward through the crowd, two of them grabbing the man by his arms, literally lifting him off the ground, while the third heavy punched him in the stomach, followed by two heavy blows to his face and head. They then ran the man away, his feet dragging through the dirt as they did so.

This could be where Sabini himself shows up, thought Comer as he discreetly followed them. He watched as the heavies continued to drag the man towards some public toilets, explaining to onlookers as they went that the man was drunk and they were helping him.

Comer watched from a distance as they dragged the man into the public toilets, where he could hear more beating and the low groans of their victim. Suddenly two more men appeared on the scene, one was a middle-aged man, short and wiry, not at all well dressed; the other was a bigger man, dressed almost like one of Oswald Mosley's thugs, in a dark suit and a roll neck jumper. "Do you want me to go in Darby? Asked the big man, "or do you want to do it?"

So this was the infamous Darby Sabini, a little runt of a man, with all that power and money. Comer could have taken him with one hand behind his back in a fair fight, but who fights fair in the underworld?

Darby Sabini sneered at the big man, "What is the point of me owning a dog and barking myself? I want you to go in and break his fingers, but no cutting, do you understand?" His accent was a mixture of Cockney and Italian; so strong he could have come straight from a pantomime.

Comer watched the big man enter the toilets; followed by a piercing scream from somewhere within. Seconds later the big man and the other three heavies came hurrying out again. "Done to order boss" said the big man, smiling as he cracked his own knuckles in a parody of what it must have sounded like as he crushed the bones on the punter's hand.

Sabini looked so small and insignificant as he walked away between all these four men, but the power he welded was something Comer had never witnessed before. Comer followed at a discreet distance and watched as Sabini suddenly stopped, and took his pocket watch from out of his waistcoat pocket. He brusquely dismissed two of the men and indicated for the other two to continue with him, towards the bookmaker's stands once again.

Comer watched as the first two men, whom Sabini had dismissed, now headed towards a large pub at the edge of the course. Could be just the right time now, he thought, for a drink himself, and hopefully some insight into how Sabini's men operated when out of sight of their boss.

The pub, appropriately named 'The Winning Post' was large and filled mostly with men, many of whom were standing by the bar. The two heavies were not difficult for Comer to spot, as they stood out, head and shoulders against the average customer there. Comer positioned himself as close to them as he could without making it too obvious. He ordered the same drink as he saw them drinking, which was a pint of Guinness Stout, which he thought seemed more in keeping with his surroundings than his usual large Brandy would have been.

The two heavies, Irish Pat and George Sprattling, were busy stuffing sausage rolls down their throats and washing them down with huge mouthfuls of Guinness as they continued to talk. Their conversation was mostly inane and light-hearted banter about the barmaid, nothing to do with their work or their boss, Mr Sabini. Comer had to edge a little closer in order to hear them properly, as they started talking in lower tones. Unfortunately the chat had now changed to what was going to win the 3.30. "I'm not asking you to believe me" said Pat, in a strong Irish accent, "I'm just telling you that I got this straight from the governor's mouth himself, it's going to be Rose of Tralee by a mile" Sprattling shook his head, as he looked at a sheet of paper with the runners, riders and prices on it, "Rose of Tralee is going to be at least fourteen to one, it's impossible" "Well don't fucking do it then," replied Pat, "I'm only trying to help you"

As Comer leant across the bar to order another drink, he purposely caught Pat's arm, knocking some of his Stout over, and onto the bar. "Oh dear," he said, "did I do that? I am sorry, here, let me buy you another drink" Pat was about to burst a blood vessel by the look on his face, which had turned the colour of a London pillar-box, but Comer had diffused the situation just in time with his offer of another drink. "Make it three more, one for each of us" he called to the barmaid.

A few minutes later, all three men were smiling and chatting as if they had known each other for years. "So what is it you do then Jack?" asked Pat. Comer smiled "Acquisitions Pat," he replied, "acquisitions" Pat looked round quizzically to Sprattling, who shrugged; he had no more idea what the word meant as Pat did. "It's all about business boys," Comer interjected, "Take-overs, that sort of thing" Both Pat and Sprattling nodded enthusiastically, even though neither had any idea of what Comer was talking about.

Desperately trying to think of something sensible to say, Sprattling asked Comer if he was having a day off today then, "From your business I mean?" he added. Comer took out his cigarette case, offered them to the two men and lit one for himself. Blowing out a cloud of smoke, he stared for a moment or two at the two men and replied "Far from it boys, I'm always working, even at this very moment" Pat looked puzzled, "What, are you planning to take this pub over then?" he laughed. "This pub?" replied Comer, smiling, "not really boys, I was thinking more along the lines of this race course"

Comer finished his Stout and slammed the glass back down on the counter, "Don't forget to tell your boss will you boys, I'm sure he'll be very interested, and don't forget to mention my name as well won't you? – Comer, Jack Comer" Pat and George Sprattling looked at each other in silence; after all, heavies are normally picked for brawn not brains. They watched Comer, not sure what to do, as he swaggered out of the pub.

• • •

The Packard was waiting for him, with Moisha at the wheel, as he walked down the steps of Waterloo Station. Sonny was already standing by the rear of the car with the back door open. "Everything go alright Jack?" he asked, as he let Comer into the car and ran around to the other side to climb in himself. "Fine, fine" mumbled Comer as Moisha eased the great car away and into the traffic towards the west end.

By the time they reached Piccadilly Circus it was quite dark; their faces illuminated every so often by the neon lit advertising signs that flashed on and off in garish colours. Comer looked up to see the Guinness sign; a clock with the words, 'Guinness is Good For You' underneath it. It made him smile as he remembered drinking it with the two morons from Sabini's gang, at the racecourse earlier that day.

"So what did you find out about our friend Mr White?" asked Comer as the car turned into Great Windmill Street and pulled up outside the Kosher Salt Beef Bar, almost opposite the Windmill Theatre. "You're going to be surprised when I tell you," replied Moisha, "shall we go inside and eat, or do you want me to tell in here?"

Comer was starving hungry and could smell the salt beef and pickled herrings from where he sat. "Let's go," he said as he opened the car door and hurried into the café. Within seconds the three men were sitting on stools by a long window shelf. The food here was like manna from Heaven for Comer, much better than Blooms in Whitechapel, and you didn't have to put up with miserable staff either.

Moisha leant close to Comer, "Remember the High Holborn bank robbery a few months back? They got away with two hundred and fifty grand?" Comer stopped eating for a moment, "You're not saying this Billy White character was involved in that are you?" Moisha nodded his head, "The word is that Billy White not only put the job up in the first place, but he also funded it"

"Hold on" replied Comer, "where did you get this information from – it is Kosher isn't it?" Moisha nodded again, "I'm telling you Jack, it's as Kosher as that schmaltz herring you're eating – I got it from Sonny

Goldberg – you know him, Sonny the thief from Stepney, he told me he was working for White until he broke his leg while he was escaping from a break-in at a big house that White had put him onto"

Moisha continued; telling Comer that Billy White had suddenly burst onto the scene about a year ago, starting with hijacking lorries, then smash and grab raids, and graduating onto armed bank raids. "How come I've never heard of him before?" asked Comer. "You've never heard of him before Jack", answered Moisha, "for the simple reason that he moves in different circles to us, while we have been stuck in east London, White has concentrated on the west end – he's got his finger in every pie, including the top clubs, you name it, and White's involved in it, they call him the governor around here now"

Comer stared at his refection in the window in front of him, as the lights of the Windmill Theatre opposite flashed on and off; one second he was alone, in the darkness, followed a second or two later by a picture of him surrounded by an aura of light. If he had been a religious man, he might have taken this as some kind of divine message, but Comer had never upheld his faith. One thing he was sure of, and that was that he had dreams and aspirations to fulfil, and come what may, he was going to do it.

Billy White was a very useful contact to have, but Comer felt that he needed to prove himself first before running to see White. First on his agenda were the race courses, and that meant getting rid of the opposition, i.e. Darby Sabini, and to do this he needed to expand his team. He had remembered what Billy Munro had told him in Brixton Prison, how Sabini used his fellow countrymen to boost his powers. This, he decided, was an option he would most definitely look into.

Chapter 10

The Red Lion pub in Clerkenwell was the unofficial headquarters of Darby Sabini and his crew. There was nothing luxuriant about this pub, with its bare wooden floorboards, yellowing walls and ceiling, dark, almost black, oak tables and chairs, and flickering gaslights. Even the publican himself looked like he was from another age, and never spoke unless spoken to first. The Red Lion did have one redeeming feature that day, for winter had arrived with a vengeance; one of the coldest winters London had experienced for many years, but tucked away in one corner was an open coal fire, where a group of four men, including Pat and George Sprattling, whom Comer had met at the races that summer, were all sitting around a table, laughing and chatting.

Sprattling was telling the others around the table that he was glad it was snowing; at least he didn't have to get up early in the morning, with all the race meetings cancelled. "You better not let Darby hear you say that," added Pat. "What's the difference?" said Sprattling, "he don't pay us if we're not on the course" "No," answered Pat, "but he might give you something else to do, in one of the spielers or something, I bet you wouldn't say no to that would you?"

Sprattling smiled and agreed that it would be nice to work in one of the spielers for a change, "But he's never asked me to work in one yet, " he said. Pat laughed, "And you know why that is don't you? He said, "because you can't fucking count or add up"

Sprattling's face turned bright scarlet as everyone around the table laughed at this comment. He slammed his beer down on the table and jumped to his feet, grabbing Pat by the shirt collar and pulling him towards him, "You'd better watch your fucking tongue Pat," he shouted, "you're not talking to one of your fucking altar boys now you know" The other two men at the table jumped to their feet and started to separate Sprattling and Pat as the table overturned, knocking all the drinks to the floor. One of the men glanced to the window beside him and saw a car pulling up. "Here comes the governor now" he shouted, "Quick, get this fucking mess cleared up" Sprattling let go of Pat immediately, while one of the other men rushed to get a cloth from the bar, which he used to start cleaning up the spilt beer on the floor while the others straightened the table back up.

It was now dark, cold and windy outside, with sheets of snow blowing along the street as Darby Sabini and his chief minder and driver, Fat Louie Russo, got out of a maroon Vauxhall Cadet and made their way across the pavement towards the door of the pub. They took no notice of the lorry, which was parked just along the street a little, but they stopped dead in their tracks, as they heard a voice shout out "Darby Sabini?"

The canvas flaps on the back part of the lorry suddenly opened up and two men appeared, both dressed in black overcoats, black hats, and carrying double barrel shotguns. They jumped down from the lorry and ran towards Sabini and Russo. The first man pulled one trigger on his gun, which released a blinding flash of light and a loud explosion, sending a thousand deadly pellets towards its intended victims. Russo flung his arms around Sabini and tried to rush him towards the pub door, but as he did another shot blasted out, this time catching Russo in the back and sending both him and Sabini to the ground. The two gunmen rushed towards the fallen bodies of Sabini and Russo and emptied their final two shots into their bodies.

The two gunmen paused for just two brief seconds; long enough to see the two lifeless bodies, their clothing splattered with blood and holes where they had been hit. A large pool of blood was now forming in the snow all around the bodies as the gunmen turned and ran back towards their lorry, where a third man was sitting at the wheel with the engine still running. The gunmen leapt into the lorry beside the driver as it roared away.

Pat rushed out of the pub, looked briefly at the two bloodied bodies of the men on the ground, quickly pulled a revolver from inside his coat and fired two shots at the lorry as it turned the corner and was gone from sight. Sprattling and the other two men now emerged from the pub. All four men stood in silence and shocked horror as they stared down at Sabini and Russo lying sprawled across the blood splattered pavement in the snow.

● ● ●

A few days later, Comer's Packard pulled up outside a row of four storey red-brick houses in Teesdale Street, Bethnal Green. Moisha, Sonny, and Comer, all got out and walked across the icy pavement to number 72, where the street door was wedged open. A long narrow passageway connected to an equally narrow staircase, where all three men ascended, with Moisha in the lead, followed Comer and then Sonny.

There were no lights on the stairs, but at the very top of the house they stopped at a small landing and a door with an electric bell set into it. Moisha rang the bell and waited. A few seconds later the door was opened by a portly woman in her fifties, who looked very worried when she saw the three men. "He isn't in," she nervously stammered. Comer looked over her head to the large room behind her, which was made up from two rooms that had been knocked into one. "Well that must be his twin brother over there then," Comer said as he pushed past the woman and headed into the room, followed closely by Moisha and Sonny.

The room was filled with women; three on sewing machines and three at small tables, where they were engaged in hand sewing men's jackets and overcoats. A large, square table dominated the room, where a middle aged man with a thick dark moustache and a bald head, was busy chalking over some dark material and then cutting it with an enormous pair of tailor's shears. This was Solly Milner, the owner of the little factory, the man whom Comer had come to see, who, according to his wife, wasn't there.

"Hello Solly," Comer smiled as he slapped Milner on the shoulder, "not the best of news was it?" Milner looked nervously around the room, where the eyes of all the women, including his wife, seemed to be fixed on him. "I did my best Mr Comer," he said, almost whispering. Comer shook his head and tutted, "Wasn't quite good enough though Solly, was it?"

The sewing machines had now stopped; the women making believe that they were re-threading the spools of cotton, or adjusting the machine in order to try and hear what was being said. Milner was looking very nervous and looked across the room to his wife, indicating for her to get the women working again. He then pointed over to a glass door, "Do you mind if we talk out there – too many ears in here?" Comer nodded and followed Milner to the door, which led out onto a small fire escape landing with metal stairs leading down to a small backyard.

Now out of earshot of the women, Comer asked Milner who he had taken with him and where were the guns. Milner stammered, "What difference does it make who I took?" he said, "the big man fell right across the other one – it was probably that, which saved his life – it certainly wasn't my fault" "So who did you take Solly?" asked Comer, "I think I am entitled to know, don't you?" Milner was now visibly shaking as he answered Comer, "Alright, alright," he stammered, "I took my driver, Jake, he drove the lorry, and I took my brother David, he had the other gun" Comer nodded, "And the guns?" he asked. "They're under my cutting table in there" answered Milner, pointing to the interior of the workshop.

Comer shook his head; "I didn't force you to take this job on Solly, did I? I asked you if you thought you could handle it, and you told me it would be a piece of cake" Milner interrupted in a raised voice, "It was an accident Mr Comer, how was I to know he would have a fucking gorilla with him, who would fall on top of him and protect him from our shots?" Comer wasn't used to having people answer him back or raise their voices to him, his face changed, his eyes hardened as he stared in silence at Milner. "Alright, alright, I'm sorry," said Milner, "so what do you want me to do, I'll do whatever you want?"

Comer suddenly grabbed Milner by his throat, twisted him round and pushed him half over the edge of the metal fire escape. "Look at the floor down there Solly - we're four floors up, if you slipped on these icy stairs you'd be dead before you hit the ground"

Milner was terrified, his eyes bulging as he struggled to stop himself from being tipped over. "I'll carry on paying you," he whelped like an injured puppy, "I'll pay you more, if that's what you want?"

Comer dragged him back from the edge and shoved him up against the door. "I don't want more money from you Solly, I want your allegiance. When you signed up with the Jewish Protection League I kept my part of the bargain didn't I? I personally beat the shit out of two of Mosley's men when I caught them painting Nazi Swastikas on your door – now I want the same from you – allegiance, that all. It won't be me who'll throw you off this balcony; it'll be Darby Sabini's boys, do you know what I'm saying?"

Inside the workroom, Moisha and Sonny were standing, silently watching the fire exit door, while the women workers tried their best to continue with their work. At last the fire escape door opened and Milner and Comer came back into the room. Milner led Comer over to his large cutting table, where he bent down and took out a roll of material from underneath and handed it to Comer. "Here," he said, "as ordered" Comer smiled and looked at the roll of material. From one end he could see just the tip of one of the shotguns barrels poking out, which he quickly covered over with the end of the material.

Milner did his best to smile and look as if everything was fine as he escorted Comer, Sonny and Moisha to the door. Comer paused for a moment and shook Milner's hand, "From now on Solly, you pay me nothing, no more weekly contributions, but I will expect allegiance from you when I call upon you in the future, do I make myself clear? Comer handed the roll of material containing the shotguns, to Sonny and then continued down the narrow winding staircase towards the street door.

Chapter 11

The funeral of Fat Louie Russo took place at Highgate Cemetery on Friday 15 March 1935. Only a handful of mourners attended the burial, including his older brother and an elderly woman, who was believed to be his aunt. Pat and George Sprattling did not attend the service, but turned up at the graveside later, with Pat pushing Darby Sabini in a wheelchair.

At least a dozen police officers watched from a distance as the coffin was lowered into the ground and Russo's brother, his aunt, and Sabini, threw handfuls of earth down the open grave onto it. The police were hoping to see more underworld figures, as is usual in these types of events, but in this instance they were disappointed, for all, they saw was Darby Sabini, who had now lost a leg and was confined to a wheelchair, and two minor underlings, Pat and George Sprattling.

"Look at him," remarked one senior police officer, referring to Sabini, "he's had one leg and half his lung blown away, and he still insists he don't know who did it" A second police officer shook his head in agreement with his superior, "They might just as well been burying him today - his days as a major figure in the underworld are well and truly finished I would say – all I see now is an old man in a wheelchair with just two hangers on – all the rest have gone, like rats deserting the sinking ship"

• • •

At long last spring had arrived, after a winter that had seemed to drag on forever. It was mid April, the start of the racing flat season. Moisha pulled the Packard into the car park at Brighton Racecourse, allowing Comer, Sonny, and himself to get out. At the same time an open top charabanc pulled in, filled to capacity with hard faced men, some with scars, others with broken noses, who definitely didn't look as though they were on a work's outing or a pleasure trip.

Comer stood to one side as the men got out of the charabanc, and indicated for them to see Sonny and Moisha, who in turn handed the men pieces of paper with bookmaker's names scrawled across them, and lists of runners and riders for this particular meeting. They were also given packets of chalk, which the bookmaker would use to mark up the prices on their blackboards. These few seemingly insignificant pieces of paper and chalk, would prove, if need be, that Comer was supplying a legitimate service to the course bookmakers.

This new band of heavies had been recruited, mainly by simple word of mouth; Comer, Moisha and Sonny had visited all the gambling clubs and east London spielers that they knew and let it be known that they were looking for men to join Comer's new organisation. With so many of Sabini's men now out of work, this didn't prove too difficult. Comer also managed to make the number up by enlisting a few members from his Jewish Protection League, who, like Solly Milner, had wanted to get out of paying their weekly fees, and earn some extra money into the bargain.

Everything was now going to plan, or so Comer thought as he led Moisha and Sonny through the pleasant afternoon crowds. He smiled to himself as he received a little wave or nod of recognition here and there; this was like an upmarket version of Brick Lane on a Sunday morning.

The smile however, quickly dropped from his face, when he was approached by two of his men, Jock McKenzie and Jimmy Buller, who told him that the bookmaker they had been given the name of had told them in no uncertain terms that he did not need them, that he already had all the protection he needed. Comer was fuming with rage, "Did you tell him you was working for me?" he bellowed. Of course they did, but it made no difference. He even threatened to have them nicked if they didn't move off his pitch straight away.

The painted sign said 'Matthew Barrett – Turf Accountant' A crowd of around thirty people were gathered around; some just looking up at the blackboard, as prices were constantly being updated, while others pushed their way to the front to place their bets as soon as the saw a price they thought favourable.

McKenzie pointed to the bookmaker, who was presumably Matthew Barrett, "That's him," he said in a strong Glaswegian accent. Comer pushed his way to the front of the crowd and beckoned Barrett with his finger, "Oi, you, I want to talk to you" Barrett looked down at Comer, a look of indifference on his face, as he then looked away and continued to take bets. Comer called him again, this time in a louder voice, which Barrett certainly heard this time. There were some anxious glances from the nearest punters, who quickly started to move away as they sensed trouble.

Barrett looked around, over the heads of the punters, and signalled to two men who were some distance away and obviously hadn't heard all the commotion. The two men came rushing through the crowd, pushing and shoving everyone out of the way as they did so. It was only as they got closer that Comer recognised them, they were none other than Irish Pat and George Sprattling, whom he had met before in the pub at Epsom Downs Racecourse, when they worked for Darby Sabini.

Barrett shouted to Pat and Sprattling and pointed to Comer; "Got a trouble maker here boys, and I want him out of here now, right?" Comer watched as both Pat and Sprattling reached into their inside pockets and started to take something out as they approached him. Comer held his ground; facing them alone as they raced towards him. Pat suddenly stopped and held his arm across Sprattling, stopping him as well; he had recognised Comer. The weapons were returned to their pockets as they now walked calmly up to him.

"We've met before haven't we?" said Pat. "We certainly have, "replied Comer, "and do you remember my name?" Pat and Sprattling looked quizzically at each other, trying their best to remember his name, "We meet a lot of people in our travels," said Pat, "your face is familiar," he suddenly paused, "yes, I got it now, you're the fellow we talked to in the pub at Epsom Downs one day; going to take over the racecourse wasn't you?" Comer nodded his head slowly and stared straight into the eyes of Pat without saying a word. "I hope you're not thinking of trying to take this one over are you?" asked Pat, mockingly.

Comer did his best to show no signs of emotion as he answered Pat, "Depends on exactly who's looking after it now?" Pat and Sprattling shuffled their feet a little closer to Comer, and brought themselves up to their full height in an obvious attempt to intimidate him. "We're looking after it," replied Pat. Comer looked around at the crowds of people, "It's a big course for just two men isn't it?" he said, He could see that he was starting to rile the two men now, and especially Pat, who moved closer still, "Darby Sabini rules this course, and we work for Mr Sabini," growled Pat. Comer nodded nonchalantly, "Oh I see," he said, "I heard that Mr Sabini was finished?"

"You heard wrong then," chipped in Sprattling, who now spoke for the first time, "and if you're thinking of taking on Mr Sabini then you are going to have a war on your hands, d'you get me?" Comer nodded as if agreeing with Sprattling, "I didn't realise," he said, "if that is the case then I admit defeat; it's all your boys" With that, Comer turned and walked away.

"Did I hear you right?" asked Moisha as Comer came back towards him. "Just keep walking" Comer quietly ordered; leading his men back towards the car park, "call the rest of the boys in straight away, we're leaving"

• • •

As Comer's men started to gather at the car park, many of them seemed to be confused about what was happening. The majority of them had followed their orders and seemed to be getting on well with the bookmakers they had been detailed to; and now this sudden call back. What was going on?

Comer took Moisha and Sonny to one side and whispered a few brief words to them, which they nodded in agreement to and quickly hurried off, back towards the course again. As soon as they were out of sight, Comer started ushering the rest of his man back into the charabanc.

Within ten minutes everyone was back on board the charabanc. Comer walked round to the side, where he could be heard and told his men not to worry, they would all be paid as normal. He then slapped the side of the vehicle and ordered the driver to pull away. As the charabanc drove out of sight, Moisha and Sonny returned. Sonny grinned and nodded his head. "OK then, let's go," said Comer. The three men looked happy as they piled into the Packard and drove out of the car park, in the same direction as the charabanc.

It was just starting to get dark by the time they reached London. Moisha pulled the Packard up outside the Mackworth Arms pub in Commercial Road, Stepney, where all three men alighted and went into the pub.

Sonny went to the bar and bought a round of drinks, while Comer and Moisha sat down at a table facing the door. Comer always insisted on sitting in this position wherever he went, as he didn't like the idea of anyone 'sneaking up on him from behind'. He smiled as he looked at his watch; it was just after 6.30 pm. "They should be leaving about now I would reckon" Moisha put the drinks down on the table and Comer raised his glass to both Moisha and Sonny, "Well cheers boys, a job well done I would say" They all chinked glasses. "To absent friends eh?" laughed Sonny as he toasted the others. "Absent friends"

● ● ●

'Leaving about now,' was exactly what Irish Pat and George Sprattling were doing. The day's races had finished, and they were walking back up the White to the road, which overlooked the car park, where Sprattling had parked their car, rather than pay the one-shilling fee for the car park. Both men were puffing and out of breath by the time they reached their car, a maroon and black, Armstrong-Siddeley four-door saloon. "Here she is, my little beauty," said Sprattling as he unlocked the car, climbed in and unlocked the passenger door for Pat to get in.

Sprattling smiled as he looked at the mahogany and chrome trim, and smelt the leather seats; he had only had the car a few days and was justifiably proud of its solid goods looks. He pulled out the choke halfway, switched the ignition switch on and pressed the starter button, "What's the betting it starts first time?" he laughingly asked Pat, who didn't show any interest whatsoever, "Just get the fucking thing started will you? It's almost seven o'clock now and we have to go and see Darby yet"

The car did exactly as Sprattling had predicted, the engine bursting into life the moment he touched the starter button, "See, what did I tell you?" He gently eased his foot onto the accelerator pedal and started to give the engine a few revs to warm it up before pulling away, "Oh fuck," he moaned as his foot slid off the accelerator pedal, "what the fuck is that all over the pedal?" He opened his door, stuck his legs out of the car, took a handkerchief out and started to wipe the pedal and the bottom of his shoes. Pat was now starting to get really angry, "What the fuck are you doing now?" he shouted, "why don't you clean the fucking spark plugs as well while you're at it?"

Sprattling was not exactly the wittiest of men, and did not understand that Pat was just being derogatory towards him. "No," he replied, "it's not the plugs, its all this shit all over the pedal, look," he said as he pointed to a puddle of dark slime in the gutter, "I must have trod in as I got into the car"

Pat looked at his watch, "Alright," he shouted, "so now you've wiped it off, for Christ sake can we go now?" It was all very well for Pat to shout and holler, thought Sprattling, it isn't his car, it's me, he thought, who had to pay for it. With the pedal now clean, Sprattling put the car into first gear and pulled away slowly up the White.

• • •

At the Mackworth Arms pub, Comer, Moisha, and Sonny were still drinking and chatting. "One thing I don't understand," said Sonny, "if Sabini is still in business, where are all his men, and how come our boys took over so many bookies stands so easily?" Comer nodded his head knowingly, like a headmaster administrating the rules to his pupils, "Firstly," Comer said, "the only business Sabini is now in, is trying to rake in a few bob for his pension – he's holed up in some little flat in Brighton, he can't go out, he's got no men beside those two idiots, Irish Pat and his gormless mate, and from what I have been able to gather, they have been minding just that one bookies stand, and that gentlemen, is what we are up against"

● ● ●

Sprattling was driving the Armstrong-Siddeley up the steep White at exactly eight miles an hour. Pat looked at his watch again and shouted at Sprattling, "For fuck's sake George, can't this thing go any faster than this?" Sprattling was getting agitated at Pat's constant barracking; he doubled his clutch and went to change up to a higher gear, but succeeded only in crunching the second gear as he did so, "Now look what you made me do," he shouted, "I'm supposed to running this car in for fuck's sake" Both men were now losing their tempers. "We're not even heading in the right direction," shouted Pat. "I know that," shouted Sprattling in reply, "I'm looking for somewhere where I can turn around"

Sprattling swung the Armstrong-Siddeley over to a patch of grass on his right, reversed back and then headed down the White in the direction they had come from. "That's better," said Pat as they started to pick up speed.

● ● ●

Drinks were still flowing at the Mackworth Arms pub. "What I still don't understand," said Moisha, "is if Sabini is well and truly finished and this Irish Pat and his mate are no threat to us, then why are we still bothering with them, and why did we....?

Comer interrupted Moisha in midstream. "Did I ever tell you about a geezer I met in Brixton Prison? Nice bloke he was, a Scotsman by the name of Billy Munro, he used to work for Darby Sabini, but fell out with him when Sabini overheard him joking about the Italians, saying they were a bunch of ice cream sellers. Billy Munro then went to work for the Collins family from south London, who also worked the racetracks, but while he was waiting for a train at Liverpool Street Station one day, he was suddenly approached by two men, one with a strong Irish accent and the other a Cockney" Comer paused for a moment to let his comment sink in. "Yeah, I think you've got the picture," he said, "It was our old friends, Irish Pat and George Sprattling – they slashed Billy down each side of his face and threatened to shoot him if ever he showed his face at any of the racecourses again"

Moisha and Sonny had listened in silence as Comer related this story. "But that's not all," continued Comer, "Billy Munro was then nicked by a copper who was on Sabini's payroll, and charged with being in possession of an offensive weapon, which was one of the cut-throat razors, that Irish Pat and his mate had thrown down as they ran away" Moisha shook his head in disbelief, "Fuck me," he said, "no wonder you asked us to take care of things"

● ● ●

Sprattling was now driving the Armstrong-Siddeley down the hill, picking up speed as he went, and swerving every now and then to avoid an oncoming vehicle. "Can't you do anything normal?" complained Pat as they picked up even more speed and hurtled around a sharp bend. He looked at the speedometer, which was now on 70 mph and still creeping up, "For Christ sake George," he stammered, "Slow down" "I can't," Sprattling shouted, "the brakes have gone"

Pat grabbed at the steering wheel, forcing the car to partly mount a grass verge as another car came towards them. The Armstrong-Siddeley scraped along the side of the other car, but still could not come to a halt. Sprattling was stamping on the brake pedal, to no effect whatsoever. Both men stared in disbelief and fear, as just ahead of them to their left, a large Tram pulled out of the Brighton Tram Shed. These vehicles were not quick at the best of times; it seemed to linger in the centre of the road for ages, as it swung round to take its course down the White in the same direction as the Armstrong-Siddeley. Both Pat and Sprattling now grabbed the steering wheel and pulled on it with all their might in an effort to swing their car around and avoid the Tram, but it was impossible, they were now too close and going much too fast. The Armstrong-Siddeley smashed into the rear half of the Tram, sending splinters of wood, metal and glass scattering across the road as the huge Tram rolled over onto its side. At the same time, the bonnet of the Armstrong-Siddeley buckled like a concertina, the windscreen shattered and the engine burst into flames, engulfing the whole car within seconds. No one could have possibly survived such a crash!

Chapter 12

With Darby Sabini, now minus one leg and a lung, and living in forced retirement in a poky flat in Brighton, Comer was the new kingpin of the racecourses in southern England.

Money was coming in fast, and he was determined to keep it that way. Any incursions by other gangs, into his territory were swiftly and ferociously dealt with. If anyone thought Darby Sabini was tough, they would be in for a real shock if ever they crossed Comer's path.

This didn't stop other gangs from trying to muscle in, as with a well-known gang from Birmingham, who showed up at a race meeting one day, armed to the teeth and ready to 'teach these southern nancy-boys a lesson' Comer had got wind of the oncoming threat and had organised over sixty men to surround a pub where he had been told the Birmingham gang would be meeting just before journeying on to the race meeting.

Comer's men ambushed the Birmingham gang as they came out of the pub, de-armed them, and forced them to run the gauntlet down a long line of men armed with pick-axe handles, hammers and police truncheons, where they were beaten mercilessly, some ending up with broken limbs and skulls; nearly all requiring some form of hospital treatment afterwards. Needless to say, that was the last time the Birmingham gang stayed out of their northern patch.

Having all this control of the racecourses didn't mean that Comer had neglected his connections in London's east end, far from it. He still saw the east end as his spiritual home, even though he had now moved from his small flat just off Petticoat Lane, and into a much larger flat near Holborn.

There were still a great number of Jews living in Stepney and Bethnal Green, and Oswald Mosley's men were still very much active in these areas, even after being routed at the infamous 'Battle of Cable Street" in 1936, which Comer often boasted that he had taken part in and helped defeat Mosley's Blackshirts. There was no proof of this of course, but Comer didn't need proof, he employed men to spread his legend; like propaganda, 'say something enough times, be it true or false, and people will eventually believe it'

The Jews, being a long persecuted race, have always tended to stick together. If a Jew needs help he goes to his family first, and possibly his Rabbi next, staying well clear of the police and other authorities. As the 1930s started to draw to a close, more and more stories started to emerge from Germany, where the Jews were being persecuted on a scale not seen before in Europe. Oswald Mosley took advantage of this and escalated his purge against the Jews in this country.

None of this helped Jack Comer personally of course, as although he was not a practising Jew, he was still Jewish by birth and proud of his heritage, but he was never too proud to take advantage of the money that was on offer. He even had Jewish businessmen seeking him out for help, after being recommended to him by their local Rabbi.

Rather than concentrating on the small businesses and shops like he had done in the past, he now decided to delve deeper into the local spielers and gambling clubs, which had opened on a unprecedented scale in the east end over the past few years. He was helped out with this when an old friend called to see him one day, while he was holding court at the Mackworth Arms pub. The old friend was none other than Billy Munro, whom he had first met in Brixton Prison. Munro had just been released from prison and remembered Comer telling him to look him up when he got out. Well here he was, and he was looking for work. After explaining how he had dealt with Irish Pat and George Sprattling, Comer offered Munro a job, helping to look after his newly acquired spielers and clubs in the east end. Munro jumped at the offer and so a new member of Comer's ever-expanding team was born.

Jack Comer saw himself as a man of taste and culture; his Holborn flat was luxuriously furnished with Persian rugs, crystal chandeliers, antique furniture and oil paintings. A large mahogany partner's desk, with a red leather wing chair behind it, dominated his living room, although he did have one piece of modern furniture, which was a Dynatron Radiogram in dark walnut, on which he would play his favourite jazz records, by such luminaries as Duke Ellington, Benny Goodman, and Louis Armstrong. There was no dining room, and the kitchen was very sparse. Comer loved his food but never entertained socially, and certainly never cooked for himself, apart from toast and tea or coffee.

At this point in his life, Comer could have sat back and lived the life of a gentleman, or at least someone who looked somewhat like one, as his gang now did all the hard work, and presented him with all the money at their weekly meetings. The gentleman's life however, was not something, which Comer took to easily; in reality, he was and always had been a street boy. He loved walking down the street and being recognised; he was big, and he was tough, and he knew it and played up to the part like a film star or a prize fighter.

He had never forgotten Billy White' invite, to look him up whenever he was in the area. He had purposely avoided such a meeting until he had thought the time was right. He didn't want to be seen by White as just another second rate east end thug, who was looking for an introduction into the world of big time crime. Maybe this was the right time? It had been a few years since his meeting with White and Comer's fortune had certainly changed for the better. It was now September 3 1939; he was 27 years old and ready to take on the world. Maybe he should tell Billy Munro, who was now occasionally driving for him, when Moisha was otherwise engaged, to bring the new Buick Straight Eight round and park it right outside White' office, that should impress him.

Comer sauntered into the bedroom, took a freshly laundered shirt out of the chest of drawers, then a light grey pin stripe suit from the two-dozen he had hanging in the large wardrobe. Yes, he was going to make sure that he looked the business when he met up with Billy White. As he went through to the bathroom, he stopped for a moment, switched on the radiogram and sorted out a Duke Ellington record,

'Mood Indigo' It took half a minute or so for the valves to warm up in the radiogram before he could put the record on, but gradually he could hear the wireless starting to crackle into life. He looked at his watch, it was 11.15 a.m. as he took the record out of its paper sleeve, brushed his handkerchief over the grooves and started to put the record onto the turntable, but as he did so, he heard the BBC announcer saying something about an important message from the Prime Minister.

Comer wasn't particularly interested in politics, but there was something about the way this was said, which made him stop and listen. There was a brief moment of silence, followed by the unmistakable, and somewhat stilted voice of the Prime Minister, Mr. Neville Chamberlain; "I am speaking to you from the Cabinet Room at number ten Downing Street. This morning the British Ambassador in Berlin handed the German Government a final note stating that unless we heard from them by 11 a.m. that they were prepared at once to withdraw their troops from Poland, a state of war would exist between us. I have to tell you that no such undertaking has been received and that consequently this country is at war with Germany"

Comer, like probably every other person in the country who had heard this message, was stunned. War; when would it actually start, he wondered, would we have German planes flying over London and bombing us? And what about people like himself, the Jews, what would become of us? He had heard stories of the way they were being treated in Germany; would it now happen here?

Comer had never been afraid of anyone in his life, and he still wasn't, but what he was afraid of was what would happen to his family and friends; he had fought Mosley's Blackshirts, maybe he would now be called up into the armed forces to fight Hitler?

Still only half dressed; he looked out of the window to the streets below. It was a fine and sunny day with people going about their business as if nothing had happened, maybe they hadn't heard? The skies were clear, no sign of German bombers, no air-raid warnings, everything seemed perfectly normal, so what should he do, should he still go and see Billy White, or should he wait and see what happens next regarding this declaration of war thing?

He decided on the latter; give it a few days, or maybe weeks to see how things progress; maybe Chamberlain and Hitler would come to some sort of agreement? Maybe it was just a storm in a teacup.

● ● ●

The following few weeks however, were not so nice, sunny, and relaxed as the scene from his window had indicated to Comer that day. Everywhere he went people were naturally talking about the war, and what was going to happen next.

There hadn't been the German planes over London, which many people had expected, but there had been an attempted bombing raid on the east coast of England, and this happened just four days after the declaration of war.

The population of the east coast had been woken at 6.45 am by air-raid warnings, wailing out their terrible drone as German bomber planes were seen nearing the coast. Fortunately no bombs were actually dropped, as it was believed that either the bombers were driven off by British fighter planes, or maybe they decided that the weather was unfavourable for their proposed attack and turned back. It was, nevertheless, irrefutable proof, if ever that was indeed needed, that Great Britain and Germany were well and truly at war with each other.

Probably the worst news to hit Comer at this time was the announcement that all British racecourses were to be closed down for the 'duration,' with the exception of Newmarket's July Course where all Britain's classic races were still to be allowed. Although Newmarket did come under his control, it was only a very small part of his business empire. He did contemplate going into the greyhound racing business, but even that had been placed under strict control. Thank God, he thought, for the spielers, which were illegal anyway, so they couldn't put Government closing orders on them.

The spielers however, were hit from another angle, when the Government brought in military conscription for all men between the ages of 18 to 41. This was the average age of the gambling man. With no racecourses and no men left to gamble their money away at the spielers and clubs, what would Comer do now?

• • •

During the weeks and months that followed, Comer naturally lost a number of his men; some were called up to serve in the forces, while others made sure they would not be called up by changing their names and disappearing to other towns and cities. Fortunately for him, his name seemed to have slipped the net, for the time being anyway, along with a number of his old stalwarts, including Sonny and Moisha, and Billy Munro. Between them they managed to carve out a living from the old remnants of his business, such as Newmarket's July Course, the few spielers, which were still limping along in the east end, and of course, the Jewish Protection League.

There were of course, all kinds of rumours going around; mainly concerning how the Germans were about to invade Great Britain, and that London was about to be bombed. Others included such fairy-tales as the Government had left the country and were now living in Bermuda, and that German spies had killed the King. There was one rumour however, that was soon proved to be true, and that was that rationing of certain goods was soon due to be introduced.

This came true quicker than most people would have predicted, for petrol rationing was announced almost immediately. Comer could hardly believe it when he read it in the paper; what would he do? He had one of the largest cars on the British roads, his Buick probably did something like 8 miles to the gallon and now petrol was to be rationed.

Just after Christmas that year, the Government ordered a number of different foodstuffs to also be rationed, including butter, sugar, meat, bacon, eggs, tea, jam, biscuits, breakfast cereals, cheese, lard, milk and canned and dried fruit. Every person in the country was issued with a ration book, from which the shopkeeper would cut out the relevant coupon, according to what the person had bought. The big problem with this for Comer and his associates however, was that they were not officially registered anywhere, so such formalities as ration books or even identity cards, which were to also be issued, would never be issued in their names.

Comer, Billy Munro, Sonny and Moisha were discussing the petrol crisis just after it was first announced, "The army have got petrol," said Comer, "the fire brigade have got petrol – even the old Bill have got petrol – if we can't buy any, we'll nick it from them; simple" What Comer didn't explain, was that when he said we will nick it from them, he used the "we" as in the 'Royal we' In other words, he would do the ordering and Billy Munro, Sonny and Moisha would go out and do the actual 'nicking'

By August 1940, Comer and his team had managed to sort out their petrol problem. With almost every young man now enrolled in the armed forces, the streets and pubs of London were teaming with soldiers, and most of them in desperate need of a few extra pounds, as wages in the British Army were notoriously low. Comer's men would watch out for military vehicles parked near a café or pub, find the driver and offer to do a deal with him. Nine times out of ten it worked, and Comer's boys would come away with probably 20 gallons of petrol, and the soldier a few pounds better off.

This little enterprise not only kept their personal cars running, it also provided extra cash, for they sold what was left over to businessmen and shopkeepers for exorbitant prices, far above the normal retail price.

On the night of August 24, 1940, Luftwaffe bombers flew over London for the first time. They were apparently looking for military targets on the outskirts of London, but for some reason, the lead plane drifted off course; the others followed, and then dropped their bombs on the centre of London by mistake, destroying several homes and killing a number of civilians in the process. Needless to say there was public outrage over this, and the Prime Minister Winston Churchill, believing it was a deliberate attack, ordered Berlin to be bombed the following evening.

Hitler was fuming, how dare the English bomb his capitol city; it was an outrage that he could not let go unpunished, and so on 7 September 1940, he launched what was to become known as the Blitz (from German, meaning lightning) upon Britain. The main objective being London, which was bombed by the Luftwaffe for 57 consecutive nights. More than one million London houses were destroyed or damaged, and more than 40,000 civilians were killed.

Many small time criminals took advantage of the Blitz, and would pilfer the homes of the victims of the bombing, sometimes stepping over the dead bodies of the victims in order to rifle through their possessions. Jack Comer was undoubtedly a criminal, but when he heard about incidents like this, he did everything in his power to find those responsible, and teach them a lesson they would never forget. In one instance, he took an iron bar and broke both the culprit's hands, as well as making him pay compensation to his victims. He classed those who carried out this type of robbery to be the "lowest of the low".

Shops and especially factories, were a different thing as far as Comer was concerned. They were insured and would therefore not lose out in the same manner as an ordinary householder would.

With London being bombed every night, there was no shortage of factories, shops, and warehouses being hit, which meant piles of loot, sitting there for the taking. Comer had bought a lorry, which he had had painted with ARP (Air Raid Protection) markings on the side. The minute he, or any of his team, heard that something 'worthwhile' had been bombed, he would send the boys round, sometimes accompanying them himself. They would all be dressed in blue boiler suits, wearing steel helmets, and carrying axes. If ever they were questioned by the police or anyone else, they would flash their false ARP identity passes, and say that they needed to remove as much as possible from the building in case there were any unexploded bombs as well as clearing the site in order to help rescue any casualties that might still be in there. Everything possible would be removed from the premises, loaded into their lorry and driven away as quickly as possible to their warehouse in Essex, which was in the heart of the countryside at the time.

Moisha and Sonny could not understand what was on Comer's mind, when he phoned them one night and told them to get Munro and the lorry and get over to a small printing works, just off Commercial Street in Whitechapel. Unless they had been printing banknotes there, Moisha couldn't see what good a pile of old machinery was going to be, especially as they had to get it outside and onto their lorry.

Luckily for them, the machines that Comer wanted were both quite small, which made their job a little easier. Once unloaded at the Essex warehouse, Comer explained that the larger of the two machines was a German printing press; "Yes, German," he said, "and so what? We'll make the fucking Germans work for us this time" The other machine was a copying machine, made in England, as it proclaimed in raised letters on the side.

"Gentlemen," announced Comer, "we are now going into the printing business" Moisha, Sonny and Munro all looked astounded, "But none of us know a thing about printing" said Sonny. "Neither do I," answered Comer, "but I know a man who does"

Chapter 13

Business was once again starting to boom for Comer. He was beginning to be seen in the east end of London as a sort of Robin Hood character, who could supply the indigenous population of east London with whatever they wanted; at a price of course, but the majority were more than happy to pay his price than to go without.

He had graduated from just stealing from bombed factories and warehouses, and now had contacts all over the country, and even in the London docks. He could supply anything, from meat to butter, eggs, cheese, bacon, clothing, wireless sets, and of course, petrol. Later on, when the Americans joined the war, he found them very obliging to deal with and consequently added cigarettes, confectionery, spirits and women's stockings to his list.

By far the biggest money-spinner in Comer's repertoire was his printing business, which he kept firmly anchored at the Essex warehouse, while taking on several other warehouses in the suburbs for his black-market goods. He hired a man named Manny Finklestein, who was a first class engraver and printer, to take charge of the Essex operation. Finklestein could produce almost anything on those two small machines, apart from banknotes, which they did try, but were not too successful with, as the paper has to be perfect, and this was one commodity, which Comer could not access. Ration books, petrol coupons, identity cards, and driving licenses were Finklestein's speciality, and Comer had a market clamouring for all these items.

• • •

It was a bright and sunny Sunday morning, with surprisingly enough, no bombs being dropped and no sound of air raid warnings wailing out over London. Comer put the kettle on, for his customary cup of tea, and popped a slice of bread into the toaster. It was just after 10 a.m. Billy Munro would be round to pick him up at 11 a.m. to take him to Barney's café in Petticoat lane, where he was to meet Moisha and Sonny.

He never found the tea to be a problem, just two spoonfuls of tea in the teapot, fill it with hot water and two minutes later he had a perfect cup of tea. Toast, on the other hand, always proved to be somewhat difficult for Comer to master; he would watch the first side until he thought it was perfectly cooked, and then open the flap, turn the toast over in order to cook the other side. It was at this point nearly every morning that the phone would ring. Needless to say the toast ended up like a black cinder, which would be consigned to the rubbish bin, and today was no exception.

Comer looked at his watch, it was 10.50 a.m. He was dressed, ready to go, and starving hungry. He looked out the window to the street below, eagerly awaiting Munro to arrive. Still no sign of him, but who was that, he thought, standing in the doorway opposite? A tall man in a raincoat and trilby, looking every inch like a typical policeman.

Exactly eight minutes later, Billy Munro swung the big Buick around the corner and eased to a stop outside Comer's block. Comer adjusted his hat a little as he walked out of the doors of his apartment block. The man in the raincoat was still standing there. He nonchalantly lit a cigarette and tried his best to act as if he was possibly waiting for someone else, but Comer could smell a 'wrong-un' a mile off, there was no doubt in his mind at all that the man in the raincoat was watching and waiting for him. He hurried to the waiting car as quickly as possible, as he didn't have any sort of weapon on him, with which he could protect himself if the man did decide to attack him.

Munro looked round at Comer as he jumped into the car and slammed the door shut, "Are you alright boss?" he asked. "The man in the doorway," said Comer, "him in the raincoat, have you ever seen him before?" Munro looked at the man and shook his head, "No," he said, "looks like a copper to me" Comer agreed, "Whatever he is I don't like the look of him" Munro was told to get moving and to make sure they were not followed.

Comer felt safe once they were in Barney's café, but even then he couldn't help looking at the crowds of shoppers outside; every time someone looked in the window he thought it was the man in the raincoat.

The first thing he did the following morning was rush to the window and look opposite to see if he was there again. Thank God, he thought, that he wasn't. Maybe it was just a coincidence, maybe he was genuinely waiting for a friend or a girlfriend, who knows?

Two days later, Comer had called a meeting of a few of his men at the Mackworth Arms pub. Munro, Moisha, Sonny and two others were all there. Comer spoke in hushed tones, even though there were hardly any other customers in the pub. He was talking about the driver of a military lorry, which was going to be loaded with rations for the troops, which would consist of various meats, dairy products, and tinned food. "The driver," he explained, "has agreed to turn over his load to us, for a price of course; all we have to do his give him a little smack on the head and leave him tied up somewhere near Hamstreet Woods in Kent" Everyone was nodding in agreement, "When's it going to happen boss?" asked one of the group. "Thursday," replied Comer, "Seven o'clock Thursday morning"

Comer downed his Brandy and smiled at his men, but as he did so, he saw the man in the raincoat again. He was standing in the other bar, but looking across to where Comer and men were. "It's him again," he spluttered, "Look, look, Billy, d'you see him, that is him isn't it?" Munro looked across to where Comer had indicated. He stared directly into the eyes of the man in the raincoat, "That's him alright Boss," he said, "d'you want me to go round there and sort him out?" Comer shook his head and told Munro not to do a thing – yet.

Wednesday morning, and a very paranoid Comer did as he had done a few days earlier, rushing to the window of his flat the moment he had got out of bed, to see if the man in the raincoat was there or not. Thankfully he wasn't. Comer breathed a sigh of relief and went about his usual duties, of making the tea and putting on the toast.

All was going well, the tea was ready, and he had just turned the toast over, after making sure the first side was cooked to perfection. A sip of tea while he was waiting, and there it goes again, the phone, ring, ring, ring, ring. Why did it always happen? Maybe he should change the time that he had his tea and toast? He picked up the phone, "Hello?" he said. There was silence on the other end, "Hello?" he repeated. After a couple of seconds he heard a man's voice on the other end, "Mr Comer?"

Comer didn't recognise the voice, it definitely wasn't one of his men or anyone else that he knew. "Is that Mr Comer?" said the man again. Comer never gave out his telephone number to anyone he didn't personally know, and they never called him by his surname, they would call him Jack or sometimes boss. This voice wasn't exactly cultured, but it was a little more refined that most of the people who worked for him. "Hello, Mr Comer?" Comer slammed the phone down and went straight over to the window again to see if the man in the raincoat was down there. The street was deserted, but what did that prove?

Jack Comer was not normally the sort of man to let something like this worry him. In the past he had been known to give someone a hiding just for looking at him, but there was something odd about this. If the man in the raincoat was a policeman, why was he making himself so bloody obvious? Not exactly police undercover work was it? And was it the same man who had just phoned him as well?

The thoughts continued to plague him as he continued getting ready. Moisha was due to pick him up this morning, and should be here any minute now he thought as he had one more look at his image in the mirror. What the hell? He grabbed at his tie and pulled it off. How the hell could he have put a light blue tie on with a brown suit? He just wasn't thinking straight. He started tying his brown and beige striped tie when the doorbell rang.

A quick glance out of the window. The Buick wasn't there yet, and there were no police cars in the street. He made his way over to the intercom; if this was the man in the raincoat, he'd make him regret this day. He pressed the intercom button and spoke aggressively into the mouthpiece, "What do you want?" The voice on the other end definitely wasn't the man in the raincoat, or any other man come to that, it was his sister, Rebecca. "Hello Jack?"

Rebecca was trembling and in tears as she sat on the settee next to Comer, who held her hands and tried to calm her down. "Let me get you a drink Becca, look at you, you're shaking"

Rebecca shook her head; she didn't want a drink. "It's papa Jack," she sobbed. Comer's jaw dropped open, "What – he's?" Rebecca interrupted him, explaining that their father was not dead, but that he had suffered a heart attack after a bomb had fallen on their street and demolished half the block opposite them. "They've taken him to the London Hospital Jack"

Comer got Moisha to take both him and his sister to the London Hospital in Whitechapel, where his father, Jacob, was lying in a cubicle, surrounded by curtains, with an intravenous drip attached to him. "Your father is going to be alright," said the doctor, "he is a very strong man, but he does need a lot of rest" He looked at Comer and asked, "Do you live in London Mr Comer?" "Why? Asked Comer.

The doctor explained that Comer's father really needs to convalesce, somewhere away from London and the bombing. Unfortunately, he said that due to all the children now being evacuated to the countryside, and troops being billeted in large houses outside London, it was very difficult for hospitals to recommend a convalescent home.

Comer could hardly believe his eyes when he saw what was left of the old block of flats opposite his father's home. Rubble was still strewn across the road, and windows of his father's flats blown out. "Another few feet and it could have been you," he said to Rebecca, "You can't live like this, I'm going to get you out of here" Rebecca told him not to worry about her, but if he could find somewhere for papa to stay she was sure it would help him immensely. Comer handed his sister a bundle of banknotes, "Get the windows fixed and give him whatever he needs," he said as he walked back to his car, "and don't worry, I'll find somewhere for dad"

Moisha looked in his interior mirror as they drove back towards Holborn, "Don't want to worry you even more Jack, but I think we're being followed" Comer turned his head and saw a little black Ford 8 some yards behind them. It was starting to get dark by this time, so he couldn't see who was driving the Ford. He instructed Moisha to pull over. "I've had enough of this," he said, as Moisha steered the Buick into the kerb. The little black Ford slowed down as it overtook the Buick. Comer opened his side window and stared at the driver of the car it slowly passed them. The driver of the Ford stared back. It was definitely him, the man in the raincoat.

"What do you want me to do?" asked Moisha, "do you want me to go after him?" Comer wound up his window, "No," he said, "not until I've found out who he is, and exactly what he wants"

• • •

An early morning mist lay like a grey blanket over the Old Dartford Road in Kent. It was Thursday morning, 6.30 am. A dark green Morris 5 cwt van was the only vehicle parked in the lay-by. Billy Munro sat at the wheel of the van, Moisha sat next to him, while Sonny and a new man on the team, Teddy Baxter, sat on the wheel arches in the back. Baxter had been introduced by Billy Munro, whom he had met in prison a couple of years earlier. Munro knew that Baxter wasn't exactly 'the full ticket' in the brain stakes, but had been impressed by Baxter's toughness and willingness to take orders. "What sort of lorry are we looking for?" Baxter asked Sonny. "It's an army lorry Teddy," replied Sonny. "What colour?" asked Baxter. Sonny rolled his eyes in exasperation, "Well it ain't going to be bloody pink, that's for sure, I just told you it's an army lorry" A daunted look came over Baxter's face, "So, what colour is it then?" he repeated. Sonny stared angrily at Baxter, "Haven't you ever seen an army lorry? They are always the same fucking colour, khaki – fuck me, I've got a six year old nephew with more brains than you"

Baxter was fuming at this remark and went to jump to his feet, to attack Sonny, but in doing so, he hit his head on the roof of the van. Moisha and Munro both turned around to see Baxter looking slightly dazed. "You're making me fucking angry now Baxter," he shouted, "the lorry's just pulled up, so shut it and do what you're told, got it?" Baxter mumbled a somewhat pathetic apology and followed the others out of the van.

The army lorry had come to a halt. The military driver opened his door and jumped down to the ground as the four men reached him. Moisha smiled at the driver, "Well done," he said, "dead on time" The driver looked somewhat nervous as he handed the ignition keys to Moisha and asked him when he could expect the rest of the money. "That's down to the governor," he said, "all we do is take the lorry from you and make it look as much like a hijacking as we can" The driver swallowed hard as he looked nervously at the four men facing him, "Make it look real," he said, "but you won't go overboard will you?" Moisha smiled, "We're professionals mate, no problem"

Moisha walked back towards the lorry as Munro got back in their van and turned it around, ready to follow the lorry. Sonny was carrying a length of rope as he and Baxter escorted the driver towards some nearby bushes, "Don't worry mate," he said, "we're just going to tie you up to make it look as realistic as possible, just sit down there," he indicated towards some grass.

As the driver did as he was told and sat down on the still damp grass, Baxter suddenly pulled out a length of lead piping from the waistband of his trousers and smashed it ferociously into the driver's temple. Blood spurted out immediately and poured down the man's face, sending him falling backwards, but before he even landed, Baxter lashed out again, this time catching the man on his cheekbone. "What the fucking hell are you doing?" yelled Sonny as he grabbed at the lead piping, trying to wrestle it away from Baxter. For a few moments Sonny and Baxter were locked in combat, rolling over the muddy ground. This finally stopped when Moisha and Munro, who had now both jumped out of the vehicles, and were now starting to separate the two men.

At last they managed to get the lead pipe away from Baxter, with Moisha pinning him down with his knee on his chest, while Munro was helping Sonny to his feet. "Check him out," shouted Sonny; pointing at the bloodied body of the driver, "that fucking idiot might have killed him"

Fortunately, the driver was still alive, but Baxter wouldn't be for much longer if Sonny could have his way. "You're a dead man Baxter," he shouted, "when Jack hears what you've done, he'll tear your fucking head off, and if he don't, I will"

Twenty minutes later the green Morris van pulled to a halt outside a large building. Moisha and Munro got out, opened the back doors and lifted the beaten and bloodied body of the military driver out. They helped him limp to a wooden bench and gently sat him down. As soon as they were sure he was alright, they hurried away, jumped back into their van and drove off as quickly as they could, passing the large sign that proclaimed 'The Southern Hospital, Kent'

As Munro drove the van down the narrow country lanes of Kent, Sonny sat in the back beside the trussed up body of Teddy Baxter, who was struggling and swearing at both of them, "Untie me you bastards, who the fuck do you think you are, I work for Jack Comer not you?" Sonny responded by giving Baxter a kick in the ribs.

Munro flashed his headlights twice as he saw the army lorry parked just ahead of them, with Moisha at the wheel, indicating that he were nearly there. The lorry pulled away, with Munro following closely behind in the van. A sudden loud humming noise caused Munro to swerve the van, narrowly missing a ditch, "What the hell's that?" he grunted as he tried to look upwards through the windscreen. The noise grew louder as they turned a bend and into more open countryside, "It's a fucking German plane," shouted Sonny. The plane, with the familiar German crosses on its wings, was a Messerschmitt fighter, now no more than forty feet above their heads. The noise from the plane's engines was deafening as it swooped in even lower, but worse was still to come, for now it opened up its machine guns, ploughing up a row of holes along the road just in front of them. "Drive faster," yelled a terrified Baxter, "we need to get to the cover of those trees ahead" "It won't go any faster," Munro shouted. "I'll tell you what," replied Sonny, "if we throw him out," indicating Baxter, "that'll give us less weight and more speed" He grabbed the trussed up body of Baxter and started pulling him towards the back doors of the van, which he now opened. Baxter screamed and pleaded with Sonny not to do it. "What did you say?" shouted Sonny tauntingly, "what did you say, I never heard you?" Baxter stared at the road, his eyes nearly popping out of his head in fear, "Fuck off you Yid bastard," he screamed at Sonny.

Sonny glanced round towards Munro, who gave a slight shrug and nod of his head. Sonny then pulled Baxter towards the open doors of the van and helped him on his way with a kick to his stomach. The van picked up speed as Baxter hit the road and bounced twice before rolling into the ditch. At the same time the Nazi Messerschmitt fighter did a loop the loop in the sky directly above them and fired off another blast of bullets, which narrowly missed the van and ploughed their way into the hedgerows and ditch where Baxter had landed.

As the van reached the cover of the trees, the noise above them grew even louder. Both the army lorry and the van pulled to a halt under a dense clump of trees, which provided shelter for them. Munro, Sonny and Moisha, all jumped out of their vehicles and dived for cover into the ditch. Through the trees, they could now see not just the Nazi Messerschmitt in the sky above them, but also two British Spitfires, who were zooming towards the enemy plane.

As the machine guns of all three planes rattled away for what seemed like an hour, but in reality was more like a few minutes at the most, Munro, Sonny and Moisha all kept their heads down as low as possible. A different sound now emanated from somewhere above them; it was the sound of one of the planes spiralling out of control towards the ground somewhere, hopefully not on top of them. Sonny raised his head for a moment and saw it was the Messerschmitt, with flames bursting forth from one of its engines, "Yes," he shouted, "our boys have done it, they've shot the Nazi bastard down" As Sonny finished his sentence, the Messerschmitt hit the ground in a field, some distance away and exploded in a ball of fire.

• • •

It was the early hours of the following morning, and Jack Comer was sitting in the canteen inside Euston Railway Station, with two suitcases next to him. He looked up as Moisha came in and sat down opposite him. They spoke in whispered tones, with Comer constantly looking around to see if anyone was watching or listening to them.

Comer explained to Moisha that he had found out who the man in the raincoat was; he had been told by an inside source that the man was detective inspector Peter Beveridge, who was trying to make a name for himself at Scotland Yard. He had apparently heard all the rumours that had been going around, and was determined to get Comer by any means possible. And if this wasn't enough, Comer explained to Moisha, he now had the added problem of his father, who had suffered a heart attack and needed to rest, somewhere away from London and the bombing.

"So what are you going to do?" asked Moisha. "I am catching the first train this morning to Holyhead," explained Comer, "from there I'll be getting the ferry over to Dublin, where someone will be meeting me and taking me to the house they have got for me there" Meanwhile, he wanted Moisha to pick his father up from his home in Stepney and take him to a retirement home in Essex, which he had found for him. He gave Moisha a card with the name and address of the home on it, and explained that it was only a couple of miles away from their warehouse and that he had taken care of everything, including all fees. All Moisha had to do was pick Comer's father and sister up and drop Mr Comer senior off there, Becca would be looking in on her father from time to time, while Comer was away in Ireland, "Oh, and don't forget to drop Becca's weekly pay packet over to her will you?"

Moisha nodded, "And what about the business here in London?" he asked. "I want you and Sonny to take care of things while I'm away" replied Comer, "I'll be in touch with you every day by phone, but ultimately it is up to the pair of you to make all the decisions – do you think you can handle this?" Moisha smiled and nodded, "No problem Jack, leave it to us"

Chapter 14

Comer was picked up by a man named Bryan Lynch at the Dublin ferry. Lynch wasn't exactly what Comer had envisaged when he had paid for the deal in London. He had been told that his contact in Dublin was a well-respected man within the Irish underworld, and was someone who could handle himself. The man who stood before Comer was a scrawny little man, probably in his late 50s to early 60s, with an Irish accent so thick that Comer thought he might have to employ an interpreter as well, in order to understand anything he said.

Lynch jabbered away something to Comer, which was completely unintelligible to him, grabbed his heaviest suitcase with surprising ease and pointed towards a row of parked cars nearby. As Comer followed the little man he eyed up the cars, in particular the large black Humber, or maybe the dark blue Rover behind it. Disappointment soon set in when he saw Lynch striding past both his preferred vehicles and stopping at an ancient Beardmore taxicab, where he practically threw the heavy suitcase into the open recess beside the driver's cabin. He then turned to Comer, "Here lemmee tack tha dorfya," he said with a smile, as he grabbed the smaller case from Comer, threw it into the recess beside the other one and buckled a leather strap across the two of them to hold them in place.

It had just started to rain as the cab pulled away. "Hawozda crahzzin?" shouted Lynch, trying hard to make himself heard above the din of the taxi's engine. Comer thought about this one for a second or two before replying, "Oh, the crossing? Yeah, it was fine thanks. "Jabedda set onda udder soyed," shouted Lynch again, "derrain comzin truder roof datside" Once again Comer understood the man, but only after a drip of water trickled through one of the small holes in the canvas roof above him and dripped down his shirt collar, forcing him to move over as quickly as possible.

From what he could see through the rain-spattered windows, Dublin looked quite similar to London, with plenty of shops and offices, and a pub on practically every other corner. Lynch mumbled and pointed to various buildings every now and then, "probably giving me some sort of tour of the city", thought Comer as they proceeded on their journey.

Lynch drove the cab across one of the bridges over the river. The shops and offices started to dwindle away and made way for small houses and cobbled streets, although there was still as many pubs, maybe even a few more than the other side of the river. "Dis ez Temple Bar" shouted Lynch, "ets where youlbe staying" Comer nodded and looked around at the small and dirty looking streets; the east end of London was supposed to be slummy, but compared to what he could see of this place, Stepney was paradise.

It was getting dark by the time Lynch pulled the cab up outside a block of flats in a dilapidated street of mostly two up two down houses that looked like the German Luftwaffe had bombed them. Comer looked up through the rain swept window of the cab, at the four storey building that confronted him, "You had better be kidding me," he exclaimed, "this isn't where I'm supposed to be staying?"

Lynch had jumped out of his cab, opened the door for Comer and was getting the now rain soaked cases out of the recess, "Dontya go drawinta any conclusions 'tillya've seen de insoide" he quipped as he took both cases, one in each hand and hurried up the steps and into the hallway of the flats. Comer followed with a look of gloom and dread on his face. It would be the top floor as well, he thought as he followed the sight of Lynch's skinny little buttocks up the four flights of stairs.

Lynch dropped the suitcases and opened the singular door on the top floor landing; which was strange, thought Comer, as all the other floors had two doors. Lynch reached inside and flicked the light switch before waving Comer to go in, "Lectricity n everyting," he said with a smile, "we call dis der panthouse suite"

Comer could hardly believe his eyes as he looked around the flat; it was large, with three bedrooms, kitchen, bathroom, lounge, and separate dining room. "Italian bloinds as well" said Lynch as he ran his finger up the wooden Venetian blinds in the living room, "Oideel fur stupping people looking in while still letting yerself looking out ifya know what oi mean?" Lynch showed Comer around the flat like an estate agent showing off his prize rental, "Dere's even a refrigerator inda kitchen and a telephone inda front room," he said with some pride. Before leaving, Lynch left Comer a piece of paper with a phone number on it where he could be contacted, "at any toime of de day or noight, well almost any toime"

By the time Comer awoke the following morning, he was starting to relax a little more. He looked through the blinds and was surprised to see that the rain had finally stopped and it was a nice, clear sunny day. He was also surprised to see the view that he had over the rooftops of the crumbling little houses opposite him, to the River Liffey and the city beyond.

He looked through the kitchen cupboards and the refrigerator to see a surprising amount of food and supplies that had been brought in for him, such as eggs, bread, butter, tea, milk; maybe Lynch wasn't so bad after all? Ten o'clock on a Wednesday morning in a completely different environment however, wasn't exactly the time to start testing his culinary skills, and he needed to familiarise himself with his surroundings, so ten minutes later he stepped out onto the streets of Dublin.

Not much life going on in his particular street, hardly any traffic and just the occasional passer by, mainly women with shopping baskets, who all seemed to be heading in the same direction. He decided to follow the shoppers, as that must lead him to a market or at least a parade of shops, where he would hopefully find a café.

His surroundings gradually started to improve with every new street he walked down, gone were the little crumbling houses, replaced now with three and four storey town houses and the occasional shop in between. Five or six minutes later he turned a corner to find himself immersed in a bustling street market, with stalls and shops selling goods of all descriptions; this was almost like a miniature Petticoat Lane.

Tony's Café looked as good as any to start his day; very doubtful if he would get anything Kosher in there but he wasn't exactly a Kosher Jew at the best of times, although he did like the occasional Beigel with cream cheese and smoked salmon. Tony turned out to be a very amiable Italian, whose food was excellent, and as no one knew him there, Comer decided to go for the home cured bacon with eggs and fried bread. As far as he was personally concerned, being Jewish was more of an art than a religion.

As Comer walked back to his flat that day, he did a little detour of the area, making mental notes of decent looking pubs along the way. Both the Stag's Head and Neary's looked very promising and worthy of a later visit. He walked through a small park and smelt the freshly mowed grass and heard the birds singing; this was a new way of life to him, he hadn't visited a park in London since he was a child.

Back at his flat he phoned Moisha in London to give him his address and phone number, and to ask how things were going. Moisha laughed, "You've only been away one bloody day Jack, nothing's changed here, still being bombed day and bleeding night – what about you?" Comer smiled to himself as he told Moisha that bombing was the least of his worries here, "Ireland's a neutral country isn't it?" "It might be neutral," replied Moisha, "but according to a paper I was reading yesterday, the Germans bombed it just a couple of weeks ago, at a place called County Wexford"

Comer was stunned by this news, how come he hadn't heard anything about it before he left England? Probably because he didn't read the papers or listen to the news enough. If he picked up a newspaper it was to read the racing results, what little there were of them.

When he woke the following morning and looked out at the clear blue sky again, he saw it in a different light; even as he took his walk through the little park on his way to Tony's Café, he didn't hear the birds singing, all he heard in his head was the terrible wail of the air-raid warning and the low monotonous drone of the German bombers. In the market he bought a paper and read through it over breakfast. There was plenty of news about the war in Europe and the bombings in Britain, but absolutely nothing about bombings or threats to Ireland. Maybe it was a mistake, a one off? Comer hadn't come to Ireland to dodge bombs; he had come to lie low for a while and hopefully reorganise his business interests.

He decided to give Bryan Lynch a call, get him to come round to him, hopefully in a different car, instead of that rickety old taxi. He needed to talk to Lynch and find out what was going on in the underworld scene in Ireland.

First things first, Lynch declared that the 'rickety old taxi' as Comer had described it, was essential to driving around the city without the police paying too much attention to it or its occupants; "The vast majority of taxis in Ireland are old," he explained, "so my old girl fits in nicely – it's the same with this area, no one will notice you around here" Comer could see the logic in this and agreed with Lynch. He was also surprised that he was starting to understand Lynch's lingo.

"Tell me," he said, "who is the boss around here? I think I should meet him don't you?" Lynch shook his head, "I'm here to help keep you invisible Mr Comer, and now you are talking about meeting up with the people who run this town – I'll tell you something shall I? The people who run things here are not exactly known to be on the best of terms with the English if you know what I mean? Do I need to spell it out?"

"You're talking about the IRA?" replied Comer. "Well I'm not talking about the fucking boy scouts," said Lynch, "and what you also need to bear in mind is that Garda Special Branch are watching the IRA twenty four hours a day, and if you are seen anywhere near them they will do a check on you and you'll be back in a prison cell in England before you can whistle God Save the King – am I making myself clear?"

"Clear as a bell old son," replied Comer, "clear as a bell – well at least you can show me a few of your legendary Irish pubs around town – I could do with a drink"

• • •

Comer could hardly believe his eyes when he walked into the Stag's Head pub; it was midweek, late afternoon and the public bar was so crowded that he and Lynch had to fight their way to the bar to get a drink. "Christ, is it always like this?" asked Comer. "No," Lynch replied with a smile, "it's usually quite crowded in here" Lynch passed a pint of Guinness over to Comer, who looked at it with a frown. "Yes, I know," said Lynch, "you probably usually drink some English pansy drink, but I don't want you standing out like a sore thumb in here, you understand? And try to keep your voice down a bit, that's also a dead give-away"

Comer wasn't used to people talking to him like this, especially people who were supposed to be working for him, but in this case he knew that Lynch was doing it for his own good. He looked around the pub, mostly men, and mostly dressed in working clothes. In an alcove quite close to him however, one man seemed to be holding court, with six others sitting around him, watching every move he made and listening to every word he spoke. "Who's that over there, in the mack?" asked Comer. Lynch shook his head, "Will you never listen to me Jack? Why can't you just relax and enjoy your drink like I am instead of constantly searching for trouble? Comer grinned sardonically and nodded his head, "I knew it was him – it is him isn't it – Mr Big?"

Lynch was starting to feel exasperated, why had he even brought Comer to this particular pub, but to be fair, he hadn't quite expected it to be so full of IRA men and their supporters. There must be something important going on. Maybe they should leave and go somewhere else, somewhere a little quieter? When he suggested this to Comer however, it fell on deaf ears, for Comer was now staring in the opposite direction. What the fuck is he looking at now, or more to the point, who is he looking at now? "Are you listening to me Jack?" he said again, "I want to show you some other pubs around here, there's one in William Street called Grogan's Castle, now I know you'll love it in there"

Comer hadn't heard a word Lynch had said, "I know her," he said. Fuck me, who does he think he knows now? Lynch thought as he tried to hone in on who Comer was talking about. "It's Ruth," declared Comer. He was staring at a beautiful young woman in an emerald greed dress, who was sitting at a small table in the corner of the room, chatting with two older ladies. Lynch now focused in on the object of Comer's attention. "If you're talking about her in the green frock," he said, "her name's Rita, Rita Portman, and her brother is - well the less you know about him the better"

Whether Comer actually heard what Lynch had been saying to him, or had he chose to just ignore him is debatable, but without saying another word he pushed his way through the crowd and stopped before the three women. "Ruth?" All three women looked up at him with puzzled expressions on their faces, "You remember me?" The women looked at each other and at Comer, who had a broad grin across his face. Rita smiled back at Comer and told him that he had made a mistake, "My name's Rita," she said, "not Ruth" "I met you in London," Comer blurted out, "about seven years ago – I'd know you anywhere"

"You have made a mistake pal – now do yourself a favour and fuck off" Comer swivelled round to see a man of his own age and size facing him with a very aggressive look on his face. Comer was not accustomed to being spoken to like that by anyone. He put his drink down on the table and pushed his face into the face of man in front of him. "And what the fuck is it to do with you?" he growled. The man slammed his pint of Guinness down on the table so hard that some of it splashed up, almost catching the women. "I happen to be Dave Portman," he snapped, "and Rita is my sister, and we don't like people who can't take no for an answer – especially Cockney bastards like you"

Comer felt the hair on the back of neck stand on end as he pulled his fist back, ready to smash it into the man's face, but he was prevented from doing so by someone behind grabbing his arm and stopping him. He swung round to see Lynch, who now stepped in between the two men. "Hey, hey, come on now" shouted Lynch, "both of you" He then turned to Dave Portman, an almost apologetic look on his face, "Calm down Dave, this is a friend of mine, he's not a bloody Cockney, he's from America for Christ sake, he made a mistake that's all"

Comer and Portman stood in silence, staring at each other like two heavyweight boxers who had been stopped in the ring for punching low by the referee, a man twice their age and half their size, but who still commanded their respect. "Now come on," Lynch said to Comer as he pulled on his arm, "let's get you out of here and back to your hotel, I think you've had enough drink for one day don't you?" Comer gave one more brief glance at Rita as he allowed himself to be meekly led out of the pub by Lynch.

● ● ●

Comer couldn't get the woman out of his mind, she was the spitting image of Ruth, whom he had met at that party seven years ago He had often thought about Ruth, and how he wished he could have contacted her again, with the death of Solly Feinstein, he would not only have a great deal of explaining to do to Ruth, but he could also have placed her in danger at the same time.

The shrill sound of the phone brought Comer back to reality. It was Moisha, calling from London, "We got a problem Jack" Not exactly the best opening line of a phone call, he had only been in Ireland a few days and already they had problems in London. "What do you mean, a problem, what sort of a problem?" snapped Comer. Moisha went on to tell him that the printer, Manny Finklestein, had been badly injured during a bombing raid and looks like he may lose a leg. "Fucking Hell," replied Comer, "just my bloody luck" There was a slight pause at the other end of the line before Moisha retorted with, "To be honest Jack, I don't think Manny is feeling too lucky either at this moment in time"

Comer wasn't thinking straight, what with this girl, Rita, and now this. He had come to Ireland to escape the problems that were threatening him back home, "Listen Moisha, I want you to go and see Manny and make sure he's comfortable and getting the right treatment, bung the doctor a few quid if you need to, we can't afford to lose Manny, he's a good man, d'you know what I mean?"

Moisha didn't sound too happy with Comer's explanation of what he should do, but at the end of the day, Comer was the boss, and all he could do was carry out his orders. Comer told him that he would make a few calls and see if he could come up with a replacement for Manny while he was in hospital, and said he would phone Moisha later in the week.

● ● ●

It was 11 am by the time Comer was tucking into his eggs and bacon breakfast at Tony's Café He raised his eyes towards the window as he heard the sound of that old-fashioned horn honking from outside, it had to be Lynch in that bloody old taxi of his, and sure enough it was.

Lynch walked into the Café with a big smile on his face and sat himself down opposite Comer. "I thought I'd find you here," he chirped, "seems you made quite an impression last night" Comer looked up at Lynch, who went on to tell him that he had received a phone call this morning from Dave Portman, the man he had the altercation with the previous night.

Dave Portman had apparently liked Comer's style; an American having the guts to stand up to him in a crowded Irish pub was something he was not used to. Comer questioned Lynch on the term American. "That's right," Lynch, replied, "don't you remember, I had to tell him you were a Yank as he positively hates the Brits" "Does he really?" Comer retorted, "well you can tell him from me that I'm not too keen on him either, even though he does have a lovely sister"

Lynch managed to calm Comer down, reminding him that he needs to keep a low profile. Portman had asked Lynch if Comer would be interested in doing a piece of work for him, which only went to infuriate Comer even more. "Me?" he shouted, "doing work for him – who the fuck does he think he's dealing with here?" "Keep it down, keep it down," whispered Lynch, "he doesn't know who you are and we want to keep it that way – I spun him a yarn that you are on the run and that the FBI are hot on your trail – he won't want to be seen anywhere near you now, believe me" "Thank God for that," replied Comer, "now let's get out of here, I want you to show me some more of Dublin in case I ever need to make a quick getaway on my own"

• • •

It wasn't exactly a comfortable ride in the back of the old Beardmore cab, with horsehair sticking through parts of the upholstery and a suspension that felt like it had gone into retirement many years earlier, but at least the windows were clean, and it wasn't raining.

Lynch took Comer on a tour of the nearby streets first, showing him little back alleys and cut-throughs that might help him, should he ever need to escape fast. He then drove into the City and around all the usual tourist spots, including St. Patrick's Cathedral, Dublin Castle, and Leinster House, the home of the Irish parliament. "Now there's a place that might interest you," he said, pointing to Kilmainham gaol, "that is real Irish history, did you know that the leaders of the 1916 Easter Rising were executed there?

Comer didn't even know what the 1916 Easter Rising was let alone who was executed there and what for. As for prisons, why, he thought, should he be particularly interested in prisons? He spent the best part of his life trying to figure out how to stay out of them. "There is one part of Irish history that I am very interested in," said Comer, "and that is Irish food and drink – now where do you suggest?"

Real Irish food, explained Lynch, is only available in people's homes, and as for drink, everyone knows about Guinness, but if he wants first class food and drink, there is only one place to go in Dublin, and that is Jammet's on Nassau Street, "That's if you don't mind hob-knobbing with odd film star or politician," said Lynch with a smile. Comer nodded, this sounded good. "What are we waiting for?" he said, "just make sure you don't park this thing right outside"

About fifteen minutes later, Comer was getting impatient, "We've been on this same road for ages," he said, "how much longer is it going to take?" Lynch explained to him that this was the South Circular Road, probably the longest road in the city. "I'll tell you something, which should interest you," he said, "this was the first road the Jews settled on after fleeing from Russia in the last century, and if that isn't enough, it also happens to be where Rita Portman, the girl you were chatting to, happens to live" He pointed to a Jewish dairy opposite as they passed it, "she has a flat right above that shop there" Comer glanced at the Dairy as they passed it; this was definitely something he would have to delve into in the not to distant future.

When they at last arrived at Jammet's, Comer made sure that Lynch parked two streets away. One thing he had always demanded, was respect, and he knew that if they were seen getting out of that old jalopy, his credibility would be at a minus zero rating. The only minor setback was when the maitre d' insisted that Lynch removed his cap and muffler and put on a tie before being allowed in.

The interior of Jammet's was sumptuous and equal to anything he had seen in the west end of London, with Mahogany wood panelling, brass fittings and marble serving tables. It looked like everything he had ever heard about Parisian restaurants; even the waiters were dressed in long black aprons with white shirts and spoke with French accents. With all this, it came as no surprise that the cuisine was also French.

Four hours and four bottles of wine later, Comer and Lynch were still seated at their table at Jammet's. Comer had never experienced food like this before, starting with soup à l'oignon, followed by confit de canard, then tart tatin, and fromage with bread to finish with. This was a lifestyle he could easily get used to. Who said Ireland was a country full of peasants?

Chapter 15

Billy White was talking on the phone at his Park Lane office as the door opened slightly and Albert Redman poked his head in. "Sorry to bother you Billy, but there's someone here to see you" White nodded to Redman and cut short his phone call, "Who is it? He enquired. Redman gave a sardonic grin, "It's Teddy Baxter". White shook his head, "What the fuck does he want?" Redman shrugged his shoulders, "Shall I tell him you're busy?" "No, no," replied White, "send him in, let's get it over with"

A few seconds later Baxter walked into the room; his head swathed in bandages and his left arm in a sling. White had known Baxter for a few years; he was a sort of odd-job man in the underworld; if you wanted something messy done, then Baxter was your man; 'thick as shit' was how White once described him to an associate. "Hello Teddy," he greeted him, "you look like you've been in the wars"

Baxter grunted, "In the wars?" "You can say that again Mr White, I had a fucking German plane trying to gun me down" White had a look of incredulity on his face as he listened to Baxter, was this another of his made up stories? "I'm not kidding Mr White," Baxter continued, "I was doing a bit of work in a van with a couple of Comer's boys when this German plane flew overhead and started shooting at us, then that fat bastard, Sonny, who works for Comer, suddenly kicked me out of the van, right into the path of this fucking German plane who started shooting at me, if I hadn't rolled into a ditch I would be fucking dead now"

Billy White didn't know whether to laugh or cry. He lit a cigarette to try and hide the emotion showing on his face. "Terrible, terrible," he muttered. Baxter's face was red with rage as he related his story. "They won't get away with it," he snapped, "one way or another I'm going to have that little team – Comer, the lot of them"

Billy White interrupted Baxter, "Before you go any further Teddy, what exactly have you come here for today?" Baxter took a deep breath and started to calm down, explaining that now he had fallen out with Comer's mob, he was looking for some work and wondered if White had anything for him. White was wary of Baxter, but ultimately knew that he might be of some use to him in the near future. "I've got a couple of things I'm working on," declared White, "which could be right up your street, but before we go any further I want you to know that you don't declare war on Comer and his mob while you're working for me, you got it?" Baxter nodded and assured White that he wouldn't dream of doing anything like that, "You can trust me Mr White," he said. "Alright, leave me your phone number and as soon as I've got a few things sorted out I'll give you a ring," White said. As he should have guessed, Baxter did not have a phone, "I'm not on the phone Mr White," answered Baxter, "but you can always get me at the Spread Eagle pub in Islington" He wrote down the pub's phone number on a scrap of paper and gave it to White.

Albert Redman came back into the room after Baxter had gone. He shook his head in disbelief, "You're not serious about taking him on are you?" he asked. White got up and walked over to the window, where he looked down onto the busy Park Lane below them, "Here, have a look at this," he said, beckoning Redman to the window. The two men watched as Teddy Baxter hobbled across the busy main road, narrowly escaping being run down by a taxi as he did so. He then held out his arm to stop a bus and just about managed to climb up onto the platform, with the help of the bus conductor. "If that's the face of organised crime in Britain today, God help us" sniggered Redman. "A cart horse isn't known for its brain power either, but once you harness it and point it in the right direction it'll do all the heavy work you want, without question" added White with a knowing look on his face.

• • •

Just five miles away from Park Lane, Moisha, Sonny and Billy Munro were holding a meeting in the Mackworth Arms pub in Commercial Road, east London. Moisha was busy reporting to the others that Comer had phoned him a few hours ago, and arranged for a new man in the printing business to meet them there in the pub. He was still talking about it when the doors of the pub flew open and a youngish man in his early thirties, tall and very smartly dressed, walked in. This was the new printer, Tony Speers, who was known to his friends as Sharp Tony.

After introductions, and a few preliminary questions, Sonny asked Speers how he knew Comer, how long had he been in the printing trade, and was he also an engraver? Speers explained that he had never met Comer personally, but his uncle Willy had grown up in the same street as Comer's family. He had worked for his uncle in the printing trade since leaving school, doing everything from typesetting, to printing and engraving, which is why his uncle Willy had recommended him to Comer. So far, so good. The next move was to take Speers to the Essex warehouse and show him the set up.

● ● ●

Comer was overjoyed when he heard the good news from Moisha. They had taken Sharp Tony Speers to the warehouse and within half an hour he had everything up and running, meaning ration books, clothing coupons and lots more would soon be starting to roll off the presses once again. It was as good as printing your own money.

Comer was at last starting to relax; he had good men working for him back in England, whom he knew he could rely on. He was also starting to feel more comfortable around Lynch, who obeyed his every order, with the exception of buying a different motor vehicle. Lynch even introduced him to a weekly card school. Dublin was looking better by the day.

Christmas came and went and apart from missing his old friends and east London haunts, Comer still managed to enjoy himself in Lynch's company. Lynch even invited him to a family party on New Year's Eve, where the whiskey flowed like it was going out of fashion, and if that wasn't enough, he was invited to another party two days later, on 2 January.

His head was throbbing when he woke the morning after the second party. It was like a sledgehammer banging against his skull. It was only 5 am and still pitch black outside. He reached for the glass of water beside his bed and took a mouthful before realising that the banging wasn't coming just from inside his head, but outside, in the street somewhere. He sat bolt upright and listened for a moment; it was that old familiar sounds of German aircraft flying overhead; he'd know their monotonous drone anywhere. The drone was coupled with the sound of bombs being dropped, whistling through the air and exploding as they hit their targets, and it didn't sound too far away.

Comer's hangover disappeared as if by magic as he leapt out of bed, rushed to the window and pulled the curtain to one side. He couldn't see the planes as there were no searchlights to pick them out like there were in London, but he could certainly hear them, and the sky to his left was glowing red from the fires caused by the bombs.

As he continued to stare towards the area being bombed a strange feeling suddenly came over him; he couldn't quite put his finger on it, but he knew something was terribly wrong. He turned from the window, grabbed the phone and started to throw his clothes on at the same time. A few seconds later a very weary sounding Bryan Lynch answered him, "Hello there – who's that?" Comer didn't have time for niceties, "It's me," he hollered, "if you look left from my window, what area is that?" There was a slight pause on the other end of the line while Lynch came to his senses and finally answered, "It's the South Circular," he mumbled, "but why?" Comer cut him short, slammed down the phone and rushed out of the house.

• • •

Comer was a big man, but very fit. He ran through the dark and deserted streets as fast as he could, following all the time, the red glow from the buildings, which had been hit by the bombs. "Which way to the South Circular?" he shouted as a man hurrying along in the opposite direction. The man turned and pointed, "It's straight in that direction," he said, "but you don't want to go there, its being bombed"

The sounds of the planes and the bombs had now stopped and had been replaced by the heavy beating of Comer's heart as he hurried even faster in the direction the man had indicated. The scarlet red sky seemed to be growing in intensity the closer he got to the scene. The sounds of fire engines police cars, and ambulances now filled the air, along with raised voices and cries for help.

He turned a corner and found himself confronted by a maelstrom of people and vehicles. Firemen were desperately dousing the building on the corner of the street, with gallon after gallon of water as they perched themselves on top of their ladders. Two fire engines and an ambulance were parked in the centre of the road, while a cordon of police officers did their best to control the ever-increasing crowd.

Comer looked up at the burning building, it was, as he had feared, the Jewish Dairy, where Rita Portman had her flat above. The building was engulfed in flames; God, no one could possibly survive that. He pushed his way through the crowd towards where the ambulance was parked, only to be stopped by a police officer as he got close to it. "I need to get to that ambulance," he shouted, "someone I know was in that building, I need to find out what's happened to her" The policeman quickly and politely explained that all the occupants had been evacuated from the building safely, so there was no need for Comer to worry.

Comer heaved a sigh of relief; he felt as if a huge weight had been lifted from his shoulders, but what for he asked himself; he had only met the girl once, after all. Then suddenly there she was, standing, staring up at what was once her flat; with a shawl wrapped around her, her face blackened by the soot and dirt of the fire, and she was just a few feet away from him.

Comer approached her and stood directly in front of her, looking down at her without saying a word. Rita stared up at him for a moment before actually recognising who he was, "What are you doing here?" she said, in almost a whisper, "I came for you," Comer replied, "come on, you can't stand here all night" He put his arm around her waist and gently guided her away from crowds and the devastation.

• • •

By 10 am that morning, Lynch had heard about the bombing, knew no one had been seriously injured or killed and had put two and two together. "Can I come round and see you?" he asked Comer, down the phone. Comer had been expecting this and naturally told him yes, but he certainly wasn't going to allow Lynch, or anyone else to start lecturing him. Lynch worked for him, not the other way round.

A very worried looking Lynch was there within twenty minutes, "What am I supposed to say to her brother?" he asked. Comer told him that he wasn't supposed to say anything to anyone, "I haven't fucking kidnapped her" Lynch nervously lit a cigarette as he paced the room; this was more awkward for him than it was for Comer. "I know that Jack," he said, "but" Comer was starting to get very angry now, interrupting Lynch and raising his voice, "But nothing Bryan, who the fuck do you think you are coming here and talking to me like this? That poor girl had been bombed out of her home – do you want to tell her brother where she is? You do it – what do you think, that I'm scared of him or something?

At this point a door opened and Rita stood there, still dressed in the shawl she had on earlier. Lynch looked eagerly into the room behind here where he could see her unmade single bed. "If it's of any significance to either of you, I will be phoning my brother myself this morning," she said.

Lynch and Comer looked at each other, Comer had a look of self-satisfaction on his face. Lynch just shrugged and gave the sort of look that men do when a woman does something they wasn't expecting.

Over the next few days Lynch started seeing more and more of Rita in Comer's company. He took them to high class stores around the city, where Comer bought her outfits and jewellery, he also took them practically every lunchtime to Jammet's Restaurant, where they would sit at a corner table and chat away like a pair of lovesick teenagers, while he was now obliged to sit separately and keep an eye out for any trouble, as Comer put it. The truth was, Comer wanted to be alone with Rita; what possible trouble could there be in a high-class place like this?

As Lynch sat there, alone, staring out of the window and thinking, two men walked in and were shown to a table at the back of the restaurant. Lynch didn't take any notice at first because the restaurant was crowded as usual, with people coming and going all the time. But then he did a double take at the two me; the first man was Rita's brother, Dave Portman, and the man with him, even though he had now grown a beard and moustache was without a doubt, Charlie Kerins. Good God, he couldn't believe it; he still didn't know for sure whether Rita had actually told her brother that she was now living with Comer or not, so that could be trouble enough on its own, but coupled with Charlie Kerins, it could spell disaster.

Charlie Kerins was a major force in the IRA, he hated the British with a vengeance, and it was rumoured that he and other IRA members had carried out several attacks on British targets in Northern Ireland. As far as Lynch knew, Kerins was now on the run from the police, for allegedly murdering a top police officer by mowing him down with a machine gun. All in all this didn't look very good news for Comer at all. What could he do, how could he get both Comer and Rita out of there without Dave Portman seeing them, or himself for that matter?

A note, that's what he would do, write a note and get a waiter to discreetly deliver it to Comer at his table, and then to show them out by the back door, which just happened to be very close to where they were sitting. He opened his wallet and took out a small piece of paper, on which he started to scribble down the note. Even as he got the first couple of words down onto the paper he glanced up to see Portman standing up and looking right at his sister and Comer. "Rita," he called. Lynch was too late; Portman was now walking across the room to where his sister and Comer were sitting.

Lynch froze as he watched Portman stop at Comer's table and then reach into his inside pocket. He is going to pull a gun out and shoot Comer. It wasn't a gun however that he took out, but a cigarette case, from which he took a cigarette out for himself and offered another to Comer, who cautiously accepted it. Lynch continued to watch as Portman kissed his sister on the cheek and shook Comer's hand.

From where Lynch was seated, he obviously couldn't hear what was being said, but there certainly didn't look like any animosity between Portman and Comer, quite the opposite in fact, with Comer gesticulating for Portman to sit down and join them. Portman smiled and nodded towards the table where Kerins was still seated. Even Kerins looked relaxed, which must have taken some doing, especially for a wanted man.

What Comer had omitted to tell Lynch, was that Rita had kept to her word and phoned her brother the morning following being bombed out of her flat on the South Circular. Portman had rushed round to Comer's flat and was very grateful to him for giving Rita her own room in his flat and looking after her so well.

While Rita went into her room to get ready, Portman quietly told Comer that he had been doing some checking up on him since they had first met in the pub. It wasn't difficult, he explained, he knew that Lynch had an interesting sideline in looking after fugitives of one kind or another, he only had to start asking a few questions in the right places and the name Jack Comer soon came up. "I had my suspicions," he exclaimed, "when Lynch tried to pass you off as a Yank – I may be from the Emerald Isle but I'm not completely green – that accent of yours is strictly Cockney Kosher, not Yankee Doodle Dandy" Comer found it somewhat difficult to suppress a smile at this assessment of him.

Half an hour later the two men were getting on like two brothers at a Bar Mitzvah. Portman explained to Comer that when he mentioned to Lynch about maybe doing a piece of work for him, that what he had really meant was working together on something. Now this might be something that could interest Comer, "Did you have something in mind?" he asked. Portman told him that he did, "I'll be perfectly honest with you Jack," he said, "last month we lost one of our main people, our chief money getter - he was gunned down by the Garda in an ambush, and this is why we need someone with your organisational skills Jack," he said, "I think you'd be perfect for what I have in mind, but I have to convince the main man about this first"

This was the first time that Comer and Portman had met again since that meeting in Comer's flat over a week ago. "Do you see the man sitting over there?" Portman nodded towards where Kerins was sitting, "his name is Charlie Kerins, he's a very important man in my organisation, if you know what I mean? I brought him here specifically to see you, Charlie goes very much on what he sees – I have told him all about you, and now it's up to him - if he likes the look of you, your in, if he doesn't – then we have both got a big problem"

Chapter 16

Ten days after his meeting with Portman in Jammet's Restaurant, Comer received a phone call from Portman, telling him that things were now moving forward and to meet him at midday in a little pub where they wouldn't be recognised by anyone. At the pub, Portman explained that Charlie Kerins was satisfied with what he had been told about Comer, and that he had authorised Portman to let Comer have the details of the job in hand.

Comer obviously didn't tell anyone about his plans, including Portman's sister, Rita, as he had been asked specifically not to by Portman. When he asked Lynch however, to drive him to the South Circular Road and to pull up just past the big iron gates of the Player Wills cigarette factory, Lynch did as he was told, but immediately turned to Comer and shook his head, "You're asking for trouble Jack, you know that don't you?" This was beginning to wear Comer down somewhat, Lynch constantly nagging him about what he should and should not be doing. He got out of the old Beardmore cab and started to walk away; he then stopped and returned to the cab, where he looked in at Lynch, "You do your job Bryan, and leave me to do mine alright?" he said, "your job is to wait here for me – I'll be a few minutes" Lynch didn't say a word, he just watched as Comer walked away towards the big brick built building.

Comer looked at the iron railings that encompassed the huge building. A pair of double gates, set with a security box to one side, where Comer could see a middle aged looking man with a large white moustache, dressed in a dark green commissionaire's uniform. This was obviously the man who checked all vehicles in and out of the factory; so no problem there then.

The building was enormous, must have a hell of a lot of people working here, thought Comer. The first street past the factory was filled with little houses, probably homes of many of the workers here. He turned into the street and walked the full length of it, only to find it was a dead-end street. Comer turned and came back out onto the South Circular Road again. There were no streets on the opposite side of the road, just more houses and a few small shops; he kept walking, feeling somewhat despondent as he did so. He was looking for an escape route, and so far it looked like the big South Circular Road might be the only way, which wasn't very good news. He stopped for a moment and lit a cigarette. It was while he stood there smoking that he noticed a tiny little alley just behind him. He stared down the dark alley, with its high blank brick walls, but where did it lead out to?

It was so narrow that his shoulders almost touched the sides of the walls as he walked along its length, and within a few minutes he reached the end, and found himself in a little square surrounded by tall Georgian houses, with three separate streets leading in different directions. A smile came over his face; perfect, this would be perfect.

Three days later, Comer took a bus, just in case anyone might be following or watching him, to the outskirts of the city where he met with Portman again, this time in a little run-down pub. "Before we go any further," said Comer, "who's going to be working with me?" Portman shook his head and told Comer that he couldn't give names at this point, but that he could give his word that they would be thoroughly reliable men. "I need to know how many?" answered Comer. "If your plan is approved, you'll be working with two of our best men," answered Portman. "Fuck me, don't overstretch yourself will you?" replied Comer, "there's still a few things I'll need to discuss with them before we go any further"

Portman agreed with Comer, as soon as they had the actual day sorted out, he would call a meeting somewhere outside the city, where Comer would meet everyone involved and be able to ask all the questions he wanted. They continued to go over Comer's plans, which Portman seemed a bit wary of at first, but as Comer continued to explain things, Portman started to warm to the idea.

• • •

It was raining as usual on the morning of Friday March 6, 1942. A small cream coloured Ford 8 HP van with the familiar Player cigarette logo on the side came into view; moving at a sedately 25 mile per hour along the South Circular Road in the direction of the Player Wills factory.

The driver of the van pulled off the main road and onto the entry road of the Player factory where he came to a halt at the gates. He turned to the man sitting in the back of the van, who was guarding the two large metal boxes containing the weekly wages of the factory's employees, "Here we are again then Patsy, let's see how long he takes this time to open up for us shall we?" The man in the back of the van grinned as he looked towards the security box where the man in the commissionaire's uniform was now looking up from his desk, as if in slow motion, "I'd say we got time for a fag before he manages it, what do you reckon?"

Patsy, the guard, was perched on the wheel arch in the back of the van; he lent back and took out a cigarette and lit it, blowing a thin stream of smoke out as he did so. He thought it best to relax for a few minutes before the commissionaire opened up the gates for them and they continued their journey into the factory. At this precise moment, the front windscreen, the driver's door window, and one of the small back windows of the van all exploded inwards, as if they had been hit by a bomb. Shotguns appeared, as if out of nowhere, their barrels shoved into the van through the broken glass, and behind the shotguns stood three men, wearing balaclava helmets, which obscured their faces. They shouted at the driver and the guard to get onto the floor of the van.

The terrified occupants of the van did what they were told immediately. The driver's door was almost pulled off its hinges as one of the masked men ripped it open and shoved his shotgun against the driver's head, yelling at him that if he made one wrong move he'd be a dead man. Meanwhile, another of the masked men tried to rip the back door open but found it locked, "Get this fucking door open now or I'll shoot your fucking head off" he shouted at the terrified guard. "I can't" the guard shouted back, "he's got the keys," indicating towards the driver, "it's locked from the outside" One of the masked men leaned in and grabbed the driver, pulling him half out of the van, "The keys" he shouted, "give me the fucking keys"

The terrified driver's hand was trembling with fear so much that he couldn't get a grip on the keys, which were still in the van's ignition. "Come on, come on," the masked man screamed, and then in desperation shoved the driver out of his way, onto the ground, and pulled the keys out of the ignition himself.

While all this was going on, no one seemed to notice the commissionaire, who had started to come out of his box, but when he had eventually seen what was going on he quickly jumped back inside and locked himself in, probably the fastest he had moved for years. He ducked down to the floor, out of sight of the raiders, picked up the phone and started dialling the police.

The guard in the back of the van moved as far away as possible from the back doors as he heard the key being inserted into the lock and could see through the broken window, the outline of one of the raiders. The doors suddenly swung open and he was faced with the huge figure of a man, dressed in a black trench coat and wearing a black balaclava helmet on his head. All the guard could see of the man was his eyes, which were dark and menacing, and the shotgun, which was pointed directly towards his head.

"Don't shoot, don't shoot," he stammered as he pushed the two metal boxes towards the masked man, "here, take 'em – it's all in there" The masked man didn't need to be told twice, he quickly grabbed the boxes, one at a time and passed them out to one of his accomplices, who was now standing just behind him. While two of the raiders now stood guard on the men inside the van, the third man carried one of the boxes over to the metal railings, where three lightweight Matchless G3L 350 cc motorcycles were propped up. He dumped the box down on the pannier of the first motorcycle, just behind the seat and quickly strapped it securely on. He then did exactly the same with the second box, strapping it to the second motorcycle. The boxes were so large and heavy, that they looked like they were about to tip the small lightweight bikes up on their ends.

The big man was now sweating; both from carrying the heavy metal boxes and from the thick woollen balaclava, which encased his face and head. He raised his shotgun into the air and fired off a shot to signal to his accomplices that everything was now ready to go. At that precise moment, another sound caused him to look round; it was the sound of police cars with their bells clanging as they sped towards the scene, getting closer with each second that passed. At the same time an alarm siren also started to wail from somewhere within the factory.

The three raiders rushed off towards the three motorcycles, which they leapt on, kick started the engines and roared off as quickly as they could, almost colliding with the two police cars, which were heading in their direction. The drivers of the police cars didn't need to be Sherlock Holmes to realise that these masked men, still carrying their shotguns, were the men who had just carried out the raid on the Player Wills cigarette factory. They slammed on their brakes and did swift U-turns, their bells still clanging loudly as they chased after the raiders.

Comer, still masked and unrecognisable, led the trio of raiders, as they now had to put on as much speed as possible to outrun the quickly converging police cars. His motorcycle was carrying one of the boxes; the second motorcycle was carrying the other one, while the third motorcyclist was carrying nothing apart from his shotgun. He glanced over his shoulder and saw one of the police cars almost upon him, looking set to run him down if he didn't act quickly. He turned again, briefly and fired a shot at the oncoming police car, which didn't manage to stop it, but it tore a gaping hole into the radiator grill, which although it didn't stop the car, it caused a huge amount of steam to start hissing out and clouding up the driver's view.

Comer, still at the head of trio, glanced around as he heard the shot, but by this time he was at his chosen destination. He turned again slightly and indicated for the others to follow him; he then roared off the road, up the kerb, across the pavement and drove straight into the little narrow alley that he had reconnoitred earlier.

The handlebars of his motorcycle just cleared the walls either side of him as he sped through the alley with the other two motorcycles close on his tail. Every now and then one of them would just clip a handlebar against the wall, sending a shower of sparks into the air.

Comer felt pleased with himself for having taken measurements and having the handlebars of the three motorcycles sawn shorter to make sure they would allow them through.

The first police car, with steam increasingly hissing out of the hole in the radiator, tried rather unsuccessfully to follow the motorcyclists down the alley; ending up with smashing into the entrance and almost tearing off both its wings. The second police car didn't fare much better; it smashed into the back of the first one, leaving the alley blocked and the two police cars completely out of action.

As this was happening, the first motorcycle carrying Comer, came roaring out of the alley at the other end, followed in quick succession by the other two motorcyclists. All three motorcycles screeched to a halt just by the gates of the square, where the men quickly jumped off, unstrapped the metal boxes and carried them to an old black Morris van. Two minutes later they were driving away from the scene, having left their motorcycles, black trench coats and balaclava helmets on the pavement beside the railings of the square.

As the old black van trundled through the streets of Dublin, no one would have given it a second look; it was a typical workman's type van; even the bespectacled man driving, with the cloth cap and muffler looked every inch a painter or decorator, or maybe even a deliveryman. Comer was indeed a deliveryman that day, for he was delivering the metal boxes containing the Players factory's wages, which they had just stolen, to a warehouse on the other side of the city.

● ● ●

Once the van was safely inside the warehouse, Comer and the other two men got out and carried the boxes containing the money up a flight of metal stairs to a small office where three more men were waiting for them. Dave Portman had a huge grin on his face as he watched them put the two boxes down on the floor and welcomed them in, "Well done boys," he said, "this is Charlie Kerins," he said, indicating the man sitting behind the desk, "you've sort of met him already Jack, haven't you?" Comer nodded, but was more interested in the contents of the boxes than long-winded introductions, "Shall we get them open?"

The third man in the room, who was not introduced and looked more like a minder than someone important, picked up a crowbar from a nearby table and proceeded to jemmy the boxes open. All six men stood in a circle around the boxes as they were opened and the contents could be seen. Bundles and bundles of banknotes, which when counted, came to £25,000, which is approximately £1m at today's values.

Comer was suitably impressed with the way everything had been organised. They even had another set of clothes there, waiting for him to change into, as well as a holdall to put his share of the cash in, which came to £6,250, or a quarter of a million pounds today, which he was more than pleased with. The one thing he had expected was some sort of transport back to his flat, instead of which he was told he would be far less noticeable on a bus.

He did as suggested and kept the holdall firmly on his lap during the whole journey back home; gripping it even tighter every time he heard the sound of police car's bells as they darted in and out of the traffic that day. This had been a big robbery by any standards and from what he could see; half the police in Dublin were out looking for the culprits.

He was sweating and relieved once he finally got into his flat. Rita had a worried look on her face as she greeted him and looked questioningly at the holdall, which he took straight into the bedroom and locked inside his wardrobe. "I have been worried sick about you Jack," she said, "where have you been all day, and what was that bag you brought in?"

Comer flopped down into an armchair and beckoned for Rita to come to him, pulling her onto his lap as she did so, "Don't you go worrying yourself about me darling," he said, stroking her hair, "I just had a bit of business to do that's all, nothing for you to worry about" Rita wiped away a tear from her eye and held his face as she kissed him, But I do worry Jack," she said, "I've seen enough of all this sort of thing with my brother, I just don't want anything happening to you" Comer pulled her closer and kissed her again, telling her that nothing was going to happen to him, "I'll tell you what," he said, "why don't you get us both a drink and then get yourself ready and we'll go out for a meal?"

Rita walked to the sideboard, took out a bottle and two glasses and started to pour their drinks, "Bryan's phoned you three times today," she said. Comer was in the process of lighting a cigar as Rita said this. A look of exasperation came over his face as he took the drink from her, "What the hell is it here?" he asked, "first you, and now him – this guy works for me for Christ sake, the way he's acting you would think it was the other way round" Rita shook her head, "He certainly knows who he works for Jack," she said, "but like me, he is worried – why don't you give him a ring?"

As if in answer to Rita, the phone suddenly rang, it was Lynch. Comer didn't mind talking to him, but he hated being ordered or told, what to do. This however, put things into perspective as far as he was concerned; if the mountain will not come to Muhammad, then Muhammad must go to the mountain, and sure enough here he was, the prophet of doom himself, Bryan Lynch.

Comer sat and listened to what Lynch had to say while Rita, now seemingly happy with the situation, went off to change and get ready. "I don't suppose you've been listening to the wireless have you? Lynch asked. Comer admitted that he hadn't and enquired why? Lynch went on to tell him that news of the raid had been on the wireless all day; the Garda are sure it was carried out by the IRA but they say that several witnesses positively identified one of the masked raiders as having a Cockney London accent, and are anxious to trace a well known character from the London underworld. "I knew it was you Jack," said Lynch, "didn't I tell you not to get involved with these fellows?"

Comer wasn't sure how to react here; on one hand he was pleased that Lynch had put him in the picture, but he was also angry, feeling that he was being lectured to, yet again. "What's it to you?" he angrily snarled down the phone, "it'll be my arse they're after, not yours" Lynch explained that he was responsible for him while he was in Ireland, if the Garda started looking for him, which they undoubtedly will, the trail would lead directly back to him as well, and not only that, he said, he would also have the 'other people' on his back, for bringing him here in the first place.

Comer started to calm down; he could see the logic in what Lynch was saying. "So what do you suggest?" he asked. "You have to get out of Ireland, and pretty damn quick," said Lynch, "and that isn't a suggestion, it's a fact"

Comer heard a click on the phone, as Lynch was finishing talking. The bedroom door opened and Rita stood in the doorway; she had been listening on the extension. "You're going to leave me aren't you?" She had tears in her eyes as she said this. Comer stood up and went to Rita. He hugged her closely to him, "I'm not going to leave you Rita, I want you with me forever" He could taste the salt from her tears as he kissed her.

● ● ●

It was almost 10.30 pm as the old Beardmore taxi cab pulled to a halt on the cobbled section of the causeway adjacent to the little fishing village of Howth port, some nine and a half miles north-east of Dublin city centre. It was almost a full moon, but fortunately for Comer, there was a lot of cloud in the sky, which kept the coastline in almost total darkness.

Comer and Rita sat in the back of the taxi in complete silence; she gripped onto his hand and stared at him and then at the suitcase that was down by his knees. Lynch suddenly turned and pointed to something moving in the sea, a little way off shore, "This looks like them," he whispered. Through the darkness, Comer could see a small rowing boat getting nearer, with just one man rowing. Comer turned to Rita and kissed her, "I'll be sending for you in a few days," he said, "just as soon as I get settled again, I want you to listen to Bryan and do what he says, he's got a small hotel sorted out for you, just stay put until you hear from me, right?" Rita just nodded in silence and watched as Comer got out of the taxi with his suitcase and hurried across to the shore, where the rowing boat had now pulled in.

Rita and Lynch watched in silence as the rowing boat headed out into the bay, where a fishing boat was waiting for it. A couple of minutes later Comer had climbed aboard, the boat's engine had started up and he was on his way.

Chapter 17

Moisha was looking particularly pleased with himself as he pulled the big black Buick onto the forecourt of the Savoy Hotel on the Strand, "How's this suit you Jack?" Comer smiled and nodded, "Suits me to a tee Moisha," he said, "to a tee"

Moisha told him that he had booked him into a one-bedroom suite overlooking the river for five nights, under the name of Jack Johnson. "That should give us enough time to find you another flat somewhere convenient – oh, and before I forget, you better take this," Moisha took a document from out of his inside pocket and handed it to Comer, "here's your new identity card, I got a feeling you're going to need this"

Comer looked impressed as he examined the card, "Hmm, not bad, not bad at all, I take it this is Sharp Tony's work?" Moisha confirmed that Sharp Tony had made it, and that he was pleased with everything he had been doing for them. At this point the doorman opened the car door to let Comer out, "I'll take your case sir?" he said, but Comer was not having any of this, and held on tight to the case, which of course contained a great deal of cash.

London was still experiencing the nightly air raids, and was now beginning to look, in parts, more like a First World War battlefield than a major capital city. There were barrage balloons hanging in the sky, like German Zeppelins, except they were there to stop attacks, not create them. Piles of sandbags were stacked outside many of the major buildings, and all windows had sticky tape criss crossed all over them. Comer had almost forgotten about the war on the home front while he had been in Ireland, but now it was here before him and couldn't be missed.

But, like the moral boosting posters that he saw everywhere, which stated, 'Keep Calm and Carry on' this is exactly what he intended to do. He felt almost like a military general, searching for a new headquarters from which to run his operation, whilst inspecting his troops at the same time and making sure everything was running smoothly and according to plan.

It wasn't very difficult finding a flat in London, as so many people had moved out to the countryside to escape the bombing. After viewing three, he settled for a luxury three bedroom flat in Cumberland Mansions, just off Edgware Road.

Over the course of the next few days, he visited the warehouse in Essex where Sharp Tony was busy turning out every form of Government document possible, with the exception of the Pound Sterling. From there he looked in on his father, to make sure he was alright, at his retirement home, which was quite close to the warehouse.

Next on his list was to get all his team together, almost like a boardroom meeting, where he could go through everything that had been happening while he had been away, and to start making fresh plans for the future.

A year ago, he would have organised a meeting at the Mackworth Arms pub in Commercial Road, Stepney, but after living in Dublin for some time, and eating French food on a regular basis at Jammet's Restaurant, he now saw himself as something of a gourmet and wanted to show off his knowledge of fine food and drink to his associates.

While he was still searching for a suitable venue, he called in on his personal tailor, David Bernard, who had a small workshop in Soho. Unfortunately for Comer, all this fine living in Dublin had taken something of a toll on his waistline in particular, and he needed Bernard to make him a few more suits. After being measured up and choosing the materials and styles, Bernard took him out to lunch at an Italian restaurant called Bianchi's on Frith Street, and introduced him to a woman named Elena Salvoni, who ran the place.

Bianchi's wasn't exactly in the same league as Jammet's in Dublin, but it was nevertheless an up-market restaurant in Soho. Comer had never eaten Italian food before, and was at a complete loss when faced with his first plate of spaghetti with tomato sauce. Elena Salvoni smiled as she placed a napkin around his neck, "To protect your lovely suit and tie" She prod his fork into the pasta, twiddled it around into a small ball and fed it to him, like someone teaching a child to eat, "See, simple"

Ten minutes later he was eating it like a native, and absolutely loving it. Elena didn't have a clue who he was, and agreed to let him use a room above the restaurant for the proposed meeting, and booked a large table for him and his entourage in the restaurant following the meeting. His problem was solved.

• • •

The meeting went to plan; everyone was there, including a few new faces whom Comer hadn't met before as Moisha had hired them while he had been away in Ireland. The printing business was going well, as was the black market goods, but there was one thing that definitely had to change, and that was the Jewish Protection League. "We are not going to take money from these people any longer," proclaimed Comer. There were looks of astonishment from around the table. Sony didn't like the sound of this at all, "But we rake in a good part of our money from this Jack?" he said. Comer's eyes looked almost black when he became angry, as they did now. He banged his fist on the table and stared at Sony, "Haven't you heard what the fucking Nazis are doing to the Jews over there Sony?" he said in a raised voice, "they are putting them in fucking camps and murdering them – Jews, Sonny, Jews, like you and me"

Silence descended upon the men round the table, like a dark cloak suddenly descending on them from above. Sony moved his mouth as if to answer Comer, but no sounds came out. "The Jewish Protection League," bellowed Comer, "will still exist, but only to do exactly that, to protect these people from the likes of Mosley and his crew, not to rob them"

Comer took a deep breath and stared at the men around the table, awaiting some sort of response, which never came. Another deep breath and he was starting to relax again, "Don't get me wrong, we are still in the business of protecting, but from now on we are going to pick our targets much more carefully – remember when we were looking after the clubs and spielers around the east end? Well now we are moving west – this is where the action is, the west end, and I aim to move in and run things around here – anyone who don't like the idea is free to get up and walk out now?"

Comer stared from man to man around the table; no one moved, then Sony offered his hand to him, "I'm with you all the way Jack" Everyone else quickly followed suit.

An hour later, the mood had changed dramatically; the whole crew was now seated in the restaurant downstairs. Drinks were flowing and everyone was happy and laughing; no more talk about business, just small talk about women, gambling, drink and food. In fact food played a big roll in the conversation, as hardly any of them had eaten Italian food before, and didn't have a clue what it was called or how you were supposed to eat it.

Elena Salvoni buzzed about their table, making sure they had drinks and helping them as much as possible with the pronunciation of the dishes and how they should eat it. She made everyone laugh when she tied a red-checkered tablecloth around Moisha's neck, like a napkin, "Here," she said in her thick Italian accent, "this'll protect your nice white shirt from the tomato sauce"

● ● ●

Over the following few weeks, Comer started putting his words into action. Soho was one part of Britain that was still relatively thriving. Clubs, pubs, bars, restaurants, gambling and prostitution, mostly legal, some illegal, but all potential money earners in Comer's eyes. Added to this melting pot were the armed forces, which now consisted of military men and women from almost every country around the globe, but the combatants that interested Comer most, were the Americans, who not only had more money to spend than the average Englishman, but were also keen to spend it in the sort of establishments, which Comer planned to control.

"I don't want you to rob the Yanks blind," Comer told his men, ""they've got plenty of dough to spend and they've got plenty of gear to sell as well, fags, booze, chocolate, they've got everything, so make 'em your friends, introduce 'em to our clubs and spielers, and do deals with them, got it?"

Comer was happy with the way his plans were now starting to take shape, but his mood changed rapidly when he received a phone call one night from a very distressed Rita, who told him that her brother Dave had been killed. He had been to a meeting with Charlie Kerins, the man behind the cigarette factory robbery. As they had left the meeting, a car load of Free State Special Branch men had pulled up opposite them and called out Dave's and Kerins' names; not thinking for the moment, they both had looked round towards them. Without another word being said, one of the Special Branch men rolled-down the window of their car and took aim at Portman and Kerins with a Thompson sub-machine gun. He emptied a full ammunition-clip in their direction. Charlie Kerins managed to escape, but Dave Portman was dead before his body hit the ground; he had sixteen bullet wounds to his body when the shooting finally stopped.

All Comer could think of was getting Rita out of Ireland as quickly as he could. She was near to hysterical; he did his best to calm her down, talking very slowly to her, after some time he did manage to get his point across to her, "Now listen to me Rita," he said, "I want you to remain where you are, do you understand me? Are you still at the hotel?" She confirmed that she was, and said that she would do whatever he wanted. He then told her that he was now going to phone Bryan Lynch, and he wanted her to pack a case and do whatever Lynch told her.

The moment he had put the phone down on Rita he phoned Lynch, who had obviously heard what had happened. "I want you to arrange a crossing for her Bryan," he said, "the same as you did for me; can you do that?" Lynch told him to leave it to him, "I'll phone you as soon as I've organised things and she's on her way"

Lynch was as good as his word. Two days later, Comer was scanning the horizon with a pair of powerful binoculars as he sat in the back of the Buick, with Moisha in the driving seat. They were parked at the quayside at Porth Penryn, just outside Bangor. "This could be it," exclaimed Comer, as he saw the small fishing boat slowly coming into view towards them. An hour later, Rita was sitting next to Comer in the back of the Buick as Moisha drove them back towards London.

• • •

Rita moved in with Comer straight away. She was so sad that she couldn't even attend her brother's funeral, but from what they had heard, it was more than her life was worth. The Irish Government of Éamon de Valera had ordered a massive clampdown and arrests of anyone and everyone connected to the IRA were being carried out on a daily basis, and that was if the Free State Special Branch men didn't get to you first, as they had done with her brother.

The first few days were the most difficult for her; trying to settle into a completely new environment, and with the shooting of her brother forever on her mind, but as the day turned into weeks and the weeks into months, Rita finally began to grow accustomed to her new surroundings, and her new life with Comer. Although he never spoke to her about his business, or what he did for a living, she was no fool, and knew that the sort of people he mixed with, the life he led, and the money that was always lying about the flat certainly didn't add up to a legitimate business source, but she didn't particularly care, she was used to living on the edge in Ireland, and she also liked the high life, which Comer was introducing her to in London.

Comer's new life of premarital bliss certainly didn't affect his business interests, which were now starting to grow beyond his expectations. He now controlled nearly all the spielers in Soho, and was doing big business in black-market goods with the help and cooperation of a huge influx of American servicemen in London.

With success however, there are always some drawbacks, and when connected to the underworld, the drawbacks can often be very painful, as happened one night when Billy Munro and one of the newer recruits to Comer's mob, a young man named Jimmy Black, called in on a spieler in Bateman Street.

Munro and Black walked to the little makeshift bar and ordered two drinks and asked to see Tony, the owner of the club. A few seconds later a weasely looking little man with a thin pencil moustache, dark, oily hair, and dressed in a crumpled suit, which looked like he had slept in it, stepped out from behind a curtained off area behind the bar. "Hello Tony," said Munro, with a smile, "got something for us I believe?" Tony looked nervously at Munro and Black without saying a word. "Did you not hear me?" asked Munro, "We've come for our money Tony"

Tony's eyes flicked nervously from Munro to Black and then to one of the groups of men, who were playing cards just a few feet away. Black swivelled round towards the men as he heard the sound of chairs being scraped back. Tony spun on his heels and disappeared in a flash, like a magician's assistant, back behind the curtain again, as the card players descended, like the four horsemen of the apocalypse, upon Munro and Black.

The first card player was a giant of a man, who stood so close to Munro that their noses were almost touching. "We're looking after Tony now, so he won't be needing your lot any more, right?" The thug was certainly a big man, but Black had a temper which he found hard to control when confronted by anyone talking to him like this, no matter what their size. He clenched his fists and began to bring his right arm upwards, to take aim at the big man, but the more experienced Munro quickly grabbed his sleeve and held him back, as he saw the other three card players had now surrounded them. "And who, exactly are you?" Munro asked the big man.

The big man snarled at Munro, "My name doesn't matter," he said, "It's who we work for that you need to worry about" "And who might that be?" replied Munro. "That's for us to know, and you to find out," snapped back the big man, "and we know who you work for by the way, Jack, bloody Comer, and you can tell Mr Comer from me, that he is finished in Soho right? We, are number one around here from now on, right?"

Munro let go of Black's sleeve and swung his right fist into the big man's jaw, knocking him several feet backward into the bar. Black followed suit with a right and a left to the two men nearest to him. What Black failed to see however, was the fourth man, who was behind him and who now brought a bar stool down upon the back of his head, which sent him crashing to the floor. Munro spun round as he saw what had just happened, but as he did so, he found himself staring down the barrel of a 38 Enfield Service Revolver; a large and cumbersome weapon from the 1930s, but one which could have split his skull apart if fired from this close.

Having quickly recovered from the blow delivered by Munro, the big man was now pointing the pistol directly between Munro's eyes. "Outside," he ordered, gesturing with the gun. Munro did as he was told, while the others picked Black up from the floor and dragged him out behind the big man. While all this had been going on, no one else in the little spieler had moved a muscle to intervene in any way; they just sat and watched in silence and fear, as the group of men left the club.

• • •

At 6 am the following morning when refuse collectors came to empty the bins in a narrow alley at the rear of business premises just off Bateman Street, they discovered the almost lifeless bodies of Munro and Jimmy Black. Both men had been stripped down to their underpants, tied up with rope, blindfolded, and beaten until hardly an inch of their bodies was left without a bruise. When they were finally admitted to hospital, it was also discovered that almost all the bones in their right hands had been broken as well.

It was two days before the police could interview Munro and Black; they were very suspicious of what had happened and were certain within their minds that the incident was gang related, but both Munro and Black denied having any knowledge of what had happened; they were set upon by a gang who sounded like Americans, they said. The police knew there was much more to this than a simple street fight; why had neither man been robbed? Why had they been stripped of their clothing? Why had both their right hands been smashed to a pulp? And why had they been blindfolded?

"So why did they blindfold you?" asked Comer, to Munro from his hospital bedside. Munro was so heavily bandaged it was difficult for him to even speak; "I don't know," he mumbled. "Did you know any of them?" asked Comer. "No, I already told you," mumbled Munro again, his face, or what Comer could see of it, obviously contorting with pain as he tried to answer Comer's question, "I only saw three of them, and I'd never seen any of them before in my life – the fourth one I didn't see anyway"

Moisha was waiting in the Buick for Comer as he left the hospital. "Did you smell anything as you got in the car Jack?" he asked as he pulled away with Comer now firmly in the back. Comer looked at Moisha's refection in the rear view mirror; he wasn't joking; "What do you mean?" Comer asked, "I mean the filth, didn't you see 'em out there – two of them, gave you a right eyeballing they did"

Comer glanced back over his shoulder through the rear window to see if they were being followed. "It's alright," said Moisha, "that's why I pulled away a bit sharpish, didn't want to give them time to get to their car, if they had one"

Comer couldn't believe what was happening, first his men being beaten up and the threat of another gang moving in on his territory, and now it looked like the law was onto him again as well. He thought he had got away from all that when he went to Ireland.

Rita; he suddenly thought of Rita, if anything happened to her. "I want you to drop me off at my flat," he told Moisha, "and then round up the boys and make yourselves seen around town tonight, right? And don't forget to be tooled up – all of you" Moisha wasn't exactly sure what Comer wanted them to do, did he want them to go collecting or what? Comer explained that he just wanted their presence felt around Soho, no collecting, just plenty of noise and bravado, and be ready for anything. "I'll join you at eleven o'clock at the Starlight Club"

• • •

When he finally arrived at his flat, Comer was relieved to find Rita alive and well and listening to one of his Glenn Miller records on the radiogram, while preparing some food in the kitchen. He watched her from the doorway, as she hadn't heard him come in over the sound of the music. He smiled to himself as he watched her dancing to 'In The Mood' She was even chopping the carrots to the beat of the music. She gave a final spin as the tune ended and saw Comer standing in the doorway watching her.

"Oh," she exclaimed somewhat embarrassedly, "you startled me, I didn't know you was there" Comer smiled as he crossed the room to Rita and took her in his arms. He hugged her to him without saying a word, she was important to him, so special, if anyone ever hurt her in any way, he would kill them.

Rita looked up at his face; was that a tear she saw in his eyes? "What's wrong Jack? She asked, "Has something happened?" "No," he replied, "everything's fine darling, and that's the way it's going to stay" He didn't want to burden her with more problems, she was still trying to get over the death of her brother, and of course there was the war and the constant bombing. He told her that he had to go out on 'a bit of business' but he wanted her to lock the door after he had gone and not open it to anyone. She should only leave the flat to go downstairs to the bomb shelter, which was in the basement of the flats, if the air raid warning sounded.

Rita had not seen Comer like this before, why was he suddenly so worried for her safety? Everyone in London had been living with the constant threat of German bombers for months now, what was so different now?

"I've been reading in the papers about this Blackout Ripper," he said, "I didn't want to worry you before, but now he's murdered four women, and all in this area" Rita was puzzled by this, she didn't usually read the newspapers, and when the news was being read on the wireless, the only part she listened to was about what was happening regarding the war. Comer explained to her that a murderer, dubbed the Blackout Ripper, has been operating in London, and that his first victim had been discovered in an air raid shelter in Montagu Place in Marylebone, which is just a few minutes away from their flat. She had been strangled and robbed.

Comer was not making this story up, it was true, but his real fear for Rita's safety was not the Blackout Ripper, or even the German bombers, but the gangsters, who were now threatening him and anyone connected to him. He couldn't tell her that of course, but he made her promise him not to open the door to anyone while he was out.

● ● ●

A short while later, Comer was sitting in the back of taxi, on his way to the Starlight Club in Soho. The air raid warning started up yet again as the taxi neared its destination; from the back of the cab he could see the searchlights zigzagging across the night sky, picking out the silhouettes of the German bombers as they dropped their deadly loads somewhere in the direction of the London Docks, where the sky was now turning crimson as the incendiary bombs took hold of their targets.

As the taxi pulled up outside the Starlight Club, the streets of Soho were deserted and pitch black, not a chink of light anywhere. Comer paid the taxi driver and hurried into the club, through the heavy draped velvet curtains, which helped keep the lights from showing outside.

Inside the club was like being in a different world. The lights were bright, the music was loud and the place was packed to capacity. At least half the clientèle were American servicemen, with a smattering other nationalities, including a very small minority of British servicemen. Comer looked around, doing a spot of mental arithmetic in his head. How much was this club paying him? Should be doubled, at least, he thought.

Comer made his way around the edge of the dance floor, towards the bar, where he could hear a lot of shouting and laughter taking place. Sure enough it was as he suspected, Moisha, Sonny, and half a dozen other members of his team, were doing exactly as he had told them, making quite a bit of noise, and making sure they were seen by all and sundry.

Moisha looked at Comer and shrugged as he passed him a large brandy, "We've been doing this all night – we've been to seven different clubs and made so much noise, no one could have missed us" Comer looked around the crowd again, he couldn't make it out. If another firm was working their pitch and were serious enough to put two of his men in hospital, then why hadn't they showed up? His men had been making enough noise; they could have hardly gone unnoticed.

Almost in answer to his thought he suddenly saw a familiar figure walk into the club, it was Billy White, who was accompanied by Albert Redman and another man, who looked like an all-in-wrestler. "Fuck" he said, almost to himself, "why didn't I think of him?" Moisha looked puzzled by Comer's remark, "But White's more into bank jobs and that sort of stuff isn't he – I didn't think he dabbled in the protection rackets?" Comer was still staring at Billy White as he continued to answer Moisha, "Times are hard Moisha," he said, "and when times get this hard, people resort to all sorts of things"

By this time, Billy White had walked right up to Comer and held his hand out to him, "Jack Comer – how are you – long time no see?" This certainly didn't sound like someone who was trying to muscle in on his rackets, but from what he had heard, White was a very slippery character, who could turn the charm on and off like water from a tap. Moisha and Sonny made a protective move forward when they saw Comer surrounded by White, Redman and the wrestler, but Comer discreetly ushered them away.

Instead of wading in like the aggressor, Comer decided to play the appeaser, the smiling friend, suggesting to White that the pair of them should go and sit down somewhere a little less noisy. Redman and the wrestler could have a drink at the bar with his boys, "I'm sure they'll find a great deal in common to talk about," smirked Comer.

A couple of minutes later, Comer was sitting in an alcove with Billy White. A bottle of brandy sat in the centre of their table. Comer opened his leather cigar case and took two of his favourite Romeo y Julieta cigars, one of which he gave to White. With cigars now lit, and large brandies in their hands, the two men got down to business.

"First of all," started Comer, "I want to say here and now, that I didn't think you operated in Soho – I thought Mayfair and Knightsbridge were more your territory?" White looked slightly puzzled by Comer's remark, "I've got a couple of clubs around here, but that's all," he insisted, "the Stork and the Blue Room, to be honest Jack, I prefer to invest my money where the old money is, as you say, Mayfair, and Knightsbridge, Soho's on a roll at the moment, what with the war and the Yanks, but I can't see it lasting"

This was getting more confusing by the minute, if Billy White wasn't involved in Soho and the protection racket, then who the hell was it who had put two of Comer's men in hospital? Comer decided to put his cards on the table. He poured them both another drink and told White the whole story of what had happened. When White heard the name of the club where it happened, and exactly when it took place, his face contorted into a grimace, "Say no more Jack, I've got a strong feeling that I know who's involved here" "So tell me then?" Comer leaned forward, eager for an answer.

"I want to talk to you about something else first," White replied, "Remember some time ago, I said I thought we could work together? Well I've got something planned now, which could make us both very rich men if you're interested?" Comer's face lit up, "If there's money involved then tell me, I'm listening"

Billy White moved in closer to Comer, "All I can tell you at this point Jack," he said, "is that it involves gold, and a hell of a lot of it" Comer could feel the palms of his hands, itching with the very thought of it, "So why do you need me?" he asked. "I need you Jack because this is going to be the biggest gold robbery this country has ever known – I do not have enough men to pull this off on our own, and you are the one person I know who has the team and the guts to pull a job like this with me, so what do you reckon, are you in or are you out?"

Two more large brandies and Comer found it difficult to keep his face from smiling. "From the little you've told me Bill, I would say I'm with you all the way, but I still need to know more details – and I still want to know who were the rats who put my boys in hospital?" White nodded, "No problem on both points Jack, I just had to be sure we were partners first"

Chapter 18

White and Comer met discreetly over the next few days, working out the details of what they would need for the robbery. They had to be ready day and night for no one knew at this point exactly when it would take place. It all hinged on White' contact, who was a Major in the British army, who had run up enormous debts at the Green Room, which was one of White' gambling clubs in Mayfair. The Major came from a noble family, and would not only be ruined if ever this came out, but would also lose his inheritance. White had put the 'frighteners' on the Major, either he came up with something or he was finished.

When he came up with this deal, White could hardly believe his luck, if it was for real and a feasible plan could be worked out, it would make him, very, very rich.

"But I have to know when?" Comer insisted, "what am I supposed to tell my men – that they have got to be on standby day and night for God knows how long?" White smiled and shook his head, "Don't you think I wish I knew that Jack?" he said, "it's not as easy as that, believe me, but you can also believe me when I say it'll be well worth waiting for – for both of us" One more thing Comer needed to know, and that was how were they going to get rid of the gold once they had acquired it. White smiled, "I wondered when you was going to ask that one," he said, "I have a contact in Switzerland, which as you know is a neutral country, as well as being a very rich one. My contact is in the import and export business, all very legitimate, and will be paying us off in cash for the gold – we'll get sixty percent of the market value, and from there he will be exporting it in small amounts back to Switzerland, does that meet with your approval?"

Comer had to agree, Billy White wasn't the sort of man to be taken for a ride by anyone, he absolutely stank of money and success, and now he, Jack Comer, was being offered an equal share in what was probably going to be the heist of the century. If his men had to be on standby for a few weeks, then so be it. In the meantime however, he still wanted to know who it was that was trying to take over his empire, and had put two of his boys in hospital.

● ● ●

It was just after 10 15 pm when Moisha and Sonny walked up to the Spread Eagle pub in Islington and peered through the cut glass window into the saloon bar. The pub didn't look very busy, just a few men at the bar and an elderly couple sitting together at one of the tables.

There was no mistaking Teddy Baxter; he was holding court in the centre of the small group of men by the bar. From his position outside the pub, Moisha could obviously not hear what Baxter was saying, but his gesticulations spoke for him; he was punching and stabbing and waving his arms about in general. This was part comedy and part extreme violence, and his admirers seemed to be hanging onto every word he said and every gesture he made.

Moisha was growing angrier by the minute, just watching this self-obsessed braggart playing to the gallery like a third rate actor in a second rate play. "I want to kill him," he almost hissed. "You know what Jack said," Sonny replied, "a good beating – hurt him badly, but no more"

The sound of the bell being rung from inside the pub signalled closing time. "He'll be out in a minute," said Sonny. Moisha agreed and signalled to a nearby doorway, where he suggested they should go and wait.

It was dark and deserted on the street as the pub door opened and the figure of a man was silhouetted in the doorway. Sonny pulled out a length of metal piping from the waistband of his trousers, at the same time, Moisha pulled out a revolver. "What the fuck have you got that for?" asked Sonny, "I told you, we're supposed to give him a good hiding, not fucking kill him"

Moisha ignored Sonny's remark and went to move forward, but was pulled back by Sonny, "Hold on," he said, "that's not him" The man had now stepped onto the street and was just one of the group of men that Baxter had been talking to. "Mask up, now" Moisha said as two more men emerged from the pub, "one of these is definitely him" Moisha and Sonny both pulled bandannas up from around their necks to cover the lower parts of their faces, "Remember Moisha, no shooting" Sonny said as they both raced across the street towards the two men.

Either the bandanna stopped Moisha from hearing properly or he was determined to shoot Baxter come what may, for he ran towards the two men, his gun raised at them as he shouted "Baxter"

Both Baxter and the other man stopped dead in their tracks for a moment, then Moisha fired the first shot, which fortunately for the two men, was well off target. The other man was a lot quicker thinking than Baxter was, and turned immediately and dived back into the pub. Baxter started running for his life as Moisha went to fire off another shot. This time, Sonny knocked his arm and made a dash for Baxter, with the metal bar raised in the air, ready to smash down upon him. "I'm going to kill you Baxter," shouted Moisha as he took aim again and fired off yet another shot. Baxter suddenly stopped and turned towards them, "Come on then," he shouted, "what are you waiting for?"

Sonny reached him first and brought down the metal bar on his head and his shoulder, but at the same time, Baxter brought out an open cut-throat razor, which he slashed at Sonny's face with, but caught Sonny's hand instead as he brought it up to protect himself. Baxter was now raging with anger as he lunged at Sonny again and this time managed to cut him across his cheek.

While all this was happening, Moisha was trying to get close and fire another shot at Baxter without hitting Sonny, but Baxter now turned his attention to him and slashed out at him, once, twice and a third time, catching his ear and his shoulder and sending a stream of blood spurting out onto the pavement. Moisha's revolver fired off another shot, causing Baxter to scream out and fall to the floor with a gaping hole in his foot where yet more blood was gushing out. Moisha hadn't aimed for his foot, he hadn't aimed at all; the gun had gone off by accident.

By this time, people had started to look out of their windows, the few remaining customers in the pub had gathered at the door and a car had pulled up opposite them. Moisha helped Sonny to his feet, "Come on, let's get out of here," he said as they both made their way off as quickly as they could, with blood dripping from both of them. As far as they knew, Baxter had been mortally wounded; it was too dark to see where the bullet had hit him. They just ran, leaving his prostrate body lying on the pavement in a pool of blood.

• • •

"Look at the fucking pair of you," shouted Comer, as he sat in the back seat of the Buick, with Sonny next to him and Moisha in the driving seat. The car was parked in a side street in the east end, where Moisha and Sonny had just had their wounds dressed by a 'friendly' doctor. "You look like you've just come straight from the battlefields of the First World War, and now you tell me you shot the fucking scumbag as well – didn't I tell you to just hurt him – warn him off – teach him a fucking lesson?"

Moisha shrugged his shoulders, "I know you did Jack," he mumbled, half apologetically, "but this guy is trouble, believe me, and the longer we allow him to stay around the worst it's going to be for us" Comer shook his head in disbelief, "That is for me to decide Moisha, not you - I've already got two men out of action," he yelled, "and now this – have you seen the papers? Gang war they're saying" Sonny mumbled a feeble excuse, saying that Baxter might have had a gun for all they knew. "Well I'll tell you what," Comer said angrily, "if he didn't have one last night, you can bet your bottom dollar he'll have one by now – for fuck's sake, don't you two realise that we have this big job in the offing, and we have to be ready at all times, not looking over our fucking shoulders every minute of the day?"

Chapter 19

Teddy Baxter was sitting in a threadbare armchair, his right foot swathed in bandages, was resting on a small cushion less stool, perched in front of him. Two heavy set men sat on hard chairs opposite him, they were Detective Inspector Bruce Cutler, and Detective Sergeant Barry Webber, both of whom used to work for Chief Inspector Peter Beveridge, who had now retired.

"I'd make you a cup of tea boys, but I can't hardly move with this foot" Baxter grimaced at the two police officers. Det. Insp. Cutler looked around the grim little bed-sit room, which looked like it hadn't been cleaned for months, and was quite relieved not to have to drink anything in there, which he considered to be no more than a hovel. "That's alright Teddy," he said, "we had breakfast at the station before we came out"

Det. Sgt. Webber stood up and went over to the window, which was so dirty that it took him a few seconds to realise that all he could see out of it was the roof and chimney pots of some houses opposite, "Does this window open Teddy?" he asked, "It's so bloody hot in here" In reality it was the terrible smell, which was like bad food or something that had died. He just wanted to get some fresh air. Baxter told him the window didn't open as he had nailed it shut, "Can't be too careful," he said, "lot of thieves living around here"

The bad smell was also getting to Det. Insp. Cutler, who got to his feet and started pacing the room in frustration, "Alright, cut the bollocks Baxter," he snapped, "you said you had something for us?" Baxter reached for his packet of five Turf cigarettes, took one out and lit it, leaving one remaining in the packet. "That's better," he smiled, "if I was to tell you there is a big diamond robbery being planned, what would it be worth to you?" "Who's involved?" snapped Det. Sgt. Webber, "Mickey Mouse or Charlie Chaplin? If you're wasting our time Baxter, we'll nick you for being involved in a serious crime and not reporting it to the police, do you understand?"

Baxter started to look worried as he took another deep drag on his cigarette. "I'm not messing around guvner, so help me I'm not" "So give us some names Baxter," shouted Det. Insp. Cutler, "and when and where this big diamond robbery is supposed to be taking place?"

"Jack Comer," blurted out Baxter, "that's the only name I've got so far – as for where, I'm not dead sure it involves diamonds, but if it does then it's probably going to be Hatton Garden ain't it?" Det. Insp. Cutler stared down at Baxter, "Give me strength," he spat out, as if he was about to spit blood, "You got us round here for that? I'm warning you Baxter, you're treading on very dangerous ground here, if you want to stay out of nick then you better come up with something feasible and fast, do you get me?"

Baxter grunted and nodded his head in silence, but let out a yelp as Det. Sgt. Webber 'accidentally' kicked the stool away from under his injured foot as the two detectives walked out of his flat.

• • •

While the fiasco with Baxter was taking place, Comer and Rita were enjoying a completely different type of day. They had been planning to get married as soon as possible, with Rita originally wanting a traditional wedding in a Synagogue, but Comer decided against this, as he couldn't afford any sort of publicity, which might have drawn too much attention to them. He didn't want to worry Rita by telling her about being watched by the police, so he used the death of her brother and the IRA connections as an excuse.

He also wanted to be around just in case he got the call from Billy White, so they decided to get married at Marylebone Register Office, which was just a ten minute walk away from their flat. Moisha and Sonny both attended, along with Billy Munro, his hand still heavily bandaged, and the new man on the team, Jimmy Black.

Comer had specifically demanded there was not to be an official photographer, just Sonny taking a few 'snaps' with his Box Brownie camera. After the very quick ceremony, they all decamped to Bianchi's restaurant on Frith Street, Soho, where Elena Salvoni had prepared a wedding banquet for them at the best table in the house.

There was no honeymoon for Comer and Rita, just a prolonged period of waiting. Comer was waiting for the now long anticipated call from Billy White, telling him to rally his troops together, for G-Day, which was their code word for the big gold robbery. Rita meanwhile, was waiting, like almost every other person in London, and indeed, all of Great Britain, for the terrible war with Germany to end.

The Blitz, as it was officially known, had ended some while ago, after consistent bombing of London and its suburbs, which lasted for 57 consecutive nights, destroying more than one million houses and killing more than 40,000 civilians, approximately half of them in central London.

The Blitz on London however, didn't just suddenly stop completely. Bombing raids were still common place, and nowhere was sacred; even Buckingham Palace was bombed, but it is when it hits someone personally that they start to realise the full extent of these atrocities, such as when the Café de Paris nightclub on Coventry Street Piccadilly was bombed. Not only was this somewhere that Comer had taken Rita to on a number of occasions, but he had also introduced her to the resident band-leader there, who was a young man from British Guiana, known as Ken "Snakehips" Johnson, who was someone Comer was proud to call his friend. Around eighty people were injured and at least thirty-four killed at the Café de Paris that night, including their friend, 26-year-old Ken "Snakehips" Johnson.

In one respect, Comer and Rita were no different to thousands of other Londoners, they had to learn to live with it, and like the Government issued poster said, 'Carry on Regardless' Money had to be brought in, and if Comer's team were not seen on a regular basis, they stood a good chance of being taken over by rival gangs, such as Teddy Baxter had tried to do.

The printing and black market business were still working well, as were the clubs and spielers, but this business with Teddy Baxter did play on Comer's mind; why had he suddenly stepped in like he did, and confronted Comer's boys like he had? Surely he must have known there would be comebacks? But then Baxter had never been known for his intelligence, and maybe after the way Moisha and Sonny dealt with him, he would think again before stepping on Comer's toes? The last thing Comer wanted or needed at this particular time was a gang war.

• • •

Days turned into weeks, and weeks into months, with still no sign of G-Day, which was very disconcerting for Comer, and could lose him face with his team if something didn't happen soon; was he being taken for a ride by White maybe?

Teddy Baxter meanwhile, was now back on his feet, limping somewhat, but definitely mobile. Being shot, to Baxter, was like a soldier being awarded the VC, he boasted of it, of how he had single-handedly seen off four armed men, beating and cutting them to pieces before escaping with just a single bullet in his leg. His other badge of courage was the amount of time he had spent in prison, "Yeah," he would boast, "I've done two years in the Scrubs, three in Reading and another year in Shepton Mallet, they all tried to break me but none of them ever did, and never will"

Although he would never admit it to anyone, Baxter had been well and truly driven out of the Soho protection business. "Not enough money in that game now," he would tell people, "you got to keep your eyes open for opportunities in this game, and believe me I've hit upon one that's going to make me a very rich man" In reality, he had recruited a small gang of young tearaways around him, mostly army deserters, who were impressed by his tales of bravado and thuggery. Their main specialities as a gang consisted of looting the homes of people who had been bombed by the Luftwaffe. This was easy pickings for Baxter and his mob, who would wait for an air raid to take place, and then rush to the area, while the home owners were either still ensconced in the air raid shelters, or sometimes even lying dead or injured by the bombing; Baxter and his mob would then rummage through their victim's personal belongings and escape as quickly as possible with whatever cash, jewellery and anything else they could lay their hands on. This was in stark opposition to the stealing from factories, which Comer and his gang took part in. As far as Comer was concerned, factories and businesses were covered by insurance, and would probably even earn money from their insurance claims. Stealing from ordinary working class people was a cardinal sin as far as he was concerned.

• • •

Comer was not alone in playing the waiting game; Billy White felt equally on edge, especially when he was at the Green Room, and confronted with the army Major running up yet more debts at the tables.

White watched as the Major spoke discreetly to one of his members of staff, who then came back to him and told him the Major was asking for a further £500 line of credit. White was fuming inside at this request, although he did not let it show at all as the Major turned from the table and caught his eye. White smiled politely at him and nodded his head, sending the staff member back to confirm the new credit line, and also telling him that Mr White would like to see him in his office in one hour.

An hour later the Major was shown into White' office above the club. He looked round somewhat nervously at the two heavies who stood guard at the door as he sat down opposite White. "Before you say anything Mr White, I know what you are thinking, and I promise you that you have absolutely nothing to worry about" The smile on White' face changed abruptly, to a snarl, as he got to his feet and walked around the desk to look down at the still seated Major. "I've got nothing to worry about?" He shouted, "d'you realise you are now in to me for over three grand?" The Major squirmed slightly in his seat and tried his best to smile and look relaxed. "I am an honourable man Mr White," he began, "I wouldn't ask you to extend my credit unless I knew for certain that I had the means to pay you back" "And do you?" snapped White. "Within five days," the Major retorted, "the operation I spoke to you about, will be taking place" White' eyes gleamed like two pieces of black coal when he heard this, "How do you know this for sure? He interrupted, "I thought you said we would only know just hours before it was going to take place?"

The Major went on to explain that intelligence were almost certain that Hitler was planning one last massive purge on London, in a bid to force the British Government to surrender. "We don't know how accurate this information is, but Churchill has personally ordered movement of all our remaining gold reserves and art treasures within the next five days. Much of our gold was moved to Canada during the first couple of months of the war, but there is still a considerable amount left in the vaults of the Bank of England, which means that operation 'Basement' as it will be known is about to begin"

Billy White had been waiting for this news for some months, and now when it had finally arrived, he felt almost overwhelmed. It wasn't often that he was lost for words, but on this occasion he was not just lost, he was stunned. He walked over to the cocktail cabinet and took out a bottle of vintage Scotch whiskey and two crystal cut glasses, which he generously topped up. "To us," he said as he raised his glass. "To us," replied the Major as they chinked glasses.

Chapter 20

The plan was that the Major would be notified by Military Intelligence the moment the German invaders were spotted on radar, heading in the direction of London. The Major was to have a convoy, consisting of two army lorries and two Jeeps on standby at a secret destination close to the City of London, probably at the Tower of London. As soon as he received the call, he was to mobilise his unit and make their way to the Bank of England, where an official, who had already been briefed, would be waiting for them with the gold already packed in wooden packing cases, and give them access to the Bank's strong rooms and the gold.

The Major's men will then load the gold into their lorries outside the Bank and head north-west out of London, taking as many minor roads as possible in the general direction of Snowdonia, Wales The total journey should take approximately six hours. The final destination would not be disclosed until the gold was safely on board the lorries and the convoy was ready to go. The Major would then telephone a secret number and be given the full details.

The Major will lead the way in the first Jeep, heading the convoy, while the second Jeep will guard the rear. All men will be armed and equipped with Walkie Talkies, which were originally called Handie Talkies, in order to keep in contact with each other during the journey.

With all this information now in their hands, all Comer and White needed to do was to work out exactly how they would execute the actual robbery, and where and when they would hit the convoy. Sounds deceptively easy at first hearing, but when faced with not knowing the exact route the gold would be taking, plus the fact that it would be guarded by a crack unit of fully armed men, the prospects of an easy job began to dwindle somewhat.

"This was never going to be easy Jack," White whispered, as the two men sat facing each other across a table in a quiet little pub in Clerkenwell, "but believe me, it's going to be worth it" Comer lit a cigar and chinked glasses with White, "I know that Bill," he said, "I'm ready when you are – I've already got a few ideas in my head – when do you want us to start drawing up some detailed plans?" Billy White took a notebook and a pen out of his pocket, "No time like the present Jack"

• • •

The plan took a lot longer than either Comer or White had imagined, even though they both had a number of preconceived ideas in the heads to start with. One of their biggest drawbacks was the fact that although they knew the general area the gold was being delivered to, they did not know the exact location or route the gold would be taking, as even the Major wouldn't know that until he was handed the details at the very last moment.

It was now a race against time, as they needed a number of different types of vehicles, as well as various arms and uniforms, all of which had to be ready and waiting to go within a couple of days, three at the latest.

Under normal circumstances, Comer was not a nervous man, but during the following couple of days he was really beginning to feel the pressure; he knew what he was doing, and he was pretty sure about White' involvement, but would he be able to rely one hundred percent on his men to do everything that was being asked of them? He was fairly certain of his men's reliability, but what he was not certain of, was their ability to work with White' men.

Comer woke early on Friday morning, would it really happen today? Was G-Day really here? He got out of bed as quietly as possible, being careful not to wake Rita, and made his way to the kitchen, where he prepared breakfast consisting of fried eggs, sausages, tomatoes, toast, and tea, which Rita was very partial to. Just a year or so ago, he would have found it difficult to cook a slice of toast without burning it; domesticity seemed to suit him very well, to a certain extent.

The surprise however, didn't quite go the way he wanted, for as he entered the bedroom, carrying the breakfast on a large mahogany tray, he was surprised to see Rita had already got up from bed, and was now in her dressing gown. "You didn't have to get up," he said, "I wanted to surprise you – look, I've just cooked it for you" Rita said that she had a slight headache and would eat it with him, in the kitchen in a while, after she had taken some Aspirin.

Rita took some time to finally come out of the bathroom and sit down in the kitchen next to her husband. She sipped at her tea, but by this time she couldn't eat anything, as her breakfast was now cold. Comer looked worryingly at Rita, who looked pale and was holding her head. "You don't look well at all," he said, gripping her hand, "would you like me to get anything else for you?" She shook her head and told him it was just a bad headache, "I'll be alright once the Aspirins start to take effect"

Unfortunately, he had to go out early today, but he was worried about her, and made her promise to go down to the air-raid shelter if an air-raid did start later on. He couldn't tell her that he was almost certain that the massive air-raid he had been informed of was going to start that evening; this was one thing he had not taken into account, but which was so important to him. To make matters worse, it would have to be this day of all days that Rita was not feeling well, but he had to go ahead with his plans, hopefully for both their sakes. He made a somewhat feeble excuse that he had to go and view the contents of a very large factory, which had just come up for sale, and might possibly be home very late.

• • •

Moisha called for Comer at 10 am and took him straight to a warehouse, which Billy White had acquired in Burnt Oak, Edgware. One of White' men was waiting as they approached, and immediately organised the large roller shutter to be lifted to let the Buick drive straight into the warehouse.

Billy White and Albert Redman stepped out of a small office to greet Comer and to show him everything that had been acquired. The vehicles consisted of two large army lorries whose front bumpers had been reinforced with iron girders one army Jeep, two ARP vans, and an inconspicuous looking family saloon car.

Over by one wall were several clothes rails, with both army and ARP uniforms in various sizes hanging from them, while next to the clothes rails were two large metal boxes, which White took great delight in opening and showing Comer a large number of army weapons and ammunition. "What I'm going to show you next Jack," said White, with a beaming smile on his face, "is our secret weapon" He opened the drawer of a metal filing cabinet and invited Comer to look inside. "What the hell are those?" asked Comer as he looked at six rectangular metal boxes, each one approximately 18 inches long and 4 inches wide on each side. The boxes had two small tubes protruding, one over the other, and were painted, like the vehicles, a sort of military green.

White smiled knowingly as he took two of the boxes out of the drawer, clicked a switch on the back of each one, and handed one to Comer, "Take it over there," he said, pointing to the far side of the warehouse. Comer hesitated, he was a little wary; it could be a bomb for all he knew. "Trust me Jack," said White, "just take it over there and put that tube to your ear" Comer was beginning to get the picture, even though he could not quite understand why or how.

When he was at the far end of the warehouse, White spoke into the box he was holding, startling Comer as he heard White' voice in his box, just like a telephone, but the difference was, there was no wires; this was magic to Comer's ears. "Press the button on the front and hold it down and then speak to me," said White into his box. Comer was almost like a schoolboy with a new toy as he did exactly what White told him, "I can't believe it," he shouted down his box, "how's it work?"

White walked over to Comer and told him he didn't need to shout down it, just to use it like you would a telephone, press and hold to speak, and press and release to listen. "I've never seen anything like it," said Comer, "what are they called and where'd you get them from?" White explained that they were called Walkie Talkies' and that he had acquired them from one of his American contacts, "Thank God for the Yanks eh? That's what I say" He went on to explain that the Major had been issued with two by his commanding officer, so that he could keep in touch with his back-up Jeep, should they lose contact. "We'll never lose sight of that gold now that we have these – it's going to be a good day Jack, I can feel it"

As the day progressed, the rest of the gang members started arriving; there was nothing much they could do now except wait and play cards. Both Comer and White gave strict orders that no alcohol was to be consumed until further notice.

At 6.30 pm the phone rang in the little office, "Yes?" snapped White, "yes, yes, fine, OK, good" he put the phone down and turned to Comer who was eagerly looking over his shoulder, "it's on," he said, "the Luftwaffe have left Germany and are on their way" Comer nodded, he could feel his heart beating fast in anticipation; would everything now go according to plan? Would the German bombers create total havoc in his beloved city? And most importantly, would Rita be alright? He had left her this morning, not looking well at all, and now he couldn't even phone her to see if she was alright as they had imposed a ban on all outgoing calls. If only she had one of these Walkie Talkies.

Got to snap out of it he thought, and quickly. "OK," he shouted, "Moisha – I want two men, straight away, the ARP vans, I want them in position as quickly as possible, and don't forget the uniforms and Walkie Talkies"

Things were now starting to happen. Moisha was passing on the orders to two of the men while others were getting into their military uniforms and sorting out weapons and Walkie Talkies.

Just after 7.30 pm the distant sound of air-raid warnings could be heard coming from the general direction of London and the City, which was approximately 12 miles away. It was dusk now, the perfect time for the cowardly invaders to arrive, thought Comer, with Rita constantly on his mind.

● ● ●

It was almost pitch black in the City of London. The only light came from the reflections of the searchlights as they zigzagged across the night sky, trying desperately to pick out the incoming Dornier Bombers. The sounds of the air-raid warnings wailing out like a banshee in the night, coupled with a heavy monotonous drone overhead, let Jimmy Black know that he was far from being alone. Black was driving one of the ARP vans and was resplendent in his ARP uniform, looking every inch as if he was there to help those in need, which in a way, he was, for he considered himself to be very much in need, and his sole mission was to help himself to as much of the gold as he possibly could.

From the little he could see from the slits of light coming from the covered up headlights of his van, he spotted the little alleyway just off

Threadneedle Street, and reversed the van into it, which enabled him a good view of the main doors of the Bank of England. Jimmy Black got out of the van and walked to a phone box, which was on the corner of the alley. Once inside the phone box he picked up the receiver to make sure it working, and then waited and watched.

A few streets away, in Cornhill, the second ARP van was also parked near a phone box, with Freddy Smith, one of White' men, at the wheel. The first bombs had now started to drop; one, two, three in a row, followed by maybe six or seven, and enormous flashes of light and fires starting from the small incendiary bombs, which the German pilots also dropped in order to light up the London skyline to get a better view where to drop their big bombs. Smith was starting to get very worried; these bombs were too close for comfort. It's alright for White and Comer, he thought, sitting comfortably back there in Edgware; no bloody bombs in their neck of the woods. He looked at the phone box, willing the phone to ring. Another enormous explosion, this time somewhere very close to him, so close that it shook the van.

Jimmy Black had also been shaken by the last explosion, and like his partner in crime, was also getting more than a little worried. He looked at his watch and at the phone box again, and at the doors of the Bank. Nothing was happening at all. Should he get out and phone Comer at the warehouse? As if in answer to his thoughts, the phone in the phone box started to ring. Black leapt out of the van and rushed to the phone, "Hello?" he gasped. It was Comer asking what the hell was going on, "You're supposed to let us know what is happening?" he snapped. Black explained the position, telling him that absolutely nothing was happening, no military lorries, and the Bank doors are still closed, "The only thing that is happening around here," he explained, "is the fucking Germans dropping bombs on us – the only gold we're likely to see will be the handles on our coffins" Comer didn't think this was very funny and told Black to get in touch with Freddy Smith to see if he has seen anything.

Freddy Smith was as mystified as to what was going on as Black was, but even as he was speaking, he suddenly saw a convoy of military vehicles emerging from a slope very near to where he was parked. Could this be the convoy? It was supposed to consist of two lorries, with a lead Jeep and a backup Jeep; this convoy had the Jeeps, but no lorries, just four much small military vans.

As the convoy continued towards him, another couple of incendiary bombs exploded somewhere nearby. The flash from one of the bombs lit up the scene just as the convoy was passing him, enabling him to get a first class view of the first Jeep and its occupants. That was him, thought Smith, the Major. He had seen him before when White was talking to him at his Mayfair club, the Green Room.

As the convoy passed him, Smith grabbed the Walkie Talkie, and pressed the switch to talk to Black. "It's on Jimmy," he almost shouted, "they just passed me and should be with you any minute now"

Jimmy Black received the message and looked up to see the convoy heading towards him. The look of excitement on his face quickly disappeared however, as the convoy drove past him and the Bank's doors, and continued heading in the direction of Norton Folgate and Shoreditch. "I don't believe it," he shouted down the Walkie Talkie, "there's no lorries, just four vans, and they've driven right past, I better get in touch with my boss straight away"

Jack Comer was fuming as he spoke to Black on the phone at the warehouse. "Go after them," he shouted, "they must have already loaded the gold before you got there, we can't afford to let them out of our sight – overtake them, let that fucking Major see you, and let's just hope he contacts you on that bloody Walkie Talkie thing, for his sake as well as ours"

Comer slammed down the phone and turned to Billy White, "Did you get that?" he asked. White nodded his head. "I think we all got it Jack," he replied, "something has got to be seriously wrong here, he wouldn't let us down at the last minute like this"

Comer banged his heavy fist down on the little desk in the office, "Wouldn't let us down?" he shouted, "he has let us fucking down – he's taking the piss Bill"

• • •

Jimmy Black drove the ARP van as fast as its small engine would allow, in the direction the convoy was travelling. Being very dark and hardly any light emanating through the narrow slits that covered the headlights, made it very difficult for him to see exactly where he was going, or even what traffic was on the road. Two small beeps from behind caused him to look into his rear view mirror and see the second ARP van, driven by Freddy Smith, coming up behind him. "I've been told to stay behind you," came the voice of Freddy Smith over the Walkie-Talkie. Black smiled to himself and answered his friend, "Good, when we do catch them up, I'll be overtaking them – you keep behind them so we don't lose sight of them until we know where they are going, got it?"

Some minutes further on, Black caught sight of the rear Jeep of the convoy as it made its way along Archway Road, north London. Black pressed the accelerator as hard as he could, down to the floor in an effort to catch up and overtake the military convoy, which was so difficult as his small engined van was certainly no match for the heavy duty military vehicles, especially as the road started developing into a Hill.

He could feel the engine getting hotter, and in his rear view mirror he could see a cloud of thick black exhaust as he slowly began to overtake the convoy. He gave two warning beeps on his motor horn, which was supposed to indicate his vehicle attempting to pass the convoy. It seemed to take forever on the outside lane, slowly but slowly overtaking the convoy until he was at last level with the leading Jeep, which contained the Major, a driver, and one guard sitting in the back. The driver glanced around towards Black and his van, and shook his head in disgust at the amount of black exhaust fumes, which were blowing all over them, "Bloody ARP, you'd think they would update their vehicles wouldn't you?"

The Major now looked and recognised the van as part of their plan. He picked up his Walkie Talkie, flicked two switches and told the driver that he was going to let the rear vehicles know which way they were going, "With all that idiot's exhaust belching out they could easily get lost"

The instructions the Major relayed to his rear Jeep driver, were also picked up by Jimmy Black in his van, which he in turn relayed back to Freddy Smith in the second ARP van. "They are now heading towards Northampton and on to Birmingham," he said, "I want you to turn off as soon as you can, park the van and make sure you make a note of where it is, then get out of your uniform and nick something a bit faster, and bring your uniform with you. I'm going to pull over at the first phone box I come to, so keep an eye out for me, I'll be waiting for you"

A few minutes later, Black had pulled up by the telephone box. He watched as the military convoy passed him again and the driver of the first Jeep looked at him as he drove past and shook his head in contempt. Black placed two pennies in the phone box slot as he heard Comer answer from the warehouse. Comer listened to what Black was saying for approximately two minutes before he completely erupted, calling the Major every expletive he could think of. In the background, Black could hear Billy White trying to calm him down. Black heard a loud bang, which at first he thought was a gunshot, but was in fact the sound of Comer throwing the phone to the floor.

Billy White somehow managed to calm Comer down a little and picked the phone up from the floor. He made notes on a piece of paper as he continued talking to Black and then turned back to Comer, "Right, we need everybody out of here straight away, I'll explain everything to you as we go"

Everyone, including Comer and White, were now dressed in military uniforms and wearing black leather gloves. The warehouse lights were switched off, and the large roller shutter opened up, allowing the distant glow of fires from London to partly light the night sky. The sounds of the German Luftwaffe's bombs, coupled with the British Ack-Ack guns deadened the noise of the army vehicles as they trundled out of the warehouse and onto the road.

Comer and White sat in the back of the Jeep; both dressed as officers, while Moisha, in his sergeant's uniform did the driving. They led the way, heading northwest away from London, with the two army lorries following closely behind. Albert Redman, who was accompanied by

Sonny, drove the saloon car, making sure to keep his distance from the military vehicles.

Meanwhile, on another part of the road, Jimmy Black had already parked his ARP van in a secret destination, and was now in his civilian clothes, carrying a small holdall, which contained his ARP uniform. He was standing outside the phone box as a gleaming 1.5 litre beige and navy blue Jaguar screeched to a halt beside him. Freddy Smith stuck his head out of the window with a big smile upon his face, "This alright for you?" he beamed, "you did say get something faster" Black nodded his consent and climbed into car beside Smith. He was instantly propelled back into the luxurious red leather seating as Smith put his foot down hard on the accelerator and the beautiful machine took off like a rocket.

At the speed the Jaguar was travelling it didn't take them very long to catch up with the Major and his convoy. Black told Smith to slow down now so they didn't attract too much attention, "Make it look like we can only just about manage to overtake them, I need to get a message to the Major" Smith did exactly as he was told, allowing Black to switch on the Walkie Talkie and connect with the Major, who in turn led his driver to believe he was speaking to his rear back-up Jeep. "Slow down," Black told the Major, "keep your speed down to twenty miles an hour"

The Major did as he was told, allowing the Jaguar to overtake his convoy and take the next turnoff to their right, which led them in an arc, back towards the direction Comer and White would be coming from.

It seemed to Smith like they were travelling in circles, which in a way they were, but they had no alternative; this was long before mobile phones were invented, and even their Walkie Talkies only had a very limited range. While Smith was driving as fast as he could, in the direction he had been told to, Black was constantly trying to make contact with Comer and White on his Walkie Talkie. They didn't have far to go before Black heard a gurgling sound over his Walkie Talkie and knew they were getting close. Another minute and he saw The Jeep carrying Comer and White, coming over the White towards him, followed by the lorries.

Smith pulled the Jaguar onto the side of the grass verge and Black leapt out, signalling wildly for Comer to see him. Black ran over to Comer's convoy as they pulled to a halt. After a quick conversation Black jumped back in the Jaguar, which Smith hastily turned around, and they were off again, this time leading the convoy down a series of country lanes, which would hopefully get them into position at a point somewhere ahead of the military convoy.

● ● ●

The Major's convoy meanwhile, was still poodling along at a leisurely 20 mph towards Stoke-on-Trent, when a military despatch rider roared up alongside the Major's Jeep and waved them down. The rider explained that he had been sent from the Home Office with sealed orders for the Major, which he passed over to him, telling him that he was to read them and act upon them immediately.

The orders explained that due to 'certain other valuable items' now being transported by a completely separate convoy, to the original destination in Wales, the Major's convoy was now to be split into two halves. The Major would continue to his original destination, while the despatch rider would lead the way for the second half of the convoy, to another undisclosed secret destination situated somewhere in the region of the original location.

The Major was greatly perplexed by this new order; there was no way he could substantiate it. The order looked genuine enough, but was it, he wondered? Or was it some sort of subterfuge on Billy White' part? He tried to look into the face of the despatch rider, in the hope of getting some sort of signal, but with the helmet and the goggles, there was not much left of his face to be seen.

The splitting of the convoy wasn't a trick; it was genuine. Churchill himself had ordered this. The 'certain other valuable items' that the sealed orders mentioned, consisted of Royal jewellery, paintings, and valuable antiques, which needed to be stored in perfect conditions to stop them from deteriorating. It had long been known that paintings and other antiques needed conditions of stable humidity and temperature. The gold, on the other hand, would never deteriorate and could be stored almost anywhere.

One serious proposal had been for the Royal jewellery, paintings, and valuable antiques, to be evacuated by ship to Canada. But the vulnerability of the ships to U-boat attack worried the Royal official, who went to see Winston Churchill who immediately vetoed the idea: 'Hide them in caves and cellars, but not one of these items shall leave this island'.

It was therefore decided at this last minute, to store the Royal items in the disused slate mine near Blaenau Ffestiniog at Manod, Wales, which had originally been designated for the gold bullion. This meant finding somewhere else, equally as secure, for the gold. There were no other caves or disused mines that were suitable in size, but two separate smaller locations were found nearby, which had been previously used as Government shelters. It was quickly decided that these separate locations would now be where the gold was to be deposited.

By this time, the vast majority of Britain's gold reserves had already been moved out of the country, to Canada, but Churchill felt that it was now far too dangerous to ship the remaining gold in this same manner. When the original gold was moved, it was taken by road to Greenoch in Scotland, where 2,229 boxes of gold ingots, worth an estimated 8 billion pounds were surreptitiously loaded at night aboard the cruiser HMS Emerald.

The ship made its way across the Atlantic, being dogged all the way by German U-Boats. It was only the bad weather and poor visibility that saved the ship and the gold, and eventually saw it steam safely into Halifax harbour, Canada, where the gold was transferred onto a train and transported to the Bank of Canada in Ottawa.

The Bundles from Britain project, as it was known, was designed to enable Britain to finance the war until help came from the USA. The operation, which eventually saw some 36 billion pounds transported to Canada, was remarkable as thousands of people were involved; yet security was maintained. The operation was a success and incredibly good fortune for the crews because 134 ships were sunk during those same three months, but it wasn't one, which Churchill was prepared to risk again at this late stage in the war.

At this point, the Major knew nothing of these last minute plans. All he knew was that this presented him with yet another problem, which meant that with the convoy being split in half, only half of the gold would now be on offer to White and his associates. How would he be able to explain this to Billy White? There was absolutely nothing he could do; as a soldier he had to obey orders, and so, with great reluctance, he let the despatch rider lead the two rear vans and the backup Jeep away, while he waited for five minutes as ordered, before carrying on.

● ● ●

Comer and White' men now took a number of small country back-roads, which eventually led them to a place called Burybank Wood, which was just outside Stoke on Trent. There, they pulled up just beyond a crossroads and parked one of their lorries on the grass verge beside a wooded area. The second lorry and the saloon car took the right fork in the road, drove about two hundred yards, and took cover behind the trees. Moisha positioned the Jeep at the centre of the crossroads and waited while some of their men started unloading temporary wooden roadblocks, which they erected across the road, along with two large 'Halt' signs. As soon as this was completed, two of the men went back to their lorry, leaving another two; both armed with Thompson sub-machine guns, in position each side of the Jeep.

As the army convoy, which now consisted of just the lead Jeep and two vans, approached the roadblock it was stopped by armed members of the gang in their military uniforms, who told them the road ahead has been closed for security reasons, and that if they are headed in the direction of Stoke on Trent, they must take the other road as a diversion. The Major recognised Billy White, who was sitting in his Jeep, even though he was wearing an obvious false moustache and dark glasses, as was Comer. The Major now knew without a doubt that 'this was it' He then ordered his driver to take the secondary road as ordered.

The army convoy moved off and got around the first bend in the road where they were confronted by two members of the gang, who were pointing their sub machine guns at them and shouting for them to halt. As the Major told his driver to do as he was told, the second lorry that Comer's men had hidden in the trees, came roaring out and drove directly into the side of one of the military vans, the reinforced iron girder, which formed the front bumper smashed into the much smaller van with such impact that it turned it over completely onto its roof.

At the same time, Comer's other lorry, also equipped with a reinforced bumper, now came roaring around the bend, heading directly for the second military van. The driver of the van however, was much quicker than they had anticipated and immediately swung his van around, off the road, and managed to dodge the lorry by driving through the trees and eventually passing the lorry in the opposite direction. Bullets from the gang's machine guns splattered the back of the van as it roared away, but failed to stop it.

Comer and White' gang were now faced with just one somewhat smallish van, instead of the two large lorries they had expected. Comer, White, and Moisha, leapt out of their Jeep, followed by the rest of their gang, all heavily armed, emerging from the two lorries. The armed guard in the back of the Major's Jeep stood up and pointed his rifle towards the oncoming gang members. As he did so however, he felt the cold steel of a .45 Service Revolver sticking in the back of his neck, and heard the voice of Billy White, telling him to drop his rifle. The guard paused for a moment, but then also saw Comer, with a 45 Automatic Pistol pressing against the Major's head. "Put the fucking rifle down or he's dead – Now," snapped Comer. The guard dropped his rifle immediately, and at the same time, received a crashing blow on the back of his head from Billy White' pistol, which sent him stumbling to the floor.

At the same time, the rest of the gang started racing towards the overturned van, but a sudden blast of machine gun fire from somewhere within the van stopped them in their tracks and caused them all to dive for cover. One of White' men had been wounded in the leg by the machine gun fire, but was not seriously injured, and was well enough to return fire upon the van with his own machine gun.

One of the van's side windows was open with a machine gun sticking out of it, and continually firing in the general direction of the gang, who were now starting to fire back. "Hold your fire," came the voice of Billy White, as he ducked and weaved his way towards his gang, throwing himself down on the ground next to the wounded man and Albert Redman, "we don't want no deaths," he said, "this is supposed to be a gift to us, not the charge of the fucking Light Brigade"

White then stood up, putting himself on offer to the armed guards in the van, "Listen," he shouted, "we don't want to hurt you, just open up the van, throw out your weapons and come out with your hands up" There was a few seconds of silence, followed by a lone voice, who shouted, "Bollocks" and then the shooting started again from within the front window of the van.

Comer had been watching what was going on from the confines of the Jeep, where he still had his gun trained on the Major. He took a pair of handcuffs from out of his pocket, snapped one cuff onto the driver's wrist and the other onto the steering wheel and then, making sure he also had the keys to the ignition, marched the Major towards the upturned van, where the shooting was still coming from. "Right," he said to the Major, "time for you to start earning your fucking money" Comer quickly dodged down next to White and Redman and told the Major to stand where he was and to tell his men to open up the van, surrender their arms and come out with their hands in the air.

The Major nervously did as he was told, shouting these orders to his men, while Comer still kept his gun trained on him. The shooting from the van stopped immediately, followed by a few more moments of silence, as the men inside obviously discussed what they should do.

There was deathly silence as Comer, White and the rest of the gang watched and wondered what would happen. The Major turned and looked towards Comer with a look of despair on his face, "They don't seem to be responding to me," he stammered. Comer got to his feet, cocked the hammer on his pistol and pressed it hard against the Major's head, "If they don't open those doors within two fucking minutes," he growled, "they won't have a Major to respond to"

Comer gave the Major a shove forward towards the van, making sure that anyone in side could see what was going on, "Open those fucking doors," he shouted, "or your Major's a dead man"

There was slight scuffling noise from within the van, and suddenly the first door of the van was slowly and carefully opened, "Alright, don't shoot," came a voice from within, "we're coming out" Now the second door opened and the four armed guards inside, who were actually standing on the upturned roof of the van, started throwing their weapons out onto the ground. As soon as Comer was sure all the weapons had been thrown out he turned and signalled to White and the rest of the gang to come forward. At the same time, the four soldiers stepped nervously out of the van, with their hands raised high in the air.

Still holding his gun to the Major's head, Comer indicated to two members of his gang to come forward, "Deal with this lot," he shouted. The two men came running forward, one of them carrying a holdall. They ordered the military guards over to some trees, opened the holdall and took out sacking hoods, which they placed over the guards' heads; they then took out several lengths of rope and proceeded to tie the guards to the trees.

The Major was visibly shaking as he watched his men, hooded and tied to trees. He turned to Comer, who was still pointing the gun at his head and pleaded with him, "You're not going to shoot them are you?" he whimpered, "and me – what about me?" Comer grabbed him by the collar and threw him to the ground, "Call yourself a soldier?" he growled, "you're a fucking coward, stay where you are down there with your face in the ground and I might let you live, d'you understand?" The Major shook with fear as he did as he was told and whispered a very weak, "I understand"

By now, Billy White and a number of his men had converged on the van and were pulling out wooden crates, and dumping them onto the grass. Comer indicated to one of the men and got him to place a bag over the Major's head and tie him up, along with the Jeep's driver, who was still handcuffed to the steering wheel of his vehicle.

Comer now joined the rest of the men with getting the wooden crates out as one of their lorries started to reverse up to them. "You have opened up one of these I hope Bill?" he asked. White smiled and pointed to a case, which had the top half opened. Comer lifted one of the gold bars out of the crate; it shone brightly and reflected a golden hew over his face as he smiled and weighed it up in his hands, "I reckon that's about a five bedroom house, and a car" Billy White stood next to him and took out another bar, "and this one's a villa in the south of France, with a swimming pool"

There were just ten crates altogether, each crate containing six bars of gold bullion. Each bar weighed 12.5 kg (approximately 27 lbs imperial) and measured 290 mm (length) x 95 mm (width) x 45 mm (height), which in Imperial measurement is 11.5 inches (length) x 3.75 inches (width) x 1.75 inches (height). Each crate weighed approximately the same weight as an average man.

One individual bar of gold was worth approximately £9,100, which at today's values, works out to £350,000. In total, the ten crates of gold bars had a value of £546,000, which works out to £21 million at today's values.

Chapter 21

The Jeep carrying Comer and White, still in their military disguises, led the way towards Edgware; followed closely by the lorry carrying the gold bullion, as well as a number of the gang members. Staying a little way back was the family saloon car, driven by Sonny, with Jimmy Black and Freddy Smith in the back; they were to keep a close watch to see if they were being followed at any part of the journey, and to create a diversion if they noticed anything suspicious.

A short while later, the Jeep and the lorry turned off the road and drove directly into the large gates of the warehouse, which were opened up from inside as they approached. Sonny drove the saloon car straight past the warehouse to a preconceived destination, where he parked the car in a small back street, and let Jimmy Black out, who picked up the ARP van again, which he had parked there earlier.

Now driving the ARP van, Sonny pulled onto another side road, where he let Freddy Smith out to pick up his ARP van. The two ARP vans now made their way back to the warehouse again.

The plan was to now load all the gold into the two ARP vans, which were the most inconspicuous vehicles on the road during this period, and move it as far away as possible from where the robbery took place. The relatively small village of Rise, which was not far from Hull on the east coast had been chosen, as there had been no bombing raids there since the beginning of the war, and White had taken a leaf out of Churchill's book, and decided to hide the gold beneath ground. This time it was not a disused mine shaft, but inside a secret underground guerrilla bunker, which had been built at the start of the war to house a special unit of men, trained in sabotage, who would form an underground army, similar to the French resistance, should the Germans ever invade Britain. The idea never came to fruition and the bunker, along with several others were all abandoned.

Everything went according to plan; the warehouse in Edgware was thoroughly cleaned and everything moved out, the bullion was delivered to the underground bunker, where it was secured and a permanent guard was posted, until White could arrange for his Swiss contact to be brought in to see exactly what he was buying.

Comer made sure that he was involved at all levels; he had Moisha posted as one of the guards, along with one of Billy White' men. He also insisted that he was present when the Swiss contact was taken to the bunker and the deal was made.

● ● ●

The feeling of elation, which Comer felt about getting away with probably the biggest robbery in British history, quickly turned to worry and depression, when he returned home and expected Rita to be there to greet him with open arms, instead of which, he found her in bed, looking very pale and sickly. She hadn't been very well when he left, but he took that to be just a sign of her usual monthly problems, but in just two short days she had deteriorated so much that he hardly recognised her. He phoned his doctor in Harley Street straight away, who was there within minutes when he heard the symptoms.

When the doctor started to examine Rita, he pulled back the bedclothes to reveal her lying in a pool of her own blood. This was the first time in Comer's life that he visibly winced and almost fainted at the site of blood; he felt responsible; if only he hadn't gone away; if he had been there with her, this never would have happened. Unlike today, the doctor didn't show much concern for what he saw as a weakness in Comer, he ordered him to go and make some tea and pull himself together while he continued with his examination.

Contrary to all preconceived notions of Comer as a man, he did exactly as he was told and meekly went into the kitchen. When he emerged a few minutes later, carrying a small tray with the tea on it, the doctor rounded on him again, and told him that he meant the tea to be for him, not anyone else, "Now take it back and get some fresh nightclothes for your wife, I have just phoned for an ambulance, which should be with us any minute now"

The doctor went on to tell Comer that Rita was just over four months pregnant and was on the verge of a threatened miscarriage if not treated immediately. The ambulance would take her to his Harley Street clinic, where he stated, a caesarean operation would be undertaken on her without delay.

Half an hour later Comer, sweating and breathing heavily, was sitting in the luxurious surroundings of the waiting room of the Harley Street clinic. He picked up a copy of the Times newspaper and tried to focus his mind on something else by quickly scanned it to see if there was any news about the gold robbery, but there was no mention of it; most of the news related to the bombing of the city, which as he already knew, had been particularly heavy. Even as he scanned through the paper, his mind wasn't really on it; he knew the gold robbery had been carried out, he didn't really need confirmation; it was just his way of trying to take his mind off what was happening to Rita in another part of the building.

"Would you care for a cigarette Mr Comer?" the receptionist asked, offering him one from the box on her desk, "might calm your nerves a little" Comer thanked her as she offered him a light from the elegant silver desk lighter. He walked over to the window and looked down to the street below, then back to his seat again, and then to the receptionist's desk, where he put his cigarette out in the ash tray. His mind was in turmoil; he couldn't stand not being in control of a situation. At that second, as if to answer the nagging in his brain, the phone on the receptionist's desk started ringing, loud and shrill. He looked at it and then at her, was she ever going to answer it; was she going to carry on writing forever?

"Yes, yes," she answered, "thank you doctor Poiser, I'll send him in now" She smiled up at Comer, and gave him directions where to go.

When Comer walked into the private room to see Rita, he could hardly believe his eyes, for although she still didn't look well, she was actually sitting up in bed, and holding their baby in her arms. Comer was now the proud father of a baby daughter.

Doctor Poiser told them that he needed to keep Rita under observation at the clinic for at least the next few days. He insisted that the baby was fine, but this was normal procedure after a woman had undergone a caesarean operation.

What an absolutely tumultuous couple of days it had been. Comer had left home an average man, if that could be possible, seeing the line of work he was involved in; he had come back an extremely rich man, even though he did not actually have the money in his hands at this time. He had also come home to find out that his wife was pregnant, something he never dreamed of, and to add icing to the cake, he was now a father. He felt as though he should be out partying and celebrating, but for some inexplicable reason, he felt downcast and melancholy.

● ● ●

Comer was woken at 5 am the following morning by the phone ringing; he leapt out of bed like an athlete, praying that it wasn't the clinic, telling him that something was wrong. It was Billy White; the meeting with his Swiss contact was to take place 11 am this morning at the bunker in Yorkshire.

He had to explain to White that there was no way he could go. Rita was not at all in good health and the clinic could contact him at any moment, he had to be at home, in case he was called. He told White to include Moisha as his representative in any deal that was made, as he was already at the bunker, and to tell Moisha to phone him as soon as he could, to which White agreed.

As soon as he had finished speaking with White, Comer phoned Sonny and explained to him what was happening. "I want you to drive to the bunker in Yorkshire straight away, and to take either Billy Munro, if he's up to it yet, or Jimmy Black – Moisha is already there, so we should be well represented if you get what I mean?"

Once Comer knew that his men were on their way to the meeting, he felt a little more relaxed; Moisha and Sonny wouldn't let him down. He was now free for a while to go and visit Rita at the clinic.

The reception area of the clinic reminded him of a stately home, with its antique furniture, rugs, and paintings, which was in stark contrast to the tiled corridors and private wards, with their modern clinical starkness. It was difficult for him to comprehend this level of cleanliness and excellence, after he had just walked through the streets of London, many of which were still littered with rubble and buildings with smashed windows, left from the recent bombing raid.

Rita's face lit up as he walked into her room, and kissed her. Comer was so overcome with emotion that he could hardly speak as he looked first at his wife and then at his daughter, who was lying in the cot next to the bed. He reached into his inside pocket and took out a small package, which he silently opened. Inside the package was a small golden Star of David, which he proceeded to place around his daughter's neck, "Now we are a real family," he whispered with great emotion as he kissed his daughter on her forehead.

During the next few hours they discussed their future, where they would possibly live now they were a family. Comer couldn't tell Rita about his latest exploits, as he liked to keep that side of his life separate, one day after the war, he hinted, maybe they would retire to Ireland, but that was still a long way away. In the meantime, they discussed a name for their daughter, and eventually settled on Miriam, which was his mother's name.

• • •

Far away from the genteel discussion and atmosphere of the clinic, Sonny and Billy Munro were just pulling up in the Buick, close to the bunker in Yorkshire. As they got out of the car they were faced with three of White' men, all armed with the same military machine guns, which they had used during the raid. They were standing just a few yards away, just outside the entrance to the bunker with their weapons pointing in their direction.

Moisha now stepped out from behind a large rock, and walked towards his comrades, purposely making sure he was directly between the two groups as he approached Sonny. "We got a problem here," he said, "they reckon they've got orders not to let us into the meeting" Sonny was fuming; he pulled a revolver out of the waistband of his trousers and tried to push Moisha to one side, in an attempt to get to the three armed guards apposite them. Fortunately, Moisha prevented him from doing this by snatching his revolver and completely blocking his path. "Are you fucking mad or what?" he growled at Sonny, "they've got fucking machine guns – what are you going to do, fight them with that fucking pea shooter?"

This was a major predicament, Comer had given them orders to oversee the deal between the Swiss contact and White, and here they were, being kept out by the three stooges, acting on White' behalf. Sonny asked Moisha if he had tried phoning Comer, but Moisha explained that the nearest phone box is four miles away, and that he had driven there when he was first ordered by White' men not to go into the bunker, but there was no answer on Jack's phone.

"They may be White' men," said a very angry Sonny, "but we are Jack's men, and I don't propose letting them walk off with our share of the dough" Munro nodded and patted his pocket, "I'm with you Sonny," he said, "I've got a shooter here, and I'm ready to use it against those bastards if you are" "We wouldn't have a chance," Moisha intervened, "they'd mow us down before we had a chance to fire one single shot off"

Moisha had to grab the arms of both Sonny and Munro to stop them from going ahead with their threat, but at the precise moment there was a loud clanging noise, which came from the metal door of the bunker. "Hold on," Moisha said, "something's happening" As they watched in silence, the metal door of the bunker opened and Albert Redman came out. He spoke to one of the guards, who immediately rushed off.

Redman now came across and held out his hand to Moisha, "Sorry about all the cloak and dagger stuff Moisha," he said, "but Billy's contact insisted he didn't want to be seen by anyone else – the deal's been done, we have the cash, and he'll be taking the gold away as soon as we've all gone from here" "What do you mean, we have the cash?" asked Moisha, "When are we going to see our share?"

As if on cue again, the metal door of the bunker opened and Billy White came struggling out, carrying two very heavy looking suitcases. Redman turned back to Moisha and grinned, "Looks like your wish has been granted Moisha"

Billy White dumped the two suitcases down on the ground in front of Moisha and the others. "Take your pick," he said, indicating the two cases, "they're both the same" Moisha turned to Munro and told him to bring the Buick over, "I want to look at both of them," he said

Two minutes later, the car was there with two doors wide open and the suitcases laying one on each the front and the back seat. White took out two small keys, opened both of the cases and stood back smiling as they all gathered around and gazed in amazement at the bundles of money, which were stuffed to the top of the cases. "Satisfied?" asked White. Moisha quickly shuffled his hands through the money; making sure both cases were filled completely to the bottom. "And we can take either one?" asked Moisha. White told him to help himself, "They are both the same"

• • •

It was almost midnight when Billy Munro pulled up in the Buick outside Comer's flat in Cumberland Mansions. Moisha carried the heavy suitcase containing the money as all three men made their way to the street door.

Comer didn't look very happy at all as Moisha, Sonny and Munro entered his flat, "Put it down there," he snapped, indicating for Moisha to put the suitcase on the floor in the middle of the room, "I want to see inside" Moisha did as he was told, took the small key out of his pocket and opened the suitcase up for Comer to see.

"I've just been talking on the phone to Billy White," he said, "do you know exactly how much money is in here Moisha?" Moisha shrugged: he could see something was wrong. "I haven't counted it Jack," he replied, "but both cases contained the same, we could take whichever one we wanted"

Comer silently walked over to his desk, picked up a pack of cigarettes and slowly lit one. Moisha had known Comer practically all his life, when he was happy or relaxed, he would light up one of his favourite cigars; he only smoked cigarettes when he was angry or tense, or maybe both.

"Both cases contained the same did they, and what about the third case, or the fourth, or maybe even a fifth? Did you check them as well?" Comer's eyes were gleaming like two shiny pieces of black coal. Moisha knew better than to argue with him when he was in one of these moods, "Sorry Jack," he mumbled, "I didn't think" Comer stubbed the newly lit cigarette out in the ashtray on the desk and spun round to face Moisha again, "You didn't think?" he shouted, "you're telling me you didn't think Moisha – you were supposed to be taking care of business for fuck's sake, and now we end up with this"

Sonny tried to calm things down by intervening and explaining what had happened at the bunker, and how the Swiss contact didn't want anyone else to see him, apart from White. This didn't bode well at all with Comer, for White had phoned him just 40 minutes before Moisha and the others had arrived. He told them how White had given him a cock and bull story, based on the story he had also told them, of how the Swiss contact would only deal with White on his own.

According to White, the contact has now paid them £100,000, (equivalent to approximately £4 million today). The balance will be paid to them over the next few weeks, as and when the contact starts to move the gold, not to Switzerland as previously thought, but to a bank in Portugal, where it can be transferred to Switzerland.

Moisha, Sonny, or Munro were not mathematical geniuses, but neither were they idiots, especially when it came to money. They had seen with their own eyes, this huge suitcase filled with cash, so what the hell was their boss griping about? They didn't actually say this to Comer; the looks on their faces said it all.

"You all saw the gold," said Comer, "but did any of you know exactly how much it was worth? Well I'll tell you, it was worth a total of £546,000. White' so-called Swiss contact was supposed to pay us 60 percent of the market value of that gold, which is £327,600. Instead of which, we have been palmed off with £100,000, and that is supposed to be shared between White, and us"

"But if he's paying us the balance within a few weeks?" interrupted Sonny. "If who's paying us the balance?" Comer shouted back at Sonny, "none of us have ever seen this so call fucking Swiss contact have we? Who the fuck is he and how do we know we'll get another penny? And as for the £100,000 did you know that Mr big shot White has even taken £10,000 from that as payment for expenses – the vehicles, uniforms, weapons, ammunition, walkie Talkies, and payments to certain people for information. That leaves £90,000, which he split evenly into the two suitcases – so what we have here gentlemen is just forty five fucking grand – we have been swindled out of £282,600"

These figures were difficult anyone to take in; by today's standards, the original value of the stolen bullion would be equal to £21 million today, making it Britain's biggest ever robbery.

Moisha had kept relatively quite so far, but what he could not understand was if all this was true, then why had Billy White phoned Comer and told him about how much was in the suitcase, and how much he had taken out as expenses?

Comer explained that White was trying to buy time; by saying that more money was on the way within a few weeks or so, he was hoping that Comer would sit back and wait for it to come in. In the meantime, White and his associates could conveniently disappear, which he assured Moisha and the others, had already happened. "When he phoned me, it was from a phone box," explained Comer, "I have since phoned his home number, his office and his clubs – he's disappeared, like a piece of shit down a bog hole, but I'll tell you now, he'll never escape me, I'll track him down to the ends of the earth – no one fucks Jack Comer up and gets away with it"

Chapter 22

The £45,000 was no mean amount by anyone's standard, but by the time Comer had taken his expenses from it, and paid all his men, it didn't exactly leave him with the sort of money to buy properties around the world and a luxury yacht. One of the few luxuries he did allow himself was a new car, a Jaguar Mark IV 3.5 Litre sedan, in maroon with light tan leather upholstery.

In the meantime, Moisha felt partly to blame for the fiasco regarding White and the money, and asked Comer to give him a car and two weeks, and he would find White for him. Comer wasn't sure, firstly he needed Moisha as his right hand man, and secondly, Moisha wouldn't exactly go unnoticed; he was a big man, who wore the scars of his trade with some pride; most people never forgot him once they had seen him. On the other hand, Comer wanted the rest of his share of the money, and he did know that he could trust Moisha. "Two weeks then," Comer fished into his pocket and took out the keys to his old car, the Buick, which he threw to Moisha, "here," he said, "it's yours" Moisha and Comer shook hands.

• • •

While Moisha was out and about, looking for the elusive Billy White, it was back to business with a vengeance for Comer and the rest of his team, the black-market, the counterfeit printing, and the protection rackets, which were all working very well indeed. In fact the temporary demise of Billy White from the London scene helped

Comer's business interests rather than hindering them, as it cut out all competition so to speak of.

Just over a week later, Moisha phoned Comer to say that a contact of his had told him that Albert Redman had apparently been seen in a gambling club in Brighton, with another man who sounded very much like he could be the Major. This was fantastic news, "Get down to Brighton straight away," yelled Comer, "take Jimmy Black with you – I want to talk to the fucking pair of them, so don't hurt them too much – let me know as soon as you have them?"

An hour later, Moisha was on the road to Brighton with Jimmy Black beside him in the Buick, while back in London, Comer was leading a last minute search of all known haunts of Billy White'. His clubs, office, and home had already been covered; "He sold out weeks ago" – " He no longer lives here" – "He's moved from here" It was the same story at all these places, but now the search was on at his lesser known haunts; his barber, tailor, cafés, restaurants, pubs, even the garage that services his car. At the end of the day a very dispirited Comer came away with exactly the same news that he had started out with – Billy White had disappeared completely from the London scene.

It was just after 10 pm as Moisha parked the Buick just off the seafront at Brighton. Both he and Black stepped out of the car and turned into a little row of narrow alleyways, known as the Lanes. There were no street-lights as even Brighton was under complete blackout restrictions; even the few pubs that they passed had blackout blinds at their windows, so not even a chink of light could show through. They manoeuvred their way through the Lanes, using the light from the moon to find their way.

Number 104 was a small shop with a sign above the door, stating, Arthur Crump, Greengrocer. Painted in whitewash on the window, was a sign, stating, 'Closed for the duration' Moisha had to light his cigarette lighter in order to make sure they were at the right door and to see if there was a doorbell or knocker somewhere there amidst the dark brown peeling paint. Sure enough it was a bell, which as he went to press it, a voice called out from somewhere behind them, telling them to put that light out. It was an air-raid warden. Moisha mumbled an apology and proceeded to ring the bell. A minute later the door was opened slightly and a large black man peered out at them from within. "We've just come down from the Smoke," said Moisha, "we're looking for a game" The black man looked at them and asked who had sent them. Moisha took a large white five-pound note out of his pocket and stuffed it into the top pocket of the black man's jacket, "Mr Peppiatt," he said. Peppiatt was the chief cashier of the Bank of England, whose signature was on every banknote.

Moisha didn't know whether the black man recognised the name or not, but he certainly recognised the banknote, and let Moisha and Black in without another word. "This way," he murmured, as he led them along the passageway and into an area, which had been luxuriously decorated and furnished, with a small bar and four card tables, where groups of men were sitting and playing cards. Moisha quickly scanned the men's faces for whom he was looking for. "Is there any other games?" he asked.

The black man nodded, "Roulette" he replied and waved them towards another door. A group of eight men stood around the table, placing bets and watching the croupier spin the wheel and watching the little ball, as it bounced in and out of the numbered spaces. Moisha saw the Major immediately, no longer in uniform, but still easily identifiable. The Major looked up briefly as Moisha and Black entered the room, there was a hint of recognition in his eyes, but his real attention was on the game.

The black man left the room, leaving Moisha and Black to close in on the table and the game. The game that Moisha and Black had in mind however, was not roulette, but a different sort of game entirely, which involved the Major and a great deal of missing money.

The Major nervously lit another cigarette as he watched the croupier rake all the money from the board, including his. As he pushed another two five pound notes across the board for his next bet, he suddenly felt pressure on his back. He angrily looked round, ready to tell whoever it was to stop crowding him, and found himself confronted with the face of Moisha, "Hello Major," said Moisha in a soft voice, "remember me do you?"

The Major tried to make a break for it, but immediately found himself hemmed in on the other side by Jimmy Black, "looks like you're on a loosing streak Major," said Black, with an evil grin on his face.

• • •

It was just after midnight when Moisha drove the Buick onto the forecourt of the Grand Hotel, Brighton. He parked as far away from the main entrance as he could. Jimmy Black got out the car first and went around to the boot of the car, which he opened as Moisha now joined him. Inside the boot, was the trussed up and gagged figure of the Major, who looked absolutely terrified as the two gangsters looked down at him. "You've got nothing to worry about," said Moisha, "just keep quiet, and if you've told us the truth, we'll be back in a while and you'll be free to go" Moisha put his finger to his lips, indicating for the Major to keep quiet, and then slammed the boot shut again.

Ten minutes later, Moisha was using the public phone to call Comer, from the reception area of the hotel, while Black sat in one of the luxurious armchairs, waiting for him. Moisha explained to Comer that they had found the Major, and taken him back to a very modest boarding house, where he has been staying in Brighton. "He has deserted from the army," he said, "after they launched an inquiry into the robbery, and from what we could see, he definitely isn't holding any money worth speaking about, he's apparently doing odd jobs and running errands for Albert Redman, who's obviously still in this country and keeping our friend the Major, in pocket money"

Moisha continued to tell Comer that after a little prompting, the Major had told them where Redman was staying. "We are here now," he said, "at the Grand Hotel, the only problem is the bloke on the desk won't tell us which room he's in, and his mate the Major doesn't know, as he usually meets him outside, so it looks like we've got to hang around here until he finally shows" Comer was pleased with the news, "What about the Major?" he asked, "you haven't let him go have you?" Moisha chuckled, and explained to his boss that the Major was in a nice safe place for the time being. "Good, good," Comer replied, "you're doing the right thing, we don't want to cause any scenes at a hotel like that, they'd have the old Bill down there before you could blink"

There was one thing that still worried Comer, which was why the robbery had not been reported in the newspapers or on the wireless? And now, to add to that, we had the Major telling Moisha that the army had launched an inquiry into the robbery, which in turn had caused him to desert. A very stupid thing to do as far as Comer was concerned. This man held a high rank in the British army, and now he had deserted the minute an inquiry had been launched. A sure sign of guilt, which would lead to a nationwide search for the Major.

Comer couldn't care less about the situation the Major was now in, as far as he was concerned the Major had no one to blame but himself. What he was more worried about, was if and when the Major was apprehended, he would, in all probability, spill the beans on the whole operation and everyone involved in it.

It was 4 am as Comer drove his new Jaguar along Brighton sea front. From the light of the moon, he could just make out the imposing shape of the Brighton Pier as he drove past it. He then turned right onto the forecourt of the Grand Hotel, which was also in complete darkness. It wasn't too difficult to pick out Moisha's Buick, it was the biggest car there; he parked directly next to it.

As Comer walked into the reception area of the hotel, he was greeted with the sight of Jimmy Black slumped in one of the armchairs and still recognisable by his mop of curly hair, even with a newspaper over his face. No one was behind the reception desk; in fact Moisha was the only one there who seemed to be alive and kicking. He sprung up from his seat as he saw Comer walk in and rushed over to him. "What's up Jack," he asked, "is everything OK?" Comer nodded and sat down, indicating for Moisha to do the same. "It's like a bloody morgue in here," he declared, "no one behind the desk, and him (indicating Black) asleep" "He's only just gone off," replied Moisha, "we've been taking it in turns"

Comer nodded thoughtfully and looked around, "What have you done with the Major?" he asked. Moisha explained that he was tied up and gagged in the boot of the Buick. "Good, good," Comer said, "I need to have a little chat with him, give me your car keys, I'll also need Black to come with me as well" "I can come with you Jack," said Moisha.

"No," said Comer abruptly, "I need you here just in case that rat Redman appears" Moisha knew better than to argue with his boss when he was in one of his determined moods; he took out his car keys and handed them to Comer and then gave Black a quick nudge, "Oi, wake up, Jack wants you to go outside with him"

After Comer and Black had gone, Moisha sat back, lit a cigarette and looked at the clock on the wall above the desk, it was now 4.30 am, and he was alone in the reception; still no one behind the desk. Strange really, he thought, surely big hotels like this are supposed to have someone on duty all the time?

On the forecourt meanwhile, Comer strode over to the Buick, with Black following up closely behind. As he inserted the key into the lock of the boot, he could hear some scuffling movements from inside; Comer turned to Black, "You got anything with you?" he whispered, "a cosh or something, just in case?" Black nodded and took a length of metal piping from out of his pocket, standing to one side, ready, as Comer opened up the boot. The Major was still tied and gagged, but struggling wildly, his eyes staring up at them in fear. "Keep still," warned Comer, "or I'll let him give you a working over, I just want to ask you a few questions" Comer ripped the gag off the Major's face, "and if you make any noise I'll kill you on the fucking spot, d'you understand me?"

Back inside the hotel, Moisha was finding it very difficult to keep his eyes open; he felt his head nod forward at one point and quickly pulled himself together, rubbing his eyes and taking another look at the clock, which now showed 6.10 am. Christ, he thought, surely that's not the right time? Still no one behind the reception desk. He got up and walked over to one of the large windows, where he moved the heavy blackout curtain slightly and peered outside, to see it was now daylight. He looked over to where he had parked the Buick, only to see Comer's new Jaguar; the Buick had gone.

A noise behind him caused Moisha to look round. It was a middle-aged man in a suit, who walked directly behind the reception desk and started checking some of the paperwork. He then glanced up as Moisha walked back from the window, "Good morning sir," he said, with a smile, "can I help you?" "I'm waiting for a friend of mine actually," replied Moisha, as he walked up to the desk, "a mister Albert Redman, the problem is I don't know what room he's in"

"I'll have a look for you sir," said the man behind the desk, with a smile as he thumbed through the visitors book, "ah, yes, here we are, Mr Albert Redman, oh dear, it looks like you have missed him sir, Mr Redman checked out just after midnight last night"

As Comer and Black pulled the Buick into the forecourt of the hotel about ten minutes later, Moisha was waiting for them. Comer was fuming as Moisha told him what he had been told. "No wonder the bloke on the desk disappeared, he must have been on Redman' payroll as well," said Comer, "he obviously warned him that we were here, and smuggled him out the back way while we were sitting there like a bunch of mugs" Comer threw the keys to the Buick back to Moisha, "Well he's not going to show up here again, that for sure, come on, we might as well get back to London" "What about the Major?" Moisha asked. "We've finished with him, come on let's go, you take the Buick, Jimmy can drive me in the Jag," answered Comer as he handed his keys to Black and climbed into the passenger seat of his Jaguar.

Chapter 23

The one thing that Comer could not stand was the thought that someone had got the better of him in any way. He kept going over it in his mind as they drove back to London, not only had Billy White conned him out of a massive share of the proceeds of the robbery, he had also disappeared completely, and now, to add insult to injury, they had let Albert Redman slip through their fingers as well. Jimmy Black tried talking to him on a couple of occasions during the journey, but Comer just snapped back at him and told him to be quiet as was thinking. Everyone in Comer's team knew better than say more when he was in one of his dark moods, as they called them.

Comer kept a low profile for the following few days; he didn't even keep to his usual morning breakfast meetings at his favourite café with Moisha and sometimes Sonny. He was in touch with Moisha on the phone, giving him orders about business matters, but he kept well away from the streets of Soho and the clubs. He knew that sooner or later he had to snap out of this dark mood; he had to wreak revenge on

White and Redman, and make sure his men knew that it was him who had succeeded in doing it.

Two days after coming back from Brighton, he had just finished breakfast and settled back to look at the morning's newspapers when he saw an article, which caught his attention; 'Man found hanging under Brighton Pier'. The article went on to say that the police had identified the man as an army deserter and were investigating the cause of his death.

A smile spread across Comer's face as he read the article. This was the slow but sure start of him coming out of his mood, he felt that he was starting to regain control once again. He didn't rush to spread the news to his men, for they were not fools, and Jimmy Black had been a part of it, but he also now felt that he could start acting like the loving husband and father to Rita and his daughter again. He was a man, and he was in charge.

• • •

Time passed slowly over the next couple of years with no big jobs on the horizon for Comer and his men, but while the war lasted he still had to carry on with his business activities as usual, but his thoughts always drifted back to Billy White. One day, he vowed, he would have vengeance.

He had never been particularly interested in politics, but being Jewish, even though he was non practising, he could not help but to be interested in the plight of the Jews all over Europe The Allied troops were starting to capture much of Germany, which meant the war was gradually coming to its inevitable end, and, people were starting to hear more and more of what had been happening to the Jews in Europe.

Still not completely back into business mode, Comer decided to take Rita out one night to the cinema, followed by a meal at a restaurant. Their daughter Miriam was now almost two years old, and was being looked after by their housemaid, who also acted as baby-sitter.

During this period in time, cinemas always showed an 'A' picture, followed by a 'B' picture, with a News-Feature in between. Rita had talked Comer into taking her to see Brief Encounter, which wasn't exactly his type of film, but he nevertheless sat back and did his best to enjoy it.

When the News Feature was shown however, neither Comer nor Rita could believe their eyes and ears, at the scenes that unfolded before them. It was a film showing a concentration camp in Germany, known as Bergen-Belsen, which the British had just liberated in April 1945. The reporter, Richard Dimbleby described the scenes of almost unimaginable horror that greeted him as he toured the camp, of piles of dead bodies, and skeletal figures, who had defied all the odds and were shuffling aimlessly about.

Comer and Rita didn't stay for the second film. They silently got to their feet, and left the cinema. This was one time in his life when he actually felt pangs of guilt and remorse. These were his people; somewhere in those terrible scenes he could have witnessed distant relatives, maybe a second cousin, maybe an aunt, and while he had been living the good life they were being massacred and starved to death. This certainly wasn't a time to be going out for a meal. They walked home, in stunned silence.

A few days later, on 30 April 1945 it was announced that Adolf Hitler had committed suicide. One week after that, on 7 May 1945 Germany signed unconditional surrender and war in Europe was finally over. Four months later, on 2 September 1945, Japan also formally surrendered, and World War Two was over for the entire world.

Everyone celebrated, there were parties and dancing in the streets of London; no more bombing and nights spent in air raid shelters; theatres would open once again and the streets would be lit up with coloured neon lit advertising hoardings.

One of the first things Comer did was organise a party for his men at Bianchi's restaurant in Soho, but he didn't forget where he came from, and at the same time, he also organised and paid for a huge street party for the children of his old school in Stepney.

It was at Bianchi's restaurant however, that Comer was reminded that with the end of the war, they were about to be deprived of a very large portion of their income, for rationing would surely be abolished, which meant all their black market enterprises would come to an end. To make matter even worse for Comer, all the American servicemen and women would be sent back to the USA, and that in turn would cut off a huge source of supply, of such goods as cigarettes, various foodstuffs, and women's silk stockings.

The next few months especially, were going to be a hard time for Comer and his team. He desperately needed a new source of income, as well as locating where White and Redman were now hiding out. He didn't just want his share of the money; he wanted revenge.

There was however, an upside to Comer's woes, and that was the return of all the servicemen, who had been fighting abroad. They should help to see a return to gambling as it was before the war, including the re-opening of the horse and dog racing tracks once again.

• • •

As the following weeks drifted into months, the race-tracks did indeed open again, but the punters did not return in the numbers he had hoped for. Servicemen and women were being demobbed, but many of them found that they did not have a job to return to, as so many businesses had been destroyed by the bombing; many of them also found that they didn't have a home either, which meant in the majority of cases that the last thing on their minds was gambling.

One thing that did not happen, as the vast majority of the population, including Comer, had expected, was the end of rationing. A General Election had been called and Winston Churchill had been ousted and replaced by a Labour Government led by Clement Attlee; consequently rationing continued, and later got worse when they decided to ration bread as well, something that had never happened, even during the darkest days of the war.

Although Comer had never served his country in the armed forces, he saw himself as a loyal citizen, even possibly a Robin Hood type character, stealing from the rich and giving to the poor, although this did not happen as often as he would brag about it. Being brought up in the east end of London, he witnessed first hand what real poverty was like, and would sometimes send a lorry load of surplus goods, foodstuff and clothing, to his old manor, making sure the recipients knew for sure it was coming from him. He saw this as possible good PR for the future.

He saw the new rationing laws as something of a dilemma; on one hand it was hurting his people, whom he felt very sorry for, but on the other hand, it was good for the side of his business, which he thought had ended; the black market and the printing of counterfeit ration books etc. For the time being at least then, Comer's business prospects were looking good, and London belonged to him.

Chapter 24

While Comer's business was going from strength to strength, in another part of London, a lonely figure, carrying a paper carrier bag, was emerging from a large Victorian building into the early morning sunshine. It was Teddy Baxter, who had just been released from Wormwood Scrubs Prison.

There was no welcoming committee of friends waiting for Baxter in a chauffeur driven limousine, no smart, up to date clothes; he didn't even have enough money to call a taxi. All he had was the scruffy clothes he stood up in, plus an extra pair of shoes, which he carried in the paper bag, and two pounds, ten shillings, which, he had been given by the Prison Board.

Although Baxter was bereft of money and resources, he certainly wasn't short of ideas. He had been plotting and scheming his next move all the time he had been in prison; no more petty robberies and playing second fiddle to east end wide boys for him any longer. He was heading for south London, where he originally came from, and where he had heard encouraging rumours about a new and emerging gang. Not only would he at last start to realise his long-term ambition, which was to be a number one face in an area, but he would also hopefully escape from the clutches of the two bent coppers who had put him away on a trumped up charge to start with, Det. Insp. Cutler and Det. Sgt. Webber.

Baxter was getting angrier with every minute that passed; he could see the two detective's faces in his mind. If only those two bastards were in front of him now he thought as his fists clenched into tight balls. "I can't wait all day," a voice called, bringing Baxter back to reality as he opened his eyes and saw the bus conductor on the platform of the bus, ring the bell and the bus pulled away from the stop where he was still standing. "Fuck it"

It was lunchtime by the time he eventually arrived at Camberwell Green in South London and made his way to the Father Red Cap pub. It was a large, sprawling pub with just a few customers, mostly elderly men, supping their pints and smoking either pipes or roll-up cigarettes. Mickey Reilly stood out like a sore thumb in there, he was the youngest person in there, about nineteen years old, dressed in a navy blue pin stripe suit, red and yellow vertical striped tie and a brown trilby with the brim pulled down, he was what was known at the time as a typical spiv.

Baxter had met Reilly in Wormwood Scrubs Prison, and was impressed with his knowledge of the underworld, especially for someone so young. He seemed to know everyone who was on the up, so to speak, and promised to introduce Baxter to two brothers, who would, in his own words, one day rule the underworld.

Two pints and a sausage roll later, Baxter was raring to go; it was take me to your leader time, and Reilly was leading the way. Past the Green, which had had all its iron railings removed some time ago as part of the war effort, then turning this way and that, through grimy little back streets and alleys until they finally came to a dilapidated building, which had once been an old stables, with the name T. Deacon & Sons painted on the huge gates in faded cream paint.

"Wait here," Reilly instructed Baxter as he gave three sharp kicks on a small door set within the large doors. The door was opened by an unseen hand from the inside and Reilly went through, closing the door behind him and leaving Baxter standing in the street. Could this dump really be the centre of operations for the gang that would one day hope to rule the underworld?

Ten minutes later the door opened again and Reilly beckoned Baxter in. He led Baxter past piles of scrap metal, stacked high to the ceiling, from old gas stoves, to parts of motor vehicles, lead piping, even cooking pots and pans. They then emerged into an open yard where two young lads were busy breaking up the various metal objects and sorting it into piles. At the rear of the yard was a wooden staircase, which Reilly led the way up to a small office.

An elderly man sat at a scruffy roll-top desk, which was piled high with paperwork and assorted rubbish. This was Tommy Deacon, the owner of the yard; he nodded for Reilly to sit down, leaving Baxter standing in the centre of the room. "Mickey's told me all about you," he said, "he reckons you're a strong geezer and not afraid to get your hands dirty, is that right?" Baxter nodded, "Sounds about right to me guvner," he answered; "I've worked with some of the toughest firms in London in my time"

Tommy Deacon seemed pleased with Baxter, and told him start work the next day. "He seems a nice old boy," Baxter remarked to Reilly as they walked back towards Camberwell Green after leaving Deacon's yard, "but he don't seem like a gang leader to me, who's he got working for him?" "The two boys you saw in the yard," Reilly answered, "they're his sons, Bobby and Georgie" Baxter stopped dead in his tracks and stared at Reilly, "The two boys?" he answered, "they're no more than fucking kids – what are they, sixteen?" "Bobby's the oldest," replied Reilly, "he's seventeen I think, Georgie's a year or two younger, I'm not sure, but don't underestimate them Teddy, they're as hard as nails and Bobbie's a fucking genius when it comes to business"

Teddy Baxter had been out of prison for less than a day, and he had already been accepted into what was to become one of London's major crime families. What he didn't know at this point, was that the old man, Tommy Deacon, had taken him on to work in the yard, breaking metal alongside his two sons. He nearly walked out the following day when a pair of overalls was shoved at him and he was told to put his back into it. Luckily for him Mickey Reilly had already spoken to young Bobbie Deacon, who quickly put him in the picture. "Don't worry," he was told, "the old man is retiring soon and we've got big plans, which you could be involved in if you play your cards right"

For once in Baxter's life he decided to bite the bullet and play along with what the brothers were saying. He didn't have any money to speak of, and Reilly had let him have a room in his flat, which was close to Camberwell Green, so he had nothing to lose, for the time being anyway.

Chapter 25

Things were starting to change in Great Britain, and especially in London, where people were fed up with the old austerity led dark grey times of the war years. The American troops had mostly disappeared from our shores, but they had left a lasting legacy in their colourful lifestyles, their clothes, and their music, even their dance, the Jitterbug, quickly caught on with London's newly demobbed young men and women and swept Britain's old fashioned ballrooms.

Jack Comer had long admired the clothes and style of the fictional American gangsters he had seen in the movies before the war; stars such as Paul Muni, James Cagney, and Edward G. Robinson. These men knew how to dress; they wore smart suits and trilby style hats, which were known as snap-brim fedoras. To Comer, this style of dress epitomised power, and he emulated it to his dying day.

The style that Comer could not stand, was that of the 'spiv' This was a greatly exaggerated version of the Americans we had seen here during the war, with their long drape jackets, rakish trilby hats, and bright patterned ties.

It was a warm summer afternoon when Comer had decided to surprise his wife by buying her a television set. Television broadcasting by the BBC, had been suspended during the war and had just been resumed, so he took a walk to Selfridges Store in Oxford Street to see what was on offer. The selection wasn't exactly great, but he ended up picking the most expensive model in the store, which was a Baird Lyric, with a 12 inch screen and encased in a beautiful bird's eye maple cabinet, with a rolling shutter to cover the screen up at night; Rita would love this. He paid cash, almost the equivalent to an average year's wages for a working man, and was told it would be delivered the following day.

As he walked back towards Soho, where he was to meet Moisha and a few of the boys, Comer cut through Berwick Street, which has a street market, selling everything from materials and haberdashery to fruit and vegetables. He received a wave and a hello here and there as he passed these premises, which always pleased him. A large number of the shops and stalls in Berwick Street were owned and run by Jews, and many of them bought the odd roll of material or silk etc., from Comer's boys.

When he heard his named being called out, he turned around to see one of the stallholders, David Hoffman, waving and beckoning to him. Comer walked back to Hoffman, "David," he said, "how are you, nothing wrong is there?" Hoffman looked up and down the road, a worried look on his face, "I don't know if you can help me Jack, but as you know I have been buying bits and pieces of schmutter from your firm for some years now, same as a lot of other traders down here" Comer smiled and patted Hoffman on the shoulder, "I know you have David," he said, "so what's wrong, tell me, if I can help you I will, you know that?"

Hoffman took Comer to one side and spoke quietly to him. He explained that his trade was being ruined lately by these wide boys, these spivs, who turn up with their suitcases full of all the same stuff that he and his fellow traders are selling, and undercut us. "They've got no overheads like we have, sometimes they stand right next to our stalls or shops, then they see a copper and they're off, but five minutes later they're back again, what can I do Jack? They're ruining me"

Comer was probably the most feared gangster in London at this time, but he still liked to see himself as a man of the people. After obtaining as much information as possible from Hoffman, he patted him on the back and told him not to worry; he would take care of things.

With his dislike of spivs, Comer kept to his word. The following day, which was a Saturday, the main market day in Berwick Street, three of Comer's men; Jimmy Black, Freddy Smith and Billy Munro, had positioned themselves in a café about halfway along the street, where they could see not only Hoffman's stall, but also a number of other stalls and shops.

Billy Munro suddenly jumped to his feet, "There's one of the bastards," he said pointing outside at a tall young man, dressed exactly to fit the 'spiv' image, he even had a small almost pencilled in moustache.

Comer's men rushed outside just as the spiv had placed his suitcase on the pavement between two of the stalls and was opening it up to show off his wares, which included various items of women's underwear and stockings.

David Hoffman looked up from serving a customer at his stall as he heard the noise. He watched as Comer's men grabbed the spiv and his suitcase, and ran him, with his feet off the floor, to their car, which was parked in a side street opposite, where they threw him unceremoniously into the back, with his suitcase following after him. All three men then jumped into the vehicle, which sped away to the cheers of David Hoffman and a number of other stallholders.

Their car screeched to a halt outside Euston Railway Station, which is literally a few minutes' drive from Berwick Street. There they bundled the spiv through the crowds, including a somewhat bewildered looking policeman, explaining as they went that their 'friend' was drunk. They dashed onto platform number four where Munro stuffed a pound note into one of the guard's top pocket and quickly mumbled something to him. The guard then opened up goods van and the spiv was bundled in, with the door being locked again by the guard. The guard blew his whistle and the train started chugging off towards its Manchester destination, running over and completely crushing the spiv's suitcase, which had been conveniently dropped onto the track.

Over the course of the next few days, three more spivs mysteriously disappeared from the area around Berwick Street market. The shopkeepers and stallholders were happy once again, and Comer had proven that he was still in charge.

• • •

Britain was certainly changing during these post-war years, but not quite as quickly as most had envisaged. Restrictions on foreign travel, which had been imposed during the war, were at long last lifted, but the average Briton couldn't have contemplated taking a holiday abroad, even if they had wanted to; not that many did want to, as they still had strong memories of the coasts of France and Italy as war-torn battlefields, not holiday destinations.

There was an alternative, which was to holiday here in Great Britain, which was being heavily promoted by both the Government and a man named Fred Pontin, who opened Britain's first holiday camp, appropriately named, Pontin's, at Brean Sands, Burnham-on-Sea, Somerset.

As far as Comer was concerned, he had absolutely no intentions whatsoever of taking his wife and daughter to a holiday camp in Somerset. He had long born ambitions of buying a villa in the South of France, which, because of the intervention of the war, and a certain well known character running off with a fortune of his money, never came to fruition, but with the war over and restrictions on foreign travel now lifted, not only could he indulge in such luxury, but he might also be able to find the whereabouts of Mr Billy White, who had often spoken about retiring to Cannes or maybe Monaco.

Rita wasn't too keen on the idea of buying a property abroad, "We don't speak the language for one thing Jack, and secondly there's still the problem of us being Jewish, or had you forgotten that?" "I'm talking about the South of France," he told her, "not bloody Berlin, and there's no Nazis there any more, they lost the war, remember?"

It wasn't easy trying to talk Rita into things; she was a very strong woman with definite views of her own. Comer decided he would bide his time with this one, work out some sort of plan and implement it a little at a time.

He liked to pride himself that plans were his forte; always had been. People came to him when they were formatting a plan and wanted expert help and advice, as did a Birmingham man named Andy Silvers.

Comer was enjoying a quiet drink with Moisha and Sonny one evening, in the Stork Club, which he had taken over since Billy White had left the scene, when the waiter approached their table with a fresh round of drinks. "Compliments of the gentleman at the bar," he said, pointing to a well-built man in his thirties, who raised his glass in a toast to Comer. "Who the fuck's he?" asked Comer, "I don't know him, d'you know him?" he asked Moisha and Sonny. "I've seen him around," replied Sonny, "he's from up north I think" "He was in Big Ronnie's spieler the other week," Moisha added, "he gave Arnie the thief a right smack, said he was cheating on him at Kalooki" Comer nodded, obviously impressed by anyone who could handle themselves.

At this point Andy Silvers, drink in hand, ambled over towards them. "Sorry to butt in gents," he said, "but I recognised you Mr Comer, and thought you might be interested in a little deal I might be able to put your way?"

Comer picked up the drink that Silvers had sent over for him; downed it in one go and slammed the glass down on the table, "I don't do deals with people I don't know or know nothing about" There was an air of tension around the table. Moisha and Sonny looked at Comer, half expecting him to lash out at the stranger, but he didn't; instead of which, he carried on with their earlier conversation, which was about horse racing, and how a twelve year old boy named Lester Piggott, had just won his first race, at Haydock Park Racecourse, "Bloody marvellous, I've got a feeling we're going to hear more about this lad," Comer stated.

Andy Silvers smiled and nodded, as if he were a part of the conversation. He then leaned down and whispered in Comer's ear, "My name's Andy Silvers by the way, I come from Birmingham, and I work as a security guard at London Airport"

Comer's eyes flickered from Silvers to Moisha and back again. He did his best to feign disinterest in what he had just heard, and then with a flick of his hand he motioned to Moisha, "Maybe you should take Mr Silvers outside Moisha, somewhere less public?" Comer then turned back to Silver, "Nothing to worry about Mr Silvers, it's just like a job interview, you don't mind do you?"

Silvers didn't have any options, he was a big man himself, but Moisha towered over him when he stood up, "Ready?" asked Moisha. The two men walked out of the club together. Sonny stayed silent for a while, sipping on his drink and lighting another cigarette, he wasn't sure what Comer had sent Moisha out to do, was he supposed to give Silvers a beating or what? Comer saw the way Sonny was looking, "Moisha knows what to do," he said, "we don't know the geezer, he could be a copper for I know"

Fifteen minutes later, Moisha and Silvers returned, accompanied by another man, Bert Curtis, who went straight up to Comer and patted him, somewhat heavily on his back. "Jack," you old bastard, long time no see, how ya doing?" Comer wasn't happy at being addressed in this manner, and it showed on his face. He had met Curtis just once before, but they had never been close friends. Curtis was a jewel thief, originally from Manchester, whom Comer had bought a consignment of jewellery from in the past. He had been passing outside when he saw Moisha speaking to Silvers and had stopped, as he knew both men. Curtis explained that he knew Silvers well, and had done business with him several times, when they both operated in the north of England. Moisha was fairly happy with this, which is why he brought Curtis into the club to meet Comer.

Curtis was over the moon to be there in the Stork Club, in the company of probably the most powerful mob boss in London, and being asked for his advice on what was obviously a very important matter. Comer, on the other hand, couldn't wait to get rid of him, and told Moisha and Sonny, with a dismissive wave of his hand, to take him off to the bar, buy him a couple of drinks as a thank you, while he had a chat with Silvers.

Silvers plonked himself down in a chair opposite Comer, "OK, so this is the plan," he blurted out, "I work for BOAC..." Comer held up his hand, interrupting Silvers in mid sentence, "Whoa, hold on, hold on," he said, "first thing you have to remember is you don't do plans – I do plans, right? Next thing is that you keep your voice down and you let me ask the questions, then you answer them, got it?" Silvers swallowed hard and murmured "sorry" to Comer.

Over the course of the next half hour or so, Comer fired question after question at Silvers; How long had he worked for BOAC? How many guards were employed at his depot? Were any of the guards armed?

Did the depot have alarms direct to the police? What did the haul consist of? How much in total value would the haul be worth? The questions continued, and Silvers continued answering them, until Comer was satisfied, for the time being at least.

The more he heard, the more Comer liked the idea, but he didn't want to show too much enthusiasm to Silvers. "Sounds interesting," he said, "leave me your phone number, I'll have a think about it and get in touch with you"

Chapter 26

No sooner had Comer, Moisha and Sonny left the club, then Bert Curtis made his move on Andy Silvers, who was also about to go. "Don't go Andy," he said, "let me buy you another drink, talk over old times"

Curtis was known as a good thief, an opportunist who kept his eyes and ears open and acted sometimes on spur of the moment decisions, quite often to his advantage. He found it very difficult to walk past an open door without investigating the possibilities, which might lie beyond, and from the little bit he had overheard between Comer and Silvers, this was a door, which was slightly ajar and ripe for him looking into.

"What luck eh? Me walking past like that just as Moisha was giving you the third degree – I reckon Jack Comer was well impressed with the way I boosted you up" Silvers could see the way the wind was blowing and tried his best to steer off the subject by chinking glasses with Curtis, "Cheers mate," he said with a hint of a smile, "so what have you been up to lately then, any good tickles?" Curtis shook his head, a glum look on his face, "If only," he replied, "all the money's moved out of London since the war, it's got so bad I've been staying in a doss house for the last few weeks"

"Well I'll tell you what," replied Silvers, "this drink's on me, I don't want you knocking out your last bit of cash buying drinks for me, especially at the prices they charge in here" "That's really nice of you mate," replied Curtis, chinking glasses with Silvers again "here's to us eh – us northerners have got to stick together, just like the old times eh?" Silvers finished his drink and slapped a pound note down on the bar, "Well must be off," he said, "maybe we'll bump into each other again soon, you never know eh?"

As Silvers went to walk away, Curtis grabbed hold of his arm, "Hold on a minute Andy, like I was saying, old mates like us need to stick together, and as you know, I'm not a fool, I can see when something big is occurring, and this must be big for Jack Comer to be involved" Silvers carefully eased his arm out of Curtis' grip. "At the moment Bert, nothing is happening, I can promise you that" Curtis moved closer to Silvers, blocking him from walking away, "All I'm asking you mate, is for you to put me in when it does happen, nothing wrong with that is there? We've known each other a long time and you know you can trust me"

Silvers was starting to sweat, he didn't want a full-scale argument with Curtis, but he felt like he was being put on the spot by him. "Look," he stammered, "I can't offer you anything Bert because I don't have anything to offer, you know Jack Comer, why don't you go and ask him?"

The two men stood there in silence, staring at each other for a few moments, both thinking the other man to be in the wrong. "I thought you was my mate," snarled Curtis as he pushed past Silvers, "I put in a good word for you, I thought at the least, you could do the same for me, don't worry, I'll find out my own way, then maybe you'll all be sorry" Curtis stormed out of the club, leaving Silvers relieved that he had gone, but somewhat worried about his last remark.

● ● ●

A few days later, Moisha manoeuvred his way through the London traffic, finally bringing the Jaguar to a halt outside the main entrance of the exhibition hall at Earls Court, London, where the first Motor Show was being held since before the war. He was immediately approached by a policeman who told him in no uncertain terms, that he could not park there. Moisha wound the window down, smiled at the policeman and told him that he was Lord Nuffield's driver and had been instructed to pick him up there. "Ah, here comes his Lordship now," said Moisha as he pointed to Comer, who had just emerged from the Show. The policeman stood to one side, and opened the rear door of the Jaguar to let Comer in. "I didn't realise it was your car your Lordship," he said as he saluted Comer and closed the door carefully once he was in.

Moisha looked at Comer, in his rear view mirror as he pulled away. "Well done Moisha," said Comer with a grin. "Did you see anything you liked there?" asked Moisha. "As a matter of fact I did," replied Comer, "I saw a dark blue Bentley – beautiful motor" Moisha was impressed, "A Bentley? Did you order one?" Comer shook his head, "No, not this time, I ordered another Jag, latest model, Mark five in British Racing Green, fast car, you'll love it, now put your toe down and take us to London Airport"

Once out of the west end of London, it didn't take them long to reach the airport, where a great deal of building work was taking place, including the demolition of rows of nearby houses along Hatton Road. There was so much work going on that they wasn't sure which way they should go, but then Moisha saw a temporary road sign with an arrow pointing to 'perimeter road'. "This road Jack?" he asked. "Yes," replied Comer, "we need to look out for the BOAC cargo building"

It was hard work for Moisha dodging the constant stream of heavy duty vehicles, which seemed to be driving all over the road and in every direction at once, from lorries to diggers to bulldozers; the once shiny Jaguar was by this time covered in a fine layer of dust and grime. "There it is over there," said Moisha, pointing to a large warehouse the other side of the perimeter fence. "Pull up," ordered Comer, "let's get out and pretend we're wiping the windscreen clean"

Moisha pulled the Jag as close to the perimeter fence as possible and they both got out of the car and started to wipe the windscreen with their handkerchiefs. "I would reckon that's about two hundred yards away from this fence at the most," Comer commented, "and If I'm not mistaken that looks like a gate just up the road there," he continued, pointing to a gate in the fence about fifty feet along the road in front of them.

Comer made mental notes in his head as he surveyed the warehouse and the site surrounding it; no uniformed guards outside, just one small alarm box, which if it did go off, would hardly be heard with all the noise of the building work and their vehicles. The only sign of life around the warehouse was one man, whom he presumed to be one of the workers, sitting on the loading platform, smoking a cigarette. "I've got good feelings about this one Moisha, very good feelings," said Comer as he climbed back into the car, "OK let's go"

• • •

Two days later Comer arranged a meeting with Andy Silvers in the private room above Bianchi's Restaurant in Frith Street, Soho. His trusted lieutenants, Moisha, Sonny and Billy Munro were also all there.

Comer, who was at the top of their table, rose to his feet, "Right, we all know why we're here, so I won't go into long speeches, the point of this meeting Andy, is to tell you that I have sussed out your offer, decided it is worth going with and decided to take it on – but, I want to tell you now that once you accept what I am going to put to you, there's no going back, and you will be expected to play a major role in the operation along with the rest of us – is that clear with you?" Silvers nodded his head and mumbled his acceptance.

Comer poured Silvers a drink from the whiskey bottle in the centre of the table, "here," he said, "you look like you could do with this" Silvers swallowed hard as he took a mouthful of the whiskey, "Er, just one thing Mr Comer – I'm willing to do my bit in all this, but I won't be expected to do any heavy work will I – like coshing and all that?"

Comer poured himself a drink from the brandy bottle, which was on the table, and of course his favourite drink; he took a large sip and smiled at Silvers, "Your role in all this Andy, will be to carry on being a security guard as far as your mates there at your depot are concerned, we'll be the bad boys, right? Silvers nodded again and took another swig of his whiskey as he listened intently to what Comer was saying to him. "Now if I remember rightly," said Comer, "you told me that at nine o'clock every morning, you and your fellow workers have your tea break, is that right?" Silvers nodded again, "that's right Mr Comer," he replied, "tea and a biscuit or a sandwich"

Comer slid the whiskey bottle up to the other end of the table towards where Moisha, Sonny and Munro were sitting, "help yourselves boys," he said. Then, turning back to Silvers, he asked, "you also told me that you take it in turns for going out to get the tea at the café on the airport site, is that right?" Silvers did his now customary nod of the head, "that's right" Comer smiled, took another swig of brandy and sat down, perfect," he said, "perfect"

Silvers wasn't the only one in the room who was at a loss as to where Comer was going with all this – Tea breaks? What the hell had tea breaks to do with planning a big robbery like this? Silvers half raised his hand, almost like a schoolboy would in class, "Er, excuse me for asking Mr Comer," he stammered, "but..." Comer held up his hand, stopping him in mid sentence, "all will be revealed," he replied, " "Well there was one other thing?" Silver interjected, "is it alright to speak freely here?" he said, looking round at the other members of the gang. "We're a team," replied Comer, "they wouldn't be here if I didn't trust them one hundred percent" "Well." replied Silver, "I hope you don't think I'm out of order saying this but I take it you are conversant with the movement of large sums of cash like this?

Comer downed what was left of the brandy in his glass, slammed the empty glass down on the table and jumped to his feet with a look of anger on his face. "You approached me," he snarled, "if you thought I was some sort of a fucking amateur, then why did you come to me?" Silvers could feel himself trembling with fear; Comer's face had changed from that of a benevolent friend, to a dark force, daring anyone to mess with him; one more wrong word and Silver felt it might well be his last. "I'm sorry Mr Comer," he fumbled with his words, "I didn't think for one minute you were any sort of amateur, I was referring to the way used banknotes are crated up in wooden boxes, which do weigh quite a bit, and the sort of vehicles needed to move them"

Comer's dark eyes bore into Silver for a few moments, but in truth, his thoughts were a thousand miles away. He was thinking of the last robbery, where he had let a vast fortune slip through his fingers. He was determined not to ever let anything like that happen again. He had been an amateur then, not that he would ever admit it to anyone but himself, a complete amateur and a fool. Never again would he put that much trust in anyone he was dealing with, and one day, he promised himself, he would track Billy White down and either get his share of the loot, which was owed to him, or kill Billy White in trying.

The sound of someone tapping on the door from outside brought Comer back to his senses, "See who that is?" he ordered Billy Munro, who immediately jumped up and went to the door. It was Elena Salvoni, the owner of Bianchi's. Their dinner was ready; she wanted to know if it could be served now? Comer looked over his shoulder at the pretty dark haired woman, who reminded him somewhat of Ruth, another dark haired girl in his life whom he had met at a party some years ago. "Yes Elena," he smiled at her, "bring it in any time you want"

Chapter 27

Unbeknown to Comer, just a few streets away from where he was now enjoying his beautiful Italian meal in Frith Street, anther man was sitting at the bar of a dingy basement-drinking club. This was Bert Curtis, who was alone and clutching tightly onto the remnants of his drink, doing his best to make it last. "Do you want another drink?" the barman asked him. "I'll tell you when I want another drink," slurred Curtis, "I'll tell you what though, a few fucking peanuts wouldn't go amiss?"

The barman ignored him and continued to wipe the bar down. There were only half a dozen customers in the club, most of them engaged in quiet talking amongst themselves and hardly any of them actually buying more drinks. Curtis dug deep into his trouser pockets and came up with a handful of small change, which he slammed down on the bar and started to count. "Here," he said, pushing the change towards the barman, "that should be enough for another one"

The barman started counting the change, "you're four pence short," he said, pushing the change back towards Curtis. At that moment, another voice from behind Curtis chirped in, "I'll pay for that"

Curtis spun around on his stool, somewhat blurry eyed but still managing to recognise a familiar face from some years back, "Teddy – Teddy Baxter," he exclaimed. Baxter passed Curtis' drink to him and ordered one for himself. "You look like you're about to fall off that stool," he said to Curtis, "why don't you go and sit down at that table over there, I've just got a bit of business to do with the chap here, and then we can have a good old chat about the old days eh?" Curtis agreed and took his drink over to a small table.

After a few minutes chatting to the barman, Baxter joined Curtis at his table. After the initial 'old times' banter, what prison they met in and how things had changed etc., the talk got around to what they were doing now. Baxter explained how he was now working with a south London firm, and was just getting into the fruit machine business, "That's why I'm here," he explained, "d'you know I've signed up over a dozen clubs just this week alone – the problem is we are still waiting for the machines, they have to be imported from America and then converted to take our money when they're in the country – what about you?" he asked, "what are you up to now?"

Curtis' first thought was to lie, tell Baxter that he was doing fine and the money was rolling in, but then he remembered the small change incident at the bar, and how Baxter had paid for his drink. His ego wanted to boost himself up, but his conscience told him otherwise. He told Baxter how the Manchester police had tried to pin a series of jewellery robberies onto him after he had refused to contribute a weekly backhander to them; his only alternative was to get out of Manchester as quickly as possible, which is why he now found himself in London, with no money and nowhere to stay.

All the time he was speaking, Baxter kept looking at his watch, showing distinct signs on disinterest. Curtis needed another drink, and hopefully a loan of a few quid from Baxter; he needed to keep his interest up somehow. "Here," he said, "you know a lot of people here in the west end, d'you know Jack Comer?" This brought Baxter back to life immediately, his head shot up, away from his watch and his eyes fixed on Curtis, "Do I know Comer? Not fucking much I do, why?" Curtis finished his drink and slammed the glass down hard on the table; somewhat exaggerating the fact that it was now empty, "Well it's something of a long story" Baxter took the hint and called across to the barman for another round of drinks.

Twenty minutes later, Curtis was still elaborating on the story of how he had seen his old mate, Andy Silvers talking to a big man outside the Stork Club and how he vouched for him and later met Jack Comer. Thirsty work all this story telling. Another drink and he was up to the part where he overheard his old mate, Silvers, tell Comer that he worked for BOAC at London Airport. "They're planning something big, I know that, and when I asked my so called friend to put me in, d'you know what he said? He as good as told me to fuck off – it wasn't his job, he said, and if I wanted to be involved I should go and ask Comer for myself"

Baxter was lapping this up like cat with a saucer of milk; he couldn't get enough of it. "Did you hear what it involves and when it's supposed to be taking place?" he asked. "No," Curtis replied, "they made me go over to the bar, out of earshot, why, do you reckon you could get me in on it then?" Baxter told Curtis that he just might be able to do that, but he needed to know a bit more first, "When are you seeing your mate again?" Baxter asked. Curtis explained that he hadn't seen Silvers for ages and had no idea if and when he would ever see him again. "He'll be around," Baxter replied, "he'll be here in London, he'll have to be, in order to keep in touch with Comer, what I want you to do is put yourself about around Soho and seek him out and find out what you can. If you do that for me I'll do whatever I can for you, right?"

• • •

Teddy Baxter's first thoughts after his meeting with Curtis, was to report his findings back to his new bosses, Bobby and Georgie Deacon. He had never been known for his business acumen, but on this occasion he actually paused for a moment to think before jumping the gun. Why should he report it to the Deacon brothers and let them earn money out of it? This could be worth a great deal of money to him personally if he played his cards right. He even lent Curtis five pounds in order for him to get somewhere to stay, and ordered him to meet him every day at 12 pm at the Dog and Duck pub on Bateman Street, Soho.

The Dog and Duck was an ordinary little Soho pub, catering to mainly local shopkeepers and businessmen. It was not the sort of pub one would expect to see underworld characters, which was why Baxter had chosen it.

Curtis was there, waiting, as Baxter walked into the pub the following lunchtime. He had managed to find a room above a café in Romilly Street, which was just a few minutes walk away, but he hadn't had any luck in locating Silvers. "Trouble is," said Curtis, putting on his best 'poor me' voice, "you need money to go into the sort of places Andy would be meeting Comer in, and I just haven't got that sort of money" Baxter looked angry at this remark, "What d'you mean?" he said, "what happened to the fiver I gave you then?" Curtis explained that as well as a deposit; he had to pay two weeks rent in advance for his room, which had left him with exactly five shillings, "not exactly splashing about money for swanky clubs is it?"

Baxter reluctantly handed over another fiver to Curtis, telling him that he had to make this last and he expected to see results within the next day or two at the latest. "Now get out there now," he said, "and put yourself about; money don't grow on fucking trees you know, I want results and if you want me to help you, then you better start working for your money, got it?" He left Curtis in no doubt that it wouldn't be wise to hang around for another drink. Curtis tucked the big white five-pound note into the inside pocket of his jacket and left immediately, with a brief 'thanks' and a pat on the arm to Baxter.

Baxter finished the beer in his glass and started to walk out of the pub, when he heard a voice from behind a newspaper mention his name, "Hello Teddy, not going already are you?" Baxter looked round as the newspaper was lowered to reveal the face of Detective Inspector Bruce Cutler, who slapped the seat beside him and ordered Baxter to sit down. "I saw you from outside," Cutler said, "and I immediately thought to myself that you must be up to no good, going into a pub like this, an ordinary pub where nice straight people go – not your usual scene is it Teddy?"

Baxter glanced towards the door. "Forget it Teddy," quipped Cutler, "my good friend and colleague, Detective Sergeant Barry Webber is right outside that door, and being the good police officer that he is, he never goes anywhere without his trusty truncheon"

Cutler pulled Baxter down onto the seat beside him and started questioning him like a naughty schoolboy. Where had he been, and what had he been up to? "Been up to?" replied Baxter, " there's not a lot you can get up to in Wormwood Scrubs Mr Cutler, beside sewing mailbags that is" Cutler knew about this little sojourn; what he wanted to know was where Baxter had been since then, and what was he doing for money? Baxter tried to play it down by explaining, "You know me Mr Cutler, I always get by – open a few doors for people and it's surprising how much they help you out"

Cutler wasn't falling for that one, he had known Baxter a long time and had never seen him so well dressed; he must be onto something. "D'you remember the last time we met Teddy, you promised me you were going to give me something on Jack Comer? I won't wait forever Teddy, if I don't get him, it'll have to be you"

Baxter tried to hide the fact that he was starting to get worried by smiling and offering to buy Cutler a drink. "I never drink on duty Teddy, you should know that, but I'll tell you what, you can buy me one tomorrow night, in here after I've finished work" Cutler stood up. "Eight o'clock, don't be late will you, and make sure you have something for me won't you? I wouldn't want us to fall out" Cutler walked out of the pub, leaving Baxter sitting there, somewhat dazed and ruminating on his future.

● ● ●

Bert Curtis had faith in Baxter, and he desperately needed money. He appreciated the cash handouts but they were not something he could rely on for his future. Getting out and about in Soho was gradually getting back to how it had been before the war, with brightly lit neon signs and club entrances with hostesses openly flouting their wares.

Curtis went from club to club, most of them just small dives that he could be in and out of within a minute or two, in his quest to find Silvers. He had been tramping the streets of Soho for over three hours, and it had now started to rain as he turned into Old Compton Street. People don't go out to clubs every night of the week, he told himself, even big time gangsters like Jack Comer; they have a night off sometimes.

Bloody rain, and he didn't even have a hat. As it started to come down even heavier he ducked into the open doorway of an amusement arcade. As he stood in the doorway, staring out somewhat forlornly as the passers by, trying to dodge from canopy to canopy to avoid the rain, while behind him he could hear the mechanical pings from the machines, accompanied by the occasional expletive from the players. He looked over his shoulder into the colourful interior of the arcade, and could hardly believe his eyes, for there was Andy Silvers, leaning over a pin-ball machine and seemingly putting all his weight into trying to guide the ball in the direction he wanted it to go without making the 'tilt' sign on the machine's display, start to flash.

"Andy," called Curtis as he walked up to Silvers inside the arcade. Silvers glanced round, but didn't look too pleased to see Curtis, who had interrupted his game. "Fancy seeing you here, I just stopped to shelter from the rain and spotted you" "Hello Bert," Silvers replied, somewhat wearily, "how are you, got yourself out of your money troubles I hope?"

Lying through his teeth, Curtis assured Silvers that he had had a nice little tickle and was now doing fine, "I'd like to say sorry for the last time we met," he said, "you know what's it like when you're skint and everybody seems to be against you" Silvers told him that he wasn't against him, it was just an awkward situation that's all, and as he explained at the time, it wasn't something he was in charge of. "Don't worry about it mate," Curtis replied, "I'll tell you what, let me buy you a drink to show there's no hard feelings – there's a little club just around the corner from here, how about it?"

Ten minutes later the two men were seated in an alcove at the Ace of Spades Club, where a jazz trio were improvising on the classic tune, 'Out Of Nowhere.' This wasn't the sort of club Curtis normally frequented; it was an upmarket establishment, which he hoped would impress Silvers into believing that his luck had truly changed for the better.

Curtis' ploy seemed to work, for an hour later, Silvers was still there and enjoying his third, or was it his fourth, large gin and tonic. "Lovely music, this," he slurred, "I love jazz don't you?" Curtis nodded in agreement, "It's American isn't it – I love all American things, they're so modern, I mean, look at their cars compared to ours – I'm going to emigrate to America as soon as I've done my next job – buy a big house with a swimming pool and sit back and relax - never have to work again"

Whether it was because Silvers was slightly drunk or just naive, or maybe a bit of both, he certainly took the bait, hook, line, and sinker. "Blimey, it must be a big job," he answered. "Big isn't the word for it mate, it's massive," replied Curtis, "Diamonds, five hundred grand's worth" Silvers almost choked on his gin and tonic, "Fucking hell Bert, makes my banknote job sound like kid's stuff"

Bingo, it had worked – banknotes. Curtis already knew that Silvers worked for BOAC, now for the final piece in the jigsaw. "I need one more man," Curtis threw in, almost casually, "I can put you in it if you want, but you'll have to be ready to go at any time within the next two weeks; how does that sound to you?" Silvers gulped down the rest of his gin and tonic and slammed the glass down on the table; a look of suppression on his face, "Shit," he exclaimed, "I can't do it, our job is set to go next Tuesday"

Curtis beckoned to a waiter to bring them another round of drinks, which would hopefully loosen Silvers' tongue even more. "It's up to you," he said, "but I know what I would do if I were in your shoes – my job's worth five hundred grand, what's yours worth – fifty, a hundred grand at the most? And then there's the risk factor – banknotes almost always involves armed guards" Silver smiled and shook his head, "Oh no," he said, "there's no risks in this job, you seem to have forgotten that I am one of the guards, and as for the rest of them, they're going to be out cold" "What do you mean out cold?" asked Curtis. "I'll be getting their tea from the café on the airport site that morning," answered Silvers, "and believe me, they won't be waking up for hours after they drink what I am putting in that tea"

That was it; Curtis now had everything he wanted.

Chapter 28

Jack Comer was ultra busy organising everything in preparation for the London Airport job. He decided to use three small vans to transport the banknotes away from the airport, instead of one large lorry, which would have been sufficient. His idea was that just in case the police were alerted to them, it would be almost impossible to follow three vans, which had all been souped up, and were to all use different routes back to the warehouse he had also organised in Twickenham, which was just seven miles away from the airport.

At the Twickenham warehouse, the wooden cases containing the banknotes would be offloaded from the small vans and onto one large lorry, which would then be driven to the next warehouse, which was in Battersea, south London, where it would be unloaded and the lorry taken out and disposed of.

Comer was once again using the private room above Bianchi's restaurant as his operations centre while planning this robbery. It was very handy; as it was central and no one would be any the wiser had they seen him or any of his gang going in and out of the restaurant.

As well as Comer, the usual close members of his coterie were there, including Moisha, Sonny, Billy Munro, Jimmy Black and Freddy Smith. One man was conspicuous by his absence, and that was Andy Silvers, without whom the job couldn't go forward. Comer took Moisha to one side, out of earshot of the others, "Have you phoned him?" he asked. Moisha assured him that he had phoned him twice that morning but no one answered the phone. Comer took a deep breath, his fists clenched into tight balls; his eyes seemed to turn black, like pieces of coal. He turned briefly to the rest of the men in the room, "Give us five minutes," he said as he walked out of the room, nudging Moisha to go with him.

● ● ●

Andy Silvers had taken temporary accommodation in a room above the Pillars of Hercules pub on Greek Street. A single Reggie of sunlight had managed to slip into the room through a small opening in the heavy velvet curtains, which were still pulled shut, even though it was almost 1 pm. His head had rolled off the pillow and his mouth was wide open as he made snorting and grunting noises in his sleep.

A metallic clicking noise next to his head brought him out of his dreams with a jolt; his eyes opened wide as he saw the 45 automatic pistol, now touching his temple. What the fuck?" he spluttered, as he looked up into the face of Jack Comer, with Moisha standing just behind him. "If I pull this trigger," snarled Comer, "It'll blow your head apart like a fucking water melon – give me one good reason why I shouldn't do it?"

Silvers was shaking with fear as Comer ripped the bedclothes from off him. "What have I done, what have I done? His voice was quivering and a wet patch was slowly forming around the crotch of his pyjamas. Comer nodded to Moisha, who grabbed Silvers and pulled him out of the bed and to his feet. "This isn't a fucking game," Comer shouted, I've invested a lot of money in this job – if I can't even trust you to get out of bed and come to a meeting, I'm beginning to get seriously worried how you'll perform on the big day – that's if you even bother to show up"

"I will show up, I will," pleaded Silvers, "I'm sorry Jack – please, it won't happen again, I promise" Comer had a look of contempt on his face as he nodded again to Moisha, who seemed to be able to almost read his mind. Moisha unleashed one powerful blow to Silvers' stomach, which doubled him in half and sent him crashing to the floor, groaning with the pain. "You've got off light this time," Comer growled, as he clicked the safety switch on his pistol to the lock position again, "now get your clothes on and come with us"

Needless to say Silvers made it to the meeting, where all aspects of the raid were proposed, times, drivers, vehicles, routes. Each man's role was laid out clearly; there was to be no deviating from the plan unless Comer decided otherwise. Last but not least was a little brown bottle, which Comer produced, "These," he said, looking at Silvers, "are the knock out pills for your mate's tea – two pills in each cup – got it? Silvers swallowed hard and looked worried as he went to take the bottle from Comer. "Not yet," Comer said, moving the bottle away from Silvers, "I'll give them to you on the morning – I hope they all take sugar and milk in their tea as this stuff is supposed to have a bit of a bitter taste?

Silvers said he didn't know if they did or not as it depended on what team was on that morning. "You never told me there could be different men?" he said. Silvers explained that the guards were from a private security firm and that he was the only one there that actually worked for BOAC. "One last thing," explained Comer, "when you put the pills in the teas, don't put them in your own will you?" Silvers looked blank for a moment, "But it's going to look a bit dodgy if I'm the only one who isn't drugged isn't it?" Comer looked exasperated, "As far as anyone will know, you are drugged, d'you get me? I need you awake to make sure when they are all knocked out and that is when you let us in – now don't fuck up on me Andy, this is crucial – you do understand me don't you?" Silvers nodded and mumbled an acknowledgement.

Chapter 29

Teddy Baxter nursed his Guinness as he sat in a corner seat at the Dog and Duck pub
and puffed nervously on a Players Navy Cut cigarette, no more cheap Turf cigarettes for him. He didn't have to wait long for Det. Insp. Bruce Cutler to arrive and plonk himself down in the seat next to him. "Hello Teddy, nice to see you made it," he said, with a sardonic grin on his face, "I'll have a large whiskey if you don't mind before we get down to business"

Two minutes later Baxter returned from the bar with the whiskey for Cutler, which he placed down on the table in front of him. Cutler accepted the drink in his usual smug manner, sipping it and staring directly at Baxter. "Well, so what have you got for me? Cutler asked. Baxter lit another cigarette and blew the smoke just narrowly missing Cutler's face, "I'll tell you what I've got Mr Cutler," he answered, "I've got a deal to offer you"

The fake smile on Cutler's face quickly dropped, who the hell did this little upstart think he was, offering him a deal? "Hold on a minute Baxter," Cutler snarled, "I think you've got your wires crossed here, you don't offer me deals, you give me the information I asked you for, and if you are very lucky I just might be able to offer you a deal, do I make myself clear?"

Baxter wasn't one bit fazed by Cutler's threats, he took another slow mouthful of his Guinness, "You haven't got any option this time," he smirked, "I'm holding a Royal flush here, while all you have is a pair of deuces at the most" Cutler could feel his hackles rising as he looked at Baxter's face, taunting him. "I can still nick you though Baxter, and send you away for a long time – you want to remember that"

Baxter still smirked as he shook his head, "You can," he replied, "but then you would miss out on your whack of probably the biggest cash robbery in British history" Cutler drew a long deep breath, he loved the sound of this, but not exactly something he should admit to, even to a notorious villain like Teddy Baxter, but could he trust him?

"In all the years I've known you Teddy, I've never known you to be straight with me, so tell me why I should trust you now?" "I have half a million reasons why you should trust me," replied Baxter, "and all in used banknotes" Cutler had difficulty in catching his breath when he heard those figures, "Alright," he said, "I'm listening"

• • •

It was 22 July, a particularly balmy evening as Bert Curtis, looking a little the worse for wear, as usual, ambled up to the Stork Club, where he had first encountered his old friend, Andy Silvers, and the infamous Jack Comer. Straightening his tie and buttoning his jacket up, he walked into the foyer of the club and was immediately stopped by the large commissionaire in his military style uniform. "May I help you sir," the commissionaire politely enquired. "No, it's alright, I'm meeting a couple of friends here," Curtis lied, as he tried to bypass the commissionaire, and go down the stairs into the club.

The commissionaire may have been middle aged and somewhat overweight, but he was used to dealing with customers like Curtis; his arm flew out like a shot from a cannon, encompassing Curtis against the wall before he could take another step, "This is a members only club sir," he said, "if you would like to give me the names of the gentlemen you are supposed to be meeting here, I will check to see if they are here, and if they are, you will need to get one of them to sign you in?"

"Silvers," Curtis, replied, Andy Silvers" The commissionaire shook his head, "Sorry sir," he replied, "We do not have a Mr Silvers on our membership list. Curtis tried to push his way past the commissionaire, but was trapped by his weight and size. "What about Jack Comer then?" Curtis shouted, "Now don't tell me he's not a member?" The commissionaire stared hard at Curtis, and pushed his face up close to his, almost touching, "Mr Comer receives guests by appointment only sir, he informs me if and when he is expecting a guest, and I can assure you that he is not expecting any today – and I can also assure you that he would not take too kindly to hearing some loud mouth drunk shouting his name at the door, so if you don't mind sir" The commissionaire grabbed hold of the collar of Curtis' jacket and dragged him to the doorway, and then threw him into the street outside.

Curtis wasn't going to be put off by a little rough handling, he had endured a lot worse than this over the years, and at least he now knew that Comer was inside the club. He had searched everywhere for Teddy Baxter, with no luck at all, so what was he supposed to do – walk away empty handed, when Baxter had more or less promised him that he would secure him a place on Comer's team?

Two hours later Curtis was perched on a doorstep on the opposite side of the road to the club. Luckily for him it was still a relatively warm night, so he wasn't too worried about a little discomfort; he was more worried about getting down to his last cigarette, which he lit with a match, cupped in his hand, and slowly drew in the sweet vapour.

As he blew out a slow stream of blue smoke he saw three people emerging from the club doorway, two men, Comer and Moisha, with a woman between them, whom he did not know was Rita, Comer's wife.

Curtis got to his feet, patted his hair down and brushed himself down as he made his way across the road, trying to catch up with the group as they approached the green Jaguar car, which Moisha started to open. "Jack," called Curtis, "Jack" All three quickly turned to see who was calling. Comer looked visibly worried, and quickly pushed Rita into the now open door of their car; who the hell was this, now hurrying, almost running, towards them; was it someone trying to kill him?

Moisha pulled a pistol from out of the waistband of his trousers and pointed it directly at Curtis, "One more step and you are a dead man," he shouted, "now put your hands in the air – now!"

Curtis did exactly as he was told as Moisha, followed by Comer, approached him and shoved him against the wall; keeping his gun pointed at him all the time while he patted him down, searching for any weapons. "Who the fuck is he?" demanded Comer. "You heard Mr Comer," Moisha interjected, "who the fuck are you and what do you want?"

Curtis was shaking with fear, he hadn't expected this type of reception, he thought they would have recognised him. "You know me Jack," he stumbled, "Bert, Bert Curtis, I met you here the other week with my mate Andy Silvers" Moisha gave him another shove, "It's Mr Comer to you" "Alright, alright, I'm sorry, Mr Comer, I just wanted to know if you had made a decision yet?"

Comer stepped forward and stared hard into Curtis' face, "What the fuck are you talking about?" he said, "decision about what?" Curtis was getting more worried by the minute, it didn't look like Comer knew anything about this. "About me being on the team, Andy told me that I should ask you myself, but when I bumped into another mate, who's a very good friend of yours, he told me he would talk to you and fix it up"

Comer shook his head in disbelief, "What's this arsehole talking about?" he said, as if to himself, "what very good friend of mine?" "Baxter," Curtis blurted out, "Teddy Baxter" Comer's jaw dropped in disbelief. He turned to Moisha, whose mouth was wide open, as he mouthed the word, "Fuck"

"Baxter?" exclaimed Comer, "a good friend of mine? The man's a fucking walking turd - Who the fuck else knows about this – you – Baxter – come on, who else?" Curtis felt his legs going weak at the knees as he fumbled for an answer; his lips were moving but no words were coming out. Moisha pushed his gun hard into Curtis' head, "Are you deaf as well as fucking stupid?" he growled, "Mr Comer asked you a question" "I know I know," whimpered Curtis, "I don't know who else knows, and that's the truth"

Comer stared at Curtis for several seconds, deep in thought; he then turned to Moisha and nodded to him knowingly. "Wait here," he said quietly, "I'm just going to walk Rita up to the main road and get a cab to take her home, I'll be five minutes"

Ten minutes later Moisha was driving the Jaguar through London as Comer sat in the back with a pistol sticking into the ribs of a terrified Curtis, who was sitting in the darkness next to him. Moisha finally brought the car to a halt in a narrow back street in east London, where they all got out and Curtis was frog marched to the doorway of a late Victorian, red brick building. After ringing the doorbell, the door was opened by an elderly man named Nat, who worked as an attendant here, and was on Comer's payroll for carrying out the odd little job for him now and then.

Nat disappeared into a small side room as soon as he had let them in, leaving them to make their way along a long green tiled corridor, which seemed to grow hotter with every pace they took. At the end of the corridor stood a large metal door with a 'Caution' sign painted on it in large white lettering. Moisha slid back the two enormous iron bolts, which secured the door, and pushed it open.

The sound that greeted them was like a convoy of lorries, revving their engines at the same time; the heat was almost unbearable as they shoved Curtis into the room. "What is this place?" he shouted, "what have you brought me here for?" Comer and Moisha took off their jackets and placed them on a chair outside. "This is the boiler room for the public baths and wash-house, this furnace is kept going twenty four hours a day – burns anything from wood and coal – even bones"

A few minutes later, Curtis had been stripped of his clothes, down to his underpants, and was chained to a metal post, just a few feet away from the furnace. "Please," he screamed, "just tell me what you want to know?" Comer and Moisha had to back away somewhat as the heat was so intense, "I want to know where Baxter is?" Comer shouted, "I want an address, a phone number?" Curtis screamed in pain and begged them to unchain him, "I don't know," he screamed, "please, I don't know" Comer wiped the sweat from his face, his shirt was dripping wet and stuck to his body, as he backed further out the door, away from the heat, "You've got five minutes to come up with what we want" He slammed the great metal door shut with the sounds of Curtis' screams echoing in his ears as he did so.

Five minutes later and still nothing from Curtis, another five, followed by ten and then fifteen. This time when they returned to the boiler room, his skin looked like the crackling on a barbequed pig. A quick word with Nat, and nothing at all would remain of what was once Bert Curtis.

This wasn't the end of Comer's problems however; he still had Baxter to find and deal with, and more to the point, who else had Baxter involved? "What are we going to do now then Jack?" asked Moisha as they drove back through central London, "are you going to call the job off?" "Like fuck I am," replied Comer, "this is the big one we've all been waiting for, and I'm certainly not letting a little rat like Baxter ruin it for us – if we don't find him in the next two days it goes ahead as planned – the only difference is we go tooled up, which is not something I wanted to do on this one"

Chapter 30

Comer didn't mention anything about Curtis to the rest of the gang. He had to mention Baxter, as he put out a big search for him, which in the end was completely unsuccessful. For once Baxter had put some forethought into his actions, and had decided to steer well clear of Soho as a precaution, not just because of Comer and his men, but also to make sure he didn't bump into Det. Insp. Bruce Cutler.

When Comer had briefed his men into why he wanted Baxter found, he purposely left out the real reason, saying it was just a personal thing. If the rest of the gang had known that Baxter knew everything it might have put some off and jeopardised the whole operation.

It was a fine, sunny morning on the day of the raid and everyone was gathered at the Twickenham warehouse, where Comer went through everything again and again. He then handed out the guns to his men and the bottle of pills to Andy Silvers, and told him his role in the operation yet again, "We're relying on you Andy, you know that don't you – you've got to get it right – there's no second chance with this?" Silvers assured him he knew what he was doing. "Good," replied Comer, "now get going, we'll see you there in a couple of hours"

Comer and his men turned up at the BOAC warehouse at the pre-arranged time of 9.45 a.m. If Silvers has carried out his part of the job properly then all the guards should be out cold by this time. Comer ordered the three vans to pull up just inside the perimeter fence after Jimmy Black had snipped the small padlock off the door in the fence.

Comer was somewhat worried at the lack of activity around the site; the only noise was the occasional plane taking off and landing about a mile away. He signalled to everyone to put their balaclava masks on. He then indicated to Jimmy Black to go and see if the door to the warehouse had been unlocked yet, as it looked locked from where he was. Black made his way across the open ground to the warehouse, climbed up onto the loading bay and gave the door, which was to one side, a gentle push. To his surprise it swung open, allowing him to peer inside. It was a strange sight' about half a dozen guards, one on the floor and the others sprawled and slumped on chairs, all unconscious.

Black turned and signalled to Comer that everything was fine for them to enter the warehouse. Comer, in the first van, signalled to the others, and all three vans drove in a convoy and pulled up beside the loading bay, where everyone got out of their vehicles and followed Black, and then Comer, through the doorway and into the large warehouse where the unconscious guards were still lying.

Comer did a quick reconnoitre of the premises. There were six large wooden packing cases stacked against a wall to the left of the loading area, he silently signalled to Black and Freddy Smith, who were armed with jemmies, to start work on one of the packing cases. The two men eased their jemmies into each side of one of the cases and started to pry the lid off.

While they were doing this, Comer looked around at the faces of the sleeping guards, but Andy Silvers wasn't there. He should have known not to trust him when he failed to show up for that meeting. What he could not understand is why had Silvers done all this work, drugging the guards and opening the door for them, just to run off before the raid actually takes place, last minute panic attack maybe? His loss, thought Comer, more cash for me.

"Yes" hissed a joyful Jimmy Black as he slipped the crate's wooden lid to the floor and pulled back a layer of waxy paper to reveal bundle after bundle of used British banknotes. "Get that lid back on," Comer ordered, "and you," indicating Freddy Smith, "get those shutters up – and I want those vans ready and loaded as quickly as possible – right?"

As the shutters were raised, Comer's men sprung into action, manoeuvring the crates out onto the loading bay, where the rest of the men were waiting with wooden boards, which the crates were edged onto and carefully slid down into the backs of the waiting vans.

Two loud gunshots suddenly erupted, bringing everyone to a standstill. Comer looked round and saw a man rushing towards him, holding a pistol in the air and firing another shot into the ceiling as he did so. "Police," shouted Det. Insp. Bruce Cutler, whom at this time, was unbeknown to Comer, "everyone stop where you are – you are all under arrest" At the same time, the 'unconscious' guards, made what looked like a miraculous recovery, jumped to their feet, while shouting, "Police – Police" at the top of the voices and taking out huge police issue revolvers, which they pointed towards Comer and his men.

Comer immediately retaliated by pulling out a large 44 automatic pistol and firing it at one of the overhead lights, and then at a metal box on the wall, which was marked 'fuses'. Within seconds, everyone in Comer's team had also drawn their weapons and a full-scale war had broken out, with the police hiding behind everything and anything they could find on one side of the huge room, and Comer's men on the other side. It was like the Blitz all over again.

Comer ducked down and noticed that his shot at the fuse box had caused some sparks to fly. He signalled to Moisha to do the same and both of them unleashed a barrage of shots at the metal box, blasting several holes in it and causing it to explode, which knocked out all the lights, and plunged the vast windowless room into darkness.

Bullets were flying everywhere, with the police officers shouting and telling Comer's men to lay down their weapons and surrender, "You're only making it worse for yourselves," shouted Det. Insp. Bruce Cutler, "back-up is on the way, you've got no chance" The answer to this from Comer's men, was two more shots zinging in the direction of Cutler's feet, causing him to fall over in the semi darkness.

Comer saw this as his chance and keeping down low he made a dash for the still open loading bay, touching Moisha and Sonny to go with him. Leaping down from the loading bay, the first thing Comer noticed was one van was missing; there was now only two. He didn't have time to start searching for the other one, or to start asking his team if they knew who had taken it. "Quick," he shouted to Moisha and Sonny, "you," pointing to Moisha, "take that one, and you," indicating Sonny, "come in this one with me" Within seconds the two remaining vans were speeding away from the BOAC site, with the sounds of gunfire, still ringing in their ears.

● ● ●

Comer, Moisha and Sonny were sweating as they manhandled the four wooden cases from out of the vans in the relative safety of the Twickenham warehouse, where they then loaded them as quickly as possible into a large lorry, with 'Carter Patterson & Co. Express Carriers' painted on the side. "I'd like to know who took our other van," Sonny breathlessly grunted as they finished lifting the last crate up onto the lorry. "And the other third of the cash that was in it" Comer answered, "we'll sort that out later, right now we got to get this lot over to the Battersea warehouse – OK let's go" Comer climbed in the back of the lorry, followed by Sonny. Moisha got in the front and drove out and onto the main road as quickly as he could.

Chapter 31

The story of the BOAC raid was all over the National newspapers and on the wireless. 'Half a million pounds in used banknotes stolen by armed gang at London Airport' screamed the headlines. 'Police captured four members of the armed gang but failed to capture at least another three, who escaped in three separate vehicles containing the vast haul'

Just off London's Embankment stood the imposing Victorian building, which housed the world famous Scotland Yard, which was the headquarters for the Metropolitan Police. Det. Insp. Bruce Cutler's office was a gloomy little room on the third floor, with oak panelling and a tiny window, which let in almost no light at all, as it faced the adjoining building. Cutler looked across his desk towards his partner, Det. Sgt. Barry Webber. "I'll be charging all four of them later this afternoon," he said. "But what about Comer and his two cronies?" asked Webber. "At the moment, we have absolutely no proof whatsoever that Comer was involved – don't forget they were all masked up, and the other police officers on the scene will testify to that," replied Cutler, "I want him to think he's slipped the net, his ego's as big as his arse, he won't be able to resist strutting around Soho showing off at least some of his new found wealth, that way he'll hopefully lead us to the rest of the loot"

"Maybe we could use Baxter again?" Webber asked, "get him to put his feelers out again maybe?" "Baxter? No way," replied Cutler," shaking his head, "he still thinks he's entitled to some sort of share of the loot from the airport job – in fact I'm in two minds whether to pull him in anyway and charge him along with the others" Webber didn't look too comfortable with this suggestion. "It's up to you," he said, "you're the boss, but if you want my opinion I wouldn't charge him with anything just yet – his defence would be to incriminate us, and we can't afford that at this stage can we?"

Webber was right of course, and Cutler knew it, but there were so many loose ends to tie up here. He had hopefully proved himself to his superiors by arresting four armed villains as they took part in the biggest cash raid in Britain's history. At a press conference later that day, after the villains had been charged, Cutler confided to the press that he was confident that he would oversee the full contents of the raid returned to its rightful owners, even though he knew this to be impossible.

Comer was of course, his biggest nightmare. He was indeed a swaggering show-off, but he was a damn clever one. Cutler knew that if he pursued Comer too aggressively, he would disappear, probably abroad somewhere, especially now foreign travel restrictions had been lifted, and along with Comer would go his trusted lieutenants, Moisha and Sonny, and most importantly, the money.

●●●

At this moment in time, Comer had no intentions whatsoever of leaving the country, or even London, come to that. He was openly flaunting his presence around Soho, just as Cutler had predicted, as well as taking his wife out to top London restaurants and nightclubs. The idea behind this was to say to the world, and especially the police, that if he, Jack Comer, had been anything to do with this enormous robbery, would he still be walking the streets of London, or driving the same car, or living in the same London flat?

Comer had also instructed Moisha and Sonny, to do exactly the same, they had all concocted watertight alibis, and there they were, Moisha and Sonny, eating breakfast in Barney's Café in Petticoat Lane, and lunch at Bloom's Kosher Restaurant in Whitechapel, both undoubtedly serving nice food, but hardly the haunts of millionaire gangsters.

Comer had pulled off the biggest cash robbery in British history, but he had lost three good men in the process. He didn't class Andy Silvers as one of his men. He had also lost one third of the loot, and had absolutely no idea of who could have taken it. He knew it definitely wasn't any of his own men, as apart from himself, Moisha and Sonny, the others had all been captured there at the warehouse, but one thing he did know, was that someone had grassed them up, which is why the police were there, waiting for them.

There was only one other person that Comer knew of, who seemed to know anything at all about the job, and according to Bert Curtis, that was Teddy Baxter. This was just the sort of double-dealing that Baxter might contemplate, but was he capable of it?

As if in answer to his thoughts, the phone in Comer's flat suddenly rang; it was Moisha, who told Comer that he was thinking of taking his old mother down to Southend in Essex for the weekend. This was a code they had worked out, in case the phone was being bugged, meaning he had something urgent to tell him, and to meet him in the usual place, which was their old meeting place, the Mackworth Arms pub on Commercial Road, east London.

Moisha and Sonny were in the pub waiting, when the taxi pulled up outside and Comer walked in. He joined them at their corner table, where his usual brandy was on the table, ready and waiting. "So what's happened?" asked a somewhat anxious Comer. "I was playing cards with a few of the boys last night," Sonny answered, "when one of the geezers started talking about a south London mob called the Deacon brothers" "Never heard of them," interrupted Comer, "No, nor me," Sonny continued, "but this geezer reckons they are making a bit of a name for themselves over there – they're not even in their twenties yet, but already they are getting a bit of a team around them and have pulled a whole string of smash and grab raids"

Comer was getting exasperated, "What the fuck has this got to do with me? You got me all the way over here to listen to a story about a bunch of snotty nosed south London kids?" No, no, no," Sonny interrupted, "hear me out Jack, I got you here because one of the people the Deacons have recruited, is none other than Teddy fucking Baxter" Comer's face froze as he took in what Sonny had just said, "This is beginning to make sense, if Baxter's now working for this Deacon mob then who better for him to pull in to help him with nicking our cash? All they had to do was hide somewhere nearby, wait for the vans to be loaded up and nick the three of them"

Comer could now see it as clear as daylight, when the shooting inside the warehouse started they would have made a dash for the vans then; started with the first one, but when they saw himself, Moisha and Sonny making their way out, they had to be content with just the one van, which they then drove back to south London, straight to their scrap yard where the van would have been cut up. As for the money, that is anyone's guess at this moment.

"So what we going to do about it?" Moisha chipped in. "I'll tell you what we are going to do," growled Comer, "we're going to find out where these bastards hang out and pay them a little visit"

Sonny interrupted again, telling Comer that according to the geezer at the card game, the Deacons have got a scrap metal yard over the water, near Camberwell somewhere, so it shouldn't be hard to find them. "I want you on it straight away, both of you," ordered Comer, find this yard and watch it for a couple of days, see who goes in and who comes out – with a bit of luck we may be able to kill two birds with one stone here – get our dough back and rip Mr poxy fucking Baxter's head off at the same time"

Chapter 32

It didn't take Moisha and Sonny long to locate the Deacon's scrap yard. Parked one day in an old butcher's van, and the next day in a dilapidated old Ford Eight, they watched the yard day and night. There were the usual scrap metal dealers, with their horse and carts and the occasional lorry, pulling into the gates, which were kept open for most of the day, selling their piles of scrap metal to the brothers, but there was also a constant flow of men, who were most definitely not scrap metal dealers; men in flash suits, who had pulled up nearby in big cars.

They also saw Teddy Baxter coming and going. He was well dressed, which was unusual for him, and often accompanied by a young man they later found out to be Bobby Deacon, who was the eldest of the Deacon brothers, but unlike the other visitors to the yard, they did not drive any flash cars, they were always in a van, similar in size to the vans, which had been used on the robbery.

A little more investigation and they quickly found out that Baxter has been installing fruit machines on behalf of the Deacons to small spielers around Soho, which was obviously what the small van was being used for.

Comer didn't like what he was hearing from Moisha and Sonny, it sounded very much like the Deacons were forming a decent size team around them, and as well as their organised smash and grab raids, they seem to be moving into the west end of London by putting their fruit machines into spielers. The problem that Comer now had is that half of his team had been arrested, and were awaiting trial for the airport robbery. He could hardly start a gang war against the Deacons with just himself, Moisha and Sonny, but he desperately wanted his money back. Baxter is the cause of all this. He must be made to talk.

• • •

The Battle of London Airport, as it had come to be dubbed, still took precedence in the newspapers and the wireless over the coming weeks and months. Scotland Yard were preparing the trial of the four men they had arrested at the scene of the crime. 'Gangsters are taking over our city' screamed the headline in the London Evening Standard, while the Daily Mirror demanded to know what the police were doing to combat the recent rise in gun crime in London?

Comer was no fool, and as much as he wanted to get to Baxter, he knew that with all this adverse publicity regarding gangs in London, that now was not the time. Even as he turned up at the Old Bailey to witness the trial of his men, he had reporters and photographers trying to photograph him or ask what he was doing there, and did he know the defendants. He would hide his face from the cameras and provide his stock answer, which was to reply that he was attending out of curiosity, and that he did not personally know any of the defendants.

Billy Munro, Jimmy Black, Freddy Smith, and Andy Silvers, were all charged with robbery with violence and attempted murder of police officers. They all pleaded not guilty, and were defended by Manfred Hendrik KC, whom Comer had secretly hired and paid for through an intermediary.

All four defendants were asked if they worked as part of a gang, whose leader and two other men had escaped with the full contents of the haul. Each man, including Andy Silvers, swore on oath that this was not true, that they had been working strictly as a four-man team. As a BOAC employee, Andy Silvers could not deny that it was him who had inside information, and that it was him who had offered this information to the others, but none of them knew a thing about what had happened to the loot.

Comer had got news to his men while they were on remand, promising to make sure that each of them, or their families, whoever they chose, would get their share of the loot, as promised. He was pleased with the way they had accepted his word as his bond and had stayed loyal to him.

Another thing he was particularly interested in, was the police officer who had been hiding there at the warehouse and made the initial arrest, Det. Insp. Bruce Cutler. From the public gallery, high above the courtroom, Comer's eyes bored into Cutler as he gave his evidence from the witness box. Comer had never had any trust or faith in the police, but as he listened to the obviously crap evidence that Cutler was spewing out, he felt like leaping over the rail and attacking him right there in the number one court of the Old Bailey.

As Comer continued to imagine the beating he would like to give this man, his mind started wandering back to his encounter at the public baths with Bert Curtis, who had alleged that Teddy Baxter was a good friend of his. The scene replayed in Comer's mind, "Baxter, a good friend of mine? The man's a fucking walking turd - Who the fuck else knows about this – you – Baxter – come on, who else?" Curtis couldn't or wouldn't, answer him on this; he was shaking with fear, "I don't know who else knows, and that's the truth" he had whimpered.

As Comer's daydreams started to drift away, the courtroom burst back to life once again. Det. Insp. Bruce Cutler was still giving evidence. He was asked by Manfred Hendrik KC for the defence, who was it that had alerted him to the robbery, to which Cutler replied that he had been tipped off by a nark, whom he had to explain to the court, was a police term for an informer, whose name he could not reveal as it could impede upon any possible future information from this source.

An informer? Now it was all coming together, it was Baxter, thought Comer, when he had asked Curtis who else had Baxter told about this, he had said he didn't know. Of course he didn't know, Baxter would hardly have told him that he was a police informer would he – the lowest of the low? Who else knew all about the job apart from the people taking part in it, and they had no reason to grass themselves up? What a fucking pair, he mused, this bent cop, Det. Insp. Bruce Cutler and Teddy Baxter.

Comer didn't attend the trial every day, as he still had a business to run, even though a sizeable portion of it, such as black market goods and much of the printing business were on the wane by this time, due to the Government's relaxation of the wartime rationing restrictions. Money-wise he was sitting pretty, but in his line of business, he needed to be seen about town on a regular basis in order to stop other gangs from getting any ideas about muscling in on his territory, and to let the club owners and other businesses around Soho and the west end, know he was alive and well and still very much active.

Week three of the trial saw Andy Silvers being questioned by the prosecuting counsel, who put it to Silvers, that he was either telling outright lies about no other people being involved in the robbery, or that he was indeed, Mr Big himself. Comer leaned forward in his public gallery seat, anxious to hear every word of what was being said; what would be Silvers' reply to this he wondered?

He need not have worried, for once again, Silvers acted perfectly, feigning absolute disbelief at the prosecuting counsel's suggestion. "I don't know what you're talking about," he replied, "all this mister big stuff, do I look like James Cagney or something?" This brought a few sniggers from around the courtroom. When he was asked about his actual role in the robbery, he said how he had devised the plan to drug the security guards' tea, but he did not know the guards were police in disguise. He carried out his part of the operation exactly as planned, but unknown to him the fake guards did not drink their teas. While he waited for them to fall off to sleep, one of them must have opened the door and let Det. Insp. Bruce Cutler in. Before he knew what was happening Cutler and one of the policemen, grabbed him and took him to a small washroom where they tied him up and gagged him. When he was at last released, the robbery was over and the other three members of the gang had been arrested. He had no idea what had happened to the loot, as he was in police custody the whole time the raid was taking place.

The trial dragged on for another week, during which time Manfred Hendrik KC the counsel for the defence, claimed the same for all the other three defendants, with relevance to the stolen money. How could they be guilty of stealing it when they were in the warehouse the whole time? By the time the police had arrested them and taken them into custody, the three vans containing the money has completely disappeared. The jury was out for just one hour and despite the gang's excuses that they could not possibly be guilty as they were all in custody at the time, the jury found them all guilty of conspiracy to rob: they were also found guilty of using firearms in order to resist arrest. The charges of attempted murder of police officers were dropped. Billy Munro, Jimmy Black, Freddy Smith, and Andy Silvers, were all sentenced to ten years imprisonment each.

● ● ●

The trial was over, but for Comer, it was back to work as usual, and his big priority at this moment was to find Baxter, which shouldn't be too difficult, as he knew he was now working with the Deacons.

Just around the corner from the Deacons' scrap yard was a small family type pub, where Bobby and Georgie Deacon would often hold meetings with their echelons after the yard had closed for the day. It was the perfect place to meet as it wasn't known to the police as a gangland haunt at all, just a small pub filled with local people, some tradesmen, but mostly families, who knew the Deacon brothers as local businessmen, and had no idea of their other activities.

Moisha and Sonny kept an eye on the pub for a couple of nights, until they saw Baxter enter with another man, who was Mickey Reilly, the man who had introduced Baxter to the Deacons. Moisha kept watch while Sonny ran to a nearby phone-box and phoned Comer, just leaving a simple coded message, "That dog I told you about has just come in at fourteen to one" Comer understood, jumped into his Jaguar and raced over to Camberwell as quickly as he could.

By the time he got there it was dark. He parked the Jag nearby and joined Moisha and Sonny in their van. Various men kept coming out of the pub and visiting the toilet, which was outside the pub, as many were at that time. "How long's he been in there?" Comer asked. Sonny replied that it must be about two hours by now. "Must have a bleeding strong bladder," replied Comer, "hold on, that looks like him doesn't it?" They all looked up as the unmistakable, slightly limping figure of Baxter, came out of the pub and entered the toilet.

There were no lights in these outdoor toilets, and no actual toilet facilities either, or even a roof, just a tiled wall with a trough at the bottom, which acted as a urinal, with the only light reflecting from a nearby lamppost on the street. Baxter unbuttoned the flies of his trousers and let out a sigh of relief as he started to urinate against the wall. Without any warning sounds, a hand suddenly grabbed the back of his head and smashed his face against the tiles in front of him. There was cracking sound as the bone in his nose splintered and blood spurted out. Comer, Moisha and Sonny grabbed him just as he started to slide, unconscious, to the floor. Less than two minutes later they had dragged him out and thrown him in the back of their van.

When Baxter awoke he found himself tied to a chair, in another tiled room, but this time it wasn't the toilet but a small room in the public baths and washhouse, where Bert Curtis had met his fate. A single light bulb hung from a long cord over his head, while the familiar sound of the furnace roaring from nearby caused him to look towards the door, wondering where he was. His shirt-front was drenched in blood but the blood around his nose and mouth had now congealed.

The single light bulb threw a sinister shadow over Comer's face as he walked slowly around Baxter, while Moisha and Sonny stood to each side of him. There was terror in Baxter's eyes as they followed Comer from side to side, "Where am I?" he blubbered, "What the fuck's going on Jack?"

Comer looked at Baxter with contempt on his face, "You know what Baxter, you're nothing but a piece of shit aren't you – the lowest of the low, look at you, mister tough guy, blubbing like a woman" "Just tell me what I'm supposed to have done?" begged Baxter. "What you have supposed to have done?" yelled Comer, "It's not what you have supposed to have done Baxter, it's what you have fucking done – you robbed me of a hundred and seventy thousand pounds and you sit there like a sack of shit asking what you are supposed to have done?" "You've got it all wrong Jack," screamed Baxter, "a hundred and seventy grand? I've never seen that much money in my life"

Comer kicked the chair away from under Baxter, sending him crashing to the floor, he then kicked him in the stomach and continued kicking him while shouting at him, "Where is it – where's my fucking money?" Comer was panting for breath as he stopped kicking and stood back for a moment to look at Baxter, writhing in pain on the floor. "Sit him up," he ordered Moisha and Sonny, who did as their boss ordered straight away. "If you haven't got it, then tell me who has?" shouted Comer. "I don't know – I don't know – I don't know," pleaded Baxter.

"You got off light last time," growled Comer, "I thought you would have learned your lesson from that, but you didn't did you? Friends told me I should have finished you off then. You know what I think Teddy, I think you've been taking me for a mug" Baxter was shaking with fear as he looked up at Comer, whose eyes were black with rage. When he was in what his men described as one of his dark moods, they all tried to keep as far away from him as possible. Moisha watched as Comer, still breathing heavily, put his hand into the inside pocket of his jacket and took out an old fashion cut throat razor, which he calmly opened just inches away from Baxter's face. "No Jack, no, not that," screamed Baxter, "please Jack, if I knew where your money was don't you think I'd tell you? It was that bent copper, Det. Insp. Bruce Cutler, and his mate, they forced me to find out all I could about the job, he said he would nick me if I didn't - I had no option Jack, honest"

Without saying another word, Comer stepped forward and ran the razor across the left hand side of Baxter's face, from the corner of his mouth up towards his ear. So much blood gushed out that Comer had to step back sharply to avoid it catching his suit. Baxter's screams were mixed with a gurgling noise from the amount of blood in his mouth. Comer took a handkerchief from out of his pocket, and threw it to Sonny, "Shut him up with you?" Sonny obeyed immediately by stepping forward and placing the handkerchief over the gaping wound.

Comer had heard enough from Baxter, "Bung him in the van," he said to Moisha and Sonny, "take him to the Royal London Hospital and dump him outside – he needs treatment" Moisha cannot believe what he is hearing, "I hope you're kidding Jack?" he said, "you know what Baxter's like – he'll grass you up as soon as look at you – finish him off Jack, finish him off now" Comer is adamant however, after what Baxter has just received he'll be too scared to come anywhere near him again. "This is something I should have done a long time ago," he says, "I've been too soft for too long" He wants Baxter to be seen as a living testimonial as to what will happen to anyone who crosses him, and that includes the Deacons – he wants them out of Soho or they will get the same – or even worse.

Comer was now one hundred percent certain that Baxter never had any part of the missing loot. It has to be the bent copper and his mate. Will he ever get the loot back again? He doubted it very much, but he was damn sure that he would do his best to make sure they wouldn't live long enough to enjoy it. Something needed to be done about this pair, and the sooner the better.

Chapter 33

It isn't easy to spring a trap on two of Scotland Yard's top cops, especially such high profile cops as Det. Insp. Bruce Cutler, and Det. Sgt. Barry Webber, who at this moment in time, were providing some very good results for their superiors at the Yard.

Comer was eager for revenge, but he was still very busy reorganising his existing business interests. Basic rationing of food and clothing had come to an end, and there was also talk that petrol rationing was due to end in the very near future. Although he was pleased as an ordinary citizen, that life was starting to return to normality in Great Britain, it also meant a huge drop in income from his numerous enterprises involving black-market goods.

Protection had always been a good source of income for Comer, but now was the time to broaden his horizons and instead of protecting other people's clubs and spielers, he decided to protect his own. Protection is usually based on how successful a club or spieler is, but his new idea was to raise the protection money to such a high rate that it made it almost impossible for the owner to pay. Comer would then give them an ultimatum, pay him by a certain given time or they would have to forfeit their business, and it worked.

He was also starting to get a bigger gang around him once again, taking some of the people who used to work the black-market businesses and integrating them into his new protection racket. He was also employing 'civilians' as he called them, meaning non-criminal types, to work in his new clubs.

Business was most definitely looking up; he was now driving, or being chauffeured in a brand new American Cadillac, and there was no doubting in the local's minds, exactly who the king of Soho was. The 1950s was underway, and Britain was changing from a black, white and grey country of austerity and dullness, to a multi coloured country, more reminiscent of America than our old and forlorn land of yesterday. King George VI opened the Festival of Britain in London, including the Royal Festival Hall, the Dome of Discovery and the strange shaped monument known as the Skylon.

Time, they say, heals all wounds, but it definitely didn't heal the wound that Comer felt regarding the two bent coppers, not to mention his ongoing search for Billy White and the money he had stolen from him. He didn't think of these people every day, but they were never far from his thoughts. One thing Comer couldn't stand was the idea of anyone getting the better of him. He had taught Teddy Baxter his lesson on this, and had not heard from him since; the same applied to the Deacons, whom Baxter still worked for, as far he knew; not that he had taught them a lesson in any way, but he had sent out a message, and so far it seemed to be working.

• • •

Another well known saying, is that 'all work and no play, makes Jack a dull boy' and Comer's wife, Rita, was becoming increasingly concerned that her husband's workload was impeding on their family life, and indeed making him a very dull boy as far as their family life was concerned; they hadn't been out together, to a club or restaurant for many months, and he hardly spent any time with his daughter, Miriam, who was by this time, ten years old.

Comer was big, and tough, and would take no prisoners when dealing with other gangsters and villains. When he snapped his fingers, people obeyed without questioning him, everyone apart from one person, and that was Rita. He admittedly spent a great deal of time away from her, but this was his job, it was purely to earn money. He had never two-timed her by going out with other women, or even flirting with them, and he did have lots of chances to do exactly that.

He couldn't believe his eyes or his ears when he walked into his flat one Saturday afternoon and was confronted by Rita and Miriam, sitting together on the settee, with four large suitcases lined up in front of them. For one awful moment he thought Rita was leaving him, but then she broke the news that they were going on holiday. Going on holiday? But what was he supposed to do? She couldn't do this to him, just run off and leave him like this. "No," she explained, "I said we are going on holiday – you, me and Miriam"

Comer, for once in his life, was stunned into silence for a few moments as he looked firstly to Rita, and then to the happy, smiling face of his daughter. He could deal with bent coppers and vicious villains, but this delicious pair of beauties had him well and truly cornered. "Where to?" he asked. "Well I haven't been back to the old country for years and Miriam has never been there" He had to admit to himself that the prospect of spending a little time in Ireland with his family did appeal to him.

"Give me a few day to sort a few things out," he said, almost as a question. Rita smiled at him and shook her head, "I knew that is what you would say," she replied, "which is why I packed your case and sorted out your passport, just in case you're asked for it" "Alright, you win," he grinned, "I'll start sorting things out straight away and we should be ready to go by tomorrow morning, how's that suit you?" "I also booked the tickets on the boat train from Kings Cross, it leaves at six this evening"

Chapter 34

Two days later, Comer, Rita and Miriam, were ensconced in a private suite at the luxurious Shelbourne Hotel, overlooking St. Stephen's Green, in the heart of Dublin city centre. A somewhat different atmosphere and surrounding, from the last time they were in Dublin. He didn't have a regular driver in his old Beardmore taxi-cab, like he had the last time he was there, but the weather was fine and sunny, meaning they could walk around the town with ease, and when they went out at night, the hotel called a cab for them. They even went back to Jammet's Restaurant, where they had practically held their courtship; the only difference this time, was that their ten-year-old daughter now accompanied them as well.

Everything was so peaceful. This was the first time in his life that Comer could remember being able to walk down a street or sit in a restaurant without having to look over his shoulder. "You know where I want to take you?" asked Rita one morning. "I want to take you to where I grew up as a child, where my granny lived just outside County Wicklow"

The taxi took just under an hour to reach County Wicklow from their hotel in Dublin. Comer had never seen anything as beautiful before. He had travelled somewhat when he was last in Ireland, but for obvious reasons, the majority of his travels were undertaken late at night, when the scenery was not so noticeable. This was breathtaking and so green, hills, valleys, woods and the sea.

They stopped for lunch at an inn, at a village called Greystones, which the taxi driver had recommended, where they had simple and straightforward, fish and chips, washed down with a pint of Guinness for Comer, a shandy for Rita and a glass of lemonade for Miriam. From the windows of the inn, they could see the cliff tops and beyond, down to the sea. "Over that way," said Rita, pointing to their left, is where my granny's house was, the actual house isn't there any more, it was blown down in a storm about fifteen years ago" "She wasn't in it at the time was she?" replied Comer.

Rita laughed, "God, no," she replied, "granny Patricia died when I was just a child, but I do remember my parents taking me to her cottage and her teasing me about my red hair, which it was believe it or not at that time – are you sure you're not Scottish she would say" Comer smiled, "Sounds a lovely old girl, very similar to my own grandmother, or bubbe as we used to call her"

Comer looked at Rita and at Miriam, they were so similar, both beautiful and charming. He was a very lucky man. But he could see a hint of sadness in Rita's eyes as she stared out at the views outside. "Come on," he said, "you want to take us and show us where granny Patricia's cottage was don't you?"

As they walked along the narrow country lanes and through the woods, Rita told both Comer and Miriam a little about her family history. Her grandmother had been named after none other that Saint Patrick himself, "And do you know where Saint Patrick came from?" she asked. Comer didn't have a clue, "Well he was Irish wasn't he?" "He became Irish," Rita replied, but he was born in Britain, his father was Roman and his mother English. He was captured by slavers when he was just a youth and taken to Ireland where he lived for six years before escaping and returning to his family in England.

As they reached the top of a steep White, Rita stopped and pointed down towards the sea. "See that port down there, she said, "that's Inver-dea, and that beach, is Travailahawk beach, they say that when Saint Patrick escaped his captors and fled the country, that he departed from that very beach, and when he returned to Ireland years later, on a mission to spread Christianity throughout the land, he chose Travailahawk beach as the place to begin his journey.

Comer was so impressed with Rita's knowledge of her country's history, and hoped it would pass on to his daughter, who seemed to be taking a keen interest. Another ten minutes and they were at the site of granny Patricia's old cottage, which had once stood almost on the edge of a cliff, looking down to the sea. All that was left standing now was a corner section of stone wall and a few rough wooden beams, which Rita lovingly touched, as if hoping to recapture a little of the magic of her childhood in doing so.

As they walked back to the inn, Rita recalled some more of her early childhood memories to Miriam, who laughed and giggled as she took it all in, until the finally reached the inn and called a taxi to take them back to their hotel in Dublin.

The receptionist at the Shelbourne Hotel stopped Comer as they walked into the reception area and told him there had been a telephone call for him. "The gentleman didn't leave a name, but he asked you to phone this number as soon as you returned," he said, passing Comer a slip of paper. "You can use the phone on the desk, or you can use one of the private booths over there sir," he said pointing to three polished mahogany telephone booths with swing doors.

Comer mooted for the privacy of a booth, sending Rita and Miriam up to their suite first, saying he would be up in a few minutes.

Ten minutes later Comer was throwing a few things into an overnight bag as Rita and Miriam looked on in despair, "I don't want you to go daddy," cried Miriam. "See what you are doing?" Rita joined in, "She wants you here, like I do – you promised us, you said how lovely it was here, and now you suddenly spring this on us, why Jack, what is it that is so important that you abandon your wife and daughter for?"

Comer went to Rita and Miriam and put his arms around them. "I am not abandoning anyone, you know that, it's just a bit of urgent business, which I need to take care of – 'I'll be back in a day or two at the most"

Chapter 35

Moisha was driving the Cadillac through London's wet and steaming streets. It was a typical summer's evening; it had been hot and sunny all day, but then, as usual, the heavens opened up, with great explosions of thunder, which seemed to ricochet off the walls of the buildings, followed by flashes of lightening that did justice to the neon signs around Piccadilly Circus. Comer sat in the back of the car, somewhat tired after his journey. Moisha looked at him through his rear view mirror as the lightening lit up his face. "Sorry to drag you back to all this Jack," he said, "but you did tell me to get in touch if it was anything really important didn't you?"

"You did the right thing Moisha," Comer nodded, "you mentioned on the phone that it involved a lot of money – I hope it is enough to have dragged me back from Ireland?" "When you hear what I've got to tell you Jack you'll be more than pleased, believe me"

As they continued their journey, Moisha related to Comer how an old friend of his Lenny Drake, had contacted him to ask for his help. Drake runs a spieler in Stepney, which has been doing quite well recently, until one day when two high-ranking detectives paid him a visit. They told him they were arresting him and closing him down, but then one of them took him off to one side and told him that it didn't have to come to this, if he decided to play ball with them, he would have a chat to his partner and see what he could do.

It turned out that they wanted five hundred quid up front, followed by a weekly contribution from him in order to let him keep his operation up and running. "Now we come to the interesting bit" said Moisha, as he watched Comer's face in his rear view mirror, "the two coppers were none other than our dear old friends, Det. Insp. Bruce Cutler and Det. Sgt. Barry Webber.

Comer sat bolt upright in the back of the car as he heard those names. "You know what I think of that pair," he said, "but what am I supposed to do about them? This is your friend's problem not mine" "Remember I told you it involved a lot of money?" replied Moisha, "well it does, and I have a strong feeling that it just might be ours"

Moisha went on to explain that Lenny Drake had seen Cutler and Webber going in and out of an old disused warehouse along Wapping Wall. Drake didn't have a clue what they were up to, he thought that maybe they were keeping observation from there. "They don't need a warehouse to watch people from," Moisha continued, "a car, a van, an old lorry, anything – I went round there and had a look for myself, it's got big doors on the front, big enough to drive a van or lorry in – do you get what I'm saying? You reckon it was them that nicked the rest of our cash, and I think you're right, and where better to hide it? Drive the motor straight in, and it's as safe as houses – I mean, who'd think of looking in an old warehouse in Wapping?" "Let's go and have a word with your friend, Lenny Drake," Comer commanded.

● ● ●

Lenny Drake was smallish man, middle aged, and slightly balding. An ex boxer, who had at one time been a contender for the British Welterweight championship, but had his boxing licence revoked when he was charged with causing grievous bodily harm to a man by smashing a chair over his head, over a game of cards.

His club was also housed in a warehouse along Wapping Wall. For obvious reasons there were no signs outside, but unofficially it was called Drake's Drum. Unlike most spielers, it was decorated to a high standard inside, complete with soft furnishings and a well stocked bar. Comer liked what he saw, and he also liked Drake, even though his first intentions had been to kill two birds with one stone, so to speak, by getting Cutler and Webber off Drake's back, whilst at the same time, hopefully recovering the cash they had stolen from him, and then installing himself a new partner in the club.

Comer felt that Drake was a man after his own heart, a man who could keep order and was respected, a man who was willing to do whatever was necessary to keep what was his. Comer, Moisha, and Drake, all sat down and discussed the situation, after which Drake showed them around. The club was on the ground floor, with all the windows blocked up. The basement had a small door, which led out to a landing bay, directly on the Thames, where a wooden boat, fitted with an outboard motor was moored. "In case I need to make a quick getaway" chuckled Drake.

● ● ●

Two nights later and Drake's Drum was busy as usual. The big man who stood guard in the hallway heard the usual four raps, two in quick succession followed by two slow, walked to the door and peered through the spy hole. It was Det. Insp. Bruce Cutler and Det. Sgt. Barry Webber. "Good evening gentlemen," said the doorman, "you know the way through don't you?" He beckoned them to walk past him towards the gaming rooms.

"Welcome to hell, you pair of thieving bastards," boomed a disembodied voice from out of a dark recess. Cutler and Webber spun around to find two large automatic pistols stuck against their heads as Comer and Moisha stepped out of the darkness in front of them. "You can't do this," screeched Webber, "We're police officers" Moisha slid his pistol down Webber's face and shoved it hard into his still open mouth, "Shut the fuck up you ponce or you'll be biting the bullet next instead of just the barrel"

Comer grabbed Cutler by his shirt and almost threw him towards another door, with Moisha doing the same to Webber. They led the terrified policemen through the door, down the steps and into the cellar, which Drake had shown them a couple of days earlier.

"You won't get away with this Comer," yelled a very frightened Det. Insp. Bruce Cutler. "Is that right?" returned Comer as he pushed Cutler up against the wall and shoved his gun under his chin, "You thought you would get away with it didn't you?" "I don't know what you're talking about," replied Cutler, "get away with what?" "With my fucking money," screamed Comer at the top of his voice. He grabbed Cutler and dragged him towards the small door, which led to the landing bay, "Come here you fucking weasel, I want to show you something"

He pulled Cutler out onto the landing bay, where the water was lapping around the small boat, which was still moored there. "See that?" he snarled as he pointed a few yards to their right, "that is an old pub, it's been closed for a few years now, probably due to the war, it was called the Prospect of Whitby, In the 17th century, a certain judge by the name of Judge Jeffreys used to stay there, he was known as the hanging judge, he used to try pirates from there and then hang them right there on that gibbet – see it can you?" he growled as he pointed to the wooden part of a gallows with a noose still hanging from it. "I'm going to put you in this boat and take you to that gibbet and hang you, just like Judge Jeffreys did with those pirates.

Cutler's feet were hanging over the edge of the landing bay. He wasn't acting so brave now as Comer held onto him with one hand and pointed the pistol into his face with the other. "You've got it all wrong Jack," he blurted out, "if anyone nicked a part of that haul it must have been Teddy Baxter" "Is that right?" Comer answered, "if you think that, then why haven't you nicked him then? I'll tell you why shall I? It's because you are a no good lying bastard"

Cutler was panicking badly; he stumbled, almost going backwards into the river. "You can't do this Jack, there's boats going past here all the time, somebody would see me" Comer grinned an evil smirk on his face, "Look at your feet Cutler, the tide is rising already, by the time I get you on that gibbet you'll have less than half an hour before the water completely covers you and you either die through strangulation or drowning, or maybe both – no one will see you until tomorrow morning"

Cutler's eyes darted from the rising tide, to Comer and onto the gibbet and back again. "Look, we're both civilised men, surely we can talk about this? Comer smiled to himself, seems like he was getting through at last. "Exactly," he smirked, "When Judge Jeffreys used to come up against a particularly awkward bastard, something like yourself, he would give them one chance, they could either play ball with him and tell him everything they knew, in which case he would save them from the gallows and deport them to some horrible place like Australia – or they could stay schtum and he would hang them on the spot – the choice is yours Cutler?"

One minute later the trembling mess that was once Det. Insp. Bruce Cutler, the scourge of London's underworld, was spilling his heart out to Comer. He explained how he and his partner, Det. Sgt. Barry Webber, had double-crossed Baxter. Webber had arrived at the BOAC depot early and hid in a now disused air-raid shelter nearby. Armed with binoculars, he watched and waited for everything to start happening and for the vans to be loaded up. As soon as he heard the first shot, which Cutler was to fire as a signal to him, he made a dash for it, jumped in the van, ready to make a jump start with the ignition wires but was surprised to find the keys already there. He raced away as quickly as he could and drove the van directly to the warehouse at Wapping Wall, just a few buildings from where they were now standing.

"And the cash?" asked Comer. "Some has been spent; some has been transferred to bank accounts, but not too much in case anyone ever suspected, the rest is still there, hidden under some flagstones" murmured a still trembling and very dejected looking Det. Insp. Bruce Cutler. Comer felt very pleased with himself. "What we are going to do now is take a little walk, you, me, Moisha and your mate Webber – we are going to your warehouse where you are going to show us where the money is – right?" Cutler was still shaking as he nodded in agreement, "When we've showed you the money, then what's going to happen to us?" "I told you," Comer answered, "we're going to deport you, just like Judge Jeffreys used to do, won't be anywhere nice and sunny like Australia, but at least you'll have been saved from the gallows, and you won't dare come back at us, after what we now have on you"

• • •

Two hours later, Moisha drew the Cadillac to a halt outside Drake's Drum. Comer got out the car and went inside the club, leaving Moisha to wait for him.

Inside the club, Drake greeted Comer with a big smile, "Everything alright?" he asked. "Good as it'll ever be," replied Comer. "Did you warn them off?" Drake asked. "Well let's put it this way, they won't be paying you any more visits" Drake was over the moon, and asked Comer how much he owed him. "You don't owe me a penny," replied Comer, "in fact I owe you something" Comer took out a roll of white five pound notes and handed it to Drake, "Take this, there's two hundred quid there" "What the fuck is that for?" asked Drake. "We had a bit of an accident with your boat out there, what with the tide coming in and everything, it started to drift away and I threw that big old anchor and chain after it to try to stop it, but instead of stopping it, it made a bloody great hole in the boat and it ended up sinking mid stream"

Half an hour later, Moisha was once again driving the Cadillac back through the streets of west London towards Comer's flat. In his driving mirror he saw Comer lighting up one of his favourite Havana cigars. Comer had three modes of smoking; cigarettes, when he was having a quick drink or chat with someone, a decent cigar when he was having an important meeting, and his favourite Havanas when he was extremely happy about something. Tonight, Comer couldn't have been happier.

Chapter 36

"I have been worried out of my life," screamed Rita, as she faced Comer in their suite at the Shelbourne Hotel in Dublin, "one or two days at the most, is what you told me – you have been a whole fucking week Jack, a whole fucking week" Miriam looked worryingly towards her mother and then her father. "Don't worry sweetheart," Comer consoled Miriam, "your mother is just upset," he then turned to Rita, "and as for you, I am so surprised at you Rita, swearing like that, especially in front of our daughter, you know how much I hate it – real ladies are not supposed to swear" Rita swung around to face him again, her face contorted with rage, "And real gentlemen don't go running off for days at a time and lying to their wives," she screamed.

Comer took a deep breath and stared in silence at Rita for a few seconds. "Alright, maybe I should have let you know," he said, "I'm sorry, alright? Now come on, I have something I want to show you"

• • •

Just over an hour later, the taxi carrying Comer, Rita and Miriam pulled to a halt outside the ornate gates of an impressive manor house on the outskirts of the village of Greystones, in County Wicklow. Comer got out of the taxi first and opened the door on the other side, for Rita and Miriam to get out.

Rita was puzzled and impressed as she stared at the lovely old Georgian building. "Who lives here then? She asked. Comer smiled as he took out a large bunch of keys and opened the gates, "Let's go and see," he said as he led the way around the oval path towards the house. After a little more fumbling with the keys, he threw open the massive street door, allowing them to step through into the marble tiled floor of the massive hallway. Rita looked at her husband, at the almost boyish and cheeky grin on his face, could it really be, she wondered? Comer predetermined her question before she had a chance to put it into words. "It's ours," he said, "I bought it for you," he took both Rita's and Miriam's hands and led them up the stairs, "I want to show you something else"

Comer threw open the French doors in the master bedroom and stepped out onto a stone terrace. "See that, over there?" He pointed towards the sea in the distance, "Just by that clump of trees, can you see it? That is your granny Patricia's old house" Rita was so overwhelmed that tears started to roll down her face. How could she ever have doubted him?

This was to become their bolthole, their country retreat. They would keep their London home, but this was to be a place where they could go to relax, and maybe one day in the future they might even retire there.

Comer stayed for two weeks before leaving again to travel back to London, he left Rita and Miriam in County Wicklow. Rita loved their new house so much, that she couldn't wait to get it exactly as she wanted it. She was to stay in the nearby inn, where they had eaten lunch that first day, and to organise everything from there, from the decorations, to the new furnishings, and even the landscaping of the gardens, which were quite large to say the least. She was determined to make this into their house, a family house.

• • •

The ever-faithful Moisha was waiting in the Cadillac outside King's Cross railway station when Comer arrived. He had conveniently left a copy of the London Evening Standard on the back seat. "Have a look at page two," he said, indicating the paper to Comer as he pulled away.

The headline on page two read 'Mysterious Disappearance of two of Scotland Yard's top detectives' It went on to say how Det. Insp. Bruce Cutler and Det. Sgt. Barry Webber had not been seen for two weeks and that Scotland Yard have launched a special investigation into their disappearance. "Just shows you doesn't it, you can't trust anyone these days," said Comer smiling to himself, "not even the boys in blue"

Moisha drove Comer to Soho, where Sonny had gathered a few of the new team together at the Hideaway Club, which they had recently taken over. They parked the car in Soho Square and walked a couple of streets to the Hideaway. On the way, Comer couldn't help noticing how many 'girls' were on the streets; they were being propositioned almost every few yards they took. Comer was by no means a prude, but he was something of an old fashioned breed of man, who still thought there was a time and a place for everything, and he didn't like the idea of sex being sold in broad daylight on the streets of our capital city.

They turned a corner from Carlisle Street, into Dean Street, where the club was situated, and was accosted yet again by a brassy blond in a fur coat that had seen better days. "Looking for business love?" she offered as they went to walk into the club's doorway. Comer paused for a moment, by this time he was getting very angry. "Fu..," he blurted out, stopping himself from swearing at the last minute, as this was another thing he never did, swear at or in front of women. He brushed roughly past her and into the club, followed closely by Moisha.

Once inside the club, they were met by Sonny, and two new recruits, Greg Saunders and Harry Myers. After a brief discussion in which Sonny updated Comer on how well his clubs were performing, plus any problems, such as late payments and defaulters. The overall picture seemed to show a distinct drop in takings over the last few weeks. The strange thing was, that it seemed to apply only to the top end of the market, the nightclubs and dance clubs, whereas the spielers were still performing as normal.

"It is odd isn't it," said Sonny, looking around the half empty club, "Friday night, it should be packed by now, but it seems to be the same all over Soho" "Tell me something," said Comer, "I've only been away a couple of weeks, so what's happened new since I've been gone?" Sonny, Moisha and the other two, all looked at each other for an answer, which wasn't forthcoming.

"The tarts on the streets," Comer replied, in answer to himself, "they wasn't there before I went away – now they're everywhere, there was even one standing right outside here, it's no wonder ordinary decent people are being put off – can you imagine a man taking his wife out for a night out and everywhere he goes he's accosted by these old tarts?"

"There's always been prostitutes Jack," replied Sonny. "Not this many there hasn't Sonny, I saw more in our little walk from the car to here than I've seen in the last six months round here" Comer was adamant, he'd always seen himself as a protector of the people, and now, the family man as well. "Find out what you can," he ordered Moisha and Sony, "I want to know why there's suddenly so many of them, and who, if anybody, is behind it?" "And you two," he addressed Saunders and Myers, I want you out on the streets, and I want any tarts you see anywhere near our clubs, to be given strict marching orders, starting with the old brass outside here, you got me?"

• • •

It took Moisha and Sonny just two days to come up with the answers that Comer wanted. Five young men from Malta, the Messina brothers, Salvatore, Alfredo, Carmelo, Attilio and Eugene were behind it. They were importing prostitutes from Belgium, France and Spain. From the information they had gathered, the Messinas had started their operation about a year earlier in Glasgow, but had been run out of town by a local gang, and had now set up here in London. It was also said that they had police protection, but so far, this was just a rumour.

While Moisha and Sonny were gathering their evidence, the only thing that Saunders and Meyers gathered, were warnings and threats from the girls on the streets, that they were being protected by the most powerful gang London has ever known, and if they didn't leave them alone to get on with their business, they would be marked for life, or even worse.

To say that Comer was fuming at this is an understatement to say the least. He felt and looked as if he was about to explode. "They said what?" he shouted, "the most powerful gang London has ever known? I'll show those Maltese bastards who the most powerful gang is"

Although Comer's intimate gang members were relatively few in number, he could always put together a virtual army of men when needs be, and now was one of those times. He decided to flood Soho with a team so strong that even the police would steer clear of them.

He put men in teams of three or four, patrolling the streets day and night, concentrating not just on his clubs and spielers, although they were to prioritise them, but on all business premises. Their job was to make the owners aware of what they were doing, and why they were doing it. They were to tell the owners that so many potential clients were being put off from entering clubs etcetera because they had to run a gauntlet of prostitutes and other undesirables in order to enter. They were to say that once the entrance areas were cleared of these people, and kept cleared, that their businesses would see a great increase in takings. This was in all probability, true, but Comer was never one to fail to grasp a new business opportunity when it was presented to him, and this would kill two birds with one stone, by ridding him of the prostitutes, and helping him to take over more clubs at the same time.

"I want you to be firm, but fair with these tarts," Comer told his men, "I don't want them slapped around, you got me? Threaten them as much as you like, but no rough stuff – after all, it is their ponces, the fucking Messina brothers that are organising all this, and it is them who we want to hit back at"

Comer's plan worked like a treat. The sight of three or four heavies approaching the average street-walker, and threatening to make her so ugly, that no man would ever want to look at her again, let alone pay her for sex, sent most girls hurrying off as fast as their clippity-cloppity high heels would carry them. There were a few disparaging remarks from the odd girl here and there, usually thrown back over their shoulders when they had well distanced themselves from Comer's boys.

Business started to pick up at Comer's clubs and spielers, just as he had predicted, and he was also raking in a lot more cash from the other premises they were now protecting. He was in fact doing, what the police should be doing, but as he well knew, the police were being paid by the Messinas to look the other way.

It had to happen, three of his men were arrested by the police, taken to West End Central police station and charged with causing an affray and demanding money with menaces. When Comer first heard about this, he naturally thought it must be one of the club owners who had fingered his boys, but when he hired a top lawyer to defend his men, he then found out that the charges had been brought about by one of the prostitutes.

There was no way in which the police would have believed this girl, if she had indeed accused these three large men of starting a fight with her, and then, according to her, they had demanding money with menaces from her? It had taken Moisha and Sonny just a couple of days to find out who was running the prostitution racket in Soho. If they could find this out so quickly, then the police would have definitely known about it. Comer could deal with other gangs; they hit you, you hit them back, but trying to deal with an increasing number of crooked coppers was another story. The papers were still dragging up stories about the other two, Det. Insp. Bruce Cutler and Det. Sgt.

Barry Webber; had they been murdered, or had they disappeared abroad somewhere, with the proceeds of some major robbery, which had never been solved?

Only Comer knew the answer to this, which made him smile to himself when he read these stories. At the moment however, he had other things on his mind, such as the Messina brothers and their friends at West End Central.

A meeting was called at Bianchi's restaurant, where Comer set out to the closest members of his team, exactly what he wanted done. First thing was to locate the prostitute who had issued the trumped up charges against three of his men. "She's got to be made to drop those charges, and then lead us to the Messina brothers" "And what do we do when we finally come face to face with them?" asked Moisha, "kill them?" Comer shook his head, "There's more than one way to skin a cat, Moisha"

Chapter 37

Four days after the meeting at Bianchi's, a very bemused looking Duncan Webb, who was an investigative crime journalist at The People newspaper in Fleet Street, was sitting at his desk, going through a pile of letters, photos and other documents, which had been delivered in a large brown envelope to his office earlier by motorcycle courier.

Duncan Webb's self-imposed raison d'etre at The People, was to expose crime, especially organised crime, and more so if it was London related. As he ploughed through the contents of the brown envelope, if true, it was as if Christmas had come early for him this year. The documents named the five Messina brothers, Salvatore, Alfredo, Carmelo, Attilio and Eugene as the men who were running the Soho vice rackets, and controlling organised prostitution in the west end of London. There were photos of many of the street girls, taken while they were actually plying their trade and importuning perspective clients on the streets of London.

The documents went on to say that the Messina brothers were importing the girls from Continental Europe and supplying them with fake passports. Most importantly there were also signed letters from over 40 prostitutes, which revealed how the Messina brothers and their henchmen forced the girls to work, supplied them with only a fraction of the money they took from clients and dished out regular beatings to them.

The last document in the envelope was a brief letter, which Comer had written, stating that top police officers were also involved in this, and were protecting the Messina brothers, but he had great faith in Mr Webb to take this matter very seriously and expose these evil people through his paper. Comer signed the letter, 'a friend' and ended by saying he would be in touch.

Duncan Webb had no idea who could have sent him all this information, someone wanting to clear up Soho of its seedy image? A local businessman or group perhaps, wanting to protect their interests, or even a local priest? He never dreamt it could have been Jack Comer, boss of the London underworld.

No newspaper hack worth his salt would publish a story without investigating it fully to start with. This had all the hallmarks of being possibly one of, if not the biggest story Webb had ever laid his hands on, but with just an unsigned letter and a promise that the author would be in touch, left him like the proverbial boatman, up a creek without a paddle.

Webb needed corroboration from an independent source, confirming that there was some truth to these allegations. He couldn't possibly interview all these prostitutes on his own, and photos of them working the streets, proved nothing. The big story would be that the Messina brothers were controlling these girls and bringing them over from the Continent to work for them in their vice empire in London. In the old days he would have approached people such as Billy White, who was then running organised crime in London. Duncan Webb had met Billy White several years earlier, when White was known as the number one man in Soho. Billy White had approached Webb with an offer to let him write a story on him entitled 'King of the London Underworld' Half of which would be complete fiction of course, which White intended using as a publicity tool for his ever growing empire.

White and Webb got on well and became close friends, but White suddenly disappeared a few years ago and was thought by some to have been murdered and his body dumped at sea. This was of course a self-publicised myth, which he wanted the police to believe in, and which they indeed did, with a little help from Duncan Webb's weekly crime column.

Rumour had it that Jack Comer was the new crime Tsar in London, but Webb had never met him, and from what he had heard of him, he didn't particularly like him either. This left him at a somewhat lose end with regard to this story, but if the worst came to the worst, he would have to do what most journalists do, and insert the odd 'allegedly' and 'possibly' here and there in the story. Not perfect by any means, but better than nothing.

● ● ●

Almost a week had gone by since Comer has sent the package to Duncan Webb. Would he go with it, he wondered? The People newspaper came out on a Sunday, so for now it was a matter of keeping his fingers crossed and waiting to see. Comer was doing his usual Tuesday morning tour of his empire, 'putting himself about' as he liked to call it. If they don't see you for a few weeks you're as dead as last week's papers. He had arranged for Moisha to meet him on the corner of Frith Street at 11 am, but now finding that he had twenty minutes to spare, he decided to have a shave in Tony's barber shop just a few doors along from the corner of Frith Street.

Tony had jut finished lathering him up and was giving his razor a few more strops on the leather belt, which hung beside the washbasin. The gentle sound of the razor being slapped up and down the leather belt was very relaxing, almost sending him to sleep, but through his half closed eyes, he stared into the mirror in front of him and saw the reflection of a man walk past outside. Tony lifted the razor, ready to start the shave, when Comer sat up with a jolt, "Who was that?" he blurted out as he leapt up out of the chair and ran to the door of the shop. With the white overall still tied around him and the shaving foam still on his face, he rushed out into the street, but the figure had now disappeared into the crowds.

Half an hour later Comer was striding through Soho Square with Moisha by his side. "It was Albert Redman, definitely, I'd know that swagger anywhere" Moisha took a sideways glance at his boss, "He'd be taking a bit of a chance wouldn't he, being seen right here in Soho?" Comer nodded, more to himself than to what Moisha had just said. "What worries me," he answered "is that Redman hasn't got the bottle to do anything on his own – if he's here, then White can't be far away – we've got enough problems with these fucking Maltese ponces at the moment. I've got a big score to settle with Billy White, but I could do without him being back on the scene until we've sorted these fucking Messina brothers out"

• • •

A black cab pulled up outside The People's newspaper office in Fleet Street. A very dapper and suntanned Billy White got out and walked into the main doors of the building. A few minutes later, he was being shown into Duncan Webb's office. "Mr White to see you sir," announced the receptionist as she ushered him in. Webb looked up from his desk and was visibly taken aback as he saw his old friend, Billy White standing before him. "Fuck," he stumbled, as he realised who it was, "Billy – Billy White, how long you been back in the country?"

"Just got back yesterday," replied White. Duncan Webb wasn't a fool by anyone's standards; he knew that Billy White hadn't just casually dropped in to see him to renew old friendships. White was a very shrewd character, who had been living abroad somewhere for the past few years. Just got back yesterday, and his first port of call was his office? As shrewd as White was, Webb considered himself to be a cut above; White needed him, otherwise he wouldn't have been there, but Webb was going to use White to get what he wanted.

"So what can I do for you Billy?" White settled back in his seat, lit a cigarette and explained that he had been living in the South of France for some time, where he had several very successful business interests on the go, "Or should I say, were very successful, until this latest bloody government took over, they're Communists, you know what I mean? They can't stand seeing anyone earning an honest living, and that is exactly what I was doing"

Duncan Webb smiled to himself, he could hardly believe his own ears, Billy White, earning an honest living? Now that was something new. "So, you still haven't told me," replied Webb, "where do I fit into all this?" White lit another cigarette and told him that he had been planning for some time to re-open his business interests here in London, and had put a few feelers out, to find out how the land lies before making his final move.

"What I have been hearing," White went on, "is that Jack Comer is touting himself as the boss of the underworld here, and I thought to myself, that if anyone knows the truth about this it has to be you?"

So this was White' plan, thought Webb, to take over as boss of the London underworld once again, and he wanted Webb's help in achieving that goal. He didn't need to ask Webb about who was in charge, anyone in Soho could have told him that. "Of course it's true Billy," Webb replied, "everyone in Soho knows Comer's the guvner, I mean what opposition has he got? You've been away; and from what I've been hearing, there's been no one else to seriously challenge him"

White became a little agitated at Webb's comments. "Alright, alright, I'll get straight to the point," he said, "we both know that you can be more powerful than the old Bill when you put your mind to it, I remember the way you smashed the north London smash and grab gang with just one article in your paper, so that is exactly what I want you to do with Jack Comer and his mob – write an expose on them, I want you to send him running – out of London, out of the fucking country, like I had to do"

Duncan Webb knew this is what White had come to see him about, and he knew that White would pay him handsomely if he cooperated. I'd like to help you Billy," he said, but firstly, I am in the middle of a major story concerning a vice ring, who are operating here in London, and secondly, I would need plenty of back up, witness statements etcetera, to show to my editor before he would give me the go ahead to tackle someone as big as Comer"

"Don't you worry about that, I'll get you all the back up and witnesses you need to nail Comer," said White waving his hand as if swatting a fly away from himself. "But, like I said Billy," replied Webb, "I'm right in the middle of this vice ring story, which I need to get out of the way before I can tackle Comer, if you can help me with this, regarding witnesses etcetera, then I am sure we can work together on the Comer thing"

A big smile broke out across Billy White' face. He got to his feet and held his hand out to Webb. "No problem at all Duncan, you just give me these rats' names and I'll dig up so much shit on them that your story will be the hottest thing in town by next week" Duncan Webb smiled to himself as the two men shook hands, round one to me.

Chapter 38

Comer was receiving daily phone calls from Rita, updating him on how the house in Ireland was coming along. Two bathrooms she had installed. Two? When he was growing up in east London, nobody had the luxury of a bathroom. They had a tin bath, which his father would occasionally use, but the general rule of thumb for Comer, his friends and family, was a weekly trip to the public baths, where they had to call out to the attendant, 'more hot water (or cold) in number six', or whatever number one happened to be in. To add a bit of fun to the event, the kids would often call out for more hot water in somebody else's bath, which would be quickly followed by a flurry of expletives from the poor gent concerned.

Rita seemed to be ordering two of everything, as well as the bathrooms, she had ordered two telephones, and two television sets. Comer couldn't remember the last time he watched one television set, let alone two. He preferred his radiogram and listening to his Jazz records. The biggest surprise she sprung on him, was when she told him that she had been taking driving lessons, and had applied to take a driving test. He had never bothered to apply for a driving licence himself, not that it stopped him driving. Would she also order two cars, he wondered?

"When are you coming over?" she asked, "I want you to see everything I've done, and I want you to help chose the wallpaper for your study" This was definitely not something he could get excited about. He liked good quality, traditional furnishings, but when it came to wallpaper and curtains he considered that to be a woman's expertise. "I want to leave all that side of things to you darling," he said, "you are so much better than me at that sort of thing" He explained that he was in the middle of a big business deal, and would definitely be paying a visit to Ireland as soon as he had everything tied up.

• • •

Two weeks later Comer sat in Barney's Café in Petticoat Lane, having breakfast with Moisha and Sonny. "How about this then?" he exclaimed, as he slapped the People newspaper down on the table in front of them, "look at that headline," he pointed at the large lettering in the paper, which read 'Arrest these five men' complete with photos of Salvatore, Alfredo, Carmelo, Attilio and Eugene Messina beneath it, complete with a sub-headline stating, 'Five debased men with an empire of vice which is a disgrace to London' followed by the full article.

Comer was ecstatic with joy about the article. "Their friends in the old Bill won't be able to ignore this lot will they, maybe now we can start getting down to business again?" Sonny however, wasn't quite as overjoyed about the article as his boss seemed to be. "Not quite as simple as that Jack," he added, "even if we do get rid of the Malts, we still have the other mob back on the scene" Comer looked quizzically at Sonny, "What do you mean, what other mob?" "I'm talking about White's mob, you saw Albert Redman for yourself the other week, now I've had several reliable reports that White and Redman have been seen together in a number of clubs throughout the west end, which could spell trouble for us – he's not back in London for his health Jack, that's for sure"

Sonny was right and Comer knew it, but at the moment he had to take things in the order they presented themselves, and his priority was to make sure the Messina brothers were well out of his way, before declaring yet another gang war. Billy White wouldn't be so easy to deal with as the Messinas.

Comer flooded Soho with his presence by rounding up every available man he could and putting them out onto the streets and clubs. "Put my name about everywhere," he told them, "I want everyone to know who's in charge, you got me?" This was like a two-pronged attack, one prong on the Messinas and the second prong there to warn Billy White.

● ● ●

While all this was happening, Duncan Webb was strutting about town, like a pig in clover. He had had a major coup with his article on the Messina brothers, and was waiting to hear the latest from his accomplice in crime, Mr Billy White. Although he saw himself as a very successful journalist, the rest of Fleet Street didn't exactly see him in the same light. As far as they were concerned, he was known as a 'band wagon journo' who created his own 'sensational' stories and then jumped on them with a vengeance, instead of reporting on real life, every day stories like real journalists did. Consequently, he didn't find a very warm welcome in the Fleet Street pubs, where they all gathered and swapped stories, instead opting for west end pubs, where he was nearly always welcomed.

About a week after the article on the Messina brothers had been published, Webb had been drinking in the George pub on D'Arblay Street, Soho, one evening. He felt a little the worse for wear as he left the pub, and started to make his way towards Tottenham Court Road Tube Station. He cut through Carlisle Street towards Soho Square, and suddenly heard the sound of a car engine, revving up from somewhere behind him. He looked over his shoulder to see a dark saloon car racing towards him, with its headlights on full beam, almost blinding him.

Webb had been crossing the street when he heard the car; he quickly jumped out of its path and onto the nearby kerb, allowing the car to pass him and slam on its breaks a few feet in front of him. This was no accident; he could see two men inside the car as it now started to reverse back again. They were out to get him.

Any earlier feelings of drunkenness had now suddenly passed as he ran across the road to Soho Square; just managing to dodge a passing taxi as he did so. From behind him he heard the sound the saloon car's tyres screeching on the road surface as it raced around the corner; its headlights were now directly behind him, illuminating his elongated shadow onto the pavement in front of him.

The car made a bumping noise as it mounted the pavement; the noise from its engine was now so close that he could feel it almost touching him. Webb made a dive for the gateway into the Square's gardens, with seconds to spare as the car scraped along the railings, causing sparks to fly off, like a giant firework, the wing and side of the car crumpled and finally came to a halt when the bumper became entangled in the railings.

As Webb made his getaway through the gardens, he realised how lucky he was; these people were trying to kill him, and if it hadn't been for the recently re-erected iron railings, which now surrounded the square once again, after the old ones had been torn down for the war effort, he would now be dead.

● ● ●

Two days after the attempted murder of Duncan Webb, Greg Saunders, who was one of Comer's latest recruits, was doing his usual twice weekly workout in Jack Solomons Gym in Great Windmill Street, Soho. Saunders was very well built, and a very promising boxer until he, much like Lenny Drake, was convicted of an assault a year earlier and promptly lost his boxing licence.

He still liked to keep fit and was a regular at the gym, and a good friend of Freddie Mills, the British light heavy weight champion. On this particular day however, Freddie Mills wasn't there, but the American, Joey Maxim was, who was about to fight Mills for the world title at Earls Court.

It was particularly busy at the gym, with press and photographers in abundance, as one would expect with someone like Maxim training there. This didn't worry Saunders, he kept to himself, over to one side of the gym, usually skipping or using the punch ball.

By 5 pm the gym was so packed that Saunders decided to call it a day. The usual smell of liniment pervaded the air in the changing room, which was empty, as everyone was so interested in what was going on outside with Joey Maxim. There wasn't any shower, but Saunders had just had a quick wash down, changed back into his suit, and was combing his hair, as another smell wafted up and overtook the liniment; it was the smell of cigar smoke.

Saunders looked into the mirror in front of him and saw the reflections of two large men standing behind him, one with a cigar. "We've been watching you," said the man with the cigar, "you've got a good physique, and you move well, are you a professional boxer?" There were often people like this hanging around in Jack Solomons Gym, managers, would be managers, talent scouts, Saunders was used to it. "Not any more," he answered, "I gave it up a couple of years ago, I just like to keep fit now" The man with the cigar nodded his head thoughtfully, "Keep fit for what?" he asked, "what is it exactly that you do for a living Mr er what did you say your name was?"

Saunders tucked his comb into the top pocket of his jacket, picked up his holdall and turned to face the two men. "I didn't say what my name was," he replied, with more than a touch of anger in his voice, "and while we're at it, why do you want to know, and who the hell are you two?" The second man stepped forward, almost touching Saunders, "No need to get angry," he said, in what sounded very much like an Italian accent, "we just wanted to help you that's all" Saunders didn't like the sound of this, it sounded more like an underlying threat than an offer of help, and help for what, he thought, "I don't need any help thanks," he replied, as he pushed past the two men and headed for the door.

Joey Maxim was leaning against the ropes of the boxing ring and answering questions thrown to him by the journalists. He must have made some sort of joke as everyone was laughing as Saunders passed on his way to the exit. A very steep flight of stairs led down from the gym to the street. Saunders was pleased to be getting out of there; he didn't particularly like crowds, and he was still somewhat worried about the two men; who they were, and what they really wanted.

He was just a quarter of the way down when a foot was shoved into his back and sent him tumbling head over heels down the stairs towards the street below. There was no way he could stop himself, it was so steep and so narrow, with no handrail that he could grab onto. He finally ended up at the bottom, flat on his face. The two men whom he has spoken to earlier were running down the stairs closely behind him. As they reached him, the one with the cigar stamped on his outstretched hand and ground his heel in until he heard the bones crunching beneath his foot. "Oh dear I am sorry," he said, "I hope that wasn't the hand you hit our girls with was it? Don't forget to give our regards to Mr Comer won't you?"

● ● ●

Comer paced up and down like a man possessed. Greg Saunders, who had his right arm in a sling, and a large dressing on the side of his head, sat on a sofa opposite him, in the bar area of the Hideaway Club. It was just after 7 pm. There were no customers in the club yet, just Comer, Saunders, Moisha, Sonny, and Harry Myers. "I never hit any of those tarts Jack, you should know me better than that, I wouldn't do it, I would never hit a woman"

Comer felt like he was hyper ventilating; he could hardly get his words out. "I'm not saying you did Greg," he wheezed as he spoke, "they are the ones who said that, not me, but what I'd like to know is how come they connected me to this, none of those tarts knew who you were, and they certainly wouldn't have known you worked for me, which means that someone has grassed us up to the Messinas"

"Don't forget the Messinas are supposed to have some tame old Bill on their team," added Sonny, "and they must have been getting a fair whack from them" "Sonny's right," answered Moisha, "I also heard on the grapevine that someone tried to run that newspaper geezer over, and now this, it has to be the old Bill" Comer ruminated on this. It made sense, the dodgy coppers would obviously know that he rules the London underworld, and now they lose a big source of their income. One of Comer's pet theories was that if you gave a copper two crimes, and then added another two; they would almost certainly come up with five.

With all the publicity the newspaper article had generated the police knew there was nothing they could legally do about it, so they get their own back on the newspaper hack and the Comer gang by employing a third party to do their dirty work for them, the big problem was, who was that third party?

"There's only one thing we can do," stated Comer, "the Messinas haven't been nicked yet, so we wage all out war on them immediately – they can't be that hard to find – watch the tarts on the streets, see who's looking after them, it won't be the Messinas themselves, but they should lead us to them"

The plan was put into action in less than an hour; Comer had twenty of his men out on the streets, watching the girls and scrutinising every man who spoke to them. It was difficult to tell who the majority of the men were; they could be potential clients or they just might be one of the Messinas men, they couldn't question every man the girls spoke to. A bowler hat and a rolled umbrella however did help to identify a lot of the men as most definitely not from the Messina clan.

When two large men in camel overcoats and trilby hats spoke to one girl in Dean Street, and pushed her roughly into a doorway, Harry Myers had a good idea he was onto something. Myers was with Dumpsy Davis, a short but stocky, new recruit to the mob. "I want you to run as fast as you can to the corner of Frith Street and Old Compton Street where you'll see Jack and Moisha, get them to come back here straight away"

Dumpsy took off as fast as he could move his little legs, while Myers continued to watch the two men and the prostitute. He saw one of them give her a back handed slap across her face. These were most definitely not potential clients.

The two men moved off along Dean Street, in the direction of Soho Square, with Myers following at a safe distance, while frantically looking over his shoulder all the time to see when Dumpsy would return with Comer and Moisha. On the corner of Dean Street and Bateman Street, the two men stopped to talk to another girl. Myers ducked into a doorway and watched as one of the men grabbed the girl's handbag, rifled through it and took out a small wad of banknotes. He then laughed as he threw the bag back into her face.

Myers was no big fan of the street girls; in fact he played a large part in helping to clear them from outside their clubs and spielers, but he never used violence towards them and hated anyone who did. He felt like running across the street and clubbing these two oafs there and then, but then he spotted Comer Moisha and Dumpsy, hurrying along the street to catch up to him.

"There they go," said Myers, pointing at the two men as they crossed the street and turned into a narrow alley called St Anne's Court, which connects Dean Street with Wardour Street. Comer spurted across the street, with the others closely behind him. "Oi, you two," he shouted, "stop there, I want to talk to you" Both the men looked around as they heard him call out; one said something to the other one and they started to run. Comer may have been a big man but he was also very fit and quickly started to catch up with the men, while Moisha and Dumpsy did their best to keep up.

Comer shouted again at the top of his voice, "Stop I said" The first man came to a sudden halt and spun round like a car doing a handbrake turn. When the second man saw what his partner was doing, he also stopped. By this time Comer was almost upon them, with Moisha and Dumpsy now making ground. "I want to talk to you" Comer snapped as he now faced the two men. The first man, who was the shorter of the two, suddenly whipped out a switch-blade-knife from his pocket, clicked on the button to reveal the blade; six inches of gleaming steel, which was now headed directly towards Comer's chest.

"Get out of the way Jack" shouted Moisha from somewhere behind Comer, as he shoved him as hard as he could and sent him tumbling, almost falling, into a nearby doorway. At the same time, Moisha threw a metal dustbin, which he was holding above his head, directly into the face of the man with the knife. The bin hit the man with such force that it sent him crashing to the ground, completely unconscious, with blood spurting from his nose, which looked like it was broken. The second man looked right, and then left, not sure what to do as Dumpsy threw himself on him and pinned him down, while both Comer and Moisha also dived in.

For a short man Dumpsy certainly knew how to handle himself, with his legs astride the big man's chest he sent a flurry of punches, left then right, then left again, knocking the man's head from side to side. "Hold on, hold on," Comer yelled, "I don't want him dead, I want to be able to talk to him"

Moisha stepped in and grabbed the man by the lapels of his overcoat, pulling him to his feet and propping him up against the wall. "The guvner wants to speak to you," he said, "so just be a good boy – do what you are told, and we might let you live to tell the tale"

"First of all," growled Comer to the man propped up against the wall, "do you know who I am?" The man looked somewhat bewildered and shook his head, "I've never seen you before in my life," he answered. "Is that right? Well here's another name for you to conjure with – Greg Saunders – does that name ring a bell?" The man shook his head again, "I've never seen you and I've never heard of this Greg Saunders whoever he is," he answered, somewhat cockily this time. Comer backhanded him hard across the face, "Don't get cocky with me son," he hissed at the man, "or I'll rip your fucking tongue out of that ugly head of yours, now just think carefully before you answer this next question, because this could well be your last chance – the Messina brothers, I want to know where I can find them?"

The man was now visibly shaking as he stared back at Comer and Moisha to his right, while at the same time Dumpsy gave a kick to the man on the floor, who was starting to regain consciousness, and rested his foot on the man's chest.

Comer reached into his pocket, took out his 38 automatic and rammed the barrel almost up inside the man's nostrils. "I won't ask you again," he snarled, "you have five seconds left – four –three –two "Alright, alright," the man pleaded, swallowing hard as he did so, "I'll tell you, I'll tell you – they have a flat in Brook Street in Mayfair, number forty two" "That's better," said Comer, smiling as he took the gun away from the man's nose, "but just in case you get any silly ideas about warning the Messinas that we about to pay them a visit, maybe this will make you think twice about it"

Comer fired two shots, up close into both men's knees. "Let's go," he said, indicating to his men to follow him, continuing through St Anne's Court towards Wardour Street, with the men's agonising screams echoing in their ears as they went.

Chapter 39

It was almost midnight when the Cadillac pulled up outside number forty two Brook Street, Mayfair, followed closely by another car, which had another four of Comer's men in it. Number forty two was a large, imposing house, looking more like a block of flats than a single house. Comer looked up at the house, through the window of the car; the only light showing in the house was from the hallway. "Looks like they're either having an early night," he said, "or they're out – only one way to find out" Comer got out of the car, indicating for Dumpsy to go with him. "Park the car around the corner somewhere," he ordered Moisha.

Comer motioned to Sonny, who was just getting out of the second car. After a brief conversation, three more men got out of the second car and joined Comer and Dumpsy, while Sonny got back in the car and followed the rout Moisha had taken.

Two minutes later, Dumpsy, who probably looked less like a gangster than any of the others, was standing at the door of the house, while Comer and all the others were lined up to each side of the door, out of sight to anyone who might open the door.

Dumpsy rang the doorbell and waited. He rang again, and finally heard a noise from within the house somewhere. "Who is it? said a disembodied voice from behind the door somewhere. Dumpsy looked round towards Comer, who gave him a nod. "I'm from the Gas Board sir," Dumpsy called out in answer to the voice behind the door, "sorry to disturb you this late, but we have detected a gas leak coming from somewhere in your house – would you please open the door sir, we need to check this as a matter of some urgency"

The sound of several bolts being thrown back and a lock being turned signalled the fact that the huge door was about to be opened. The elderly man who opened the door was puffing and breathless as he peered out at Dumpsy. "You had better come in," he said. "Mr Messina?" Dumpsy enquired. "No, I'm just the caretaker," the man replied as he let Dumpsy into the house. As the man said this, Comer and the rest of the gang barged their way in. "Where are they?" Comer shouted, "the Messina brothers, where are they?"

Comer didn't believe the caretaker, if he was indeed who he said he was. He grabbed the man and practically lifted him off his feet as they all surged forward and raced up the stairs. "There's no one here, look, see for yourself" pleaded the caretaker as he was pushed from room to room. "Where are the Messina brothers?" Comer shouted again at the now very frightened man.

The caretaker explained that he had never heard of the Messina brothers. "I was sent here by the agency," he explained, "to look after the place after the last tenants had suddenly moved out about a week ago"

By this time it was obvious that no one was living there and the man was a caretaker, but if this was true, thought Comer, then why were those two heavies still collecting for the Messinas, and why were the Messinas attacking his men and trying to kill the newspaper hack?

After Comer was completely satisfied that every inch of the house had been thoroughly searched, he ordered everyone out and back to their cars. Just before leaving he took two crisp white five pound notes from out of his wallet and stuffed them into the caretaker's hand. "Here," he said, as he handed him the money, "take this and forget everything that happened OK?" The caretaker nervously bundled the money into his trouser pocket, "Thank you," he answered with a nervous smile on his lips.

● ● ●

The Golden Guinea Club in Swallow Street, by Piccadilly was an upmarket club that Comer had had his eyes on for some time, but because of its political and other connections, he had found it impossible to work his way into. Its clientèle was made up from the upper echelons of British society, businessmen, politicians; it was even rumoured to have Royalty on its membership list.

At 12.45 am precisely, a somewhat battered Austin van with Arthur Pullen, Wines and Spirits, painted on the side, pulled up just a few yards along from the Golden Guinea's entrance. Two men, one carrying a wooden box and both wearing brown overall type coats and cloth caps, got out and walked towards the club. They paused for a moment close to a doorway next to the club, where the man carrying the box opened the lid to reveal four wine bottles inside, but instead of corks, they had pieces of rag stuffed into each one.

The first man placed the wooden box down on the pavement and gave a knowing nod to the second man, who quickly took out his Ronson cigarette lighter and quickly put the flame to the petrol soaked rags, which were stuffed into the necks of the bottles. The rag went up in flames immediately and the men grabbed two bottles each and ran as fast as they could towards the Golden Guinea and threw the flaming Molotov cocktails into the entrance, where they burst as they landed, spraying the elaborate entrance and curtains with petrol that exploded like an erupting volcano into a ball of flames.

The two men turned and ran, throwing themselves into their van, not even having time to close the doors properly as they accelerated away with the tyres screeching as it made it to the end of the street and turned right onto Piccadilly and headed in a westerly direction. By pure coincidence, Comer's Cadillac and the other car containing his men, were travelling on the same road, but going in the opposite direction, passing each other without knowing it.

● ● ●

The shrill sound of the phone ringing woke Comer early the following morning; it was Moisha, "Have you seen the papers?" Christ, doesn't he sleep at all? Comer looked at his watch, which was lying on the bedside table beside him, it wasn't even eight thirty, he would hardly have had time to see any papers. "The Mirror, The Sketch, The Telegraph, they are all full of it," blurted out Moisha's distorted voice down the phone, "Gang War in London, two men shot in Soho, and listen to this, Top West End Night Club Firebombed"

Twenty minutes later, Comer looked at his reflection in the bathroom mirror as he shaved. He thought the world of Moisha; he was his right hand man, but if only he wouldn't get up so bloody early in the mornings. Another ten minutes and he was ready to go, dressed in a dark blue single-breasted suit, and light grey tie. He placed his grey fedora on his head, gave one last approving look at himself in the mirror and headed downstairs to where Moisha was now waiting for him in the Cadillac outside.

"Soho?" asked Moisha as he pulled the big car away from the kerb. "No," replied Comer, as he settled down in the back of the car and started thumbing through the papers, which Moisha had conveniently left on the seat for him to see, "from what I can see here, the law will be all over the place around there, take me to Barney's in the lane, we'll phone Sonny from there"

Barney's café was as noisy and busy as ever, even though it wasn't Sunday, when Petticoat Lane was in full swing. There was still the usual throng of stallholders and market porters from the nearby Spitalfields Market. Comer, Moisha and Sonny sat at a window table, where they could keep watch on who was coming and going.

People in the know, knew that Sonny was a close associate of Jack Comer, but he had an air of nonchalance about him, which set him apart from the usual gangsters and heavies who inhabited the darker side of Soho. When Comer walked into a club, all eyes would be on him, the level of conversation would automatically drop to a lower level; it had often been said that he had an air of menace about him. Sonny on the other hand, was accepted by most people as a friendly face, rather than a threatening one. It was because of his general demeanour that he became Comer's eyes and ears of what was happening in and around Soho.

Comer's instructions to Sonny, was to find out exactly who was behind a number of things, starting with the firebombing of the Golden Guinea club, followed by who had attacked Greg Saunders and why? And if the Messinas had really done a runner, then why were two of their boys still collecting for them?

Sonny wasted no time in putting himself about in Soho; clubs, spielers, cafés, pubs, anywhere in fact that the denizens of Soho would gather. It is surprising what a round of drinks here and there can do to loosen people's tongues. By the end of the day, he had learned more about what was happening in Soho, than a team of police officers would learn in two months.

Firstly, the Messinas had quietly skipped the country on a tip off from their tame detectives in the Met that Scotland Yard were about to pounce on them. There were varying reports about which country they had fled to, but the top betting was on France, somewhere near Paris, from where they were still allegedly running their empire.

One thing that didn't add up was the beating of Greg Saunders at Jack Solomons Gym, where the two men responsible had spoken to Saunders, and accused him of inflicting injuries on 'their' girls, which obviously meant the Messinas girls. The big problem with this, was that the Messinas had already left the country before this attack had taken place, so why would they have bothered to send a couple of heavies to hand out a beating to someone who never actually touched any of the girls? The Messinas by this time, would have had a lot more on their minds to worry about than organising the beating one of Comer's men.

The firebombing of the Golden Guinea club was also a mystery, which no one admitted knowing anything about, but it was now a well known fact throughout Soho, that Albert Redman was most definitely back, and, according to some, had been seen in the company of his old boss, Billy White. Could they have been behind the firebombing? This seemed very likely, but then Sonny found something else out, which really worried him. Their other old adversary, Teddy Baxter, along with Bobby and Georgie Deacon had also been spotted on the Soho scene again, and were apparently not only offering their fruit machines to the clubs, but also their protection to go with them. This was like a double-edged sword, with Billy White' mob on one side and the Deacons on the other.

Chapter 40

Sonny and Moisha were sitting opposite Comer in the lounge of his London flat, where Sonny had come to report what he had found out. "From what you have said," mused Comer, "I reckon that whole thing with Greg being attacked at Jack Solomons Gym was a complete set-up, all that crap about crushing his hand because it was the hand he had hit their girls with, with the big emphasis on 'their' girls. Firstly, Greg never hit any girls, and secondly, why would they give the game away by saying 'their' girls?"

Moisha looked slightly puzzled, "I'm not really with you on this one Jack – you say it was a set up, a set up for what?" Comer looked across to Sonny, "Haven't you told him Sonny?"

Sonny wasn't used to talking about their business unless he was specifically asked to by his boss. He took out a packet of Craven A cigarettes and thoughtfully lit one before explaining to Moisha exactly what he had learned was now happening in and around Soho, with Billy White's mob and the Deacon brothers both moving in at the same time.

"Whoever it was that done Greg, wanted me to think it was the Messinas," Comer interjected, "force us to start a war with the Messinas, place a few choice stories with a bent copper here and there, and before you'd know it, we'd have all been nicked, leaving Soho ripe for them to step in – what they obviously didn't know, was that by the time they gave Greg that beating, the Messinas had already done a runner"

"I see what you mean now Jack," Moisha answered, "and from what you say, it was well planned, which make me think it has to be Billy White. The Deacon brothers are a tough little mob, but I don't think they are that well organised to set something up like this" Comer nodded, "I agree with you one hundred percent Moisha – White already owes me a bundle of money, I think now's the time to hit that double crossing little rat so hard that he'll never bounce back again"

"But what about the Golden Guinea?" Sonny butted in, "no one seems to know anything about that – do you reckon that was White as well trying to set us up for that as well?" Comer nodded thoughtfully, "That's just what we are about to find out"

As if on cue, the door opened and Rita and Miriam walked into the room. "Would you like me to make you all some tea?" Rita asked. Comer smiled as he looked across the room at his beautiful wife and daughter; he was so proud of both of them and it showed as he got to his feet and embraced them both. "Look at them," he said proudly to Moisha and Sonny, who hadn't seen either of them for about a year or more, "how did I end up with two such beautiful ladies?"

Moisha got to his feet and took Miriam's hands in his, "Look at you," he said, "so grown up, and so lovely" "Thank you," said Miriam, smiling shyly. "How old is she now Jack," asked Sonny" Comer gave Rita another hug, "If you're talking about Rita," he said, "you should know better than to ask a woman her age, but if it's Miriam you're asking about, I can tell you as a father, that she's eleven years old now and top of her class in school"

"Top of her class?" Moisha chipped in, "Where does she go to school round here?" "She goes to school in Ireland," Comer replied, they have some first class schools there, much better than the one I went to here in the east end," he laughed, "and she's not the only clever one, Rita's turned her hand to interior decorating, and has been doing up our house over there, and from the photos I've seen, she's doing a great job of it"

Rita smiled radiantly at all the compliments both Miriam and her were getting, Jack usually kept this type of thing for when he was alone with her and Miriam, it was no nice to see him relaxing and speaking out as a family man, which he didn't normally do in front of friends. "You still didn't tell me if you wanted tea or not?" she asked again. Comer told her no, he had an important business meeting to attend. He gave both Rita and Miriam a kiss and then reverted to being the boss once again as he turned to Moisha and Sonny, "come on," he said, "we have to go"

• • •

Once outside, Comer told Moisha to take him to The People newspaper offices in Fleet Street, "In the meantime I want you and Sonny to get over to Soho and round up as many of the boys as possible, get them altogether at Bianchi's. I'll get a taxi back from Fleet Street and see you all there about twelve thirty"

Comer had not told anyone about the information he had sent to Duncan Webb regarding the Messinas, and he wanted to keep it that way; as far as he was concerned, even Duncan Webb himself didn't know that the information had come from him.

The reason for his visit this day however, did not concern the Messinas at all; today's visit was in relation to Billy White. Comer had thought long and hard about this and was more determined than ever not to give up one single iota of his hard won empire to White. Put yourself in White' shoes, he had told himself, he wants us out the way so he can take over Soho – what would I do if I was him? I could wage an all out gang-war against us, which would be very dangerous, and would bring too much attention to him, or I could get some crooked copper to fit us up, but again that would involve a lot of work and trumped up evidence, which the copper would have to be able to back up in court, and as White has been out of the country for so long, where would he and his tame copper get all this evidence from? There is of course another way, and that is to do what I did with the Messinas, and get Duncan Webb on his side, and that wouldn't be difficult at all as he already knows Webb, who did a big self promotion article on him some years ago.

There was only one way Comer was going to find out the truth about any sort of White, Webb collaboration, and that was to do exactly what he was now doing and force Duncan Webb's hand with a face to face meeting.

After being dropped off at The People newspaper offices in Fleet Street, Comer strode confidently across the pavement, through the large revolving doors and introduced himself to the girl on the main reception desk "Mr White to see Duncan Webb" He had decided on this tactic to gain access as he thought it very unlikely that Webb would have granted him an audience. He kept his fingers crossed that the receptionist didn't know Billy White personally, which seemed to work, for three minutes later he was being directed upstairs to Webb's office, which was on the third floor.

Not quite the sumptuous layout that he was expecting; a windowless corridor with two chairs next to a small door with a faded plastic sign on it, proclaiming simply, Duncan Webb. After a couple of minutes a young lady poked her head around the door, "Mr White?" she asked. Comer nodded, once again keeping his fingers crossed that he would pass as the notorious Mr White, which he obviously did, as she smiled and told him that Mr Webb would see him in two minutes.

A few minutes later the smiling girl opened the door again, "Mr Webb will see you now sir" she said as she showed Comer through the large cupboard, which served as her office and into a slightly bigger room, where Duncan Webb sat behind his 4 x 2 desk. At least he had a window in his office, which let in a small amount of light.

Webb's jaw literally dropped open as he saw Comer. "Jack, Jack Comer," he almost spluttered, "I thought," Yes, I know," answered Comer as he sat himself down opposite Webb, "you thought you were seeing Billy White"

There were no pleasantries or polite exchanges between the two men. Webb had been conned into seeing Comer and was not happy about it at all; at one time even threatening that he could call the police and have him removed from the building. "You could," replied Comer, "but then you'd have to rely completely on your mate Billy White to protect you around the clock wouldn't you? Remember what happened last time you crossed someone? The Messina brothers – nearly got yourself killed there didn't you? Next time you might not be so lucky"

Webb turned red with rage at Comer's remark and jumped up out of his chair, "I'm not standing for this," he bellowed as he reached for his phone, but the much bigger and more powerful figure of Comer lent across the desk, snatched the phone away from Webb and shoved him back down in his seat again. "I came here to talk to you Duncan," snarled Comer, "not to get into an argument, but if that is what you want?"

Webb straightened his tie and took a swig from the glass of water which was on his desk, "So what is it you want to talk to me about then – I'm listening?" "That's better," replied Comer, "Billy White, pure and simple, I want to know what he's cooking up?"

Webb insisted that he knew nothing about Billy White, "As far as I know, he's still living abroad somewhere isn't he?" Comer stood up and walked around Webb, to the window, which he opened up and looked down at the traffic below him. "Long way down from here isn't it?" he commented as he calmly took a cigarette out, lit it, and turned to face Webb again. "I can't stand idiots Duncan," he said, "but even worse, I can't stand people who take me for one, do you know what I'm saying? Webb turned his head to look up at Comer, but received a sharp slap across his face as he did so. "You're a little man Duncan, a little man who likes playing games with the big boys, but you should know that one day you're going to get seriously hurt playing these games, and that day my friend, is fast approaching, so I am going to ask you one more time, what is Billy White up to?"

● ● ●

The large room above Bianchi's restaurant was noisy and filled to capacity with Comer's men, with all the seats around the large table taken, as well as more seats around the walls of the room, and even more standing. As Comer walked in the general level of conversation lowered somewhat as he took the one available seat at the head of the table, with Moisha to one side of him and Sonny to the other.

Moisha banged his glass down on the table, hard like a gavel, calling for silence and allowing Comer to speak. It wasn't a long speech, as practically everyone there knew roughly what it was to be about. Comer explained that he wanted everyone to group into teams, three men if possible, at the very least two. He wanted every club and spieler visited, no matter how big or how small. "No more of the old pals routine, or giving them time to pay, no matter how well you might know some of these people, I want a new order instilled, I want money collected immediately, and if they don't pay, I want a few things smashed, which could include their heads, do I make myself clear? I want you to make sure that everyone knows that Jack Comer runs this town and anyone opposing that will be severely dealt with, no matter who they are"

When he had finished speaking, Comer told everyone, with the exception of Moisha and Sonny, to go downstairs to the restaurant, where they would all be served with a meal, paid for by himself. "Now get down there," he hollered, "and don't be too long, you've got a lot of work to do"

As soon as the men had all filed downstairs, Comer turned to Moisha and Sonny, and explained to them what he had found out from Duncan Webb, which was that Billy White had moved back to England and was intent on taking over Soho and the west end of London once again. "It was their mob who had given Greg that beating and did their best to make it look like the Messinas, so that we would concentrate all our efforts into doing battle with them, it was also them who fire-bombed the Golden Guinea, which as we all know is a strictly non-touchable club, frequented by the aristocracy and the top men in the old Bill. On top of all this, Billy White was now asking Duncan Webb to do a story, naming me as the man behind everything – I think I've managed to talk him out of that one"

Both Moisha and Sonny found all this hard to believe. "And this Duncan Webb geezer told you all this?" asked Sonny. "Well he did after a little persuading," answered Comer, "Surprising what a little slap will do isn't it?" said Sonny with a mocking grin on his face. "To be honest," answered Comer, "I sort of threatened to throw him out the window" There was a stunned silence for a couple of moments, followed by all three men bursting into raucous laughter.

Chapter 41

There were no wailing sirens, no planes dropping bombs, or people running to shelters, as in World War Two, but the battle for Soho had certainly started that very day. Comer's men were out in force and making themselves heard and seen in every club and spieler in Soho. "Hello, just a couple of quick questions – do you have these premises covered by insurance, and if so, who with?"

The majority of club owners or head barmen were taken aback for a moment, and not sure how to answer, in which case they were given a quick prompt, such as a bottle being thrown through a mirror. "Now if you were covered by our insurance, you could avoid that sort of thing"

Not everyone took this sort of thing as lightly as it was said, and needless to say fights broke out, which inevitably ended with yet more breakages, including furniture, fixtures and fittings, stock, and in some cases, the owners or managers heads as well. As the night wore on, Comer's men ran rampant through Soho, there were fights, stabbings, slashings, and even the odd shooting here and there. Some clubs even had their drinks and furniture thrown out onto the streets, including in three cases, their fruit machines as well. but what Comer's men didn't know at the time, was that these clubs were not under Billy White' protection, but were controlled by the Deacon brothers, who at this point were not at all involved or aware of what was going on.

This wholesale destruction didn't end on that first night, it continued, although on a lesser scale for three more days and nights, as not all club owners or managers were available on that first night. It wasn't just the club owners and managers who were injured, many of Comer's men were also injured, some even hospitalised. One set of people who were conspicuous by their absence during this period of time, were the police. This could of course been down to the fact that the majority of club owners paid the police to stay away from their premises, for various reasons.

Comer lost a decent size number of his men during this exercise, but he did exactly what he had set out to do, which was re-establishing himself as the boss of the London underworld.

Almost a week later and he still hadn't heard a thing from Billy White, which really surprised him. He had been expecting an attack of some sort, be it upon his clubs, his men or him personally. Another big surprise came when Sonny told him that he had heard that the Deacon brothers had decided to cut their losses and pull their fruit machines out of London, and move them to Birmingham. "Thank fuck for that," replied Comer, "at least that'll get rid of that other thorn in my side, Teddy fucking Baxter" Sonny told him not to count on it, as from what he had heard, the Deacon brothers were still keeping their London operation going, but without the west end and Soho. They see the Birmingham thing as an expansion to their empire. "Good for them, let's hope they keep it that way"

• • •

Tuesday 12 July, Comer made sure he was home early, as Rita was off to Ireland the following day, as Miriam was about to view her new school, and spend the rest of the summer there. He had promised to take them out to dinner at the Ritz, and was looking forward it, but when he arrived home he found Rita in tears, with Miriam sitting opposite her, also looking very sad. "What's wrong," he asked, "what's happened?" Rita dabbed at her eyes with her handkerchief and looked up at her husband, "They're going to murder that woman tomorrow," she sobbed. "What woman, what are you talking about?" "You must help her Jack," she continued to sob, "you know people, you must be able to help her"

Comer sat down beside his wife and tried to console her, and find out exactly what she was talking about. When he eventually did get it out of her, she was talking about Ruth Ellis, who was due to be hanged the following day for shooting dead her lover, David Blakely, outside a pub in Hampstead, last Easter. "She murdered him for Christ sake Rita, what can I do about it? No one can help her now"

Comer felt terribly sorry for his wife, he never knew she had such strong feelings about capital punishment, or was it purely because it was a woman about to be hanged? He accepted capital punishment as an occupational hazard, something that would happen to anyone, including himself, if ever they were found guilty of murder. "I'll do what I can," he lied, "in the meantime I want you to snap out of it and get ready – did you forget we are going out tonight – me and my two beautiful ladies?"

Rita nodded and dabbed at her eyes again as she got up. Comer hugged her and kissed her, and turned to Miriam, "And as for you my darling, I have got a special present for you – something to help you with your school work" he took a slim package from out of his pocket and handed it to her, smiling as he watched her open it. It was a Conway Stewart floral design fountain pen, with 14 ct gold fittings and nib; a rare and beautiful pen, which at this time would have been the envy of most school children, not to mention most adults. Miriam was overjoyed with it.

An hour or so later Comer was smoking one of his favourite Havana cigars, adjusting the knot in his tie and admiring himself in the mirror as Rita and Miriam came back into the room, now looking as glamorous as Hollywood film stars. "You both look just perfect," Comer smiled as he opened the door for them and started to usher them out. Before he could even close the door, the shrill sound of the phone started to ring. Why is it that phones always rings when you are going out or you are in the bath? "Start making your way outside," he said, "I'll just get this in case it's anything urgent" It was Moisha. "Sorry to interrupt your evening Jack, but I just got a message from Billy White, he wants to set up a meeting with you"

● ● ●

Dinner at the Ritz went very well, with one exception, which was when Comer agreed to try the escargots à la bourguignon, as a starter, which the waiter recommended for them, "The escargots have just arrived from Paris this morning sir, and are particularly exquisite" Comer liked to portray himself as a man of the world, more-so in front of his daughter, and didn't like to admit that he didn't have a clue what escargots were. The smile on his face quickly froze however when the waiter finally arrived at the table and presented them with three plates of snails in garlic and herb butter.

Comer looked aghast at Rita, who in turn looked at Miriam, whose face summed up exactly what they were all thinking. "They're snails," murmured a disgusted looking Miriam, as she tried her best to push the plate away from her as delicately as possible, "snails" Comer held his hands up in an apologetic gesture to both Rita and Miriam. "Why did you?" began Rita. "I didn't know," Comer answered apologetically as all three of them now pushed the offending snails away from them. Their eyes all met each other as the plates touched each other, in the centre of the table and they started to laugh as the waiter returned and knowingly asked if he could bring them something else.

In his business dealings, Comer had to fight every inch of the way to get what he wanted, in general his methods worked, but were never an easy ride, but he accepted this as it was a way of life he had chosen. His home and love life however were a different thing; he looked across the table to Rita and Miriam and wondered how he had been blessed with such a wonderful wife and a wonderful daughter.

The following day, Moisha arrived early at Comer's flat, and took Rita and Miriam to the station where they were to catch the train to Holyhead and then onward to the ferry for Dublin. By the time he returned, Comer was ready and waiting for him.

Billy White had originally asked for his meeting with Comer to take place at his new office, which was above a secondhand car showroom in Warren Street, just off Tottenham Court Road and Euston Road. "Not exactly on a par with his last office, which was in Park Lane," Comer sniggered, "but I'm still not going to let him dictate to me where we should meet" "What about Bianchi's?" offered Moisha, but Comer wasn't happy with that either, "I don't want him, or anyone else for that matter, to know we regularly use Bianchi's – I want somewhere neutral and private, where we can't be ambushed, somewhere the old Bill would never expect us of holding a meeting"

● ● ●

"Are you sure this is right?" Billy White looked out the car window as Albert Redman brought the navy blue Rover P4 90 to a halt outside a shabby building near the Highway in east London. Redman looked at a piece of paper and nodded his head, "It's the right address," he said as he started to get out of the car, "wait there, Moisha said to ring the bell"

White watched from the relative safety of the car as Redman strode up to the huge double doors and pressed the ancient bell push, which was mounted on the stone door surround. He waited a couple of minutes before pressing the bell once again. This time it was opened almost immediately by an elderly looking man in a brown overall type coat. "I'm supposed to be meeting someone here," Redman said in an exaggerated loud and clear voice, which assumed the elderly man was possibly deaf. "What's your name?" the man asked. "My name's Albert Redman, and that's my boss in the car, Billy White"

The elderly man glanced over to the car and told Redman to move the car and to get himself and his boss inside as quickly as possible. "I'm off home now," he said, "you'll find Moisha and Mr Comer inside, they are waiting for you, and will let you out when you're all finished"

A few minutes later, Billy White and Albert Redman found themselves in the dark and dusty hallway of the building. The door slammed loudly, sending an echo through the building as the elderly man made his exit. "I hope you're tooled up?" White asked Redman, who nervously nodded, as he took out a small automatic pistol and started making his way forward, "Comer," he shouted, "are you there?" No answers just silence and echoes of his own voice as White and Redman continued fumbling their way along the dark corridor, which seemed to be getting even darker as they groped their way forward. "This is fucking stupid," White moaned, "if he's here why won't he answer?" "Comer," Redman called again, "Jack, are you there?"

The sound of a key turning in a lock from somewhere in the darkness surrounding them made White and Redman stop dead in their tracks. "I'm here," called the disembodied voice of Comer, "and I can see both of you" White squinted his eyes and peered into the darkness, "Where the fuck are you Jack – what's this all about? I'm not in the mood for silly games" "We agreed no weapons Billy, remember? Comer replied, "I want you both to put any weapons you've got, on the floor where you are and then to continue walking until you reach the doorway in front of you"

Redman looked questioningly at his boss, who nodded in approval to the demand, Redman put down the pistol he was still holding and White took out his own pistol from the waistband of his trousers and did the same. "That's better," called the disembodied voice of Comer once again, "in case you're wondering, I'm up here, above you" White and Redman both looked up as a beam of light from a torch Comer was holding, shone down on them from where he was standing on an iron gallery some twenty feet above them. "And I'm here behind you" called Moisha, as he stepped out of a recess in the wall and quickly scooped up the two pistols from the floor, "straight on boys"

Billy White and Albert Redman reached the end of the corridor, gave the large metal door a shove, and entered a large room, which as least had some form of lighting, although still quite dim. Comer came down from above them, the sound of his feet clanging on the metal treads of a spiral staircase as he made his way towards them. At the same time, Moisha entered the room from behind them, emptied the bullets from the pistols, put the weapons down on top of a packing case and then shut the door behind him.

Billy White did a quick look around the room, which was filled with packing cases, old furniture and stuffed animals. "Bit theatrical all this isn't it Jack?" "You asked for a meeting Bill, not me," replied Comer, "I had to be sure firstly, that no one else knew about the place, and secondly, that we wasn't walking into a trap" "You wasn't?" answered Redman, "what about us?"

Comer explained that if he had wanted to kill White and Redman he could have done it before now. "I'm here because I am interested in what you have to say," replied Comer, "gang wars are no good for either of us, all they achieve is a renewed interest from the old Bill, which neither of us want or need"

As trust, of a sort, started to build up between the four men, they decided to sit down around an old refectory table and thrash out their differences, not that Comer was aware of having any. As far as he was concerned, he was the boss of Soho and Billy White was just a pest from the past, someone who still owed him money.

Billy White on the other hand, had different ideas. He claimed that he had been forced by bent coppers to leave the country after their joint venture had gone wrong and that the bent coppers had stolen all the money from him. All he wanted now was a little of his empire back, he didn't want a gang war any more than Comer did.

Could this be true wondered Comer, who knows? He had two options, disagree with White and end up fighting over it and possibly losing men, money, power and maybe even freedom if the police decided to act, or he could agree and give White what he was asking for, or maybe just a part of it?

After a long and drawn out debate, Comer finally agreed to end the war and let White have his three old Mayfair clubs back again as long as he promises to stay out of Soho, no more setting up ridiculous stories with his old mate Duncan Webb, and starts to pay off some of his old debt to Comer. Billy White doesn't look too happy about all this but eventually agrees. Did Comer detect a slight sneer on White' lips as he agreed to his demands? Is White really happy with this new arrangement, or is he planning something else? Only time will tell.

Chapter 42

Comer had most definitely re-established himself as the boss of the London underworld, but in doing so had lost a large number of his men. In order to keep control, he needed men on the street, his name had to be kept alive, "In this game," he would say, "you are only as feared as the last man you were seen to have shivved" (cut or stabbed) "We need to recruit more men," he told both Moisha and Sonny. "What do think, I'm not trying?" replied Moisha, "I'm putting myself about every day, always on the lookout for fresh young blood, but for some reason almost everyone I talk to has already been taken on by either Billy White or the Deacon brothers" "What the fuck does Billy White or the Deacons want more men on their firms for?" Comer shouted, "White is not supposed to be involved in the protection business and the Deacons are supposed to have moved their operation up north?" Sonny shook his head in disbelief, "I wouldn't trust Billy White as far as I could throw him, and as for the Deacon brothers, they're nothing but a bunch of fucking scrap dealers who have Teddy Baxter on their firm – don't say a lot for them does it?"

Comer knew that what Moisha was saying was the truth, but it didn't help matters. He had a larger empire to take care of, and less men to do it with. Rita was still away in Ireland and his closest aids, Moisha and Sonny, along with a few other trusted men, out constantly on the streets of Soho, Comer found himself quite often alone, drinking more and ruminating about old times.

It was on such a foray into one of his clubs that he was approached at the bar by a youngish man who politely asked, "You're Jack Comer aren't you?" Under normal circumstances, Comer wouldn't entertain anyone approaching him like this, and would have told the man in no uncertain terms to get lost, but this wasn't normal circumstances, and Comer felt pleased that someone had recognised him and wanted to talk to him; maybe he was looking for a job? "That's right," he answered, "here, let me get you a drink"

The young man declined the drink, and told Comer that he was risking his health by drinking there, in fact, he warned, it would be far safer for Comer to stay out of the West End altogether. The friendly smile dropped from Comer's face as he slammed his glass down upon the bar, "D'you realise who you're talking to?" he snarled at the young man, "I own this fucking club" The young man was not to be scared easily, "I'm just trying to give you some friendly advice my friend," he said with a condescending smile on his face, and placing his hand on Comer's shoulder at the same time. Comer's eyes turned black as they always did when he was extremely angry, like glittering pieces of black coal. Without warning, he grabbed the back of the man's head and smashed his face down onto the bar, once, twice, three times. Blood was spurting everywhere as Comer let the man slump to the floor, where he then proceeded to kick his already unconscious body, while the rest of the club's clientèle either walked out or turned their backs, preferring not to see what was happening.

It wasn't until later on, that Comer found out that the man he had beaten was a friend of Albert Redman, who had recently been recruited into Billy White' mob. "Less than a month," he screamed, "less than one fucking month, and already he's reneging on our deal" Moisha, Sonny, and a few others were sitting around the large table upstairs at Bianchi's, listening to Comer as he ranted and raved about Billy White. "I gave him those clubs in Mayfair and this is the way he repays me? Sending a fucking boy into one of my clubs and warning me to stay out of the west end – I'll show him who's going to stay and who's going to get out of the west end, and it definitely won't be me"

Comer dispatched two of the newer members of his team directly to White' clubs in Mayfair. He purposely didn't want any known faces being seen there. All they had to do was look round and see if White or Redman, or any of their associates actually hung out in any of them, and to report back to Comer.

Meanwhile, another two men were sent round to White' flat in Warren Street. "I don't care what you do," he told them, "smash down his fucking door and throw the cunt out the window for all I care – all I really want to know is if he's still there or not"

Both searches proved negative, had Billy White disappeared yet again? Comer doubted it very much; why would he walk away from such a lucrative scene? This was typical Billy White, as crafty and cunning as a fox. "Well he ain't going to outfox me, not this time," confided Comer to Moisha, "especially here on my own territory, do you know how Soho got its name? It goes back hundreds of years to when huntsmen spotted a fox and used to cry Soho, meaning they had spotted it – and that's exactly what we're going to do, we're going to be the huntsmen, and we ain't going to stop until we bag our fox in Soho"

• • •

Comer tried his best to look calm and collected as Moisha and Sonny turned up outside his flat in the Cadillac. "Frith Street," commanded Comer as he slid into the back seat of the car. Moisha looked at Comer in the interior mirror of the car; this was definitely not a time for small talk. Comer was fuming inside with rage and indignation, and couldn't wait to get to their destination, where he planned a tour of the Soho club scene.

Parking in London has never been easy, and especially around Soho and the west end, with its narrow streets and roads. But in the 1950s is wasn't prohibitive, there were no parking meters or wardens, it was just a matter of finding a space and easing your car into it, which was easier said than done, when your particular vehicle was an eighteen foot long Cadillac, but that was Moisha's problem, not Comer's. "Here," he said, pointing at a gap between a van and a motorcycle, "this'll do"

Moisha pulled the massive car level with the space, which was quite obviously too small, "I can't get in that space," he grumbled, "it's much too small" Comer got out of the car, stepped back and beckoned to Sonny, who followed him, "Get that fucking thing out the way," he growled, as he indicated the motorcycle Sonny did as he was told and physically lifted the motorcycle from its parking space and placed it against a lamppost on the corner of Frith Street. Moisha smiled to himself as he looked on at Sonny's handiwork and then quietly and efficiently manoeuvred the car into the now enlarged space.

Five minutes later Comer, Moisha, and Sonny were at the bar of the first of the many clubs that were under their control, and which they would visit that day. "Billy White," growled Comer to the barman, "he hasn't been in here at all has he?" "No," replied the barman, "he must know this is one of your clubs surely?" "What about his mate, Albert Redman?" demanded Comer. The barman confirmed the same with Redman, "They wouldn't dare" Comer nodded to Moisha and Sonny and turned to leave, pausing for a moment as they did so and turning back to the barman, "Just in case either of them do decide to drop in, give 'em a message from me will you? Tell 'em I'm going to kill the fucking pair of them, and anyone else in their little mob who is stupid enough to stand by 'em" The barman nodded silently as Comer, Moisha and Sonny walked out.

Over the course of the next few hours, they visited almost every club and spieler, which were under their control in Soho. The same questions were asked, the same threats relayed as loudly as possible. They hadn't managed to actually come face to face with Billy White or his chief lieutenant, Albert Redman, but by this time there couldn't have been hardly anyone left in the criminal fraternity who had not heard the threats made by Comer and his entourage against White and Redman.

Word had reached White almost immediately that day, but he was not absent from the Soho scene and had moved from his flat because he was scared of Comer, far from it. Anyone who had been listening to the wireless that day, would have heard the news about a large bank raid in the City of London, which had netted the raiders more than £45,000, which is the equivalent of three quarters of a million pounds today, and this was a job that White had masterminded.

At this point, Comer didn't even know a big robbery had taken place, and he certainly wasn't aware that White was involved in anything. In a way it would have pleased him, for it would mean he had more chance of getting some of his money back from White.

Two days passed, in which Comer heard about the robbery and the rumours that White was indeed involved, but he still couldn't locate where he was hiding out; France again maybe? The truth was that White was alive and well and renting a small cottage near Brighton, where he discussed with Redman exactly what he wanted done about Comer and his threats, "We can't have him running around all over the west end talking about me and threatening me as if I was some sort kid, I want him sorted out once and for all, do you know what I mean Albert?"

Redman knew exactly what he meant, and within hours had hired an ex-American soldier, Jimmy Donovan, who claimed to have previously worked as a hitman in Chicago. "We want Comer dead, do you understand? Not just fucking injured or slashed, we want him, and whoever happens to be with him, stone cold dead, can you do this? Donovan smiled as he continued to chew his gum, and pulled back his jacket to reveal a leather shoulder holster, just like Redman had seen in so many gangster films, "No problem" he replied, sounding as much like George Raft as he possibly could.

• • •

Less than twenty four hours later, Donovan turned up outside a club in Soho where he had been reliably informed that Comer was holding court inside. He was stopped by the doorman as he tried to walk in and informed that it was a members only club. Donovan insisted that the doorman should check with the owner, whom he knew. As the doorman left to go and check, Donovan ducked in and made his way down the stairs into the club.

Moisha and Sonny were talking to two other men at the bar, while Comer was in deep conversation with another man, Bobby Osborne, an ex boxer, whom he hoped to recruit to his mob. Osborne looked up as Donovan walked in: he wasn't hard to spot as he was dressed in a light beige wide brimmed fedora, and a long black overcoat, exactly as he had seen pictures of Al Capone wearing, and this was still the middle of summer. "Fuck me, look whose just walked in," exclaimed Osborne. "Who the hell is he then?" asked Comer. "Al Capone," sniggered Osborne, "or at least that's who he thinks he is, "bloody Yank who's been putting himself about as some sort of hard-man"

Donovan paused where he was and looked around the room, slowly and deliberately until his eyes set on his intended victim, Jack Comer. He dramatically swung back his overcoat, reached into his shoulder holster and pulled out his US Army issue 45 automatic. Unfortunately for Donovan, almost everyone in the room saw him at the same time; some dived for cover under the relative safety of tables, while others ran behind the bar. Sonny however, saw who Donovan was pointing his gun at and rushed towards Comer, shoving him quickly to the floor as Donovan released two shots from his pistol. The first shot thudded into the bar, whilst the second shot caught Sonny in the arm and sent him crashing to the floor next to his boss.

All this happened in a just a few seconds at the most. Donovan saw his chance and ran forward in a bid to finish Comer off. He was now towering over both men, Comer and Sonny; his face contorted into an evil grin as he pointed the gun at Comer's head and pulled the trigger, "Die you son of a bitch," he growled in his best gangster accent. Click, click, click, three times he pulled the trigger but it did not fire, his gun had jammed.

At this point, Moisha leapt upon his back and started grappling with him, but Donovan was a big man, probably about the same size as Moisha, and could give as good as he received. The two men bounced off the bar and into some furniture, sending bottles and glasses flying everywhere. As this was happening, both Comer and Sonny were getting to their feet, but suddenly Donovan was on top of Moisha and starting to smash him in the face with his pistol. Suddenly, as if from out of nowhere Bobby Osborne reappeared, he grabbed Donovan from behind, swung him round to face him and stabbed him in the stomach with what looked life an enormously long knife, but which turned out to be an army bayonet. Osborne pulled the bayonet out and then thrust it in again, this time with two hands, directly into Donovan's chest.

There was a sudden silence in the room. Moisha stepped back; both Comer and Sonny stared as Donovan's mouth dropped open and blood gushed up from deep inside him. He seemed to stand there in a state of suspended animation for ages, which in reality was probably no longer than five seconds, before dropping to the floor in an ever deepening pool of blood. He was dead before he even hit the floor.

By this time the owner of the club had also arrived on the scene and looked mortified at the blood soaked body on the floor and everyone else, still standing and starring, in silence. "Oh my God," he exclaimed, "what the hell's happened here?" Moisha quickly sidled up to him and whispered something into his ear. Moisha then turned to the half a dozen or so onlookers, "Did anyone see what happened?" he called out, "I think he must have been some sort of nut-case, he had a gun and started firing at people, next thing I know he collapsed on the floor – looks like he had a heart attack to me" "He was stabbed wasn't he?" answered one of the onlookers. Moisha looked menacingly at the man who had just said this. "What?" The man quickly realised that he had said the wrong thing, "No, I meant he fell to the floor so quickly – course it must have been a heart attack" Moisha nodded, "That's better," he said, "now just go and forget all about it" He took out a roll of money and stuffed a white five pound note into the top pockets of each man there. "Get yourselves a drink somewhere else, we'll see you all again soon won't we, you can be sure of that"

Moisha had said this with just enough menace in his voice to get the message across to the men, who now quietly filed out of the club as the doorman appeared from a storage room with a large old rug, which he threw down on the floor next to the body of Donovan.

Moisha, Sonny and Osborne started to quickly roll the body of Donovan in the rug, while the barman mopped the blood up from the parquet flooring. Comer watched Osborne as he got on with the work without having to be told anything. Osborne had put his own life on the line while protecting him from a man with a loaded gun, and would make an excellent addition to his team. Comer had a quick word with Moisha and told him to get rid of the body at the the old washhouse in east London, and to make sure Osborne was in on their meeting the following day.

Chapter 43

Moisha's veiled threats to the denizens of the Soho club where Donovan was murdered, seemed to have done the trick, as no word of what had happened to him that night got out, and as far as White and Redman knew, the job they ordered on Comer had been carried out, and White was now safe to return to London.

Unfortunately for White, the police swooped on him the moment he put his key in the door of his Warren Street flat. Redman wasn't with him at the time but White was taken into West End Central police station and questioned about his alleged involvement in the big bank raid in the City of London. He was held in custody and questioned for three days, during which time he managed to get word to his solicitor, who in turn contacted Albert Redman.

On his third day of being held, his solicitor strode into West End Central police station, accompanied by Duncan Webb, who claimed that on the day of the robbery Billy White was at the offices of his newspaper, the Sunday People, where he was being interviewed by him for a possible article he was contemplating. With this cast iron alibi, the police had no option other than to release White immediately.

"What happened about Comer?" he demanded from Redman. He had scanned all the newspapers and spoken to numerous people, and as far as he could tell, Comer was alive and well and still running Soho. "Tell me about it," replied Redman, "that fucking Yank took our money, did nothing and has now pissed off somewhere, no one has seen him since"

• • •

Bobby Osborne sat at Comer's right hand side at yet another meeting above Bianchi's restaurant in Frith Street, the usual crowd were there, but Comer wanted everyone to hear what Osborne had to say. "I have this direct from the horse's mouth," he started, "the would be hit man from America was definitely hired by Albert Redman, on Billy White' orders to kill you Jack" Comer leaned back in his chair, lit up a cigarette and looked up at Osborne, "Sounds about right Bobby, but where'd this information come from?" "My brother-in-law, he works for White, does little odd jobs, runs errands, that sort of thing"

Osborne continued, telling how Billy White, now flush with money from his big bank job, is recruiting more men to his organisation, with the sole intention of taking over the whole of Soho and the west end. He also has his pet newspaper man, Duncan Webb, back on his payroll, who is supposed to be planning an article for his newspaper, entitled The Downfall and Death of Jack Comer.

When Comer heard this last sentence, he almost exploded. "I'll show Billy fucking White, who's going to be dying, I'll show the fucking lot of them," he screamed, "I want White and Redman found and this time we finish them off for good, no more pussy footing around, we do it, and we do it now" Everyone around the table agreed that this is what was now needed. "Only problem is Jack," added Moisha, "if White' now got all these extra men on his team, it leaves us at something of a disadvantage doesn't it?" "I'll do it on my fucking own then," screamed Comer, "you're either with me or you're against me, and that goes for everyone here – anyone who wants to leave just do it, walk out now"

There was silence around the table for a few seconds with everyone looking at each other. Moisha broke the silence, "I didn't mean it like that Jack, you can always count on me, you know that" "And me," added Sonny. Everyone else around the table nodded in agreement. "There is something else, which I've been meaning to talk to you about," Osborne interjected, "have you ever heard of the Kray twins?" Comer shrugged his shoulders; he hadn't heard of them at this time. Osborne explained how they were childhood friends of his from the east end, and how they were starting to make a name for themselves in Bethnal Green. "And?" Comer shrugged again.

Osborne explained that he thought he could get them to join forces with Comer. "They're still relatively young," he continued, "but believe me, they put the fear of God into their enemies – they'd be an asset Jack, trust me, I know them" Comer conceded and told Osborne to set up a meeting with them.

● ● ●

Two days after this meeting, Duncan Webb received a phone call from a man who said he was calling on behalf of Billy White; White needed to see him urgently, he said, as he was in terrible trouble. A meeting was set up straight away for Webb to meet White outside a furniture store in Tottenham Court Road.

When Webb reached the store that evening, he was not met by Billy White, but by two men who introduced themselves as friends of White. "It is too dangerous for Billy to meet you here," they said, "he's waiting for you just around the corner" They then walked Webb around the corner, into a small, dimly lit side street. "Where is he?" asked Webb.

As he said this, Jack Comer stepped out of a doorway, while his two men grabbed Webb's arms and pinned him back against the wall. "Planning on doing an article on me are you Duncan?" growled Comer as he smashed his fist into Webb's stomach. "The Downfall and Death of Jack Comer?" he unleashed another punch, this time connecting with Webb's jaw, "how about this for a title, The Downfall and Death of Duncan Webb? How's that sound to you?" Webb groaned in pain and struggled to get away from the grip of the two heavies who were pinning him against the wall.

"You got it wrong Jack," he pleaded, "that was White' idea, not mine" "You're not only a coward Duncan, you're also a fucking lying coward," Comer said as he slipped a brass knuckleduster onto his fist and brought it with full force against Webb's nose The sound of the bone splintering and the blood spurting out, even made one of the heavies wince. Webb fainted with the pain, but was held upright by the two men as Comer continued his onslaught against him until he was a pummelled mess of gore and blood. "Let him go" Comer ordered, and started to walk away. The two heavies did exactly that, letting Webb collapse to the ground, in a heap.

Less than an hour later, Comer was calming down and enjoying a drink at the bar of the Hideaway Club in Soho, with a few members of his team, when two Scotland Yard detectives entered and walked directly up to him. "Jack Comer, I am arresting you on suspicion of assaulting Mister Duncan Webb, at Alfred Mews, London, earlier this evening, you do not have to say anything unless you wish to do so, but what you say may be given in evidence" Comer looked at the two policemen in incredulity as one of them snapped a pair of handcuffs on him and started to lead him out. "He's been here all day," called Sonny. The first policeman looked round to see who had called out and paused for a moment, looking at Sonny. "Is that right?" he said, "maybe you'd like to accompany him to the police station then and prove your point?" "No need for that," Comer butted in, "you haven't got anything on me, come on let's just go" The first policeman was a little reluctant to walk away without taking Sonny with him, but his colleague thought otherwise and gave his sleeve a tug, "Come on, we've got who we came after"

Comer was taken to West End Central police station, where he was searched, fingerprinted and questioned for several hours by detectives regarding his whereabouts that day. He of course denied everything, stating that he had been drinking at the Hideaway Club all day, and that he had nothing more to say unto he had seen his lawyer.

• • •

A heavily bandaged Duncan Webb meanwhile, was lying asleep in a private room of the Middlesex Hospital in Mortimer Street, which lies at the back of Oxford Street, W1. Outside his room, sat a police officer, trying to keep awake by reading a newspaper. He looked up as he heard the sound of the rubber lined wheels of a hospital trolley, squealing on the linoleum lined floor of the hallway. A male nurse, dressed in a white surgical type gown and mask, was pushing the trolley, which also had an intravenous medical drip attached. He paused for a moment beside the police officer, nodded silently to him and then entered the room.

Duncan Webb opened his eyes as the nurse shook him gently to wake him. The nurse then removed his own mask to reveal the face of Moisha, who quickly clamped his hand over Webb's mouth to prevent him from calling for help. "Shhh," hissed Moisha, putting his finger up to his lips.

Webb's eyes were practically bulging out of his head with fear as he starred up at Moisha, who now bent down, almost touching heads with Webb, and started to whisper in his ear. Webb kept nodding as if in agreement with whatever it was that Moisha was saying. "I want you to be absolutely clear on what I am saying to you Duncan, you do understand this don't you?" whispered Moisha. A terrified looking Webb nodded again. "Good man," whispered Moisha in answer to Webb's acknowledgement, as he tapped his finger on the dressing that covered Webb's broken nose, causing him to shiver in acute pain. "Don't let us down will you? I wouldn't want to see you in more pain"

Moisha pulled his surgical mask back up over the lower half of his face and wheeled the trolley back out again, nodding once again to the police officer outside, and offering him a softly spoken "Good night officer"

• • •

Twenty four hours had passed since Comer had been arrested. The metallic clanging sounds of the lock being turned and the bolt being withdrawn on the outside of his cell door at the police station caused Comer to look and see one of the detectives who had arrested him, alongside his lawyer and the station sergeant. "Come on Jack, your free to go," his lawyer exclaimed to a somewhat surprised Jack Comer.

As Comer was given back his personal possessions at the main desk of the police station, his lawyer explained to him that no charges were being preferred against him in relation to the alleged attack on Duncan Webb. "You are a very lucky man Comer," the detective added, "seems Mr Webb has had a memory relapse and now says he can't remember even being attacked, let alone who carried it out" Comer looked angrily at the detective; he hated the police, and this one in particular, who had relished in the fact of arresting him the day before. He had done it because he was Jack Comer, and this would be a proverbial feather in his cap, not because he thought he had committed a crime.

Comer moved forward towards the detective, his fists clenched, his mouth twisting into a sneer, "You fuck." he muttered, half under his breath. His lawyer quickly turned him around to face the door and start to walk out in an effort to stop him saying what he was about to, and to diffuse the situation.

Moisha was waiting in the Cadillac, outside the police station as Comer and his solicitor emerged. The solicitor politely refused a lift, saying that he had his own car parked just around the corner, while Comer climbed into the back of the Cadillac and was whisked off to Bianchi's in Frith Street, not to the upstairs meeting room this time, but to a large table in the actual restaurant, where the rest of Comer's gang were waiting for them and a celebratory meal was waiting.

During the course of the meal, Bobby Osborne told Comer that he had spoken to Reggie and Ronnie Kray, and they had expressed a great interest in helping out any way they can, "Call the meeting for when and where you want Jack," he said, "and they'll be there"

Chapter 44

While all this was going on, Billy White was still going about his business and openly laughing at Comer's antics, as he sarcastically dismissed them. He was secretly angry at Comer's attack on his friend, Duncan Webb, but he preferred not to discuss this, as it could be seen by some as a weakness on his part, not being able to protect his friends. "Comer wants to be the king of the underworld again does he?" said White, "he's getting more like king of the fucking comic world as far as I can see – he'll be putting adverts in the Beano and Dandy comics next for new kids to join his mob," which brought a solid round of laughter from the sycophantic close coterie of White' mob.

In the relatively small world of Soho, word quickly spread, which of course it was meant to; Billy White was deliberately trying to provoke Comer into a confrontation, which he, with the larger number of gang members under his control, would undoubtedly win.

Jack Comer might well have been jealous of White' growing support, but he was not a fool, and instead of staying the course with what was left of his 'old timers' as White and his associates were now calling Comer's gang, he took Bobby Osborne at his word, and started to make plans for his new alliance with the two up and coming stars of the London underworld at this time, the twin brothers, Reggie and Ronnie Kray from Bethnal Green in east London.

Comer had a number of spielers, and pubs and other establishments around east London that he was still 'looking after', in other words, collecting protection money from. One such establishment was a billiard hall in Mile End, which had gone from being a thriving business a few years earlier, to a rather tired and down at heel place. Much of the hall's demise was due to Comer constantly milking it of any small profit it did manage to make. The billiard hall was becoming too much like hard work for Comer, having to constantly send men there, who came away most of the time with little or no money to show for their endeavours.

Comer told Osborne to organise a meeting with the Krays at his old haunt, the Mackworth Arms pub in Commercial Road, which was literally a stone's throw from the old billiard hall.

Comer, Osborne, Moisha, and Sonny were waiting at a large circular table in the corner of the bar, when the door opened, dead on time, and the Krays' minder, a giant of a man, known as Big Pat, walked in, Big Pat was enormous, he was so large that he blocked much of the light coming in from outside. He stood for a moment, looking silently around the pub, and at Comer's table and the men around it, whom he obviously recognised, he then looked back outside and beckoned for whoever was out there that it was safe to come in.

Big Pat held the door open, letting Reggie and Ronnie Kray into the pub. They were almost identical in their looks, both well dressed in dark suits and ties, and well built, with slicked back, dark hair and a swaggering walk that told everyone who saw them that they were not to be taken lightly.

Bobby Osborne jumped to his feet and shook Reggie and Ronnie's hands as they approached the table. "This is Reggie and Ronnie Kray," he said to Comer, with a smile on his face as if he was introducing him to the Pope. Comer nodded to the Krays, making sure not to overdo the big introduction thing, after all, he was the boss of the London underworld, not them, and he was 'interviewing' them, not the other way round.

Comer invited the Krays to join them at the table, and told them how he had been hearing good things about them from Bobby Osborne, who had suggested they all met, with the possibility of forming an alliance. Reggie Kray, who seemed to be the more friendly of the two, smiled as he told Comer that was what they were there for. "We've heard a lot about you Mr Comer," he said, "and would like very much to work with you" "Two things," Comer interjected, "firstly, no need for Mr Comer, you can call me Jack, and secondly, if you do decide to go with what I am about to offer you, you'll be working for me, not with me, do I make myself understood?"

Ronnie Kray didn't look very happy at this, but Reggie, ever the affable businessman, smiled again and held out his hand to Comer, Of course Jack, slip of the tongue that's all, we are both very excited about meeting you and eager to hear any propositions you want to put to us" Ronnie Kray's face didn't show any sign of emotion, apart from a sullen stare at Comer, he suddenly dipped his hand into his inside pocket, which caused a stir around the table, as both Moisha and Sonny thought he might have been pulling out a gun, instead of which, he pulled out his wallet, took out a five pound note, which he handed to Big Pat, "Get some drinks in," he solemnly grunted.

While Big Pat went to the bar and started ordering the drinks, Comer laid out his plan to the Krays. He didn't mention that he had helped to run the Regal Billiard Hall into the ground, he just told them that he part owned it, which was true, and that the current manager didn't have a clue how to run it. "What I propose," he continued, "is that you boys take your little firm and march in there and tell the manager, Mr Angel, to fuck off, as you are now the new bosses" Ronnie Kray actually smiled at this, for the first time, Little firm," he chuckled, "I like it"

Comer wasn't exactly sure what it was that made Ronnie smile; he later found out that it was his use of the word 'firm' to describe their gang, a word that the Krays used from then on to describe themselves. "And has this Mr Angel got a 'firm' of his own?" asked Ronnie, "someone who might decide to take up battle against us when we march in on him?" Comer laughed at this, "Angel, got a firm? You must be joking, there's just him and his seventy year old brother, you'll get no trouble from them" The smile dropped from Ronnie's face, "That's a shame," he said, "I was looking forward to a bit of bone breaking"

Comer wasn't too sure of Ronnie's remarks, but decided not to question him on them, directing the rest of his conversation instead towards Reggie. "When you do take over the billiard hall," he said, you can do what you want with it, make it your headquarters, run it as a straight business, it'll be yours to do as you want with" "And what do you want from us in return?" asked Reggie.

"I'll tell you what I want," replied Comer, "I want you to come whenever I call you, to stand by my side and be counted as a part of my team, to be seen with me and fight my enemies with me, how's that sound to you?" "Sounds fine to me," answered Reggie, "what about you Ron?" he asked, turning to his brother. Ronnie was smiling again, probably at the part which mentioned fighting, "I'm with you all the way Jack," he answered, offering his hand out to Comer.

● ● ●

Both Comer and his team, as well as the Kray 'firm' went away from the meeting very pleased with the outcome. Comer's first job was to start putting it about all over the west end and Soho that the Krays were now with him.

The Krays, on the other hand, set about moving into their new headquarters. It was exactly as Comer had said, no opposition whatsoever from Mr Angel and his brother, in fact he seemed almost pleased to be getting out. Reggie organised a team of men to clean and decorate the place, replace the green baize on some of the twelve full size snooker tables, which they had there, and also build a small café area.

Word quickly spread around the east end that the Krays now had a billiard hall, and that everyone was welcome. Although still quite young, the Krays already had such a reputation that people who had never played snooker in their life started going there just to be in their company, and to be able to say to their friends that they knew Reggie and Ronnie.

The Regal Billiard Hall not only became quite a successful business, it also became a great recruiting centre; thieves, fighters, bank robbers, getaway drivers, you name it, they went to the Regal Billiard Hall, where some were merely tolerated, while others were drawn into the ever growing Kray firm.

Comer was happy at this time just to keep bandying their name about the west end and Soho, he kept hearing stories about them dishing beatings out to various people and club owners, especially the Maltese, who now seemed to be centred around Aldgate and east London, and whom he didn't particularly like anyway, after his own run in with the Messina brothers a few years back. They were taking off in and around the east end with lightning speed, which didn't worry Comer one bit. The west end and Soho were his manor, and he had the Krays on call day and night.

One summer, Comer had another idea, which was to liven up his old empire of the racecourse pitches, which he had neglected over the last few years, but had recently been told that more people were now visiting the races once again, so why not, and while he was trying it, why not bring the Krays in as well?

He wanted the Krays to be seen as a part of his organisation not just in London, but everywhere he operated, and so he took them along to Epsom with him and put them in charge of several bookmakers' pitches there, where all they had to do was stand around and look tough, which they undoubtedly did.

Billy White meanwhile, was certainly aware of what was going on in London, but when he got a phone call from Albert Redman, direct from Epsom racecourse, telling him Comer was down there, strutting about like he owns the place, and with the Krays doing the business for him. White was absolutely furious when he heard this, "Who the fuck does he think he is," shouted White, ""just because he has the Krays on his team that he's indestructible now?" he shouted, "just keep an eye on things there while I work out what we're going to do"

The Epsom race meeting had worked well for Comer. Once the bookmakers saw the Krays were with Comer's team they were practically lining up to give him their money.

Back in Soho, Jack Comer felt like a new man, swaggering about like his old self, he was even starting to attract new offers of 'jobs' from various sources, who now saw him as someone who had the money and the clout, to pull off such ventures. One such offer came from an old 'friend' who was now working for a bank security firm. "This is right up your street Jack," the security man explained, "you're the only mob in town now who could pull this off, and it'll put thousands into your pockets"

Comer was more than pleased with this, and saw it as yet another step towards redeeming himself as the number one man in Soho. He hit a big stumbling block however when he asked the Krays to be in on it; they didn't exactly turn him down but they intimated that if they were to be a part of it, they would want an equal share of the profits with himself, which of course was out of the question as far as Comer was concerned. He saw the Krays as a part of his team, not as partners.

"Don't worry about them," he told Moisha and Sonny, "We'll do it with just us and our old team, we always have done it like that, so I can't see any reason to bottle out now, just because Reggie and Ronnie don't want to take part – they're still handy to have around to take care of any heavy work we might want done"

This wasn't a perfect situation by any means, and Comer knew it. One minute the Krays were a part of his mob, and suddenly there seemed to be this split, and the problem was that Soho, being such a relatively small place, almost like a village, the word soon started to spread.

Jack Comer was certainly no fool, and knew that normal type 'gossip' does happen, but this was more than that, this was a whispering campaign set up against him; he had his suspicions as to who was behind it, but needed more proof before he was ready to strike back. Within a couple of days he received a phone call, which answered his dilemma. It was from Albert Redman, who told Comer in no uncertain terms that his time was up in both Soho and the racetracks. Comer exploded, firstly at the very thought that this second-rate messenger boy even had his phone number; imagine if Rita and Miriam had been there and picked up the call? Luckily they had just gone back to Ireland yet again. "We'll see whose fucking time is up," he yelled down the phone at Redman, "I am the boss of the underworld and don't you or Billy fucking White ever forget it- d'you hear me?"

Comer slammed the phone down so hard it left a crack on the hand-piece; without even noticing it, he snatched it up again and dialled Moisha's number, telling him to get over to him straight away.

Twenty minutes later Comer was in the back of his new car, a 1958 Chrysler Imperial in gleaming black with cream leather upholstery. This was the first time he had seen the car as Moisha had just picked it up for him that morning, but he barely looked at, he just wrenched the back door open, slid in, slammed the door behind him and grunted, "Windmill Street," to Moisha.

Moisha could see his boss was in one of his dark moods, and when he was like this, knew better than to question him. The Nosh Bar?" Comer grunted a sort of yes, and Moisha kept driving, he knew there was nowhere else Comer would want to go to in Great Windmill Street at this time in the morning apart from his favourite salt beef bar. He dropped his boss off outside the Nosh Bar as it is too narrow to park in the actual street itself. As soon as Comer had gone inside the salt beef bar, Moisha drove on to the end of the street, turned left into Brewer Street and parked the Chrysler in the multi storey car park there.

Five minutes later Moisha returned to the Nosh Bar where Comer had already ordered their salt beef sandwiches and coffees and was sitting at his favourite window seat, where he could watch the world go by. "Look at those dirty old bastards," Moisha said with a grin, pointing to the queue of mainly elderly men, who were buying tickets at the box office window of the Windmill Theatre, which was opposite. He was just trying to make light talk, to break Comer out of his dark mood. "Have you noticed how so many of them wear raincoats?" he chuckled.

Moisha almost succeeded, as a slight grin did appear on Comer's face with this last remark. At the same time, the phone started ringing from behind the counter. "Nosh Bar," answered the owner in a sing song voice, "who?" he looked up towards Comer and Moisha, a slight worried look on his face, "who wants him?" he continued. He then held his hand over the mouthpiece and beckoned over to Comer, "Geezer here wants to speak to you Jack, he won't give his name"

Comer frowned as he walked over to the counter and took the phone off the owner. "Hello, who's that?" Moisha anxiously watched as Comer listened to whoever it was on the other end of the phone. Comer continued to listen to the the voice on the phone, Charlie Belcher, who was a small time crook, who usually earned his money running messages and doing odd jobs for the major criminals, "I got a message for you Jack, it's from Albert Redman – he wants to see you" Spot went berserk, almost choking on his salt beef sandwich, "He wants to see me?" he blurted out, "he wants to see me? – You tell him mister fucking messenger boy that if he wants to see me he can come and find me – I'm not that hard to find" Comer slammed the phone down and stormed back to where Moisha was still sitting, "Pay him, we're going," he said as he walked out into the warm August sunshine, leaving Moisha to pay the bill. "I need to walk," he told Moisha as he joined him outside, "you get the car and I'll see you in Frith Street" Moisha silently obeyed his boss, leaving him to walk as he requested.

• • •

Comer could feel his heart beating fast as he walked through the Soho streets and thought of the words that little shit, Belcher had delivered to him on the phone, "he wants to see you". Fucking Albert Redman wants to see me, he thought over and over again. It was mid August; a warm but perfectly normal day in London's west end as he trudged along Old Compton Street and eventually turned the corner into Frith Street. There was a crowd of about half a dozen men standing on the opposite corner not far from the Continental Fruit Store, and in the midst of them was none other than the object of everything despicable in Comer's mind at that moment, it was Albert Redman in all his glory, sharp suited and holding court as if he owned Soho.

Comer didn't stop to think or plan what he was about to do, he just darted across the street and pushed his way through the small straggle of men who were talking and listening to Albert Redman. "Oi, Redman, I want to talk you" he growled. Redman heard Comer's words before he actually saw him; he spun round to find Jack Comer confronting him, just inches away from his face. "Do me a favour Comer" he retorted, "I don't need all this, here on the street, if you want to talk to me, then give me a ring and let's do it in private somewhere"

Comer used his elbows to shove one of the other men out of the way, and moved in even closer to Redman, if that was possible, "You don't need it on the street?" he snarled, "you get poxy messenger boys to phone me demanding I should see you, and you have the nerve to say you don't need it on the street - from what I've heard you think you own the fucking street"

Comer's face was now contorted with rage; sweat was dripping off him, and Redman could see big trouble brewing if he didn't move away pretty quickly. He moved his hand in a throw-away gesture and went to walk away from Comer, saying as he did so, "Face up to it Comer, you're finished, now, why don't you just fuck off before you end up getting hurt" As he said this, he gave Comer a shove and tried to walk away from him, but Comer was in no mood to have anyone walk away from him, especially Albert Redman, and especially in front of a crowd of witnesses. Comer gave Redman a straight right, which landed directly on his chin, sending him staggering back and onto the floor. He followed this up by wading into him and kicking him about the face and body.

At this point, one of the men whom Redman had been speaking to tried to pull Comer away from Redman. Fortunately by this time, Moisha had pulled up along the street and seen all the commotion going on and had realised it was almost certainly to do with his boss. He rushed to the scene as quickly as possible, grabbed the man who now had hold of Comer from the back and threw him to the ground.

With this extra fight now taking place and somewhat distracting Comer, it gave Redman time to get to his feet and launch a fresh attack upon him. The two men grappled with each other and stumbled into a pile of fruit boxes, which were piled outside the Continental Fruit Store on the corner of the street. As they continued with the fight, they fell over some of the boxes and stumbled into the interior of the shop together, by which time Redman had pulled a knife and stabbed Comer several times with it, inflicting wounds to his arms, leg, and body.

Comer was in great pain and hadn't intended this to be a major battle, just a confrontation and a few slaps, which he had thought would suffice, but now Redman had produced a knife and was slashing and stabbing at him, he had no option, other than to pull his gun out of his inside pocket and aim it towards Redman.

He didn't pull the trigger as he thought the sight of it alone might be enough to scare Redman off, and he also didn't want to start shooting with so many witnesses about.

The owner of the fruit store was Sophie Glickstein, a large lady who was used to dealing with problematic and unruly customers; after all, this was Soho, not Mayfair. "Get out of my shop" she yelled at the two men, completely oblivious to Redman' knife and Comer's gun, "Do you hear me? Get out" Needless to say, her calls to evacuate the shop fell on deaf ears as Comer and Redman, both now covered in blood, continued their battle.

By this time Moisha had given the other man a good beating, and forced him to make as swift an exit as possible before he got more. A large crowd had now gathered outside the fruit store, watching and in many cases, thoroughly enjoying the battle which was still raging inside.

The store's proprietress, Sophie Glickstein couldn't care less which one of the two protagonists was to blame, all she wanted was to get them both out of her store, and the quicker the better. She looked round for something suitable to possibly throw at them or hit them with, starting with apples and then potatoes, which she threw at their head, but obviously to no avail. She then picked up the large brass scoop, which was used to weigh the potatoes and vegetables, and started attacking both men with it. It certainly hurt both Comer and Redman, but not enough to stop their ongoing onslaught on each other. In desperation, she started grabbing the cast iron weights themselves and hurling at them, "Stop it, stop it," she screamed as she continued to throw the weights, each one more heavier than the previous one, "Stop it, do you hear me? Get out of my shop" The last weight was the largest and heaviest, and caught Comer full on his head, causing yet more blood to spurt out and run down his face.

Moisha had seen the gun in Comer's hand, and had now managed to push his way through the crowd. He needed to take the gun away from his boss before he ended up murdering Redman in full view of a huge crowd of people.

By this time in the proceedings, both men were feeling somewhat weak, due to both of them loosing a considerable amount of blood. Comer looked through his blood-stained eyes and saw Redman coming at him with the knife yet again; he pointed the gun directly at Redman' head and started to squeeze the trigger as Moisha reached him and grabbed it away from him, "No Jack, not here," he growled. Comer was so dazed that he just staggered backwards for a moment, allowing Redman to pull away and limp towards the open doorway, where a third party quickly grabbed him and held him up for a moment in order to regain his strength and composure.

The second man then helped Redman across the pavement and into a waiting taxi, which sped away as quickly as possible. Moisha then did almost the same thing with Comer, holding him up as they emerged from the fruit store, Comer's fine Italian suit ripped and covered in blood, his face red and swollen. He stared for a moment or two at the faces of the crowd, which looked like they were spinning round in a circle, facing him. "Where's the bastard gone?" he mumbled, "Where's he gone?" Moisha tried his best to hold his boss up, but Comer just slipped through his fingers and crashed to the pavement.

Moisha grabbed hold of his boss, "Jack, Jack," he called, "can you hear me Jack?" but Comer could not hear anything at this point, he was out cold. The majority of the crowd started to slink away as they heard the sound of police cars approaching from somewhere near by. Moisha lifted the almost lifeless body of his boss, back to his feet, "Come on Jack," he said with some urgency, "We've got to get you away from here" He looked round and saw the nearby Italian barber's shop, where he half walked and half dragged his boss. "Some water and towels, quick" Moisha demanded. The owner and his assistant obeyed without hesitating and started to do their best to clean Comer up, but within minutes the police cars had screeched to a halt outside, where everyone was pointing towards the barber's shop. Three uniformed officers came rushing in and arrested Comer. They ignored the large man in the barber's chair with the shaving foam all over his face, luckily for Moisha.

Chapter 45

Comer had lost a considerable amount of blood and was in a semi-concious state in the back of the police car, as they rushed him to Charing Cross Hospital, where he was put on the critical list, given a blood transfusion and general anaesthetics to control the pain. Even while he lay in his bed, still unconscious, the police constantly harassed the hospital staff into letting them question him, which was obviously impossible at this time.

In the meantime, Albert Redman had also been traced and arrested as the other man involved in the fracas, after the owner of the fruit store had picked him out from mugshot photos she had been shown. Redman was taken to the Middlesex Hospital, and put under a 24 hours a day police guard presence.

When both Comer and Redman were eventually pronounced as being well enough to be questioned, they were suffering from strange cases of 'memory loss', for when they were questioned, independently by the police as to what had happened on the day of the fracas, they both responded by saying they couldn't remember a thing.

Moisha and Sonny, meanwhile, had plenty of work to do, with Moisha contacting Rita to tell her what had happened, and arranging her travel from Ireland back to London, while Sonny started to put himself about in Soho; his boss needed witnesses, and it was Sonny's job to make sure they would be friendly ones, who had seen the whole thing strictly from Comer's perspective, of how an armed and dangerous Albert Redman had attacked him in the street and tried to murder him.

While Sonny was doing the rounds of the Soho clubs, bars and spielers, he also got wind of Billy White' mob, who had wasted no time at all in making their presence felt in the area. "Comer's on his death bed," they were saying, "he won't last the night" Sonny couldn't believe what he was hearing. "Tell me the truth Sonny," pleaded one club owner, "I need to know? White' mob is breathing down my neck and demanding I pay them from now on, just tell me, what should I do?" "I'll tell you what you should do," replied a very angry Sonny, "tell White' mob that Jack is far from dead and neither are his mob, but White and his weekend gangsters will be if they dare show their faces in any of our clubs again"

Sonny still had lots of work to do, and it was getting more difficult by the minute. He made a few phone calls and rounded up a few of the boys, telling them to make themselves busy in the clubs, "Deal with any troublemakers as you see fit, and you all know who I mean by that" He then got in touch with Bobby Osborne and told him to get over to the Ronnieal Billiard Hall and put the Krays in the picture, "I want them tooled up and over here as soon as possible," he told Osborne, "and to bring their firm with them, I want White and his cronies run out of Soho once and for all"

• • •

By that weekend, Comer was fit enough to be properly questioned, after which he was taken to West End Central Police Station and formally charged with causing grievous bodily harm and possessing an offensive weapon. He was kept in a police cell over the weekend and appeared on Monday morning at Marlborough Magistrates Court. Standing next to him in the dock that morning was his nemesis and co-defendant, Albert Redman. The charges were read out and both men were denied bail and remanded in custody at Brixton Prison.

Comer and Redman appeared again at Marlborough Magistrates Court five days later when the prosecution called witnesses against them. Some said they were so afraid, especially of Jack Comer, that they asked for their names to be kept secret and only seen by the court in writing. At the end of the hearing, Comer was remanded in custody while Redman was given bail, which needless to say, infuriated Comer.

Comer desperately needed witnesses on his behalf if he was going to walk free from this charge, but this was easier said than done. Sonny had visited him and explained what was happening around Soho, and what an uphill battle it was becoming, but now, he explained how he had brought the Krays in to keep order while he was away, and it looked like he was starting to connect with the people they needed.

A few days later, a man walked into West End Central police station and said he would like to make a statement regarding the Jack Comer and Albert Redman' case. The man was Christopher Jackowski, an ex fighter pilot during WWII, who had won the Polish Military Cross and the French Croix de Guerre; in other words he was something of a hero whose word in court would be unanimously accepted. Jackowski said that he had been there in Frith Street when the Comer and Redman incident occurred; it was Redman who first attacked Comer with a knife, said Jackowski; all Comer did was argue with Redman and give him a shove.

It was later alleged by the prosecution, that Jackowski had met earlier that same day with Moisha and Sonny at Comer's flat at Cumberland Mansions. If the police could prove there was any truth in this, then Comer's case would be blown out of the water.

Comer's luck was about to change for the better however, when Moisha and Sonny were paying a regular visit to the Hideaway Club one evening, and were accosted by a man named Peter McElroy, also known as Tall Pete, who was in debt, not just to the Hideaway, but also to other Comer run clubs and spielers. Tall Pete said that he thought he could help Comer out, if they would help him regarding his debts. Moisha and Sonny were willing to listen to anything, which could possibly help their boss, and so Tall Pete told them how his wife had a regular income, which was earned by renting out small flats in a large house she owned in Upper Berkeley Street.

One of the tenants of the Upper Berkeley Street flats was a vicar, known as the Reverend Basil Arnott. Reverend Arnott originally came from a small parish in Oxfordshire, where he lived with his wife and young son. One day however, Arnott and his family mysteriously disappeared from his parish. There was talk among the villagers that he had been found out womanising, but this was never proven. He turned up some years later, minus his family, at a small church in north London, and quickly became a part of the local community, especially the part of it associated with pubs, where he became quite famous as someone who could drink most other regulars under the table! Not only was Reverend Arnott a very heavy drinker, he was also an inveterate gambler. It was about this time that he moved into one of the Upper Berkeley Street flats owned by Tall Pat's wife, and eventually met Tall Pete. As both the Reverend Arnott and Tall Pete were gamblers and nearly always in debt to the bookies, they had a common bond. The vicar, said Tall Pete, would literally sell his soul for a few more drinks and a gamble or two.

A huge smile broke out on Comer's face when Sonny visited him in Brixton Prison, "Sounding good Sonny," he beamed, "wouldn't it be wonderful if this old priest geezer had actually have been in Frith

Street and seen the fight that day – a jury would have to believe him wouldn't they – a priest, if he said Redman had a knife and had attacked me, and that I didn't have any weapon at all?"

Sonny assured his boss not to worry, "Tall Pete is fixing up a meeting with the vicar" he said, "the guy is in debt – I'm sure he could do with a little help, if you know what I mean?" Comer smiled as he went back to his cell, knowing that he still had good friends like Sonny and Moisha whom he could rely on.

• • •

Things were most definitely hotting up in and around Soho, while Comer was safely ensconced in his Brixton prison cell. The Krays had moved in, supposedly on Comer's behalf, with a vengeance. Beatings and slashings were being handed out to almost anyone who dared look at them in the wrong way. Moisha was fuming when he heard that one of his team had been stabbed in mistake for one of White' boys. "What the fuck is going on here?" he shouted at Bobby Osborne, "Jack will go fucking berserk when he hears this" Osborne tried to calm Moisha down, "You know what Ronnie's like," he said, "he didn't know who the geezer was – so when he told him that he was looking after that spieler, Ronnie naturally thought he was one of White' boys"

Moisha was beginning to have misgivings about getting the Krays involved, especially Ronnie, who seemed to act before thinking about anything. He was a loose cannon, who definitely needed reining in if they were to be able to work together, but for now, the main thing on Moisha's mind was getting his boss out of prison, a free man.

Luckily for Moisha, if not for Comer, the prosecuting counsel took almost two weeks in preparing his case. Moisha and Sonny sat in the public gallery of of the Old Bailey and could hardly believe their eyes when both Comer and Redman were brought into the dock together. The court heard from both men's defence counsels as well as from the police. The big question for the court to consider was who had attacked whom first and who owned the knife, which was seen to be used in the attack. Redman' defence was that Comer had attacked him with a knife and that he had wrestled it off Comer and turned it on him in order to defend himself. Fortunately for Comer, by the time he had produced his gun, Redman was so fatigued and his eyes covered with blood that he never even saw it.

At the end of the first day, the judge adjourned the trial after deciding that both men should be tried separately. Comer was once again remanded in custody, while Redman was granted bail, which for some strange reason, the police did not oppose.

On 22 September, Comer once again graced the dock of the Old Bailey with his presence, but this time he faced the charges alone. His counsel was a very smart Jewish lady named Rose Hendrik who had a fearsome reputation in the legal profession.

Sophie Glickstein, the proprietress of the Continental Fruit Store, where the fight took place, was called to the witness box and described how Comer had chased Redman into her shop and had something metallic in his hand, which he was lashing out at Redman with, her husband, Herman Glickstein, corroborated her story. The prosecution asked the pair if they were afraid of Jack Comer, to which they both answered that they were very much afraid of him.

It was quite a warm day and Sophie Glickstein was a rather large lady. She had started to sweat profusely and her face had turned bright red. The judge asked Mrs Glickstein if she felt alright and asked if she would like to take a few minutes break and have a glass of water. At this point Rose Hendrik interrupted, and asked Mrs Glickstein if her appearance was due more to the fact that she was a very frightened woman, than to the heat in the courtroom. Mrs Glickstein didn't seem to know how to respond to this, when the judge interjected by asking, "Perhaps you are frightened of Mrs Hendrik?" Mrs Glickstein responded rather angrily that she most definitely was not. This caused much laughter in the court, but Hendrik waded straight in again, this time aimed at Mr Glickstein, suggesting to him that in all the confusion, was he absolutely sure who the actual aggressor was that day, "Might it not have been Albert Redman who was the aggressor and that all Jack Comer was was doing was holding onto Redman' wrist, trying to force him to drop the knife?"

Rose Hendrik's tactics were obviously fashioned in a way to make the jury believe that Mr and Mrs Glickstein were quite old and somewhat confused by all that was going on around them. "Are you absolutely sure of the actual sequence of events that happened that day?" she asked Mr Glickstein. She was doing an excellent job and Mr Glickstein seemed to be falling into her trap, "Sequence?" he blurted out, "I know what I saw, I was there" "Yes, of course you were" said Rose Hendrik, rather smugly.

The next witness to be 'interrogated' by Rose Hendrik was Papa Stagno, also known as Charles Marshland, who was described by the prosecution counsel as a bookmaker. Stagno told the court that he had known Comer and Redman for a number of years and that Comer was a very much-feared man around Soho. Rose Hendrik pursed her lips and slowly shook her head as she looked direct into Stagno eyes. "Mr Stagno," she said, almost disparagingly, "is it not a fact that that in some quarters, you have been described as being one of the most feared men in Soho, not my client, Mr Comer? I also put to you that the term bookmaker doesn't really describe your chosen profession at all does it?" She didn't wait for an answer from Stagno, but continued with, "Is it not a fact that you once ran a thriving vice empire in Soho for a number of years before the war?" "That was a long time ago," Stagno shouted, "I have been a bookmaker for.." "I am not finished," Rose Hendrik interrupted, "Is it not also a fact that you approached several witnesses in this case and warned them that they would have you to deal with if they didn't support Albert Redman? "Lies, lies, lies," Stagno shouted until the judge warned him that he would be charged with contempt of court if he did not desist from calling out and disrupting the proceedings

When it came to Comer's turn in the witness box, he spoke in a very subdued voice, completely out of character to the real Jack Comer. The judge had to ask him to speak up on one occasion, when he was describing how he had been stabbed by Albert Redman. He looked around the court like a frightened rabbit caught in the headlights of a car; luckily for him no one seemed to notice the wink he gave to Rita, who was sitting close to Moisha and Sonny in the public gallery. At one point in the proceedings, his counsel, Rose Hendrik, asked the court if her client could possibly have a seat and a glass of water before carrying on any further. This was granted and Comer went on to complete his almost Oscar winning performance before being dismissed for the time being, and the next witness was called.

Chapter 46

Unbeknown to Comer and the Soho crowd in general, the Deacon brothers had just moved back to their south London headquarters, from Birmingham, after being chased out by a local gang due to Teddy Baxter crashing a lorry into the gang boss' home and seriously injuring his ten year old daughter.

Their fruit machines had all been either taken over by the Birmingham gang, or smashed by the local police, who were in the pay of the Birmingham mob. This didn't exactly leave the Deacon brothers skint, as they did still have their scrap metal business, but it did mean they now needed to find a new business proposition in London.

Teddy Baxter threw the Daily Mirror down on Bobby Deacon's kitchen table, "Have a look at that," he grinned, as he pointed out the front page article about Comer and Redman and their Old Bailey trial, "I hope the prick goes away for life" Bobby Deacon glanced quickly at the paper and brushed it back towards Baxter. "What's the matter with you, can't you ever forget fucking Comer? I've got more important things to worry about than him, especially after the fucking aggravation you caused us in Birmingham"

Baxter didn't like being talked down to like that, especially as it had been Bobby Deacon who had ordered him to attack the house of the boss of the Birmingham mob, how was he to know the geezer's family would be in there at the time? But this wasn't the right time to answer Bobby Deacon back. "I'm going out for a drink," he said as he picked up his paper and left Deacon's house. Deacon in return just glanced up without saying a word more to Baxter. There was certainly no love lost between these two.

An hour later and Baxter was propping up the bar of one of the more seedier Soho clubs, which was half empty. He placed his Daily Mirror on the bar next to him, with the headline facing upwards, in the hope that someone might see it and make a comment about it, which he would then join in and hopefully find out a little more about what was going on in Soho.

● ● ●

While Baxter was trying to hatch his little plot in the Soho bar, things were still moving at the Old Bailey, where Christopher Jackowski, who had been described as a Polish war hero, had just been called as a witness. Rose Hendrik arose from her seat, "Can you tell the court, Mr Jackowski, why you are here today, you were not summonsed by the prosecution to appear here were you?" Jackowski straightened himself up in the witness box, patted his jacket down and straightened his tie, looking every inch like the war hero he had been portrayed as. "I came here of my own volition," he replied in his strong Polish accent, "I had read reports in the newspapers about what had supposedly happened, and realised it wasn't true. I was there that day"

"Can you describe to the court exactly what you saw happen in Frith Street, Soho, that day? asked Rose Hendrik, "Of course," he replied, "I saw the two men, Albert Redman and Jack Comer, arguing with each other near the corner of Frith Street, Comer pushed Redman and looked as if he was about to walk away, but then Redman took a knife out and charged at Comer, stabbing him in the arm and then slashing his face"

There was deathly silence in the court as Jackowski continued his evidence, "The two men then grappled with each other and staggered into the fruit shop where they continued to fight – I could see them through the wide doorway, which was open. They were knocking over boxes of fruit as they continued to fight. At this point a large crowd had gathered and I could not see so well, but I heard a loud metallic noise and someone in the crowd said that the woman in the shop had just hit Comer with the metal scales" "And then what happened?" asked Rose Hendrik. "The next thing I saw was Albert Redman stagger out of the shop, followed a few seconds later by Jack Comer; both men were covered with blood" "Was either man carrying a weapon of any kind at that point Mr Jackowski?" Hendrik asked. Jackowski frowned as if trying hard to remember, "I am not one hundred percent sure, but I thought I saw something gleaming in Albert Redman' hand as he ran off towards a waiting taxi" "And Jack Comer?" Hendrik continued. "No, he was definitely not carrying anything, I know this because he collapsed on the floor right in front of me" "Thank you Mr Jackowski." said a very satisfied Rose Hendrik.

The prosecuting counsel's questions to Jackowski were very brief and to the point. He was asked if he knew either of the two men, Comer or Redman, on a personal level, to which Jackowski replied that he did not, he had never met either man, he had read about them and seen their pictures in the newspaper, that is all, he said. At this point the proceedings were adjourned for the day.

Moisha and Sonny were very pleased with the way things were going and decided an early celebration drink would be in order. They did ask Rita if she would like to join them, but of course she said no; firstly because she needed to get back to the flat, where Miriam was being looked after, and secondly, and more close to the truth, was the fact that drinking in Soho bars was most definitely not her scene.

After Moisha had run Rita home, he drove over to Hideaway Club in Soho, where he met Sonny and a few other members of the mob. Half an hour later, Bobby Osborne came in along with Reggie and Ronnie Kray, and Big Pat. Moisha still wasn't too sure about the Kray's involvement, but on this occasion he was willing to bite his tongue, as the Krays did offer his mob a much needed boost.

"Sorry we haven't been along to the trial Moisha," Ronnie Kray quietly said, "but we have been doing what you asked and looking after things around here" "That's right," Reggie Kray butted in, "and not only that, but I don't think it would have done any of us any good, if we had been spotted at the Old Bailey, d'you know what I mean?"

Moisha nodded in agreement, but secretly wondered who exactly were they worried about, Jack or themselves? Moisha was deep in his thoughts as he felt someone nudge him in the back. He looked round to see Sonny, who was silently indicating for him to look over towards the door. "What the fuck is he doing here?" Moisha murmured, almost to himself. It was Teddy Baxter, who was staggering and obviously somewhat drunk. "We've got to get him out of here," answered Sonny, "he's going to cause trouble, and Jack would have our guts for garters if he knew we'd allowed him in here"

Ronnie Kray had overheard what was being said and moved in closer to Moisha and Sonny. He pulled open his jacket and pulled out a German Luger pistol, "I'll take him outside and shoot him for you if you want?" "Fuck me no," replied Moisha, "he's as pissed as a fart, a good slap and a warning not to come here again is all he needs for the time being" Moisha had to be really careful, the last he had heard of Baxter, he was working with the Deacon brothers and he didn't want to start a war with them now, as well as White' mob.

"Put it away Ronnie," It was Reggie Kray, who had now moved in and was shoving the gun back into his brother's waistband. "See who's over there?" he said, nodding towards a somewhat shortish man in his mid to late thirties, who had just walked into the club. It was Detective Superintendent Leonard 'Nipper' Read, who was dressed exactly as one would suspect a detective to dress, in a raincoat and small brown trilby hat. Nipper hadn't walked in expecting not to be recognised, he had walked in with a hint of a smile on his face, which said, "I know you lot, and I am watching you"

"Get rid of Baxter as quick as you like," Moisha said, "but like I said, with a slap and a warning, and do it quietly for fuck's sake" Reggie Kray whispered something to his brother, who nodded in agreement and beckoned Big Pat over to them.

Two minutes later, while Nipper Read was ordering himself a drink at the bar, Big Pat sidled up to Baxter and edged him toward the exit by using his enormous bulk alone, "Outside," he mumbled, "outside, now" Baxter didn't have much option as he was quickly moved, as if by a steamroller, out of the club. A few minutes later Big Pat returned and mumbled to Ronnie Kray and Moisha, that the job had been done, "He won't be back in here for a while," he smilingly said, "that's for sure"

Moisha noticed Ronnie Kray lift his drink in a toast to someone along the bar, it was the ever smiling Nipper Read. Moisha and Sonny looked at each other, both thinking the same thing, whatever had they let themselves in for here?

• • •

When Comer's trial at the Old Bailey convened the following day, the first witness to be called was the Reverend Basil Arnott. This witness was something of a surprise to many in the court that day, especially as he was a man of the cloth and he was appearing as a witness for Comer's defence. A hushed silence fell as he was sworn in. He told the court, in a rather quiet and clipped manner of speaking, how he had read the newspaper article about the fracas in Frith Street, to which he had been a witness, and had decided to contact Mr Comer's solicitors as the account he had read in the newspaper was totally wrong. "Goodness me," he quipped, "I couldn't just stand back and let an injustice like this take place without telling the authorities what really happened now could I?"

Rose Hendrik asked Arnott to describe in his own words what exactly did happen then, to which he replied, "All I know is that I saw the defendant, Jack Comer trying to defend himself from a darker looking man with a knife, whom I later saw a photograph of in the newspaper, where it described him as an Italian named Albert Redman.

When Rose Hendrik summed up for the defence, she pointed out to the court that her client, Jack Comer, had suffered the worst injuries of the two men involved, which wasn't consistent with someone who was allegedly doing the attacking. She also pointed out that in the statement Albert Redman had made to the police, he seemed to know a great deal about the knife that had been used in the attack, even though it had subsequently disappeared.

Rose Hendrik had handled the case very well, even swaying the judge, Sir Gerald Bullock, who in his summing up, referred to Redman as a strong-arm man, and whom he thought Comer was right to defend himself against.

When the jury finally retired to consider their verdict, they took just 65 minutes and came back with a unanimous verdict of not guilty.

There were celebrations at Comer's flat in Cumberland Mansions that evening. All his crew were there as well as a few trusted members of the the legal profession. Outside the flat however, were members of the press who were watching who was coming and going and eagerly waiting for a story. One visitor they almost missed, because he used a side entrance, was the Reverend Basil Arnott, but one eagle eyed reporter did see a taxi waiting around the side, with its engine running. The reporter put on his best friendly face, and armed with a crisp white five pound note, questioned the taxi driver about who his passenger might be. "I don't ask their names guvner," replied the taxi driver, as he pocketed the fiver, "but he was wearing one of those dog collars if you know what I mean, probably a vicar I would say"

Within no time, word leaked out about the party and the Reverend, and by the following morning the papers were full of it. More reporters showed up on Comer's doorstep demanding interviews and asking if he knew the Reverend Arnott before he appeared in court. The papers also ran hastily made up stories about the Reverend, his gambling habits and how much he owed to Soho bookies.

Rita had only been in London a couple of weeks, but Comer was getting seriously worried about her staying at the flat with all the press constantly pressurising them. Luckily, their daughter Miriam was still in Ireland, but as much as he wanted Rita beside him, he had to relent and send her back to Ireland once again, promising to join her as soon as possible, for a long awaited holiday together.

With Rita safely out of the way, Comer placed several gang members outside his flat day and night to ward off the press and anyone else that who could cause trouble, especially after Moisha told him that Teddy Baxter was back and trying to make his presence felt once again. He wasn't too worried about Billy White now that he had the Krays in his team, but he warned both Moisha and Sonny to keep a close eye on them, in case they became too ambitious.

Just over a week later, it was Albert Redman' turn to appear in the dock of the Old Bailey to answer the almost identical charge that Comer had faced, which was that of causing an affray in Frith Street, Soho.

Redman' counsel, Alan Banister QC, stated that there was no charge to answer, as all his client had been doing, was trying to defend himself from someone who was attacking him with a knife. Redman, he alleged, had run away from the knife wielding Comer, he had run into the grocery store to try to get away from this villain, and had also wrestled the knife away from his attacker in the process. "There is no possible evidence," he claimed, "against my client, Mr Redman, to suggest he wounded with intent to cause grievous bodily harm to Mr Jack Comer" "It is not," he said, "for my client to prove he was acting in self defence, it is for the prosecution to prove he was not"

The judge was starting to look very dissatisfied with the way the proceeding were seemingly not going anywhere, He drew a deep breath and addressed the counsel for the prosecution, "Mr Broadbent," he said, with great sufferance in his voice, "do you have any witnesses at all to corroborate the accusations against Mr Albert Redman?" Mr Broadbent swallowed hard and thumbed through the pages of notes in front of him, which caused even more impatience from the judge. "Come along Mr Broadbent, surely you know, do you have witnesses or do you not?" "I am sorry your honour," replied Mr Broadbent, "I do not"

The Judge shook his head as if in complete disbelief, "What an absolute waste of time" he mumbled almost under his breath. When the summing up began, the prosecution listened to the judge, who obviously had no option other than to agree with Mr Banister, and unanimously agreed to withdraw the charges against Redman. Albert Redman walked from the Old Bailey, a free man.

"What a stitch up," growled Comer, when he heard the result, and conveniently seeming to forget that he had done the same sort of thing, "so the old Bill brings a case to court with no fucking witnesses? Do me a favour"

Comer was seething inside at the fact that Billy White' right hand man had got away with stabbing and cutting him, but in reality it was Comer who had won the day. He had walked away from court a free man, and the case had greatly enhanced his reputation as the boss of the London underworld. All he needed to do now was to get rid of Billy White and his gang for good, and London would belong to him, lock stock and barrel.

The day following Redman' acquittal, the newspapers were full of the story, 'Gangsters' fight in Soho never happened'. The press, the public, and the police, all wanted answers; how could two of the leading men in the underworld cut each other to pieces in the heart of London, and yet both walk free from court without a stain on their characters?

Everyone knew that certain witnesses could not have possibly been telling the truth. They also wanted to know what had happened to possible witnesses for the prosecution of Albert Redman. The police had sent undercover officers to watch the witnesses in the Comer case, to see if they were approached in any way by members of the criminal fraternity, but unfortunately for them the criminals were not as stupid as the police imagined they might be, and consequently no evidence of witness 'nobbling' was ever brought to light.

Even though the police could find no evidence, the Home Secretary, Gwilym Lloyd George opened up an enquiry into the affair, explaining that the British public need to know the truth about what happened and if indeed there was any evidence of corruption from any of the parties concerned.

The press, on the other hand did not have to strictly abide by the law and at least two National newspapers decided to launch their own investigations. It didn't take long before underworld minions were crawling out of the woodwork and offering their stories, for an agreed sum, of what had happened that day.

By the following Sunday, one major National ran a story about the Reverend Basil Arnott and his gambling habits, telling of how he had run up a string of bad debts and how the London bookies were now searching for him. The Reverend had by this time, disappeared from his usual Soho haunts, but according to him someone obviously knew his whereabouts, for he was now alleging that he had received a death threat in the post.

As much as the Reverend was used to mixing with the criminal fraternity, it was normally based around his gambling habits, but when he received this threat to his life he didn't hang around or start asking questions, instead he went directly to yet another National newspaper and offered to sell them his story.

The paper bought his story, which was in the form of a letter, which he dictated to them. The letter stated that he did not lie in the witness box and that he did not therefore commit perjury.

The newspaper printed its story, and the Reverend Basil Arnott received his forty pieces of silver from the paper, but he also received an invitation to attend an interview with Commander Ted Greeno at Scotland Yard. The Reverend was questioned for hours by Greeno and his team, and then taken to a safe-house for his own protection.

It didn't take long for word to spread that the Reverend Basil Arnott was being questioned by Scotland Yard, and that he was ensconced in a private dwelling somewhere in London. Comer was understandably worried when he heard this. From what he knew of the Reverend Basil Arnott, he was a man of little principals, who would sell out to the highest bidder. "We have to find out where they're keeping him," he ordered Moisha and Sonny. "And if we find him, then what?" asked Sonny. Comer looked grim as he drew his finger across his throat. "Top him?" exclaimed Moisha, "we can't top a fucking vicar" "If necessary get the Krays to deal with him," answered Comer, "it's what we're paying them for"

Unbeknown to Comer, the Reverend wasn't his only worry at that time, for Scotland Yard were continuing to interview more and more people in what was now known as the Frith Street fight enquiry. One of the major witnesses in the case had been the Polish fighter pilot, Christopher Jackowski, who became so worried that he issued a statement through his solicitor to the press, saying that he might have been approached by a woman just before the trial, but he was not absolutely sure; in other words he was trying to portray himself as a somewhat confused character, rather than a dishonest one.

Meanwhile the press continued to compile more and more stories and statements from the seedier side of Soho, to their ever-growing list, which they gleefully published in their rags, and apparently intended to hand over to The Home Secretary and the Director of Public Prosecutions.

One such story, which came to light involved yet again the Reverend Basil Arnott. The story referred to a young girl in her early teens, whom the Reverend had once described as his niece. It was alleged that the young girl had suddenly married an elderly man, and that it was none other than the Reverend Basil Arnott who had conducted the marriage ceremony for them. There is nothing illegal or strange in that one might think, until it suddenly came to light that the Reverend owed money to the elderly man, and that the elderly man had handed over £365 to the Reverend, which was a sizeable amount of money at the time. The Reverend never confirmed or denied the story, and his 'niece' and her elderly husband mysteriously disappeared from off the radar.

The police did not show an active interest in these stories, for neither the story regarding the Reverend and his so called 'niece' nor the one concerning Jackowski, were thought of as marking these people as potential criminal cases in their own right, but the police were secretly delighted, as they did bring to light the fact that they were certainly very unreliable characters and possibly unreliable witnesses in the Jack Comer case.

A battle was going on within the press as newspapers vied with each other to be the first with an exclusive on London's gangland. Snippets of news kept appearing, with promises of more to come, but in general it was nothing more than rehashed stories under different banners.

Suddenly the Daily Sketch published a 'major scoop' proclaiming that they had uncovered a dramatic new story regarding the gangs who were running the London underworld. So important were their findings they said, that they could not publish the story until they had sent the full details to Scotland Yard, which they claimed to be doing immediately.

Other papers quickly followed up with demands for a major enquiry into the Comer and Redman affair, as well as a complete investigation into why these characters and their henchmen had been allowed to rule the underworld for so long, without any apparent intervention by the police.

Chapter 47

Reggie and Ronnie Kray sat in their little office at the back of the billiard hall and listened to Sonny explaining what Comer wanted done. "I'm not sure about this Sonny," Reggie said, shaking his head, "we can give him a slap if you like, and warn him what would happen to him if he does decide to talk to the old Bill, but if he goes missing the first person the law will turn to will be Jack, and then us – no, not a good idea at all" Sonny wasn't at all happy with Reggie's answer, "You do realise that you are supposed to be working for Jack?" he said, "it was Jack who gave you this place and put you in the position you are now in"

"I know all that," replied Reggie, "and I'm grateful to Jack for what he's done, but murdering a vicar is something else, and I'm not prepared to do it"

"Hold on Reg," Ronnie interrupted, "I think we should consider this more carefully, from what I've heard this so called vicar is about as religious as I am - he lied in court for Jack, what's to stop him lying again, this time for the old Bill?" Reggie Kray shook his head, he didn't like the way this was going. He had always considered Ronnie to be the more headstrong of the two of them and liable to dive into the deep-end without taking the risks into consideration first. "I know that," Reggie replied, "It's not the religious part I'm personally worried about, but can you imagine what the papers would say once they got hold of the story, vicar murdered by gangsters? They'd fucking crucify us"

Ronnie lit another cigarette, inhaled it deeply and blew out a thin jet of grey wispy smoke. "Let's say we agree to this," he said to Sonny, completely ignoring his brother's last remarks, "how would we find the vicar, and how would we get rid of his body?"

Sonny explained that the police had got the Reverend Basil Arnott hidden away in a safe house somewhere, but one of the coppers involved in the case, also happens to be as bad as the vicar in his gambling habits, and owes us a lot of money. "He's done us little favours before," added Sonny, "so we don't see this as a problem, if you get my drift?" Ronnie Kray nodded, "And getting rid of the body?" he asked.

Sonny had the perfect place in mind, which was the old wash-house in east London, but he didn't want to give too many secrets away at this point, and just told Ronnie that they had a one hundred percent foolproof scheme for that.

A smile started to break out on Ronnie's face as he weighed up the situation in his mind. Reggie was now starting to get worried and quickly interrupted the conversation, "I think we need to talk about this Ron," Ronnie ignored his brother, got to his feet and held his hand out to Sonny, "Leave it with us Sonny," he said, "and tell Jack not to worry"

As Sonny drove back towards Comer's flat, he kept wondering to himself if they had done the right thing in getting the Krays involved. Maybe Reggie was right, maybe the police would come down on all of them if the vicar suddenly disappeared, but what if he didn't just disappear, what if Ronnie gunned him down in front of witnesses, and the thought of that wasn't entirely improbable?

Inside the flat Comer weighed up the situation carefully in his mind as Sonny explained to him exactly what the Krays had said, and the way Ronnie had acted. "He can be a bit of a loose cannon, I know that," he admitted, "but I don't see what other options I have, the old Bill will get the vicar to say whatever they want, you can bet your life on that"

At the end of the day, Comer was the boss, and as much as Sonny disagreed with letting the Krays handle this, his job was to act upon his boss's orders. Comer was pleased with the outcome of Sonny's meeting with the Krays, and told him to get onto the bent copper straight away. "We need to find that old rogue of a vicar as soon as possible," he said, "before the old Bill start putting another case together about us" "Leave that to me," replied Sonny, I'll go straight round to his brother now and make a meet with him for tonight"

As Sonny walked towards the Chrysler, which was parked outside Comer's block of flats, he noticed something stuck on his windscreen. What the fuck was this now he thought as he pulled the piece of paper off and looked at it. It was a parking enforcement ticket, probably the first one to be issued in that part of London. Sonny had never even heard of such things, Yes, he thought, I'm going to pay to park in the fucking street – like hell I am. He screwed the piece of paper up, threw in the road and drove off.

• • •

"This had better be good Teddy," said Billy White to Teddy Baxter, who was sitting opposite him and Albert Redman in a café in Berwick Street market, "I've got an important meeting in half an hour, so make it good and make it quick"

Baxter did his best to come straight to the point, which was a story that he had heard from a reliable source, that the law were preparing a new case against Comer. "So tell me something new?" replied White, somewhat sarcastically. "I know there's been rumours going around for a long time Mr White," added Baxter, "but this time it's definite, a mate of mine who used to work for Comer, was pulled in just two days ago – the old Bill threatened to charge him with being an associate of Comer's gang, robbery with violence, attempted murder, and Christ knows what else if he didn't play ball with them"

Billy White and Albert Redman looked at each other and at Teddy Baxter. Could this be true they wondered? They had heard some of Baxter's stories in the past. "So why are you telling me this Teddy?" asked White, "you want something, I know that, so what is it?"

Baxter explained that he had an ongoing grudge against Comer, and was willing to do anything to see him deposed. "Now he's got the Krays with him as well, he is strutting about like Lord of the fucking manor" "Hold on," Albert Redman interrupted, "one minute you are saying the old Bill are preparing another case against him, and now you're saying he he's still a threat to us, which is it Teddy, make your fucking mind up?"

"It is definitely true that the law is preparing this new case against him, but look at the way he got out of the last case where he attacked you Albert, he bribed and threatened witnesses and then walked free, do you think he won't do the same again?"

Billy White was starting to get despondent, this was going absolutely nowhere. He looked at his watch and then back to Baxter again.

"You've got five minutes left Teddy, either you come up with something worthwhile or I'm walking out of here"

"I'll kill him for you – I'll kill Jack Comer" This made White and Redman sit up and take notice, straight and to the point, most unlike the usual Baxter garbage. "All I'm asking you for," continued Baxter, "is a permanent place on your team, and protection afterwards"

Less that a mile away, Sonny had parked the car in Soho Square and made his way to the Back Door Club, which was an illegal gambling club above a café in Meard Street, just off Dean Street, Soho. It was a little more classy than the average spieler in the fact that it had roulette wheel there, with an attractive female croupier.

Sonny stood behind one of six men who were playing the roulette wheel and watched as the croupier raked in all their chips. This happened three times in succession "You should stick to cards Barry," he said to the man in front of him. Barry Turner looked round and grinned at Sonny, "You're probably right Sonny," he answered, "what are you doing here, this isn't one of your clubs is it?" Sonny leaned forward and whispered in Barry's ear. He told him that he needed to speak to his brother urgently. "No problem mate," replied Barry, "He's been waiting for you, I'll arrange it straight away"

• • •

Early the following morning, at West End Central Police Station, P.C. Gerald Turner whistled nonchalantly as he walked along one of the corridors, carrying an enamelled tin mug full of tea in his hand. He paused as he came to a door marked Detective Chief Superintendent T Butler. P.C. Turner paused, looked around and then gently tapped on the door. After a couple of seconds he tried the door handle, found it to be open and went inside.

P.C. Turner moved quickly once inside, straight to the filing cabinet, which he opened and started riffling through the beige coloured paper files with various names on. He stopped at the Jack Comer file, opened it up and flicked through the documents inside until he came to the Reverend Basil Arnott. He took out his notepad and pencil and quickly copied something from the file, put everything back and made his way out of the office.

• • •

Comer was beaming as he leaned back in his armchair and lit one of his favourite cigars. "Nice work Sonny," he said, "and Reggie and Ronnie are going to act on it immediately are they?" Sonny nodded as he sipped the large brandy that Comer had just given him, "That's what they said Jack" "Nice work," replied Comer. "I'll tell you what though Jack," added Moisha, who was sitting next to Sonny, "I reckon you should get yourself an alibi ready, be as far as away from London as you can when this happens"

Comer paused in thought for a moment, summing up what Moisha had said to him. "Depends when they're going to do it," he said, "did they give any indication as to when it might happen?" Sonny shook his head, "Immediately, was the word Ronnie used"

"You're right, have you got the car here?" Comer asked Moisha. "It's around the corner," replied Moisha, "can't park out here any more since they put those bloody parking machines in, the car's too big for the space anyway" "Don't worry about that," Comer replied, just go and get it as quick as you can, I want you to run me to the station straight away, I'm going to Ireland - now"

Chapter 48

The Reverend Basil Arnott smiled smugly as he moved his white Queen to check his opponent's black King. "Checkmate" The police officer didn't look too happy, but this was his first game since he was a child, and it had taken the Reverend Basil Arnott almost two hours to reach this position.

From the outside of this little semi-detached house in Shepherds Bush everything looked completely normal. No police cars parked outside, just one light green Ford Anglia sitting in between other cars of a similar type. The suburban neighbours would have had a fit if they realised the house was being used a safe house to guard a major witness in an infamous gangster trial that had recently taken place.

They would have had a double fit if they had also seen the large man in the front garden of number twenty seven, who was peering in the window, through a slight gap in the curtains. The large man suddenly turned and made a quick dash across the street, to where a Bedford Dormobile van was parked. He slid the passenger door open and jumped inside. The man was Big Pat, inside the van was Reggie and Ronnie Kray, and the driver of the van, Dave Williams. "The copper's been playing chess with him," said Big Pat, "and from what I could hear, he's just popping out to get some fish and chips for supper" "There he goes now," said Ronnie Kray as the police officer came out of the house, got into his Ford Anglia and drove off. "Get over there, quick" Ronnie ordered. Dave Williams punched the Dormobile's engine into life and pulled across the road and into the space left vacant by the police officer's Ford Anglia.

When the doorbell rang, the Reverend Basil Arnott went immediately to the door and for one second was almost about to open it, just remembering what he had been told in time. "Who is it?" he called out. "Detective Sergeant Reece," replied the voice from behind the door. Arnott smiled as he unlocked the door and opened it. The smile quickly disappeared from his face as Big Pat and Ronnie Kray grabbed him, bent him double, ran him to the Dormobile, and threw him into the already open doors at the back, where Reggie was waiting for him, and threw a sack over his head. Everything was over in seconds, the van doors were slammed shut and they were on their way.

Less than an hour later the neighbours in the leafy, tree lined street had no second thoughts that something was most definitely going on at number twenty seven, for there were now three police cars parked outside and police officers coming and going, and making a great deal of noise as they did so.

"Fish and chips?" shouted a senior offer at the policeman who was supposed to be guarding the Reverend, "you were supposed to keep him under strict surveillance around the clock, do you know what that means?" The police officer nodded, "Yes sir," he murmured lowly.

At this point the police did not suspect foul play, they assumed the Reverend had simply had enough of court cases and had decided to abscond and maybe revert back to the simple life of a man of the church.

• • •

While the police continued with their investigations, the Dormobile pulled up outside the old wash-house in east London. "I hope this is right," Ronnie Kray said, "what's the name of the geezer Sonny said runs this place?" "Nat," answered Reggie, quietly. Big Pat pulled out a cosh and glanced over at the prostrate figure of the Reverend, still lying on the floor of the van with the sack over his head. "Do you want me to give him a whack before we take him in? he whispered. Ronnie Kray smiled evilly and took his Luger pistol from out of his waistband. "Leave it to me," he sneered. Big Pat got out of the Dormobile and rang the bell of the wash-house A few seconds later, Nat answered the door. "Sonny sent us," said Big Pat. As he spoke, a loud bang reverberated from inside the van. Nat stared for a moment at the van, "You better come in, quick as you can" he said.

• • •

Scotland Yard were informed of the Reverend's disappearance, and police patrol cars were sent out all over London, in the hope of finding him. They had decided to keep the story secret, but P.C. Gerald Turner, who was working at West End Central Police Station that night when the news came in, thought otherwise and the story ended up in the hands of one of the National newspapers. By the following morning, the Daily Mirror's headline proclaimed, 'Major Witness in Gangster Trial Disappears' While the story, which accompanied this headline didn't actually name the Reverend Basil Arnott, it did speak of a 'man of the cloth' which left readers in no doubt as to exactly who it was referring to.

The Polish fighter pilot, Christopher Jackowski, read the article in the Daily Mirror, the following morning regarding the Reverend's disappearance. There was no reason to believe the Reverend had been harmed in any way, in fact the article more or less suggested that he had run away, rather than face Jack Comer in a courtroom again.

Jackowski started to get very worried as he continued reading the article, especially as he had also been recently interviewed by the police regarding him being called as a witness for the prosecution in a new case against Jack Comer. If the Reverend Basil Arnott was so scared of what might happen to him if he turned against Comer and became a witness for the police, then he certainly wasn't going to hang around and become the star witness and the star target for Jack Comer's gang.

By that afternoon Jackowski had packed his suitcase and made a hasty exit from his London home to the relative safety of Europe, in all probability Poland, his native country. This of course now meant that the new case, which the police were building against Comer, was nothing more than a dead duck in the water, now that the two star witnesses has disappeared.

• • •

While the police were desperately trying to play down the story of a new trial for Comer, someone else had something entirely different on their mind. It was 9 pm and a dark grey Vauxhall Cresta was parked on the opposite side of the street to Cumberland Mansions.

The nearest lamp-post was directly outside Cumberland Mansions, which shone no light at all into the Vauxhall's interior or the figure of the man at the wheel inside it. The man looked up towards the block of flats, in particular at one floor, where all three front windows were lit and the silhouette of someone inside could be seen walking back and forth.

As he continued to watch, first the lights in one room went out, then the second room, and finally the third. The man in the car now focused on the main doorway to the flats, where the inside hall light now came on, showing through the frosted glass windows of the street door.

The door opened and the unmistakable figure of Jack Comer emerged, complete with his navy blue Crombie overcoat and matching blue fedora hat. He paused for a brief moment on the doorstep to light a cigarette before making his way down the steps to the street.

The door of the Vauxhall Cresta burst open at this point and the driver leapt out, carrying a double barrelled sawn off shotgun, "Comer," he shouted as he took a few steps forward and levelled the shotgun towards his target. There was an almighty blast and a flash of light as he fired the first shot, this was followed immediately by him emptying the second barrel of the shotgun at his victim, knocking him backwards as the lead shot hit him and sending him sprawling across the pavement.

The protagonist paused for a moment, almost as if he intended to fire another shot, but then realising that there were no more shots to be fired; two barrels, two shots. Teddy Baxter had borrowed this weapon from a friend, and knew very little about such guns. He threw the shotgun into the car, took one last look at Jack Comer, lying prostrate on the pavement opposite, and quickly drove off. If he had bothered to learn anything about such a weapon, he would have realised that it is only deadly at very close quarters as the shot, which it fires, is made up of hundreds of tiny lead pellets, which scatter widely the further they travel.

On closer inspection, Teddy Baxter would have also seen that the man lying sprawled out on the pavement was not Jack Comer at all, but his close friend and right hand man, Moisha, who had been visiting Comer's flat to pick up a few things and to phone his boss, who was still happily ensconced with his wife in Ireland. Teddy Baxter, however, had never been known to delve too deeply into anything, be it guns and their workings, to actually making sure he was firing at the correct target.

By the time Baxter's car had reached the end of the road, nearby neighbours who had the shots, had raced down to the street to see if they could be of assistance to the man lying on the pavement. Moisha was starting to move and groan as they reached him, obviously not dead. In fact far from it. His heavy Crombie overcoat had taken most of the flack, and was pitted with tiny rips. One side of his face was also bleeding, where two fragments of the shot had caught him, one in his left ear and one in his cheekbone, other than that, he was fine, and started to pull himself to his feet as the first neighbour asked if he was alright. Moisha thanked them and mumbled something about an accident as he quickly made his way off into the darkness before anyone had a chance to call the police or an ambulance.

Chapter 49

"The job's done," hissed Baxter. He was talking from a public telephone box in Tottenham Court Road. "What?" he replied to the voice on the other end of the line, "It's me, Teddy – Teddy Baxter" He listened to the voice of Billy White on the other end, "Sorry Mr White, I just wanted to tell you..." White cut him short, forcing Baxter to listen in silence for a few moments before mumbling an apologetic, "Yeah, sorry, I will," and then putting the phone back down onto the cradle, pressing button B and trying to get some of his money back, which didn't happen. "Bollocks," he exclaimed as he slammed the phone down again and walked dejectedly out of the phone box, into the cold rainy London air.

Billy White passed the phoned back across the bar to the publican of the Three Greyhounds pub in Greek Street, Soho. He turned to Albert Redman, who was standing next to him, "He reckons he's done it," he said quietly to Redman. Albert Redman looked quizzically at his boss, "Who - done what?" "Comer – Teddy Baxter says he's done the job" White whispered in reply. Billy White gulped down his drink, slammed a pound note on the bar, and started to walk out, "Come on," he said, "we've got work to do"

White and Redman left the pub and started a walking tour of the clubs, pubs and spielers of Soho, gradually picking up old members of their crew along the way, as they spread the word that Jack Comer had been shot and killed and that Billy White was the boss of Soho once again.

By midnight, White and his entourage had made it to the Hideaway Club, which was akin to Hitler marching into Poland. The Hideaway was known to everyone in Soho as Comer's club. This was an outright declaration of war, an affront on what was left of Comer's gang.

It took until ten minutes to one in the morning for Teddy Baxter to actually trace White down to the Hideaway Club, by which time White was hosting a big party and plying drinks to all and sundry in the hope of gaining their loyalty and support. Baxter had a huge grin on his face as he approached White. "I told you I'd do it didn't I?" he beamed.

• • •

Comer stood on the terrace of the large house, at the wonderful views of the surrounding Irish countryside. He turned as he heard the unmistakable sound of Rita's footsteps behind him. She had brought them both a drink. "You're taking to it more aren't you?" she said as she passed him one of the drinks. "I've never been not taken to it," he answered, "it's just that I am so busy with work in London, you know how it is" Rita looked up at him and chinked glasses with him, "Cheers," she said, "to us, our family and one day, not too far away, our life together, here in Ireland – promise me?" Comer smiled at Rita, pausing for a moment, his thoughts always drifting off to his work. "Of course I promise you Rita, what would I do without you eh?"

At this moment the phone rings, saving Comer from promising too much. It is Sonny, who tells him that Moisha has been shot but still alive. "From what he has told me," says Sonny, "it looks like he was mistaken for you, as he was picking up some paperwork from your flat, and as he came out someone shouted your name and then fired two shots at him from a double barrelled shotgun" Comer can't believe his ears, "how the fuck did he survive that lot?" he asks. Sonny tells him that the guy with the gun was obviously not used to using that type of weapon and was too far away to make it effective. Comer is furious and must return immediately to sort this lot out.

So, once again, Comer has to make yet more excuses to Rita and return to his old haunts in London, hoping that by this time the police will not connect the vicar's disappearance with him.

• • •

Moisha was sitting at their usual corner table in the Mackworth Arms pub in Stepney when Comer and Sonny, now with a moustache, walked in. Apart from a couple of plasters on his face, Moisha seemed to be perfectly well. "Was it just the one person?" asked Comer. Moisha shook his head, "I honestly don't know Jack," he said, "It was dark, I heard a car door open and this voice called out your name, I then saw someone standing just in front of the car, and bang – bang, two shots. I was on the floor, I thought I was going to die for a moment, and then I heard the car door slam again and it pulled away. I pulled myself up and realised that I had only been nicked, there was hardly any blood on me at all, thank God"

Comer was pleased that Moisha hadn't been hurt badly, but he couldn't stop thinking of what might have happened. In a more competent gunman's hands, Moisha could have been killed. In fact, a more competent gunman would have made sure of exactly who he was aiming at to begin with, and Comer knew that the real target was him. He had a number of enemies; he had to find out exactly which one of them was behind this and eliminate them pretty damn quickly, or the next time he might not be around to even think about it.

"Is there something you are not telling me?" Comer asks Sonny, who has been unusually quiet during this meeting. Sonny says that everything is alight, he has a headache, that is all. "I have known you since we were kids Sonny," says Comer, "I know when something is wrong with you" After a few more minutes of interrogation, Sonny finally admits that he is worried about something. "Maybe I'm wrong," he says, "but since you have been away I get the distinct impression that the Krays have been overstepping their mark, if you know what I mean?"

No, Comer didn't know what Sonny meant at all, but he soon found out, when Sonny started to elaborate. It had been difficult for Sonny to put himself about in the clubs and spielers without being spotted and asked where Comer was, but he had done his best, with the help of the moustache he was now sporting, and a flat cap. "Most people's eyes seemed to have been concentrating on Billy White and Albert Redman, who have been lording it up around Soho, like they own the bloody place," said Sonny, "so naturally when I saw Reggie and Ronnie walk in to one of our clubs one night, I thought this was it, that there was going to be a big showdown, instead of which, they all ended up buying each other drinks and doing lots of back slapping like they were the best of friends"

This was worrying for Comer. What should he do, ask the Krays outright if they were now siding with Billy White' mob, or walk into the clubs and act as if nothing was wrong?

• • •

The Hideaway Club was particularly busy for a Wednesday night. Ronnie Kray was perched on a bar stool in the corner of the bar, where he was talking quietly to a youngish looking man with fair hair. Reggie Kray was standing near to the centre of the bar, surrounded by a bunch of his acolytes, including Big Pat, Bobby Osborne, and a new addition to the firm, a young man from east London, named Tony Pistone.

To the casual onlooker, this scene looked perfectly normal, a group of men enjoying themselves, having a drink and telling the odd joke here and there. There was no hint of menace or rowdiness; the only hint of anything not quite normal was that there were no females in their company. It was strictly all male like a football team enjoying some time off. Osborne looked up towards the entrance as two men entered the club. He looked slightly alarmed, and quickly nudged Reggie, "See who's just come in?" he whispered. Reggie Kray looked up to where Osborne was indicating. The two men were Bobbie and Georgie Deacon. Reggie looked over to his brother, Ronnie. Even though Ronnie was deep in conversation, he looked up as if Reggie had just called out to him. Reggie and Ronnie had this thing between them, always seemed to be knowing what each other was thinking. Reggie nodded his head towards the Deacon brothers. Ronnie Kray pushed the young man he had been talking to out of his way and went for his gun, which was nestling in the waistband of his trousers, where he always kept it. No, Reggie silently mouthed. Reggie then turned to Big Pat and Tony Pistone, "See what they want," he told them, "tell them it's members only, and they definitely ain't members"

Big Pete and Pistone hurried over towards the Deacon brothers, stopping them in their tracks before they got any further into the club. Ronnie Kray meanwhile had removed himself from his corner stool and joined Reggie and the rest of their boys. All eyes were now on Big Pat, Tony Pistone, and the Deacon brothers.

Ronnie could hardly contain himself in his eagerness to join in but Reggie held him back, "No Ronnie, not yet, let's see what happens first" Ronnie sneered, "What are we supposed to do, wait 'till the fuckers start shooting at us?" he sneered, "you heard what they said to Bernie, about taking over all our clubs" This was in relation to an acquaintance of theirs, Bernie Hatten, who had bumped into Georgie Deacon a few days earlier, after just being thrown out of his local spieler, and Georgie Deacon told him not to worry as they would be taking over all the clubs in the west end soon, including the Krays'. Reggie shook his head, "talking about it and doing it are two different things"

As Reggie said this, a fracas started to break out between the Deacon brothers and Big Pat and Tony Pistone. Bobbie Deacon tried to shove his way past the two big men, but found more than he had bargained for with Big Pat, who just stood his ground and barred him from going any further. Pistone then moved closer and pulled out a long baton, which he slapped up and down, threateningly on his hand. "Now fuck off like good little boys before you get hurt," sneered Big Pat.

"We don't want any trouble with your firm," snapped Bobbie Deacon, "we're looking for Teddy Baxter" "What do you think this is then?" asked Pistone, "a fucking matrimonial agency? Teddy Baxter works for Billy White now doesn't he, which means he's hardly likely to be seen around here is he?" Bobbie Deacon looked quizzically at his brother Georgie, and then back to Pistone and Big Pat. "But this is one of White' clubs isn't it?" asked a somewhat dazed Bobbie Deacon.

Big Pat put his enormous hand on Bobbie Deacon's shoulder, looking like a bunch of bananas had just fallen there from a tree, almost hiding his shoulder completely, "I think you should have listened to what I said the first time," he growled, "this is our club, right? Reggie and Ronnie Kray's, it don't belong to Billy fucking White or anyone else – now are you going to turn around and walk out on your own, or do you need help?"

Bobbie Deacon didn't like being bossed about by anyone, but Big Pat was twice his size, and Tony Pistone was still wielding his baton, ready for instant use, not to mention the rest of the Kray firm, which were poised at the bar, all looking very much like they were ready for action. Bobbie Deacon looked across the room to the bar, where for a brief second he caught Ronnie Kray's eyes, staring at him like a dead fish, his mouth twisted in an evil smile. Bobbie Deacon nudged his brother and turned without saying a word. All eyes were on them as they walked out of the club.

Chapter 50

Victoria Park is one of the largest parks in London, set in between Bethnal Green and Hackney, with its laid out flower gardens, Lido swimming pool, lakes and children's areas, it is a regular haunt for many east London families, especially on a Sunday. Ronnie Kray loved the park; it was where his mother used to take him and Reggie when they were children.

It was late September, a particularly bright and sunny autumn morning as Big Pete drove the pale blue Ford Fairlane into the park and pulled up just inside the gates. Ronnie Kray got out from the back seat, accompanied by 'Bomber' his newly acquired German Shepherd dog. He told Big Pete to go and park down by the lake, where he would meet him later as usual. Big Pete drove the car off, leaving Ronnie and his dog by the park gates where there was a statue of an Alsatian dog with its head tilted backwards, as if howling. Legend has it that many years ago the dog had jumped into the lake and saved the life of a drowning child. Ronnie Kray smiled to himself, almost proudly, as he looked at the statue and then compared it to his dog.

Bomber strained at the heavy leather lead as it led the way through the park, stopping every now and then to bark at a pigeon or the odd duck that had strayed out of the lake and onto the path. This was Ronnie Kray's other world, far away from his world of darkness and crime, a world where he could walk in the sunshine and the trees. He looked at the wooden bridge that led over to the old Chinese Pagoda, which was built on one of the islands in the lake, where he and Reggie used to play all those years ago, and imagine it was haunted.

He crossed to the other side of the road, to the trees and bushes, where he undid the lead from Bomber's collar and let him run into the bushes where he could do his toilet. While he was waiting for Bomber, he turned to look at the lake, where a few people were idling away their time in rented out rowing boats. Just past the lake he could see the Ford Fairlane with Big Pat at the wheel, patiently waiting for him. One day, he thought, he would live in a big house in the country, with his own forests and lake, like a lord of the manor.

He turned again as he heard a rustle in the bushes somewhere behind him. "Bomber?" he called, "come on boy, come on Bomber" Another rustle, but it was not Bomber, Ronnie saw the vague figure of a man behind one of the bushes. A hand with a gun pushed through the bush, the gun pointing directly at Ronnie. "Fuck it," exclaimed Ronnie as he turned as quickly as he could and started running in the direction where Big Pat and the car were waiting. A shot rang out from behind him, followed by another, both narrowly missing him. "Bomber," he shouted as he kept on running, "Bomber, come on Bomber"

Ronnie glanced over his shoulder and saw a shadowy figure from somewhere in the bushes. Suddenly Bomber was there, bounding along at his side, then another shot, and another, and another until all six shots in the chamber of the revolver had been fired. Bomber whimpered and fell like a stone beside him as the last bullet thudded into him. Elsewhere in the park, people had started to scatter and run for cover. Ronnie looked down at Bomber, who managed to turn his head up towards him for a moment, almost like the dog portrayed by the statue.

Ronnie Kray looked back towards the bushes, where he could now see the shadowy figure running at full speed in the opposite direction. He opened his mouth as if to shout but no sound came out, he then looked down once again at Bomber, dead in a pool of blood. A distant shout made him look up again for a moment, it was Big Pat calling his name, "Ronnie," he shouted, "Ronnie, stay where you are, I'm coming to get you"

Big Pat moved incredibly swiftly for a man his size, and was with Ronnie in two minutes, "Ronnie," he panted, "are you alight, Ron?" Big Pat had never seen either of the Krays cry before, but tears were running down Ronnie's face as he stared down at the body of his dog. "Look what they did Pat," he sobbed, "look what they did"

• • •

"Ronnie Kray's gone into mourning over his fucking dog," sniggered Billy White, "word has it that he's dressing in black and has ordered a big wreath in the shape of a bone for Fido's funeral," he burst out laughing. White was sitting in a barber's shop chair with a white apron around him, while the barber used a lighted taper to singe the hairs around his ears. Albert Redman and another man were sitting opposite, laughing at every word their boss uttered. "This is supposed to be the man who was helping out Jack Comer – no wonder Comer's done a runner with people like him around"

The barber looked in the mirror at the reflection of Billy White, "Comer's done a runner?" he mused, "I'm sure I saw him walk past here just the other day, with that big bloke who's always with him" The smile quickly evaporated from Billy White' face as he looked in the mirror at the barber, "Are you sure?" he asked. The barber assured him that it was Comer, "If it wasn't him, then he must have a double walking about round here," he answered.

This was worrying for White, he thought he had driven Comer out of London, once and for all, and now it seemed that like some awful spectre, he had returned to haunt him yet again. At this moment in time, the Krays were not causing White much consternation; he saw them as a bunch of young tearaways who had jumped onto Comer's bandwagon. He had purposely given them his blessing about taking over the Hideaway Club, as he assumed it would keep them off his back for the time being. As far as he was concerned, they could be dislodged at a moment's notice, and when the time was right, that is exactly what he planned to do. In the meantime however, Billy White' priority was to find out if there was any truth to the sighting of Comer back on the streets of Soho, and if so, to deal with it without delay.

If proven to be true, this also raised another matter, which had been playing on White' mind for some weeks, which was the so called murder of Jack Comer by Teddy Baxter, who had sworn to White that he had done the job. He had even come up with the story that Comer's men had quickly removed his body from the scene in order keep the whole thing quiet, and not alert either the police or his enemies. This, he said, would potentially allow the likes of Moisha and Sonny to take whatever was left from Comer's ailing business, and run with the money before they ended up the same way as their boss.

Billy White couldn't believe that he had been taken in by the likes of Teddy Baxter, and to make matters worse, not only had he agreed for Baxter to be a part of his team, he had also loaned him one hundred pounds as an up-front payment on future earnings.

• • •

Although he didn't know it, Baxter was now in deep trouble, not only was Billy White out to get him, but also Bobbie and Georgie Deacon, for not only had Baxter deserted them to align himself with Billy White' mob, he had also managed to consign half a dozen of their fruit machines to his own use.

"He's got to go, that's for sure," bemoaned Bobbie Deacon, "but he's not the only one, those fucking Krays are also getting too big for their boots" The Deacon brothers were in their shabby little office at the back of their scrap metal yard in Camberwell, where one bare light bulb lit the gloomy room. As they discussed what they should do about Baxter and possibly the Krays, another man, Sid Winters, who was new to their mob, was sitting by a workbench, where he was toying around with a metal box, which looked similar to a car battery charger. He plugged it into a nearby wall socket and touched the two electrodes against each other, causing it to crackle and throw off sparks. It also caused the single light bulb in the ceiling to flicker on and off.

Georgie Deacon looked over at Winters and shook his head in despair, "Can you stop doing that Sid?" he demanded rather than asked, "you'll fuse this fucking light in a minute" Winters mumbled a sort of apology and kept on tinkering with the metal box while the brothers continued their plans. A loud bang interrupted them, and sent Winters flying off his chair, "Aghh," he screamed out in pain as he dropped the two wires he had been holding, "that could have fucking killed me"

Bobbie Deacon rushed over and unplugged the contraption from the wall, "You silly bastard," he shouted at Winters, "it would have been your own fault if it had, what's it supposed to be anyway?" Winters explained that he had found it in the scrap and didn't know what it was, he thought it might be a battery charger but wasn't sure. "I'll tell you what I'd like to do with it," added Georgie Deacon, "I'd like to attach it to Teddy Baxter's fucking balls when we catch him" Bobbie Deacon chuckled, "might not be a bad idea," he added.

Chapter 51

Moisha swung the Chrysler onto the forecourt of the Regal Billiard Hall, where Comer, Sonny and himself got out and hurried into the hall. They were met inside by Tony Pistone, who told them that the Krays were not there at the moment. "What do you mean, not here?" asked a very agitated Jack Comer, "Sonny set this meeting up yesterday" Pistone shrugged his shoulders, "What can I do Jack?" he asked, "I'm only the messenger here, they had to go out on some very important business" Comer was fuming, It's not good enough Tony, who do they think they are? I gave them this hall, I gave them a job in my team – what's so fucking important that they think they can just ignore me, after all I have done for them?

Pistone explained to Comer how someone had tried to kill Ronnie Kray, and how he had managed to escape but his dog had been shot and killed. "So his dog's been killed, I'll give him ten bob if he's that hard up so he can go down Brick Lane and buy another one," grumbled Comer, "you tell them I want to see them, urgent – I'll be at the Hideaway tonight, right?" Pistone looked somewhat taken aback, "The Hideaway?" "Yes, that's right," added Comer, "something wrong with that?" "No, no," lied Pistone, "I'll tell them"

● ● ●

Moisha looked at Comer's reflection in his interior mirror as he drove back towards the west end of London. Comer sat there in silence, with Sonny next to him. There was a dark uneasiness, which Moisha had seen in Comer many times before, and which usually ended up in something terrible happening. He had to try to talk Comer round before they reached the west end and Soho.

Moisha switched the car radio on, an upbeat version of an old song came on, 'Slow boat to China' by Emile Ford and the Checkmates. Moisha started to click his fingers in time with the tune, "Good one this isn't it?" he said, trying his best to sound relaxed and happy. "Turn that fucking racket off and stop at the first pub we come to," growled Comer, "I need a drink"

That certainly didn't work then, thought Moisha, as he switched the radio off again, pulled off the main road, into a small side-street and came to a halt outside a small east London pub.

• • •

Less than a mile away from the quiet little pub where Comer was sitting and drowning his sorrows in brandy, another very similar pub was was full of men in working clothes, mostly dockers from the nearby London Docks. Drinks were flowing and deals were being made between each other, of goods, such as cigarettes and watches, which they had purloined from their places of work. This type of bounty was classed at this time as the perks of the job.

Billy Fisher, a young man in his twenties, was holding court at the bar. He stood out from the crowd, in his well cut mohair suit and the wad of money that he readily flashed about as he bought various packages from the dockers, and passed them onto his bag-man, who stood nearby.

Fisher was the king here in the docklands of Stepney and was not scared of anyone, not even the Krays, who had tried unsuccessfully, on several occasions to take over his little empire. Ronnie Kray had been so cock-sure of himself, that he had sent a junior member of the firm to warn Fisher, 'Get out and turn your business over to us or you're a dead man'

Needless to say, Fisher didn't like this at all, and sent the Kray's messenger boy skedaddling back to his masters with a severely bruised face and a warning for Ronnie to stay out of his territory or it would be him who would end up a dead man, not the other way round.

The chatting and laughing of the men in the pub, ended suddenly as a metal milk crate came crashing through one of the plate glass windows, showering everyone with splinters of glass. At the same time, the doors of the pub came bursting open and three masked men came bursting in. The first man was armed with a pistol, which he fired into the ceiling as a sort of warning shot, the second man carried a metal bar and the third, a bayonet. "Billy Fisher," shouted the man with the gun, "we want Billy Fisher"

Within two seconds every man in the pub had moved as quickly as possible, away from Fisher, leaving him standing alone at the bar. "Fisher?" shouted the gunman again. Billy Fisher braved it out and did his best to smile, "And who are you?" he condescendingly asked, "more messenger boys from the Krays?"

The gunman never said a word, he just lifted his gun, pointed it at Fisher and pulled the trigger. As with so many of these old WWII weapons, it didn't work. Click, click, click. Fisher saw his chance and picked up a bottle from the bar, smashed the end off, and made a lunge towards the gunman. As he did so, the man with the bayonet quickly moved in and plunged the weapon into Fisher's stomach, bring him to an immediate halt.

Fisher's mouth dropped open and the bottle fell from his hand as the man with the bayonet pulled it out of his body and then brought the blade down in a slashing movement against Fisher's neck.

"Let's go," shouted the man with the gun to his accomplices. As the three men ran from the pub, the last thing they saw was Fisher, lying on the floor, his hand up to his throat, his mouth moving as if trying to speak, and blood gurgling out from deep within his throat.

●　●　●

By the time Comer and his men had reached the Hideaway Club in Soho, he felt a lot more 'relaxed' which was how he often described himself, when other people saw him as slightly drunk.

Ronnie Kray greeted them with his usual big, twisted smile, bought them all yet more drinks and said how nice it was of them to drop in. Drop in? This was like a red rag to a bull. As far as Comer was concerned, he always considered the Hideaway to be his personal club. He had come there as the Krays' boss, to ask them what was happening about Billy White.

"Don't you go worrying yourself about Billy White," said Ronnie, "we're taking care of him – look, do you see anything of Billy White or his cronies in here? He knows better than to make enemies of us"

Moisha looked at his boss and could see he was getting angry with the way Ronnie Kray was talking to him, especially after they had not even bothered to turn up for their meeting earlier. He needed to diffuse the situation and calm Comer down before he erupted in a fit of anger, which in all probability would end very badly for the three of them, as almost everyone in the club was either a member of the Krays' firm, or a friend in one way or another.

"The two geezers over there," Moisha interjected to Ronnie, in a low voice as he nodded towards two well built men at the end of the bar, "do you know them?" Ronnie Kray glanced over at the two men, "No, why, should I?" he asked. "They're definitely old Bill," replied Moisha. "Nah," mumbled Ronnie, squinting his eyes to get a better view, "they don't look like old Bill to me"

Sonny could now see the way Moisha was deflecting the situation away from a possible conflict between Comer and Ronnie Kray. "Be fair Ronnie," he interrupted, "you'd hardly expect them to turn up in here in pointed helmets and hob-nailed boots would you?" Ronnie Kray swung round to face Sonny, with a look on his face that was scary to say the least. Sonny braved it out and faced him back, both staring at each other for what seemed like ages, but in reality was probably no more than a few seconds. Ronnie then started to laugh. He slapped Sonny on the shoulder, "You bastards" he laughed, "I thought you meant it for a minute"

Moisha now moved closer to Ronnie, "We do mean it Ronnie," he whispered, "they're not just local plod, they're flying squad. Ronnie Kray stared over again at the two men, "Fuck me," he said, "we could be in big trouble here with filth like them hanging around, I don't know whether I should give them a slap and throw them out or what – what do you think Jack, you must have had to deal with shit like this in the past?"

The red flag was being raised to the proverbial bull once again. Comer could feel his eyes starting to glaze over, but fortunately his time in the bullring was lengthened once again; this time not by one of his own men, but by the sudden appearance of Reggie Kray, who smiled at Comer and held his hand out to him. Jack, how you doing? Come and sit down," he offered, pointing to a table at the other side of the room.

A short while later, all five men were safely seated around the table, drinks and cigars were being freely imbibed and talks were in full swing. Considering the amount Comer had drunk by this time, he was still very coherent and put his case clearly to the Krays. Comer wanted to know exactly what was going on, were the Krays still working for him or not? Comer also asked about Billy White. He had been told that Billy White had been seen in the Hideaway Club, and that the Krays were being very pally with him. What was all this about he wanted to know?

Ronnie Kray, as usual, was very reticent and just sat there in silence, looking around the table, from one to the other, with the occasional glance over at the two men, still standing at the bar, whom Moisha had described at members of the Flying Squad.

Reggie Kray however, was much more forthcoming and smiled at Comer as he took a large brown envelope out of his inside pocket and passed it under the table to him. "Take this Jack," he said, "I don't want those bastards at the bar to see, in case you are right and they are the old Bill" Comer glanced down at the envelope and felt it. It was obviously filled with banknotes. "What's this about then?" Comer asked as he quickly stuffed the envelope into his pocket. "It's yours Jack," Reggie replied, "from now on you'll be receiving an envelope like this on a weekly basis, and you don't have to do a thing, except collect it, do you know what I mean?"

Comer could feel the envelope in his pocket, it was thick, must have been a considerable amount of money in there, which in one way he was pleased with, but when he thought again he realised that it was his by rights anyway. The Krays were giving him a percentage of his own business. This wasn't right. "This is from the profits of my own club," he asked, "the Hideaway?"

Reggie and Ronnie looked at each other with some unease. "Partly Jack," answered Reggie, "it's from all your clubs and spielers" For once in his life Comer was speechless. He took the cigar from his mouth and slowly started stubbing it out in the ashtray, twisting it around and around until all that was left was a pile of grounded tobacco leaf and a pile of ash.

He had come to the Hideaway Club to discuss business with the Krays, but from what Reggie had been saying, they had already made up their minds without any sort of discussion with him.

"Don't take it bad Jack," said Reggie as he laid his hand on Comer's hand, stopping him from continuing to stir what was left of the cigar butt round and round the ashtray, "all we're doing here is making life a little easier for you – at your age you should be sitting back in comfort and relaxing, instead of waging wars and being threatened on a daily basis"

Comer stared at Reggie for some moments in silence, trying desperately to weigh up things in his mind. He felt that he had two options at this particular time, the first being to say bollocks to Reggie's proposal, or demand as it was in reality, but he knew that if he did this, it would start off an immediate war, in which he was hopelessly outnumbered at this moment in time. He looked around the club, where so many eyes now seemed to be focused on his table, at Moisha, Sonny, and himself.

The second option was to trick the Krays into believing that he was ready to play ball with them; walk out with a smile on his face and a pocketful of cash, but once outside he could, and would, start planning his revenge.

Option two came into play immediately. "You know what Reggie," said Comer, with a look of self resignation and defeat on his face, "I think you are right, it's been at the back of my mind for some time now, none of us are getting any younger, and I think I owe it to my wife and daughter to settle down and spend what should be the best years of my life with them"

Comer got to his feet and held his hand out to both Ronnie and Reggie.

Chapter 52

Once outside the club, Comer explained himself to Moisha and Sonny, "There is no way I am about to roll over like an old dog and let those two young tearaways take over my business," he explained, "we are going to hit back – rebuild our old team and fight the fucking lot of them"

He ordered Moisha and Sonny to put themselves about and seek out Dave Newman, the bank security guard who offered him a nice bank job some time back, "He usually drinks at a pub in Leather Lane, called the Two Archers, you'll know him when you see him – find him and tell him we're ready to work with him now"

At the same time that Comer was briefing Moisha and Sonny, Reggie Kray was putting his brother in the picture back at the Hideaway Club. . "Are you kidding?" he said to Ronnie, "pay Jack Comer every fucking week? All I want him to do is relax and stay out of our hair for a few weeks, then we can strike when he's least expecting it and get rid of him for good" Ronnie smiled at his brother's remark; this was his sort of talk. "Like we did with Billy Fisher?" he asked. "Exactly," replied Reggie, "just like we did with Billy Fisher, and after Comer, it'll be Billy White, and after him, anyone else who gets in our way"

• • •

A few days later at New Scotland Yard, and Nipper Read had a meeting with Sir Joseph Simpson, Commissioner of the London Metropolitan Police. The murder of Billy Fisher in broad daylight in a London pub has been reported and the press want to know what the police are doing about the gang wars in London. Nipper Read explains that he is making slow but steady progress in his surveillance of the gangs, and has several teams of undercover officers working Soho clubs and pubs etcetera, that are regular haunts of known gangsters. "It is all very well saying you have these people under surveillance," stated Sir Joseph, "What I want to know is when we can expect some arrests? I have both the press and Parliament now breathing down my neck, they are fed up with seeing the likes of Jack Comer and Billy White openly flaunting themselves as Kings of the underworld, and us not seemingly doing anything about it" Nipper explains that according to his sources, both White and Comer are on their way out, and it is the Krays and the Deacons that he is now working on. "I just pray to God you are right in your estimation," replied Sir Joseph, "and that we have some results to show pretty damn quick"

• • •

Sir Joseph Simpson wasn't the only one looking for results. The results Jack Comer was looking for were not to be forthcoming at all, as Sonny had since found out that Dave Newman, the contact who Comer had in the bank security firm, had been arrested since his tip off to Comer, and was now serving three years in HM Prison for attempted robbery.

Not a happy day at all for Comer, far from it, as it now brought to a halt his plans to raise a large fighting fund, with which he was going to recruit more men to his team and retake the west end from the likes of Billy White and the Krays.

Billy White, meanwhile, was quite content with his lot, as at this point, he was unaware that the Krays had been slowly muscling in on Soho's clubs and spielers. He knew they had the Hideaway Club, and he was happy with that, but any problems he was having with collecting from other clubs, he had been putting down to Comer, whom he now saw as a dyeing ember, someone whose flames could be 'pissed out by a woman' as the Lord Mayor of London had once famously said about the Great Fire of London.

At this point in time, Billy White was more interested in finding and exacting revenge on his old adversary, Teddy Baxter, whom he had paid to kill Comer and had bodged the job completely.

Albert Redman had just returned from the Turkish Baths in Ironmonger Row, Clerkenwell, where he went once a week, more to pick up gossip amongst the fellow thieves and vagabonds than to cleanse the pores of his body. He met White for lunch in their usual café in Frith Street. "You know what I just heard down the baths?" said Redman, "I heard that we're not the only people looking for

Baxter, apparently that other little mob from south London, are also after him"

White looked up from his steak and chips, "Who, the Deacon brothers?" Redman smiled and nodded in agreement, "Apparently the Deacons have heard that Baxter is working for us, and listen to this, that he's nicked a load of fruit machines from them and is setting them up in our clubs"

Billy White took another bite from his fat juicy steak and shook his head in disbelief, "What is it with these people?" he mused, "if I wanted fruit machines I'd get my own, not a hooky lot from a nutter like Baxter, I'm going to have a word with this Deacon lot"

Redman sneaked a chip off White' plate and continued, "I've thought of something else a lot better than that Bill, we could kill two birds with one stone here" Billy White stared reticently at Redman and then at his plate of food, "As long as it doesn't involve nicking any more of my chips, I'm listening"

Five minutes later White had finished his steak and chips, and Redman had finished setting out his elaborate plan to White. White rose from the table and nodded approvingly at Redman, "It's going to take a bit of work, but I like it and I think it might be just what we're looking for"

● ● ●

It was not exactly a big event at the York Hall in Bethnal Green that evening, no big names, but almost always the fighters concerned, put on a good show. Albert Redman walked in, with a welterweight fight already in progress, and made his way down towards ringside, where there were quite a few empty seats. He paused for a moment, looking round the crowd before deciding upon a second row seat.

A short while into round three of the welterweight fight, Redman lent forward and put his hand upon the shoulder of the man in front of him, "Hello Frank," he said. The man, Frank Wilson, an ex boxer in his mid forties, looked round at Redman, "Hello Albert, long time no see, how you doing?"

After a brief conversation, and an offer of a 'nice little earner' from Redman, the two men left the arena for the more subdued atmosphere of the bar, where the offer could be discussed with a little bit more privacy.

First thing that needed to be established, was if Wilson was still in the market for a bit of skulduggery, as he had once been a very promising young middleweight, who had to retire early due to a car crash that had left him with what the doctors described as impaired vision.

"I'm not exactly skint," he said, "but a little bit more cash in the old sky rocket wouldn't go amiss either, especially with Christmas coming up" "How's your eye now?" asked Redman, "are you still driving OK?" Wilson laughed this off and told Redman that he had been doing a bit of lorry driving for a firm in Spitalfields Market, "So I can't be that bad can I?" he answered. "And if it involved a little bit more than just driving?" asked Redman.

The affable smile quickly faded from Wilson's face, "I didn't think you'd be offering to pay me just to drive you around like a taxi driver Albert," Redman was happy with Wilson's response and promised to contact him again within the next few day.

Part two of Redman' plan was now put into action. He put out a number of men to seek out Teddy Baxter in the pubs and clubs of Soho and the east end, and to tell him that he had nothing to worry about from either Billy White or himself, we all make mistakes, and now we are giving him one last chance to rectify his last one.

● ● ●

Comer meanwhile is starting to get very worried about his lack of ability to attract more men to his mob, everyone he approaches seem to be either working for Billy White now or the Krays. "You seem to be forgetting some very old and very useful contacts," says the ever faithful Moisha to him one day. Comer looks quizzically at Moisha, "And who might that be?" he enquires. "The Irish," replies Moisha, "you met some of the top people when you were over there, I reckon it's worth asking if they could send us some of their people, what do you think?"

Comer had known Moisha and Sonny, since they were all kids, and they were as reliable now as the day he had first met them. He hated to think what he would ever do without them.

• • •

Teddy Baxter stood at the bar of the French House pub in Soho. He nervously checked the inside pocket of his jacket, where he had carefully placed a cut-throat razor, as he still wasn't sure if this was an offer of appeasement or a trap. When the door of the pub opened and he saw Albert Redman walk in with Frank Wilson, he froze for a moment; was this going to be an attack on him? Why did he have this other man with him if it was supposed to be a friendly meeting?

Baxter put his drink down on the bar, so that he had both hands free as the two men walked towards him. Redman held his hand out to Baxter and smiled in a friendly way, "Hello Teddy, how are you?"

Baxter gripped Redman' hand, the longer he held onto this hand the more difficult it would be for Redman to attack him. "I'm getting by Albert," he answered, "how about yourself?"

After these few preliminary greetings were out the way and drinks were bought all round, Redman got down to business, he introduced Wilson as a first class getaway driver, whom he had known for years. "What we want you to do Teddy," he said, "is get yourself another man to work with you on this, needs to be someone good, who you know you can trust, we can't afford any more cock-ups, and Frank here will be your driver on the job, he knows London like the back of his hand, especially the area where Comer lives. He'll do all the prep work to start with, when and where Comer is going and coming – everything, and we'll supply you with the shooters, proper ones this time, no more farmyard rabbit guns like you used in your last attempt"

Baxter listened intently and seemed very happy with Redman' proposal. He had just one question; When? "The quicker the better," replied Redman, "we want to try to set it up within the next couple of days if possible – are you happy with that?" Baxter was very happy with that. He knew just the man to help him as well, Mickey Reilly, who had introduced him to the Deacon brothers just after he had come out of prison. This was his last chance of getting back in with Billy White.

Chapter 53

Frank Wilson pulled the big American car over beside a red telephone box, leaving Teddy Baxter and Mickey Reilly in the back of the car while he went and made a quick phone call. Less than a minute later he hurried out of the phone box, jumped back in the car and pulled away again, edging the car through the dark streets of west London, "Looks like we're on lads," he said to Baxter and Reilly, "he's making his way back home right now"

A few minutes later Wilson pulled the big car to a halt at one end of George Street, where Comer's flat was situated. "See that entrance over there?" he said, turning to Reilly and pointing across the street, "see the light to the right hand side of the door? I want you to undo the catch and take the bulb out – then hide yourself there and wait for Teddy to make the first move, be quick as he could be along at any minute now"

Reilly got out of the car, hurried across the street and up the steps to the light fitting, which was as shoulder level. He did as Wilson had told him and immediately plunged the doorway into darkness and stepped back, out of sight.

Baxter turned and looked out the rear window of the car, "This is him," he said, "fuck me, he's got his missus with him, you didn't say she would be here" Wilson waited for Comer and Rita to walk past them and then started the car's engine again. He pressed down hard on the accelerator and screeched to a halt just as Comer reached the entrance to his flat. "Go, quick, go now" he commanded Baxter, who pulled out a pistol in one hand and a large knife in the other hand as he leapt out of the car. "Comer," Baxter shouted as he ran across the street.

Wilson sat and watched from the relative safety of his car as Baxter and Reilly gave all they had in their attempt to kill Comer. Shots were fired, punches and kicks were traded and Wilson also witnessed Baxter's knife reflecting flashes of light from the nearby lamppost as he attacked Comer with it. And while all this was happening, Comer's wife screamed incessantly.

Wilson looked up as he also heard windows from other flats nearby starting to open, and neighbours poking their heads out to see what was going on. This wasn't going well at all. The job should have been finished by now, Comer should have been dead. The sound of police cars' bells caused Wilson to look round again. He could see their headlights starting to approach. Fuck me, he thought as he started the engine again and raced the car across the street. "Quick, get in," he shouted as he lent round and flung open the back door, "it's the old Bill" Baxter and Reilly didn't have to be told twice, they left Comer, looking decidedly dead, and lying in a pool of blood on the ground, as they leapt into the car and Wilson accelerated away as fast as he could.

The police had no option other than to pull up when they saw the two bodies of Comer and Rita lying on the floor outside the flats. This gave Wilson extra time to make a clean getaway through the backstreets and out of the immediate area within minutes.

"Where the fuck are you going?" yelled Baxter, as Wilson twisted and turned around corner after corner, finally getting onto the Embankment and then onto Westminster Bridge. "Leave it to me," Wilson answered, "I know what I'm doing" He slowed down somewhat, so as not to cause unnecessary attention and continued towards south London, finally pulling to a halt under a railway arch. Baxter looked at Reilly, a look of bewilderment on his face. "What have we pulled up here for?" asked Reilly.

Wilson turned around in his seat, "For this," he said as he lifted his hand and pointed an automatic pistol at Reilly's head and fired one shot directly into his head, killing him instantly. Baxter's eyes stared in horror as Wilson now pointed the gun at him, "No, please Frank, don't do it," he begged. This time Wilson did not pull the trigger, but kept the gun pointing directly at Baxter, keeping him in suspense until the rear door of the car was suddenly wrenched open and Bobby Deacon was standing there, also with a gun in his hand, with his brother Georgie, standing just behind him. "Out you get Teddy," growled Bobby Deacon, waving his pistol towards Baxter.

Baxter didn't know whether to laugh or cry at the sight of the Deacon brothers. They had actually rescued him from the jaws of death, but why, and what fate awaited him now? Bobby Deacon led Baxter away to a small van, which was parked nearby, roughly shoved him in the back and climbed in beside him. Meanwhile Georgie Deacon winked at Frank Wilson, "Nice work," he said as he stuffed a wad of money into Wilson's breast pocket, and quickly made his way towards the van where his brother and Teddy Baxter were waiting.

Wilson waited until the Deacon's van had driven away and then glanced once again at the body of Mickey Reilly, still propped up in the back of the car. Wilson smiled to himself as he had one last look around to make sure he had not left anything incriminating in the car, checked his leather gloves and then got out and walked away.

• • •

When the police did eventually find the body of Mickey Reilly in the car, they were stumped as to who might have possibly killed him and why. It had all the hallmarks of a gangland murder, but why him? He was just a petty thief, a person of no particular significance in the world of crime. One person they knew who couldn't have committed this particular crime was Jack Comer, as he was laid out in St Thomas' Hospital, where he was undergoing treatment for stabbing and gunshot wounds.

Nipper Reed however placed more importance in this killing than the local south London police force seemed to be doing, and was sure in his mind that there could be a strong link between the attack on Comer and the murder of Mickey Reilly, especially as they both happened within an hour or so of each other. Nipper Reed grew even more suspicious when the car was dusted for fingerprints and those of Teddy Baxter were found. Nipper put all available men on an alert to find Baxter without delay.

• • •

Most of the local police around Camberwell in south London, were on the payroll of the Deacon brothers, which meant they turned a blind eye to almost all their illegal activities. If a house or a shop was robbed in the same vicinity as the Deacon's scrap yard, the locals would call on the Deacon brothers to sort it out for them, rather than go to the police, which meant, the sight of a policeman patrolling in their street was a very rare sight indeed.

As one would expect, there was always a lot of noise in and around the scrap yard, but how no one seemed to hear Baxter screaming in pain beyond belief. Bobby and Georgie Deacon had Baxter locked up in a windowless cellar beneath their yard. A single light bulb lit the tiny brick built room, and the only piece of furniture was an old camp bed and a small table. He had been stripped of all his clothing apart from his underpants.

When Bobby and Georgie Deacon entered the cellar with their new man, Sid Winters, who was carrying the black metal box, Baxter groaned at the thought of having this box attached to him yet again, "Oh no, please, not again," he begged them as Winters slapped him across his face and told him to be quiet, "If you've got anything to say, then tell Bobby what he wants to know" shouted Winters. "I haven't got any machines of yours," begged Baxter, "if I had, don't you think I would have told you where they are by now?"

Winters looked around to his bosses, who both nodded their acknowledgement. Winters then threw a leather strap over Baxter's neck and pulled him back with it, buckling the other end over the end of the camp bed, which meant that every time Baxter struggled, the belt became tighter around his neck.

He then attached the two electrodes onto the nipples on Baxter's chest and started to turn the handle of the machine. "Now tell us where our fucking fruit machines are?" screamed Bobby Deacon. "This is your last chance Baxter," yelled Georgie Deacon as a back up to his brother. Winters turned the handle of the machine faster and faster, causing Baxter to scream at the top of his voice before passing out.

Chapter 54

It had been just over a week since the attack on Jack Comer, and now he was finally home again with his wife and daughter. He eased himself into his favourite red leather armchair and smiled as Rita handed him a little package, which turned out to be a gold Star of David, on a gold chain. He asked Rita to put it on for him as his hands were still bruised and swollen from the altercation he had suffered earlier.

Comer looked lovingly at Rita and Miriam and then stood up to look at himself in the mirror, to see how the Star of David looked on him. The Star looked fine, but he looked a mess, bruised and battered with bandages and plasters still covering much of his face. How the hell can they love me, he thought, I'm like a fucking monster now?

A phone call from Sonny brought Comer back to reality. He had to go to a meeting he had prearranged with Sonny and Moisha, at their old meeting place, the Mackworth Arms pub in east London, to discuss the proposed collaboration with the Irishman, whom Comer had met up with on the night he was attacked. Rita didn't want him to go, "Not on your first day home Jack," she pleaded, "remember what the doctors said, that you should have complete rest for at least a few more days before doing anything strenuous?"

Comer smiled at Rita and kissed her on the cheek as he struggled painfully into his overcoat, "Don't worry about me," he told her, "it's only a meeting at the Mackworth Arms pub in Stepney with Moisha and Sonny, and hopefully that Irish fellow we met the other night, I'll be back before you know it"

• • •

Nipper Reed meanwhile, was growing ever more furious with his team regarding the disappearance of Teddy Baxter. "I've got Sir Joseph Simpson breathing down my neck about this," he shouted, "how difficult can it be to find a man like Teddy Baxter, a loud-mouth who's never been known to leave London? We've been given another forty eight hours to find this scumbag – and if we don't, he's disbanding our team" The four man strong team looked at each other, their mouths gaping open as they tried to take in the severity of what their boss had just said to them. "Well don't just stand there," yelled Nipper, "get out onto the streets and start talking to people"

• • •

Comer, Moisha, and Sonny were sitting at their usual corner table in the Mackworth Arms. "He's late," stated Sonny. "I know he's fucking late," answered Comer, "an hour late to be exact" Sonny shrugged his shoulders in an indecisive manner, "I was only saying," he murmured.

The mood wasn't good as they sat there in almost total silence; Comer was starting to regret ever asking the Irishman to become involved. He was still in some pain, and feared that in the eyes of his men, he was not looking at all like the leader whose judgement they had always relied on.

The shrill sound of the phone ringing from behind the bar suddenly brought all three men to their senses. All eyes were on the publican as he answered the phone in a quiet voice, "Yes?" he said into the phone, "Just a minute, I'll see if he's in here"

The publican put the phone down on the bar and came around to Comer's table. "It's someone asking for you," he said to Comer, "do you want me to tell 'em you're not here?"

Comer leapt out of his seat, "No, I'll get it," he shouted as he made his way over to the bar and picked up the phone. Moisha and Sonny watched him intently as he spoke into the phone. "Hello?" he snapped, "What? What do you mean? I don't understand, how could?" Moisha and Sonny knew instinctively that something was seriously wrong. Comer's face had turned ashen white as he put the phone back down and almost limped back to their table. "They've got Miriam," he stumbled the words out, "they've kidnapped my daughter" He collapsed back down into his chair.

Neither Moisha nor Sonny had ever seen Comer in such a state before; he was literally trembling as he explained to them what had happened. That was Rita on the phone, he said, she had told him that about half an hour ago, their doorbell had rung, and when she went down to answer the door, two large men, both armed, had pushed their way in and made her take them upstairs to the flat where Miriam was.

The two men tied Rita up loosely and gagged Miriam. They demanded to know where Comer was but when she refused to answer them they slapped her across the face and told them Miriam would get a lot worse if she didn't play ball with them. Rita was sobbing as she told Comer what had happened and how she had no alternative but to tell the men where he was. They then started to bundle Miriam out the door, pausing for a moment to tell her not to phone the police or do anything else for at least half an hour. She did exactly as she was told as her bonds were quite lose and then phoned Comer.

Moisha placed his hand caringly on Comer's shoulder "I can't believe this Jack, who the fuck would do a thing like this?" Rita had never seen either man before, he said, and they didn't give any sort of explanation as to who they were or who they might have been working for. "They told Rita to tell me not to move from here, and that they would contact me here and give me instructions as to what I need to do next"

"Put me in my place if you think I'm wrong Jack," Sonny said as he stood up from the table, "but I don't see why we all need to sit here and take orders from these toe-rags like this – I'm all for putting myself about and seeing if anybody knows anything"

Moisha can see from the way Comer is acting that his mind is in a turmoil, and it is up to Sonny and himself to take action. "I agree with Sonny," Moisha says, "we need to act quickly on this, let him go back to Soho and start asking a few questions, maybe even put a bit of money about – in the meantime, I'll stay here with you until we hear from these ponces"

A somewhat dazed Comer, nodded in agreement to Moisha, "As long as it doesn't jeopardise Miriam's safety, that has to be our number one priority, you have both got to understand that"

· · ·

Sonny left Comer and Moisha in the Mackworth Arms, and caught a taxi to the west end, where he started an immediate tour of the clubs and spielers. He couldn't exactly walk in and start asking if anyone knows who has kidnapped Jack Comer's daughter, but he could drop little hints here and there, such as were there any new gangs on the scene lately, or fresh trouble for instance.

The big problem was that Sonny didn't have time to hang around, if he was to find out anything that might help his boss, then it needed to be found out pretty damn quick. What he did discover almost immediately, was that Billy White' mob had been very scarce on the ground lately, and that the Krays' firm seemed to everywhere. "What about Teddy Baxter?" he asked, as this seemed just the sort of stunt that Baxter would pull. "Nope," he was told, "No one's seen hide nor hair of Teddy Baxter, he's disappeared off the face of the earth, or at least Soho"

● ● ●

Earlier that day, a farm worker in Kent had noticed one of his pigs eating a strange looking object, which on closer inspection turned out to be a human hand. The farm worker managed to get what was left of the hand away from the pig and called the police immediately. Scotland Yard and Nipper Reed in particular, took this very seriously and took fingerprints from the hand, which were proven to be those of Teddy Baxter. Nipper now had a major murder investigation on his hands, and his team certainly wouldn't be scrapped now.

● ● ●

Sonny had just left a small spieler as he heard someone call his name. He looked round to see a large but friendly faced man, who was standing in a nearby doorway. "Are you Sonny?" asked the man. Sonny walked over to him and said he was and what did the man want? The man explained that he had just bumped into a friend who told him that Sonny had been asking questions. Sonny didn't like the sound of this, what did he mean by 'asking questions?'

The man was like a gentle giant, probably a bit simple, and just shrugged his shoulders and said he didn't know, he had been told by his friend to fetch Sonny as his friend had some information he thought might interest him. "Who is this friend of yours?" asked Sonny, "and where is he?" The gentle giant looked each way, up and down the street and then indicated for Sonny to follow him, "He's in here," he said, indicating a narrow doorway, with various 'Model for Hire' signs pinned to the wall, "upstairs," he said as he led the way up the rickety winding staircase, past various doors where the 'girls' carried out their business.

• • •

It was starting to get dark now. In Greek Street a man came out of a tobacconist shop and paused to take a cigarette out of the packet and light it. He inhaled the smoke deeply and blew a thin stream of it into the air above him. As he did so, he looked up at the building where the gentle giant had just led Sonny into, He could just make out the two figures of men on the roof, one of whom looked over the small handrail, down into the street. The second man suddenly grabbed the first man's legs and tipped him over the rail. Sonny screamed as he flew through the air and crashed to his death on the pavement just a few feet from where the man smoking the cigarette was standing.

Chapter 55

The telephone on the bar in the Mackworth Arms rang. Comer rushed over to it and listened while Moisha watched and waited. Comer clicked his fingers at the publican and asked for some paper and a pencil, which he quickly started writing down some details on. "OK, let's go," he said to Moisha as he hurried out of the pub.

Once inside the car Comer started explaining to Moisha what was happening. He still didn't know who has kidnapped his daughter; it was an Irish voice on the phone, but not one that he had recognised. The kidnappers want £20,000, which is the equivalent to approximately £400,000 today. "What the hell are you going to do?" Moisha asked, "where are you going to find that sort of money?" "We've got it," explained Comer, "Rita and I, it's our retirement money, for when we go to Ireland"

Some time later, Moisha was sitting in the car, waiting outside Comer's flat. He checked his inside pocket to make sure he has his gun with him. He had a feeling he might be needing it. Two minutes later Comer came hurrying out of the door to the flats and jumped into the back seat of the car, carefully placing the suitcase he is carrying next to him on the floor. He leaned forward and handed Moisha the piece of paper that he had written the details on in the pub, "here's the address" Moisha started the car up again and looked at the piece of paper, "Fuck me Jack, you know where this is don't you?" he said with aghast. "No, where?" "It's the old baths," replied Moisha as he pulled away, leaving Comer stunned into silence.

It was dark and deserted as Moisha pulled the car to a halt outside the old baths in east London. Comer got out of the back of the car, carrying the suitcase full of money with him, with Moisha naturally starting to get out to accompany him. Comer stops him, telling him that he has been told that he must go in alone if he wants to see his daughter alive again, "Just wait here in the car," he says, "I shouldn't be too long"

Comer looked up and down the street, making sure there wasn't anyone hiding in a doorway somewhere and proceeded to press the large bell push, but at this moment he noticed that the door is slightly ajar. This didn't seem right, was it a trap maybe? He pulled out his gun out and gingerly entered the building, pulling the door closed again behind him. It was pitch black inside, just like the last time he was there. A very faint light from somewhere ahead of him helped him to navigate his way along the narrow passageway.

"Hello," he called, "is there anybody there?" He continued moving along the passageway, straining his eyes to try and see in the almost total blackness, "Hello – hello?" Still no answer. He seemed to be getting closer to the boiler room as he could now start to hear the roar of the furnace, Again he called "Is there anyone there?"

● ● ●

It had now started to rain as Moisha sat in the car outside, his eyes nervously moving from what is going on in front and around him, to the interior mirror, where he suddenly saw the dark reflection of someone approaching. As the figure got closer, Moisha realised that it is a policeman, probably doing his nightly patrol, he thought, but what is he going to tell him if he asks why he is waiting there outside the old baths at this time of night?

By this time the policeman had drawn level with Moisha's car and spotted him sitting at the wheel. There is the repetitive tap on his side window, which Moisha was dreading. Putting on his best friendly smile, Moisha wound his side window down. "Good evening officer," he said in his best 'friendly' voice, "bloody cold tonight isn't it?"

"Can you please step out of the car sir?" the policeman demanded. Moisha wasn't sure what to do, but he didn't want to arouse the policeman's suspicions, so he did as he was told and opened the door of the car and moved forward to get out. "I'm not doing anything wrong am I officer?" answered Moisha, "to be honest I'm just waiting for my lady-friend to meet me here" "It's up to you sir," the policeman said as he reached inside his overcoat and pulled out a large pistol, which he pressed directly into Moisha's eye and pulled the trigger, which sent a spray of blood all over the interior windscreen and dashboard as Moisha was propelled back against his seat.

● ● ●

From inside the old baths Comer heard the shot, but didn't put two and two together as the noise from the furnace was now roaring very fiercely. At the same time he also heard Miriam calling out to him from what sounds like somewhere within the furnace room, "Daddy, Daddy"

He stopped in his tracks, his face aghast and white with fear, Oh God, she is in there, he thought, whatever is he going to do? "Miriam," he called, "Miriam, where are you Miriam? He kept calling out but all he could hear was Miriam crying and calling out for him again and again. He could now hear that Miriam's voice was definitely coming from inside the furnace room. "Don't cry darling," he called as he tried the handle of the furnace room, and found it unlocked, "I've come to take you home, you're safe now"

The roar of the furnace and the intense heat hit him as he walked into the room and quickly looked around for Miriam, but there was no sign of her anywhere, "Miriam, where are you?" he called again. "Daddy, Daddy," she sobbed again, "please daddy, help me daddy" Comer's eyes darted about the room, what the hell is happening here, she is there somewhere but he still couldn't see her.

He looked to a dark corner where the voice seems to be coming from and there on a small table was a Grundig tape recorder with the tape spool actively spinning round and round and the voice of Miriam repeatedly calling him, "daddy, daddy"

Comer stared at the tape recorder for a few seconds, realising by this time that he has been tricked. A metallic clicking sound from behind him caused him to look round. His jaw dropped in horror as he saw a figure in the darkness with a Luger pistol pointing directly at his head. "Oh no, not you" were Comer's last words as the hand holding the gun squeezed the trigger, sending a single bullet directly into the centre of his forehead.

Chapter 56

It was New Year's Eve 1960, and the opening night of the Kray's lavish new club, the Starlight Rooms in Soho. The place was crammed full with well dressed men and their wives and girlfriends, and Reggie and Ronnie Kray, both in evening suits and bow ties, smiling and playing the convivial hosts to everyone.

Outside the club, people were lining up to get into the club, with many people being turned away. Two burly bouncers on the door were looking at their lists to see who has a genuine invite and who had not. One man who got out of a taxi, most definitely looks like he shouldn't be on the list, he was Nipper Reed. The bouncer glanced at Nipper's printed invite and waved him in without a second glance.

● ● ●

Outside Comer's flats in George Street, a black taxi-cab pulled up. The driver turned without saying a word and opened the rear door of the cab. Miriam got out, looking somewhat bedraggled but otherwise unhurt as the taxi-cab pulled away again. She stood there, on the pavement, not attempting to move, with the yellow light of the nearby lamppost shining down on her like a spotlight in a stage play. The street door of the house suddenly opened and Rita ran out to her daughter with tears streaming down her face, and threw her arms around her.

• • •

Back at the Starlight Rooms, Reggie Kray was chatting to a group of people including his brother Ronnie, when he suddenly saw Nipper Reed standing at the end of the bar, sipping a glass of champagne, "What the fuck is he doing here?" he asked Ronnie, who grinned, seeming to think it was very funny, as it was him who had personally sent an invitation to Nipper. "It's not funny Ron," he growled, "he is one copper we can't bribe, his sole purpose in life is to bring us down" Ronnie Kray sneered and stared over at Nipper, "No one's going to bring us down Reg, we're bigger than the fucking lot of 'em"

Reggie shrugged his shoulders and shook his head at his brother's remark, whilst at the same time across the room, their guest of honour, Judy Garland, had just stepped up to the microphone. The pianist played out a little introduction, "Ladies and gentlemen, the fabulous Miss Judy Garland"

Everyone in the room turned and applauded as Judy smiled and whispered something in the pianist's ear before starting her song. The pianist tapped one of the piano keys a couple of times, producing just a dull thud instead of the intended note, which should have been heard. He shrugged and whispered something back to Judy, who didn't look very happy at all. "Sorry ladies and gentlemen," the pianist announced, "we seem to have a slight technical hitch with one of the piano keys – Miss Garland will not be able to sing Over The Rainbow as intended, but will instead sing her own special rendition of You Made Me Love You"

• • •

The lively atmosphere of the club couldn't have been more different from that of Billy White' flat. He was sitting alone in his living room watching TV. The only concession to New Year's Eve was the bottle of Scotch by his side and the large cigar he was smoking.

White smiled to himself as the flickering black and white images of the BBCs regular New Year's Eve programme, The White Heather Club spluttered into life, with Andy Stewart, Kenneth McKellar and Moira Anderson.

White poured himself another large Scotch and puffed happily on his cigar, completely unaware of a movement of the curtains behind him, or the looming figure of the man who stepped out of the shadows and silently crept up behind him and slipped the length of piano wire around his neck.

White' mouth gaped open, the cigar fell from his mouth and the glass of Scotch crashed to the floor as the piano wire cut into his windpipe and a line of blood around his neck trickled down onto his shirt.

• • •

Everything was in full swing at the Starlight Rooms, Judy Garland had now finished her numbers and was sitting, laughing and chatting with her entourage. Reggie Kray looked at his watch, which was showing 11.55. "Only five minutes to go and it'll be 1961," he said, but Ronnie had other things on his mind at this moment in time, "We only have the Deacon brothers to take care of now," he said, "and then London's ours"
"There is another south London firm you might want to have a look at," Bobby Osborne interrupted, "according to what I've heard, these people are major players and are planning a massive raid on a Royal Mail train, which, according to my source, will be the biggest cash raid ever"

Ronnie Kray grinned evilly, "If that's right, I want to make sure we get our share of that as well" At the other end of the bar, Nipper Read was quietly taking it all in.

Ronnie Kray looked at his watch, "It's nearly 1961 - Out with the old and in with the new" He started the countdown, which everyone in the club joins in with, 9 – 8 – 7 – 6 – 5 – 4 – 3 – 2 – 1 – Happy New Year. Everyone starts to sing, Auld Lang Syne.

Printed in Great Britain
by Amazon